THE
KATHARINE MOORE
OMNIBUS

THE
KATHARINE MOORE
OMNIBUS

Her three novels

Summer at the Haven
The Lotus House
Moving House

Allison & Busby
published by W. H. Allen & Co. Plc

An Allison & Busby book
published in 1987
by W. H. Allen & Co. Plc
44 Hill Street
London W1X 8LB

This omnibus edition first published 1987

Printed and bound in Great Britain by
Anchor Brendon Ltd, Tiptree, Essex

ISBN 0 85031 772 X (hardback)
ISBN 0 85031 773 8 (paperback)

SUMMER AT THE HAVEN

To Josephine Fry

1

THE HAVEN

THE HAVEN, a private Home for elderly ladies, was by now not unlike its inmates, but it had originally been the proud achievement of a prosperous Victorian merchant who had pulled down the old Tudor farmhouse, once a Manor, and erected on its site a handsome structure in the fashionable pseudo-Gothic style with a side turret and stained-glass windows over the porch and on the stairs and even in the proud bathroom. His sons had been killed in the 1914 war, the family had faded out and the house, untenanted throughout the Second World War, had at length been sold off cheaply to be converted for its present purpose. It was thoroughly unsuitable for this, being just too far away from the large village of Darnley for convenience or company. Its rooms were big and had to be divided, which made them disproportionately lofty and a queer shape, and the menace of worn floors and windows and roof tiles was always present to the harassed house committee. It was also too secluded to attract domestic staff and there was not enough money available to tempt them by high wages.

The house made a brave effort, however, though this was never enough to achieve an all-over effect. Some sections peeled obviously away while others showed a distinct facelift and, where once there had been an elegant conservatory, a square annexe containing the offices, which looked rather as if it were constructed of cardboard, had been painted a bright pink.

The Victorian merchant had found nothing much in the way of a garden. There were a few old fruit trees growing out of a rough grass space ending in an ancient ditch, on the other side of which was a little copse of oak, ash and thorn. He had laid out a lawn and flowerbeds and, though he had left the old trees, he had planted near the house a monkey-puzzle and a deodar which had grown to fine proportions. As with the house, there was now a struggle to keep the most visible and utilitarian part of the garden trim and flourishing. The narrow beds each side of the gravel sweep were filled with neat bedding plants, begonias and geraniums in the summer, chrysanthemums and dahlias in the autumn. Spring bulbs were not encouraged because they were untidy. In fact, all the cultivated parts of the garden were rather like the shelves of a self-service store with rows of the same sort of goods kept orderly and separate. At the back of the house, a short strip of the old lawn was regularly mown and there were two beds of floribunda roses, one pink and one red. There was a small trimmed shrubbery of privet, laurel and lilac and, in a discreet corner, ranks of vegetables. Only under one window, was a plot where well tended but not very tidy flowers were happily mixed up together like the goods in an old-fashioned village shop.

The Haven, when full, could accommodate eight old ladies. Each had their own room containing their remnants of furniture, china and pictures. It also housed the warden and whatever resident staff that could be scraped together.

Mrs Thornton's room was the larger of the two attics. It had originally held three narrow iron bedsteads in which had slept a parlour maid, a housemaid and an underhouse-maid. The smaller attic had been the cook's and was now used as a boxroom. Mrs Thornton had chosen her room because she did not like the sound of people tramping above her and because, as the other attic was empty, she felt an assurance of comparative privacy. The shape of the room, too, appealed to her – the interior of the absurd turret opened out of one corner – this had been where the parlour maid had slept, thus claiming her superiority over the other two maids, and Mrs Thornton in her turn had thought it very convenient for her own bed, which was the one on which her son had been born. From the little turret window she could see the railway line and the trains, now, alas, much depleted in number, that connected the branch station with the main line, seemed to her like a link with the outer world. The other window looked on to the front drive, used by whoever called in from this outer world. So, although the lift stopped short of the attic floor and it was cold there in winter and hot in summer and the sloping ceilings allowed little wallspace, she felt the advantages outweighed the disadvantages.

Besides her bed, she had brought with her her mother's rocking-chair and her husband's bureau, the gate-legged table they had bought together when furnishing their first home, and as many books as she could find room for. All these articles were thickly encrusted with memories. On the whole, if no longer happy, she was content. When tempted to indulge in melancholy she would take herself in hand and at such times she would hear the voice of her Scotch nanny quite clearly, as though she were in the room: "Count your blessings, Miss Milly." It was her favourite maxim and perhaps next came: "Eat up everything on your plate, now. I canna have a faddy bairn in my nursery. There's many a poor callant would be glad to have what you are wanting to leave each day." At the time, when suffering from some childish grief or lacking appetite – for she was a delicate little girl – Nanny seemed not only unsympathetic but stupid. Any other blessing but the one denied her then and there seemed quie unreal, and as for the unwanted dinner, how she wished the poor child would come and take it away from her. But in old age and at The

Haven, while more profound advice was forgotten, Nanny's precepts remained and stood her in good stead both at the rather unappetizing meal times and in moods of dejection.

One wet cold May morning, then, she began deliberately to count her blessings. She was not deaf like old Miss Brown, only a little hard of hearing; she was not going blind like old Miss Norton, only with gently failing sight; she was not crippled and wracked with arthritis like old Miss Dawson, only troubled at night by one hip and one knee; she was not bald like old Miss Ford underneath her wig, only going a little thin around the temples; she was not asthmatical and bronchial like old Mrs Perry; above all, unlike poor dear old Mrs Langley, she was still in her right mind; only proper names eluded her in a stupidly arbitrary manner. It was strange, she realized suddenly, that she was thinking of everybody as old when she herself was as old, or in some cases, even older than they. She must try to remember this. One other blessing occurred to her – her heart was not all that strong, unlikely, as in some cases she knew, to outlast the rest of her. She gave it all the work she could, walking up and down to her attic, for instance, disdaining the help of the lift for the first two floors.

She had got thus far in practising Nanny's maxim that morning when she was disturbed by a voice, not altogether unlike Nanny's own in tone, and when she was not at her best either. It was the voice of Miss Blackett, the warden, from the landing below.

"Mrs Langley, whatever are you doing?"

A foolish little laugh in reply floated up through Mrs Thornton's half-open door and then she heard another door firmly shut and Miss Blackett's steps ascending the stairs. The warden could only be called a mixed blessing and Mrs Thornton braced herself for the encounter. Hardly waiting to knock, Miss Blackett marched into the room.

"Mrs Thornton, I wonder that with your door ajar you didn't hear Mrs Langley wandering about. I have just found her playing absolute havoc with the linen cupboard – sheets and towels all over the floor and herself actually standing on a pile of blankets trying to reach the upper shelves; and when I asked her what she was up to she said she was looking for her baby's clothes and that her husband was coming this afternoon to fetch them both. She thinks that this is a maternity home and that she's just had a child. She shouldn't really be here now and I don't think we can keep her any longer. She must go into the geriatric ward at the hospital."

"Oh, no!" exclaimed Mrs Thornton, "surely not, Miss Blackett. She is so happy and she never does any real harm, it is only that she doesn't live in the present any more. She believes her husband and her friends she has loved in the past come to see her every day – she never stops believing it and so of course they do."

Miss Blackett stared at her blankly and Mrs Thornton swore inwardly. Would she never learn not to make remarks like that to people like Miss Blackett? No, she supposed at her age she never would. It would almost certainly make it worse now if she went on, but go on of course she did.

'If she goes into a geriatric ward she will be treated like an invalid and she'll have to leave everything behind, all her things, I mean, and then she may wake up, you see."

"Well, wouldn't that be desirable," said Miss Blackett crossly, "though I fear it isn't at all likely, senility never regresses – and as to her things, she has far too many of them and she never dusts them."

Residents at The Haven, if able-bodied, were expected to do their own dusting. It gave them something to do and relieved the domestic situation just a little.

"She says that Susan, her housemaid, who has been with the family for years, sees to all that whenever I mention it," went on Miss Blackett, adding with a rare touch of

7

humour: "I only wish I could lay my hands on that Susan."

Immediately Mrs Thornton felt herself thaw and she noticed for the first time, too, how tired the warden looked and that she was leaning against the door as she talked.

"Isn't Brenda due back tomorrow?" she asked. Brenda was the latest living-in help and away for a week's holiday.

"She isn't coming back at all," said Miss Blackett. "She phoned last night that she's taken a job in a shop – too quiet here, she says. She didn't even have the decency to give in her notice."

Mrs Thornton looked distressed, she and the warden both belonged to the generation that expected a month's notice and could not easily accept modern casualness.

"Oh, dear, that leaves only Gisela and Mrs Mills," she said. Gisela was the au pair from Germany who was a recent arrival. Miss Blackett did most of the cooking herself. She was an adequate but not a good cook, not being interested in food. Mrs Mills, the gardener's wife, came in to do cleaning.

"Yes," sighed Miss Blackett, "I shall have to let the committee know and try advertising again, I suppose".

"I'll do Mrs Langley's dusting," said Mrs Thornton.

Miss Blackett merely sniffed in response, recalling Mrs Thornton's remarks about Mrs Langley with irritation. She had thought Mrs Thornton had more sense, but they were none of them to be relied on. She turned and went downstairs. Why ever Mrs Thornton chose to stay on in that attic when there was now a good room available on the second floor, she failed to understand. If she moved down the attic floor could be left to take care of itself, which would save a good deal more work than doing the dusting for Mrs Langley, who ought not to be here any longer anyway. But none of them thought of anyone but themselves. The old were so self-centred.

After lunch and resting time were over, Mrs Thornton knocked on Mrs Langley's door. She had thought out her plan of action carefully and marched in flaunting her duster about and talking rather loudly and quickly.

"I know it is Susan's day out, Mrs Langley, and I wondered, as you are sure to be having visitors for tea, whether you would like me just to go over your lovely china so as to have everything looking just as it would if Susan were here."

Mrs Langley, who was in her nineties, was sitting by what should have been the fireplace but was now only a cold radiator, for the heating was turned off, it being May by the calendar though nearer November in temperature. She was a pretty old lady with large faded blue eyes and white curls done up with a narrow green velvet ribbon on the top of her head. Her face was singularly smooth and unlined. She was wrapped in a none too clean little grey shawl and Mrs Thornton's heart smote her as she saw it.

"Dear Jessie," said Mrs Langley, "how very kind."

She always called Mrs Thornton Jessie, but who Jessie really was she had never discovered. She preferred it, however, to her own name, for Milly, rhyming inexorably with silly, filly and frilly, had been unfortunate for her in her schooldays.

"I am expecting the vicar," went on Mrs Langley. "He said he'd come about the christening – not that he's likely to notice a little dust, gentleman don't, do they – but it's well, perhaps, to be on the safe side."

The lovely Chelsea shepherdess on the mantelpiece had the same slightly neglected, soiled look as her owner, but Mrs Thornton soon put her to rights and her attendant shepherd, too. Between them was a row of enchanting tiny china houses and a Dresden flower piece. But Miss Blackett was right, the room was really too cluttered up with ornaments and furniture, and all the wallspace was completely covered with photographs in dark oak frames and pale watercolours in gilt ones. There were far too many chairs and small tables and they none of them seemed to

9

know what they were doing or where they were meant to be. Yet Mrs Thornton was sure that everything in her room was significant and precious to Mrs Langley. She dusted them as carefully and quickly as she could and finished just as Gisela, the German girl, appeared with tea – a brown teapot, a plastic cup and a plate upon which were two slices of bread and butter and a dull little cake.

Mrs Langley clicked in disapproval. "Would you mind getting out the Worcester cups from my corner cupboard? My husband will be here directly, I always hear the carriage at about this time." She seemed to have forgotten the vicar by now. "My husband likes to drive himself, you know, though he brings James with him to hold Bessie and Brownie while he is here, such a dear fine pair they are."

Mrs Thornton found the cups and placed them on the tea tray where they looked sadly out of place. Such as the happy expectation in Mrs Langley's voice that she caught herself listening for horses and carriage wheels as she went upstairs to her own room. She did not hear them but she knew that Mrs Langley would.

Meanwhile Miss Blackett was having her own welcome cup in her office sitting-room and making notes in preparation for the house committee meeting on the following day. These were held only quarterly unless a crisis arose needing immediate attention. On the whole, Miss Blackett enjoyed them. She was listened to with respectful attention when she gave her report, for the committee knew she would be difficult to replace.

"Granted that Miss Blackett is not the ideal warden," said the chairwoman, Lady Merivale, to her secretary, "but she is conscientious and hard-working and she is also cheap, which, I need hardly say, is a sad but inevitable necessity in these times." The secretary had been hinting that Miss Blackett seemed sometimes to lack sensitivity.

She had been a matron in a boys' preparatory school for some years but had then thought that old ladies might be easier to manage. She found she was mistaken. You generally knew where you were with small boys, but with "them", as she always thought of the old ladies, you never knew – they were so unreliable. "Unreliable" was her favourite term of disapproval. She bore "them" a grudge for the mistake she had made but she did not feel like another change.

Miss Blackett's room was the extreme opposite of Mrs Langley's. It was spotless and very neat, her papers stacked in tidy piles on her desk, on the top of which stood the one picture in the room, a small faded photograph of a kitten. Miss Blackett sat at her desk and wrote:

(1) Mrs Langley, to be removed to the geriatric unit of the hospital as soon as possible.
(2) The deodar tree to be cut down. It makes Miss Dawson's room very dark and also damp, as it is far too near the house and in wet weather its branches drip down the walls.
(3) Report on Brenda's leaving and discuss replacement.
(4) Report on repairs to gutters and bathroom pipe and request for repainting of front ground-floor window frames and needful repair of old stable door and lock.

As she finished the last note, a large ginger cat rattled imperiously at the door and was immediately let in. He sat down at once on the top of Miss Blackett's papers. She sighed resignedly and stroked him. This was Lord Jim, so christened by a Mrs Wilson, a late resident, the widow of a naval officer, who had read nothing but Conrad's novels and made his wife read them too. Miss Blackett knew nothing of Conrad and thought the name a compliment to her cat's proud manners. She was therefore pleased with the name. Everyone knew that Lord Jim could do no wrong in her eyes and everyone thought her one photograph was of him, but in this they were wrong. It was of her

11

only childhood's pet, passionately loved but put to sleep when he reached maturity because the aunt who had brought her up said he ruined the furniture and harboured fleas. Miss Blackett could not believe that Lord Jim was not a privilege and pleasure for all the old ladies and good for them, too. This happened to be true as regards Mrs Thornton, Miss Norton and Miss Brown, but quite untrue of Miss Dawson and Mrs Perry. Mrs Perry's passion was flowers and she it was who lovingly tended that herbaceous border beneath her window. Unfortunately Lord Jim's favourite daybed was precisely on this plot. It was sunny and sheltered from cold winds and he enjoyed both sleeping there and trying to catch the butterflies that hovered over the lavender and pinks and buddleia.

"Lord Jim does love your little garden, Mrs Perry," said Miss Blackett approvingly. "He's made quite a nest for himself so cleverly there, do you see?'

Poor Mrs Perry did indeed see, but she said nothing for she knew the situation was hopeless both from Miss Blackett's point of view and Lord Jim's. As for Miss Dawson, her passion was for birds and ever since Lord Jim, with that inspired tactlessness not seldom to be observed in cats, had laid a dead thrush at the door of her room, there had been a bitter one-sided feud between her and the warden – one-sided because Miss Blackett was quite unaware of it. Even had she seen the thrush, she would have considered it a signal sign of regard for Miss Dawson on Lord Jim's part for which she should have felt gratitude. Birds, after all, were designed by Nature among their other uses to provide healthy amusement for cats.

Unfortunately the thrush was not an isolated casualty and with each pathetic little corpse, whether laid at her door or found elsewhere, poor Miss Dawson suffered anew and raged inwardly.

2

MISS DAWSON AND MRS PERRY

MISS DAWSON'S room on the second floor was always in a green gloom. Very close to the window were the boughs of the deodar tree. This tree was a perpetual joy to her, not only in itself, its alien mysterious world, the association with a far country of great mountain peaks, but also for its population. Miss Dawson had travelled and bird-watched wherever she went, and photographed and lectured on birds, and her walls were decorated with beautiful prints of rare birds. Seen dimly in the shadowy room, they sometimes seemed alive. But there was no doubt about the busy life that went on among the branches of the deodar. Miss Dawson knew all the tree's regular visitors and residents better than she knew the residents of The Haven, for she was something of a recluse. There were tree creepers, wood pigeons, of course, robins and tits, best of all a pair of gold crests. Miss Dawson was never tired of watching them and listening to their varied conversation. She knew many of the other birds besides, not just the ones that belonged to her tree. The thrush that Lord Jim had brought her had nested for three years past in the old shrubbery lilacs. He had become very tame, which of course was his undoing. Painfully crippled though she was with her arthritis, and only able to walk with sticks, Miss Dawson had managed to wrap up the thrush in a handkerchief and placing it in the bag which she always wore slung round her neck, she edged herself down to Mrs Perry who promised to bury it out of reach of Lord Jim. Not that actually he ever did eat his prey, he was too well fed for that and killed merely for sport.

"I believe you know every bird in this garden," said Mrs Perry to Miss Dawson.

They were having tea together in Mrs Perry's room which had been the morning room. It was one of the lightest and most cheerful in the house, on the south side and with a bow window overlooking her own garden patch. She suffered from a chronic bronchial condition and was always grateful that she had been able to have this particular room. Though she would not admit it, even to herself, Miss Dawson was sometimes quite glad, especially on chilly days when the radiator didn't radiate much, to leave her dim retreat for a time. She had eased herself into the comfortable chair that was always kept free for her and was enjoying the pleasant illusion of an early summer's day provided by the jar of warm coloured wallflowers on the round table and the row of robust polyanthus and primula pot plants on the windowsill. Though a born solitary, she was human enough to feel the need of congenial company sometimes and she had discovered that she and Mrs Perry shared a love of nature, though in somewhat different aspects and ways, for Mrs Perry's feeling for flowers was not in the least professional. They were drawn together, too, by the treatment they had suffered at the paws of Lord Jim.

"It's a wonder there's a bird left for me to know with that wretched cat around," said Miss Dawson.

"He's been taking his usual siesta on the top of my poor pansies," mourned Mrs Perry gently.

"As if birds hadn't enough to put up with," went on Miss Dawson, "with all the destruction of nesting sites that goes on and ghastly pesticides poisoning their food, without cats, and there seems more of them about every year."

14

"I don't blame Lord Jim so much," said Mrs Perry, "but he is so spoiled. Miss Blackett lets him do just as he likes. She has never attempted to train him."

"You can't train cats," snapped Miss Dawson. "The only thing to do is to get rid of them."

Mrs Perry was silent. She respected her friend too much to contradict her but she knew that you could train cats. Their family cats had all been trained to take "No" for an answer, to keep off flower beds and never to thieve food from tables. She poured herself out another cup of tea.

"I believe Miss Blackett takes the top off all our milk for him," she said, "it's so thin."

"*Most* likely," said Miss Dawson.

"But to do her justice, she probably gives him all the cream off hers first."

"More fool her," said Miss Dawson.

They were interrupted in this comforting talk by Gisela coming in to collect the trays. She seemed upset and nearly dropped a cup. She was easily given to tears and appeared on the brink of them now.

"What's the matter, Gisela?' asked kind Mrs Perry.

"It's that Miss Norton. I do not understand at all. She had beautiful picture of a white horse and many dogs and I try to please and I say: 'Miss Norton, what a beautiful picture of a white horse and many dogs,' and Miss Norton speak quite cross, and she say, 'They are hounds not dogs and the horse, she is grey,' and the horse is white, white, WHITE," her voice went up the scale almost to a shriek, "and I speak English, *not* German and say 'dog' properly and not 'hund'."

It seemed too difficult to try to explain so Mrs Perry merely said, "Never mind, dear, you are getting along very nicely with your English."

Miss Dawson, who took not the slightest interest in Gisela or Miss Norton, simply waited until the room was quiet again.

"Yes, the only way with cats is to get rid of them," she then repeated.

"I can't see how Lord Jim is to be got rid of," said Mrs Perry.

"Where there's a will, there's a way," said Miss Dawson, so firmly that Mrs Perry felt a little disturbed. She wished Frances Dawson had something else to think about than her birds and her tree. She herself had a loving family most of whom, though they were at a distance, regularly phoned or wrote, and there were a couple of nice grandchildren who managed to visit her fairly frequently, and sometimes brought her cuttings and plants, for gardening was a family addiction. She was afraid, too, that Frances was often in pain, she was such a valiant creature that she never complained, and sometimes perhaps it was better to complain a little. She thought she would change the subject.

"The apple blossom's scarcely shown yet, it's been such a cold spring, but the lilac's brave as usual, and the warden was picking a lot of it this morning, for the committee meeting tomorrow, I suppose. It's a funny thing about lilac, sometimes it behaves well when it's picked, but more often than not it wilts in a most tiresome fashion."

"Oh, if there's a committee, I suppose the dining-room will be out of action and we'll have meals in our rooms," said Miss Dawson with some satisfaction.

"Why don't we ask Gisela to bring yours in here and we'll have them together," suggested Mrs Perry.

"No, thank you, Mary," said Miss Dawson. There was a limit to her capacity for companionship and this was reached fairly quickly and often quite suddenly. She was subject, too, to a queer feeling, almost of disloyalty, if she were absent too long from her room and her tree. Mrs Perry did not press her, accepting though not understanding her friend's ways by this time, so that she was sorry but not in the least offended.

The two continued to chat amiably until it was time to

prepare for supper. Although the main meal at The Haven was in the middle of the day, the old ladies had been used in past years to changing for dinner and as long as they were able, they did so still. It was part of the courageous losing battle that was perpetually being waged within those discreet walls. Miss Blackett, who shared the midday meal, only "saw to" the supper. She and Lord Jim ate together later when the day's work was almost done and she could relax. It was the favourite hour of her day when, with her television set switched on and Lord Jim purring expectantly at her feet, they could enjoy a snack of whatever took their fancy.

The ladies, in their brave array, a few pieces of jewellery sparkling on old fingers or fastening wraps, sat at an oblong mahogany table in the dining-room. Like them, this table was a relic of a more dignified and prosperous past and made the plastic and steel chairs look like the undeveloped embryos of real furniture. The ladies had to trust themselves to these, however, three on one side and three on the other and one at the end facing the warden.

In the centre of the table was a pot of bright pink hyacinth lolling their top heavy blooms over the edge. Mrs Perry didn't exactly hate them – she couldn't hate any flowers – but she compared them unfavourably with every other spring flower she could think of and their particular shade of pink with every other colour. She herself always grew the more delicate Roman hyacinths that never lolled.

Supper consisted of tomato soup (Heinz), macaroni cheese, not very strongly flavoured and the kind of bread-and-butter pudding that lacked all pleasant surprises. Miss Blackett considered it a good nourishing supper and very suitable for the old. Mrs Thornton, mindful of Nanny, classed it as one of those meals to which she would willingly have summoned as a substitute for herself a starving citizen from the Third World. Miss Dawson did not notice what she was eating, Miss Leila Ford enjoyed it because she

17

loved all food, Mrs Langley smiled happily to herself throughout. Who knows what bygone meal *she* was consuming. Miss Norton, whose sight was very bad, was concentrating too hard on getting the food to her mouth without degrading spillings, to care what it was. Mrs Perry, controlling an itch to tie up those hyacinths properly, thought complacently of a little secret store in her own room which was regularly replenished by thoughtful relatives and friends. She decided that after supper was over she would take some particularly nice shortbread, sent by a niece in Scotland, to cheer up Miss Brown who was eating as little as she dared without attracting Miss Blackett's attention.

The ladies always sat in the same places and when the warden had once tried to change them round, it met with such obvious disapproval that, as it did not really matter at all to her, she gave up the attempt and let the old sillies have their own way. Mrs Thornton, whose seat was between deaf Miss Brown and Mrs Langley, would herself have benefited by a change, but she understood and partly shared in the half-conscious desire for territorial security which, having lost their homes, made each cling to their own place at table and the same chair in the common sitting-room. Conversation at meal times could not be called animated unless the day had brought any unusual visitors or news of any interesting happening from the outside world. Miss Blackett, used in the past to the chattering of noisy small boys, welcomed at first the negative calm of meals at The Haven, but after a while it oppressed her.

"I'll be getting as dumb myself, shut up day after day with the old things," she had complained to Brenda and Gisela one day. She felt it was beneath her dignity to talk in this way to the girls but they hardly noticed. As far as they were concerned, she was already almost in the same category as the old ladies and neither she nor they possessed any real relevance to life.

Supper over, all but Miss Norton, Mrs Thornton and Miss Dawson went into the sitting-room to watch television. As no one was allowed to touch the controls because the warden thought, probably correctly, that this would cause friction, the majority decided on the programmes and she switched them on, very loud and very bright, as she thought this was both necessary and nice. Miss Norton never watched because of her defective sight, Mrs Thornton had her own small set which from her attic fastness she knew could disturb no one. Miss Dawson vehemently disliked all television on principle. This evening, too, she felt very tired but she knew that the pain from her arthritis would only become worse in bed and although allowed two pain killers, doled out to her each evening, she did not allow herself to resort to these so early in the night. She wrapped herself in shawls and a rug and sat in her favouite chair by the window and prayed for the miracle that sometimes some kind magic worked for her. She never knew when it would happen and it was not often, but when it did it was far better than any pain killers. Somehow she thought it might tonight. There was a full moon rising and the softly moving branches of the deodar tree threw shadows on her walls, for she had not switched on her light. The window was slightly open and the distant hoot of an owl floated into the room. Nearer at hand a blackbird was still hard at it and Miss Dawson knew that a thrush or two would follow, singing late into the May night.

The bird's song, though so native, did not seem to conflict with the faint exotic scent from the deodar but mingled subtly with it, creating in Miss Dawson's mind a strange compound of past and present, of scenes near at hand and far away in time and space. Gradually these impressions became more vivid and more compelling. Frances Dawson was now a girl in her father's garden, listening to the promise of summer in the evening bird chorus all about her, excited beyond measure at the mysterious summons of their song. Almost simultaneously she was a much older but a no less happy Frances Dawson. The curtains of her room had changed to the canvas flaps of a tent open to vast distances glimpsed through a fringe of Himalayan pines, standing like huge sentinels round her camping site. She was so high up in the world that she felt almost as free as the bright tropical birds she had been watching all that day. The deep peace of that freedom enveloped her. She turned and stretched luxuriously on her campbed – she nodded and slipped down in her old chair at The Haven and slept deeply and dreamlessly at last. Her miracle had worked once again.

3

MISS NORTON, MISS BROWN, MISS FORD

MISS NORTON negotiated the hall and passage and stairs successfully with the help of her stick which she used for guidance only; she was still erect and agile and needed no prop. She shut the door of her room with relief and triumph. Another day conquered and she could relax completely.

Mrs Thornton, who was the only person likely to visit her, would tonight, as she knew, be listening to a favourite music programme. Since her sight had worsened, each day was a battle to retain her dignity and independence. But she came of fighting stock in which self-pity in misfortune had had little part, though she allowed herself the indulgence of exasperation now and again. For instance, when she realised that she could no longer play her endless games of Patience, that it really was no good (even the largest cards got muddled up), she threw the pack across the room and it took her a long while to locate and retrieve each card. "That'll teach me," she said to herself. But such outbursts were few. In her own room, unless someone had moved any of her things from their accustomed places, she could manage pretty well still and she remained the most immaculately neat, clean and well turned out of all The Haven's residents.

She did not sit down now before she had taken off her beautifully fitting though ancient black velvet gown

21

(definitely a gown and not a mere dress) and hung it carefully in her cupboard. She folded the little muslin scarf she had worn round her shoulders and placed it in her top right-hand drawer among her lavender-scented embroidered handkerchiefs. She took off a pair of elegant pointed shoes and fitted them with their trees, then felt for her slippers beside the bed. They were warm and comforting to her cold feet. Then she put on a loose wrapper and at last seated herself in an upright armchair and switched on her radio to hear the sporting news.

The picture which had caught Gisela's attention dominated the room. It was an oil painting of her father on his favourite hunter with two cavorting foxhounds in the foreground and, behind, a grey stone house of pleasing proportions. Though Miss Norton's eyes could no longer see the picture well, she did not need them to recall its every detail. Beneath it hung two miniatures, one of two children, a boy and a girl, the boy with an arm flung protectively round his sister, for it was easy to see the likeness between the two, though he was dark and straight-haired and she had pale brown curls. It was not difficult either to trace in old Miss Norton the same fine bone structure and the same small head set on a long neck, as in the child's portrait.

The other miniature was of a very fair young man in an army officer's uniform which seemed to eclipse his identity. He looked too young for it. He was indeed, like so many of his contemporaries, too young for what it signified at the time when the picture was painted. Miss Norton had been engaged to him once. He was her twin brother's closest friend and both had passed out of Sandhurst together in the summer of 1914 and had been killed in Flanders in the first battle of Ypres. Her short romance seemed now as if it had happened to someone in a book she had read long ago and when she thought about it, she felt ashamed that she could hardly recall Paul's face or his voice – the miniature had never seemed real. She could only remember how the back of his hands and his arms were covered with fine golden hairs and that he had a habit of softly whistling to himself, whereas she could always still see her brother vividly and hear him speak and laugh.

There was no one else left to marry among the families that her parents knew and "afterwards", as Miss Norton always referred to the years immediately following the War, her parents anyway needed her at home. Her father, always keenly interested in racing, grew reckless. "One must do something, Meg," he had said to his daughter, "you understand, don't you, a man must do something, but promise me you'll never bet yourself." Gradually racing debts piled up and, at his death, the estate and the old house and most of its contents had to be sold. Miss Norton and her mother took a flat in Darnley and there her mother died and, eventually, Meg Norton, whose sight had begun to give serious trouble, moved into The Haven.

She did not make friends there easily. "Stand-offish," said Miss Blackett, but it was really that she had never learned to mix in a wider circle than the narrow one in which she had been reared. She found herself more at ease with Mrs Thornton than the rest. She had been the Squire's daughter in a village and Mrs Thornton's girlhood had been spent in a country parsonage. They had inhabited the same vanished world. It was Mrs Thornton, though, who had made the first overture. She noticed how blind Miss Norton was getting and wondered if she would like the morning papers read to her sometimes. Miss Norton agreed to the suggestion with some hesitation, though grateful for the offer, and Mrs Thornton soon found that she was not much interested. It took several sessions equally boring to both before Miss Norton brought herself to ask for the sports pages. She had kept her promise to her father but retained the interest which she had shared with him. By this time, however, Mrs Thornton had taken note of the row of silver cups on the long shelf opposite the window and was not altogether surprised.

"What a beautiful array you have there, Miss Norton," she said.

"I used to be quite a successful show jumper as a girl," said Miss Norton, "but most of these cups were won by my brother – he was a fine all-round athlete."

Mrs Thornton felt a pang of sympathy and pity, while at the same time she was glad that her shelves held books and not silver cups. She possessed a living heritage from the past and she thought, not for the first time, that old age bore more grievously upon those whose main interests had been in physical activities. So from then on she patiently ploughed through reports of race meetings and when these were exhausted, accounts of cricket, tennis and football events in their due seasons, and followed the careers of notable sportsmen and women of many nationalities for Miss Norton's sake. And then, one day, when she had finished reading about how "Sandhurst Prince won the Sirena Stakes at Kempton Park with consummate ease", Miss Norton surprised her by asking if she knew anything about "Talking Books".

"Indeed I do," said Mrs Thornton. "I have a blind cousin who would not know what to do without them. There is a great variety to choose from, too. Is there any special author you would like me to try and get for you?"

"Do they have any of Shakespeare's plays?" asked Miss Norton. "I am very fond of the plays."

"Now," said Mrs Thornton to herself, "this just shows that nobody really knows anything about anybody when they think they do."

Miss Norton went on, "Of course, I don't understand them properly but you don't need to understand Shakespeare, do you? I mean, not when you have seen him acted. We lived near Stratford, you see, and Harry – that's my brother – was very fond of the theatre. We used to go off together in his holidays, on our bicycles. Coming home at night in the summer it was never really dark. Sometimes there was a bright moon – the honeysuckle smelt so nice in the hedges. It was the old theatre that was burnt down, you know, it had an outside stircase by the river. We used to go down to the river in the intervals – there were no crowds in those days. Then, 'afterwards', I used to go alone. It didn't matter riding home alone at night, then, did it? You might think I wouldn't want to go afterwards, but I did. *Twelfth Night* is my favourite play and then *Henry V*."

So then Mrs Thornton read Shakespeare aloud, too, quite regularly. She tried once or twice to interest Meg in other authors but it was no good. Shakespeare and the sports pages of *The Times* were enough for her. When the plays were being read, Meg Norton would sit perfectly still with her eyes shut and her lips a little parted in rapt attention, as though she were seeing again the long dead actors and actresses playing their various parts.

"She looks like 'Patience on a monument smiling at grief'," thought Mrs Thornton, and then the aptness of the phrase pierced her. "Smiling at grief", "Count your blessings", "Smile at grief". "It ought to be written up over our front door."

But Mrs Perry, seated before the television on the evening when Miss Blackett had picked the lilac and Miss Dawson had experienced her miracle and Mrs Thornton was listening to her music, had really no grief to smile at. She was quite happily knitting a garment for her second great-grandchild and looking up now and again at the Box. She always knitted while she watched. She had been taught as a child that idleness was a sin and though she no longer believed this, the habit of constant employment remained with her. Besides, she liked it, and her knitting was a refuge when the programmes became boring or unpleasant: Mrs Langley did not mind what she watched, she liked the animation of movement and sound and it was for her like the constantly changing kaleidoscope patterns that had delighted her as a child. She nearly always dropped off to sleep after a while, Miss Ford and Miss Brown generally preferred ITV, so ITV it was. Mrs Perry felt ashamed that what she often enjoyed most were the advertisemens. Many of them were really clever, she thought, and funny too and the voices that accompanied them, cajoling, menacing, sensational and portentous by turns, never failed to entrance her – they were so ridiculous. She liked it when there were gardening programmes but the best of these were often on the other station and, generally, while supper was in progress, so she missed them. But she liked travel films, too, and some science fiction ones and pleasant family series. What made her concentrate on her knitting was the drearily monotonous sex pictures, always the same with hideous close-ups of people embracing. Really, the human face when blown up to giant proportions was too grotesque. She had read *Gulliver's Travels* once at school and sympathised with Gulliver's disgust at the huge Brobdingnags. The other boring activity was men hitting each other or firing off guns that made her jump and there seemed more of these every week. Still, it all made a change and when she had had enough she gently woke up Mrs Langley and took her safely back to her room before she went to her own. Invariably she left the other two still watching.

Leila Ford, who had been a third-rate actress in her youth, was really only interested in the personalities of the various performers, but Dorothy Brown, whose experience of life had been largely vicarious, lived out each drama, identifying herself, where possible, with the characters and the action so thoroughly that it was a recurring shock to hear Leila's comments. But tonight it was the background rather than the story or actors that gripped her. The scene was set in Greece and for Dorothy this was the land of pure enchantment, where long ago "the light that never was on land or sea" had shone for her once and for all. And, as if it were not enough to be drunk with its beauty, it was in Greece that she had first met Leila, not the monstrously overweight Leila with her bronze wig, now seated beside her in the only really comfortable chair in the room, but a Being in tune with all the magic of the wonderful country around her, a nymph with flowing red-gold hair and a dazzling smile, and outrageously daring clothes and exotic scent unknown in Dorothy's world – and this glorious Being unbelievably had chosen her as a friend and confidante for the rest of that marvellous holiday. The meeting with Leila had shaped the rest of Dorothy's life, whether for better or worse she was not the sort to enquire.

"Look, Leila," she said, "it's Greece!"

"Oh, is it?" said Leila indifferently. "Well, wherever it is, it's not worth looking at any more. That woman is far too old for the part and as for Derek Jones, he's the same boring understudy for Noel Coward whoever he's playing. Let's go to bed."

"Oh, no, Leila," said Dorothy, "do let us stay a bit longer; they might go to Delphi."

Leila turned her head slowly and looked at her. She had singular eyes, large, dark and opaque. "You can stay if you like," she said, "but you know I can't sleep if I don't get off when I feel like it."

Dorothy knew it too well, and she also knew that Leila could not easily undress herself now. She said no more but helped Leila to her feet, as she did so looking her last on all things lovely, the golden glory which the warden would switch off at the regulation time of ten o'clock.

Dorothy Brown was formerly an unsuccessful school teacher. In a modern large comprehensive school she would have been a total failure, but luckily for her when she started her career the times were not yet ripe for this and the girls' school in which she taught was on the whole well mannered and misbehaviour was unobtrusive.

"Oh, heavens! I haven't done my Latin prep. What *shall* I do?"

"Do it in Brownie's geog. lesson; she'll never notice, and if she does, she won't say anything."

Unhappily this was true. Dorothy suspected that her lessons were dull and inefficient, and poor exam results confirmed this, but geography was a second-class subject and so results did not matter all that much and she kept her job, staying on and on because she did not know what else to do until, most unexpectedly, an uncle left her a house and quite a substantial sum besides. Her mother, who had died when Dorothy was a girl, had been his favourite sister but he had lived mostly abroad and she scarcely knew him. She had a stepmother and a father who were not very interested in her, nor did she see any reason why they, or indeed anybody else, should be. She was not particularly able or amusing and, though she had nice grey eyes behind her spectacles, the rest of her appearance was easily forgotten. She could hardly believe in this legacy. She gave in her notice at once and at the end of the next term she left without regrets. Unreasonably, though, she hoped against hope for some sign of regret in others. Two more of the staff were leaving at the same time and they had presents and cards. On the last morning there was actually a card in her pigeon-hole, but it was only a regulation one from the Headmistress – a photograph of the school with "All good wishes for your future" written on it. This somehow made things worse, but travelling home with a wait at a railway junction, her eye was caught by a picture of the Parthenon on a magazine cover. On an impulse she bought it, read an article on "Touring in Greece" and thought wildly, "Why not? I could go there if I wanted to, I, Dorothy Brown, could go to Greece."

She fell in love with Greece when she got there, even before she met Leila. Dorothy was always falling in love with no hope and indeed with no great wish for any return. To be in love was enough. As a girl she had fallen in love with her geography mistress, which was a pity as it led to her taking up a subject in which she had never really been much interested. Then her loves succeeded each other in quick succession. There was Leslie Howard, and Jessie Matthews, and Laurence Olivier, and Vivien Leigh and the young local Conservative candidate who came one day to speak to the school and for whom she afterwards licked many election envelopes, and there was a headgirl, who looked like a fawn and had acted Juliet in the school production so movingly that Dorothy could hardly restrain her tears, and then there was Greece and Leila Ford.

In this, as in much else, Leila was her opposite. Leila had only loved once and for all in her life and was as constant and ardent a lover as any immortalized in literature. She was the only child of a late marriage, but her parents had not wished for any other children who might have deprived their Lilly (for so she had been christened) of their undivided attention. They believed her to be the prettiest and the cleverest little girl in the world, and as soon as she was old enough, which was remarkably soon, she fully agreed with them. Nothing was thought too good for her, but unfortuntely this resulted in nothing being quite good enough. As soon as she went to school the trouble began.

'Lilly, teacher says you are to be an angel in the Christmas play."

"But I want to be Mary." And it went on like this.

Lilly really had striking looks but she possessed little real ability and the stage, which had seemed to offer so much glamour as a career, proved hard going. After a few minor engagement with touring companies, she decided marriage was preferable to continuing to cast her pearls before swine. But once again she was dreadfully disappointed.

"Darling," she confided to Dorothy as they gazed together at the columns of Sumnian, "I gave up everything, yes, everything, for him and on our honeymoon I discovered —" she paused and lowered her voice and

Dorothy caught her breath in delicious suspense – "I discovered he was a pervert."

Dorothy only had the vaguest idea of what this could mean but obviously it was some almost unmentionable horror, and she thrilled at the thought that this tragic victim, almost in fact an Iphigenia or an Antigone, was actually pouring out her heart to *her*. Yes, the marriage stage which should have only brought more gifts to lay at the feet of Leila, the loved one, had had the impudence to demand unpleasant and inexcusable returns. It became obvious to Leila that she must be loyal to her first love – one could not serve two masters.

"It was, of course, impossible to stay with him," she said, "so I went back to my parents, my life ruined."

"Couldn't you have gone on with your acting?" said Dorothy. "You must have been *such* a loss. How I would have loved to have seen you!"

"Darling, the blow was too great, you don't quite understand. Look, we must go, the coach is filling up."

Later, Dorothy learned that it was not long since Leila, who was some years younger than herself, had lost her mother.

"It was her heart. She had just nursed me through influenza and I was away convalescing. She had caught it from me, you see."

"Oh, dear!" said Dorothy. "How you must have suffered not being with her."

"Yes," said Leila, "I was in no state to look after my poor father. He has gone into a very nice Home. I felt I needed a thorough change after all the upset, so I booked this holiday. Darling, you are such a wonderful friend, there is no one here that I could possibly have told of all my troubles."

This was probably true, as Dorothy Brown and herself happened to be the only unattached members of the party, all the rest being married couples or pairs of close friends.

30

In return for such confidences, Dorothy felt that the only item of interest in her own life was her legacy and indeed that seemed to interest Leila greatly.

"And where are you going to live now, dear? she asked.

"Well, besides the legacy," said Dorothy almost apologetically, "my uncle left me a house in Darnley. I don't suppose you'd have heard of Darnley, it's a little town, really only a large village, in Warwickshire."

"The very heart of old England!" exclaimed Leila.

"But it's really too big a house for me,' went on Dorothy, "and my solicitor advises me to sell it, so I may get a flat there instead, or somewhere else I suppose – I don't quite know."

"You vague little thing!" said Leila affectionately.

The day after this conversation, while admiring the stupendous views from Delphi, Leila resumed the subject.

"I think it would be a shame to sell your dear uncle's house. Why not get a friend to share it with you? Two living together is so much cheaper than one."

"I haven't any friend who would want to, I am afraid," said Dorothy. There was silence; the sun was disappearing behind the vast violet mountains and a wild impossible idea invaded her.

"I don't suppose . . .' she faltered, "oh, of course not, but you're so kind, you'll forgive me asking, but I don't suppose you could think ever of sharing the house with me yourself."

"You darling thing!" cried Leila. "How marvellous of you to propose such a thing! It might, d'you know, it might be possible, it just possibly might. Let's sleep on it, shall we?"

Peacefully Leila slept on it, but Dorothy alternated between huge hopes and fears. She settled for fears, it would be too good to be true. But it wasn't.

In the morning Leila said, "Well, darling, shall we give it a trial?"

When Leila actually saw the house, it obviously wouldn't quite do as it stood, but after getting the willing Dorothy to throw out an extension and put in an extra window to the best room – "After all, dear, it's improving the value of your property" – she found it took in her furniture quite satisfactorily, and so they settled down together and the long years passed, bringing, almost imperceptibly, unhappy changes to both.

For Leila, discontent became a way of life, only assuaged by eating and sleeping; Dorothy, for whom the glory had long departed, was always tired. One day, climbing the hill to Leila's favourite Delicatessen to shop, she had fainted and was brought home in an ambulance. The doctor said she was suffering from severe anaemia. It was just about then that Leila had developed her nervous headaches – she was approaching seventy and Dorothy five or so years older – what was to be done? The answer was found in The Haven where there actually happened to be two rooms vacant at the same time – two adjoining rooms, one large and one small. It was providential.

"How cosy this is," Leila had said, looking round the small one. "you'll be so snug in here, Dot dear."

4

THE COMMITTEE MEETING

MOST COMMITTEES consist of one member (usually the chairman) who appears to be doing a great deal of important work, and another (usually the secretary) who really does it. Besides these two essential components, there is often someone who is constantly puzzled to find themselves on a committee at all, and another who seems to have been born there and whose lifelong hobby is to serve on as many others as possible. Most committees also contain certain ex-officio members of one sort or another and a spare part or two.

The house committee of The Haven was no exception to this. Lady Merivale had a reputation for philanthropy to keep up in her own eyes, as well as among her neighbours, and she was successful as a chairwoman, ordering people about quite naturally and without giving offence. Her secretary, Miss Honor Bredon, was capable, intelligent and hardworking, in fact a good secretary. The treasurer, Colonel Bradshaw (retired) did not do so badly either in what was a somewhat thankless and difficult job, for the finances of the Home were complicated and inadequate and what with inflation and his own kind and conscientious disposition, he spent quite a number of worried hours over The Haven's affairs.

The vicar, an ex-officio member, was more interested in bees than in anything else in this world, or, it must be confessed, in the next. He was secretary to the County Apiary Society and often wished his parishioners were as industrious, clever and orderly as his beloved bees. But he accepted that this was not so, nor ever would be, and he did his duty by them manfully, which included serving on this particular committee and visiting the old ladies from time to time. Miss Hughes, one of the spare parts, possessed a surplus of both money and leisure and too few friends or interests, and so, on looking through her distressingly empty diary, she hailed with delight the entry for May 10th – "Committee Meeting at The Haven, 2.30 p.m." She had been proposed as a member by Col. Bradshaw at the instigation of his wife, who had refused the honour for herself.

"Yes, I know you are right, Dick, there should be another woman on the committee, considering The Haven is a Home for Old Ladies, but really, what with the Wives' Fellowship and the Conservative Association and the secretaryship of the Bridge Club and the children and the garden, I really can't undertake anything more, and Miss Hughes would love it.'

Miss Hughes did love it, only she wished she could think of something important to say at the Meetings. However, she could always assent or dissent heartily to show that she really was deeply involved and interested. Col. Bradshaw cherished a secret hope that one day it might occur to her to donate a small portion of her large income to ease the financial straits of The Haven, but his hope was unlikely to be realized. Her money being her one asset, she naturally clung to it with tenacity. The sixth member of the committee was an architect, a little restless man with a sandy moustache. Someone had once suggested that he could be helpful about problems of conversion and maintenance and might be in touch with cheap or even reasonable contractors. This had not hitherto been so. He spent the time during meetings wondering why he was pointlessly

34

wasting it and drawing little plans and pictures on his agenda paper. Seventh and last was a Mr Martin, the committee enthusiast, passionately addicted to irrelevant detail, but a mine of accurate information which was useful enough to outweigh the irritation he aroused.

Their number happened to be the same as the number of the residents and they sat round the same dignified solid table on the same uncomfortable and far from solid chairs. Only Lady Merivale was provided with an imitation Chippendale, the usual function of which was to lend tone to the entrance hall. The hyacinths, certainly now past their best, had been removed to the sideboard and were replaced by the lilac, picked by the warden the day before, but this had already elected to turn bad-tempered and was lifeless and droopy.

"Flowers always make a place look so homelike," cooed Miss Hughes to Honor Bredon. "Our good Miss Blackett never spares herself, does she, to make everything as pleasant as possible for the old dears."

Honor responded with a little grunt. She found it impossible either to agree or disagree.

Miss Blackett had had a strenuous morning and was looking hot in a too tight flowered artificial silk dress. With only Gisela's inefficient help she had had to prepare the tea which was always provided after the meeting, to see to the dinner trays for the residents, to polish the table and set out the pads and pencils, never used, for members always had their own, but in her eyes the right and proper regalia for any committee. But, as she sank thankfully into her chair, she congratulated herself that all was as it should be and she looked forward to hearing the accustomed expressions of appreciation and confidence which she felt were certainly her due.

The vicar and Col. Bradshaw were discussing the local agricultural show, the architect (who felt the cold) had secured the place nearest to the radiator and was fidgeting about already with paper and pencil, Lady Merivale was condescending pleasantly towards Miss Hughes, when Mr Martin hurried in, having swallowed a hasty sandwich in the train on the way from another meeting. Immediately everyone stopped talking and Lady Merivale picked up her agenda paper and said:

'Well, ladies and gentlemen, I think perhaps we should begin. The first item for discussion, as you will see, is the matter of Mr Jackson's bullocks." Mr Jackson farmed the land adjoining The Haven. "They have apparently broken through the boundary fence and trampled over the copse. Miss Blackett reports that Fred Mills had great difficulty in chasing them back and that their hoof marks are all over the lawn, not to speak of damage done to the fruit trees and the copse."

Col. Bradshaw frowned, Miss Hughes murmured, "Dear, dear, what a pity!", and Mr Martin said: 'Madam Chairman, may I ask whose responsibility it is to keep the fence in good repair and could it reasonably be said to be an adequate protection before this invasion?"

Col. Bradshaw said he was afraid the supports of the fence were on The Haven side of the ground, so legally the responsibility for the fence was not the farmer's, but as far as he had ascertained, it was in a fair condition and the bullocks seemed of an exceptionally inquisitive and adventurous breed.

The vicar said he supposed that lot would soon be sold and the trouble wasn't likely to recur. But Mr Martin rustled through his papers, of which he always had a stack, and finding at last the one he wanted, said with some satisfaction:

"Madam Chairman, it appears that this is not an isolated occurrence, in fact it might almost be said to be an annual event. Perhaps Miss Bredon will confirm this?"

Honour, who had already been looking up past Minutes, agreed that earlier bullocks had acted in the same way at least twice before.

Col. Bradshaw admitted that unfortunately Jackson owned a favourite cow, "a fine animal too", who regularly produced a very agile and bold son who was a natural leader, and wherever this troublemaker led, the rest of the herd followed.

The architect remarked that this behaviour was not peculiar to bullocks. Mr Martin ignored this irrelevance and asked what should be done to stop the nuisance.

Miss Hughes echoed him with: "What indeed!"

Col. Bradshaw said that what was really needed was electric wiring and Mr Martin said that it was only right that Jackson should contribute to this or sell his cow.

Lady Merivale then proposed that Jackson should be approached by Col. Bradshaw as to the carrying out of some form of effective barrier between his field and the copse. Miss Hughes enthusiastically seconded the motion and the committee moved to the next item, which was the preliminary arrangements for the annual summer fête. The object of the fête was threefold – to arouse and maintain local interest in The Haven, to raise a sum of money for "extras" – no really substantial amount could be hoped for – and to give the ladies a chance to contribute articles for sale, so providing them with interest and suitable occupation and the satisfaction of feeling of use.

"Well, Miss Blackett," said Lady Merivale, "who can we count on among our flock?"

"Mrs Perry will have some pot plants ready, I am sure, though I feel bound to say that she is not always prepared to give of her best."

"She regards them as her children," explained the vicar, "and finds it hard to part with any of them, but she is a charming old lady, and when it comes to the point, she'll be generous, I'm sure, and all her plants are well worth buying."

Miss Hughes, who had never set eyes on Mrs Perry or her plants, assented heartily.

Miss Blackett sniffed a little resentfully and continued: "Mrs Thornton is making some quite pretty little patchwork cushion covers."

"Now, I've always longed to do patchwork," said Miss Hughes.

"Miss Norton is too blind to produce anything herself, but she has written to a nephew who has just returned from service abroad and she is sure he will send us some attractive foreign articles."

"Splendid," said Lady Merivale.

"Miss Ford is knitting squares which Miss Brown will make up into a coverlet," continued Miss Blackett. Knitting squares was always a last resort for the least capable of the ladies.

"And they can be very pretty and useful," said Lady Merivale, "I see that as usual you have home supplies well in hand, Miss Blackett. Colonel Bradshaw, I hope Mrs Bradshaw will undertake the produce stall as usual?'

'Yes, I think you may count on her. Oh, she did ask me to mention that she hoped her stall could be sited in the shade this year. Last summer she said all the shady positions were taken before she could get here and the Produce Stall she feels, by its nature, should have priority. Her goods really did suffer rather badly," he added apologetically.

"Oh, what a pity!" exclaimed Miss Hughes.

Honor Bredon made a note to see what could be done, but the question of sites was a tricky one.

"Madam Chairman," said Mr Martin, "I believe it is the custom for the committee to provide the raffle prizes and that these are promised well in advance."

"I'll send along a bottle of sherry," said Col. Bradshaw.

"A pot of honey from me," said the vicar. "My white clover is a general favourite."

Mr Martin said he knew of a firm that would let him have fancy notepaper at a wholesale price, Lady Merivale always gave a large box of chocolates and the architect, with a decent show of diffidence, promised a framed drawing of the Old Market Cross done by himself.

Col. Bradshaw then looked encouragingly at Miss Hughes, who was reviewing in her mind the contents of her gift drawer. It contained, as far as she could remember, an orange silk lampshade and a set of plastic ashtrays, pink, blue and green, a pink satin nightdress case, a stuffed fashion doll bearing a faint likeness to Marilyn Monroe, a large tartan pincushion, a handbag in the shape of a rabbit with artificial fur and glass eyes, and a smart looking stainless-steel (but thoroughly unreliable) clock. All these articles had been bought as bargains or as the cheap left-overs from Bring-and-Buys, and were useful for the birthdays of her domestic 'helps' or for occasions like the present one. She decided on the clock as her raffle contri-bution, it really did look very well.

The next matter was not disposed of so easily – it had to be decided every year: should there be a band? The Boys' Brigade was available but it was quite expensive and con-sumed a good deal of refreshments besides. On the other hand, a band always attracted people. But then should there be a marquee in case of rain?They could not afford both. As it was a chilly afternoon, the committee were quite illogically inclined to be gloomy about future weather prospects; rain seemed more likely than not and rain with-out a marquee would be disastrous, so the marquee won the day. Miss Blackett felt relieved; she hated uncertainty and the strain of watching the weather. It was decided to appoint a small sub-committee nearer the date to help with all the other arrangements.

The afternoon was slipping by and Lady Merivale brought the business of the fête to an end and passed on to the next item, which was to record the vacancy left by the departure of Mrs Wilson for the local hospital where most of the old ladies ended their days when they had passed beyond the care of The Haven. The next name on the waiting list was a Mrs Nicholson who was unable, owing to heart trouble, to continue to run her own home. Miss Blackett felt that the time had now come for a protest and an appeal.

"Lady Merivale," she said, "I am sorry to say that Brenda Jones, my only domestic help beside Gisela, the German au pair, and Mrs Mills who, as you know, only comes to me twice a week, has left me without notice. This Mrs Nicholson does not sound as though she will be able to do much for herself and I feel I cannot undertake this fresh responsibility and the extra work a new resident entails under present conditions. Then Mrs Langley's condition has deteriorated during the past year and she needs constant supervision. I feel she should receive better attention than I can give her, certainly now without Brenda, and I think she should be removed to the geriatric department at the hospital as soon as they have a bed free."

There was a general murmur of sympathy and assent.

"Of course, Miss Blackett," said Lady Merivale, "we cannot let you be overworked and it does seem as though Mrs Langley is not a case for The Haven any more. Will you get Dr Moss to see her and then I am sure he will be able to arrange matters for you."

But the vicar looked uneasy. His visits to the geriatric unit were not among his happiest.

"Mrs Langley is very contented here," he said, "it will be a great change for her. No doubt she will get every physical care at the unit but has she not any relatives who might give her a home? I believe there is no lack of means to provide help and considering her age, it cannot be for very long."

"She has a son close on seventy – the last time he visited her, which was some years ago as he is not in good health, she could not be persuaded that he was not her father. There is a married daughter in Canada and one grandson, a businessman in Birmingham," said Miss Blackett.

"I presume he or his father have powers of attorney," said Mr Martin. "They should be informed of the position."

Honor made another note.

Miss Blackett felt she had done well so far and continued firmly: "If Mrs Langley goes there will be another room vacant. I don't think I can cope with two new residents at once and besides I think it would be far better for Mrs Thornton to move down from the attic floor which is really not suitable for an old person and it would ease the work considerably."

"Quite, quite," said Miss Hughes, but as no one else spoke she felt she had been too precipitate.

"It has always been the custom, as I am sure you know, Miss Blackett," said Lady Merivale after a short pause, "to allow residents their choice of rooms whenever possible but I quite see your point and, if Mrs Thornton agrees, there perhaps should not be any objection."

"It will reduce our income," said Col. Bradshaw.

"Do you know what Mrs Thornton thinks about it?" asked the vicar.

Miss Blackett was an honest woman. She knew that Mrs Thornton had reacted unfavourably to the hints she had thrown out up to the present, but she also believed her to be a sensible person at heart, in other words that she would come to see things as she, Miss Blackett, saw them, so she replied with conviction that though the old always took a little time to adjust to any change, she was sure Mrs Thornton would welcome it quite soon.

"I think then we should wait for the decision to come from her," said the vicar firmly. Mrs Thornton was a clergyman's daughter.

"But, Madam Chairman," said Mr Martin, "if our warden has insufficient help for too many duties, all the residents will suffer. I suggest that we advertise for help at once in the local papers and explore every avenue."

41

Miss Blackett knew too well all those dead-end avenues but she merely said a little tartly, "The papers are already full of such advertisements."

The vicar cleared his throat and this time spoke with some hesitation.

"I do happen to know of a lad who is quite handy and very willing and is anxious to find work. If you would consider him, Miss Blackett, merely as a stopgap, you know, until you can find someone more suitable, and take him on trial, it might 'bless she who gives and he who takes'," he finished with a nervous flourish.

"Beggars can't be choosers," said Miss Blackett ungraciously, "but I must say I wouldn't choose a boy. What sort of a boy is he?"

"Well, you may not think the sex the only disadvantage," said the vicar hesitantly and paused.

"Come, come, out with it, Vicar," said Mr Martin. "He isn't a Borstal boy on probation, I hope?"

"Oh, no, no nothing of that sort," said the vicar hastily, "but he's a simple fellow, definitely E.S.N., so his school says, but they speak quite highly of his character and I have been employing him a little on odd jobs and find him an attractive lad, though a bit odd – he has a wonderful way with bees."

"But I don't keep bees," said Miss Blackett.

"No, no, of course not," said the vicar sadly.

"If he's E.S.N. he can't expect much in the way of wages," said Col. Bradshaw.

"Where does he come from?" asked the architect.

"He has been living with his grandmother, old Mrs Hobb at Sturton," said the vicar. Sturton was the hamlet about three miles from The Haven. "But she is anxious for him to learn to be independent of her though she seems very fond of him. She wouldn't expect anything but pocket money and his keep."

"Hobb, did you say?" said Col. Bradshaw. "Family's

42

been in these parts since the Conquest I should think but nearly all gone now. The old woman is quite a character, I've heard."

Miss Blackett was silent. The boy sounded very unreliable but she thought of piles of dirty dishes, of unswept floors, of beds to be made, trays to be set and carried about, vegetables to be prepared and all the cooking and the shopping and the fête ahead, not to speak of the possible crises that were apt to occur at any time, and so at last she said: "Well, I'm used to looking after old loonies, so I suppose I can take a young one on, and if the vicar can assure me that he is honest and clean, I dare say he'll be better than nobody."

The committee was relieved at her decision, though not for the first time deploring the warden's way of expressing herself, but still, so they told themselves, her bark was worse than her bite.

"I'm sure you won't regret it," said the vicar. "When can I send him round to see you?"

"Tomorrow evening," said Miss Blackett.

"The next item," said Lady Merivale, "and one that Miss Blackett feels is urgent to put in hand before next autumn, is the felling of the deodar tree."

"It's a fine tree," said Col. Bradshaw. "Must be over a hundred years old."

"It is far too near the house," said the little architect. "People will make that mistake in planting trees. They seem unable to grasp the fact that trees grow and houses can't run away from them."

Miss Blackett looked gratified at this support.

"That is exactly the case here," she said. "The tree makes poor Mrs Dawson's room very dark and cheerless and in wet weather the rain collects on the branches which brush against the walls. I feel sure this causes damp."

"Then there seems a strong case for the felling," said Mr Martin.

"It's a fine tree," repeated the colonel sadly, "and it will cost a good deal to fell, though the timber ought to fetch something."

The architect was asked if he knew of any reasonable and trustworthy tree doctors, but it was Mr Martin, of course, who was able to supply names and addresses. The matter of repairs and repainting was soon dealt with and at last the meeting was over. The warden went to help Gisela bring in the tea. The architect and Mr Martin both swallowed a hasty cup and disappeared. Col. Bradshaw, after disposing of one of Miss Blackett's uninteresting little cakes, asked Honor Bredon to come and inspect the damage done by the bullocks. Lady Merivale was left with Miss Hughes. Lord Jim, who had been sulking at having been shut out of the dining-room all the afternoon, had bolted in as soon as the door was opened and after taking a look from the window to make sure that nothing of note was happening in the drive, made straight for Miss Hughes, who disliked all animals but perhaps more especially cats. He wrapped himself ecstatically round her ankles. She exclaimed, stepped back hurriedly and jerked Lady Merivale into upsetting her cup of tea down her pale grey linen suit. Miss Hughes apologized effusively, Lady Merivale said it really didn't matter in the least, and Lord Jim went to the door which someone had closed again and demanded to be let out immediately.

"A very useful meeting, don't you think, Miss Hughes?" said Lady Merivale pleasantly.

"Oh, yes, very!" agreed Miss Hughes.

"I wonder if you could spare some of your valuable time to help with the fête," went on Lady Merivale, "perhaps as a stallholder?"

"I think I could manage it," said Miss Hughes delightedly.

"That would be most kind," said Lady Merivale drawing on her gloves. "Well, I think I must be off now, Miss

44

Blackett. Thank you as usual for all your splendid work for us and for your hospitality this afternoon. I am sure you have decided rightly in giving this poor boy a trial and I do hope he will prove a real help to you."

"I hope so too," replied Miss Blackett, but the hope was faint. Life had not taught her to be very hopeful.

5

TOM

THE VICAR often liked to go about his business on his push bicycle. He said it was good for him and besides, it left the car free for his wife. She was the better driver and by far the better mechanic of the two. On the morning after the committee meeting, he set out to visit Tom Hobb and his grandmother. The weather at last had taken a turn for the better. The east wind which had blown relentlessly since early April had veered to the south-west and everything beautiful could stop looking brave as well and instead rejoice in shining with a quite remarkable loveliness. The vicar sped along the road leading to the hamlet and as he passed The Haven he waved courteously to the house, thinking that one of the old ladies might chance to be looking out of a window and be cheered at the gesture. Soon he turned into a lane bordered thickly with cow parsley, the hawthorn was out in the hedges and there were great clumps of campion on the banks and here and there a single foxglove reared up like a sentinel. A few white clouds were rapidly disintegrating in a sky of deep secure blue and the sun felt really hot for the first time that year.

The vicar could not contain himself. "Praise God from Whom all blessings flow," he roared out and flew down the lane at a dangerous speed. He was a man given to happiness. He had his bees, a wife who was admirably fitted to be a vicar's helpmate, two pretty small daughters and an

46

uncomplicated mind. Of course he was sometimes troubled about erring or sorrowful parishioners, and he made himself miserable for a short time once a day by reading or listening to the news. But this he felt was enough. His wants were few and he had no ambitions to speak of, so on this fine May morning he sang the Doxology as he sped through the sunshine.

Tom Hobb's grandmother lived at the bottom of a steep, rough little footpath leading off the lane that continued on its way to the hamlet. The vicar proceeded down this path on foot. The Hobbs' cottage was tiny, humped and thatched, and sat square across the path with a lilac bush and an old apple tree, both in flower, on either side of the gate. On the crest of the thatch, which was in need of repair, crouched a black cat watching the sparrows and in the cottage doorway sat old Mrs Hobb stirring something in a basin. She was noted in the hamlet for her herb potions and her homemade wines and was held to be very ancient and crafty. "A hundred years or so ago she would certainly have been the village witch," thought the vicar, as he propped his bicycle against the hedge, and indeed she looked the part, with her black cat and her pot. The village children were a bit frightened of her, though they all liked Tom. She had had a husband once, it was supposed, and children and other grandchildren, but Tom now seemed to be the only one left. He had always lived with his grandmother and no one could remember his parents being around.

"Good morning, Mrs Hobb," shouted the vicar, coming up the path, "what a lovely day at last."

"And so it be, sir," said the old woman looking up at him with eyes surprisingly bright in a face as brown and crumpled as a winter leaf. "And what can I do for you today?"

It was, as a greeting, the other way round from those he was used to, and took him a little aback.

"Well, it's about Tom. He's been helping me with my bee swarms after school, you know, and now he's finished his schooling, he tells me you'd like him to find a regular job away from home, but not too far away, and I think I've found just the place for him." He paused, she had not taken her eyes from his face and now she nodded vigorously.

"T'would be best for the lad to see a little more of the world," she said.

"I'm afraid you may miss him and the help he is to you," said the vicar. He had thought of this before and wondered if the old woman would be all right on her own, but her gaze did not falter.

"I can manage, sir, and if you have somewhere in mind that is not too far, perhaps he can come and see me of a Sunday."

"It's at The Haven," said the vicar. "Miss Blackett, who is warden there, needs help now, though it may be only temporary."

"The Haven," said the old woman slowly, "that's what they calls the New House that was raised where the Old Farmhouse stood."

"Well, it's scarcely new now," said the vicar smiling.

"Why, no to be sure, but my Mammy, she allays called it the Old Farm when she were a slip of a girl. She'd be pleased for Tom to go there, I expect, even though it is the New House now."

"Miss Blackett wants to see him first," said the vicar, and felt bound to add: "Of course, she may not think him suitable."

"My Tom will suit all right, there'll be no need to be wary of him – there's more corn than chaff in Tom," said the old woman quietly.

"She's as proud of him as if he had left school top of the class instead of not knowing how to read or write and only counting on his fingers," thought the vicar, but aloud he said: "I know he's a good boy and will do his best. Miss Blackett would like to see him this evening. Where is he, by the way? I'd better have a word with him if I can."

"He be gone to gather a bit o' fire wood, sir, and I can't say exactly when he'll be home again." Then, "Ah yes, but I can," she added smiling, for the black cat had suddenly leapt to the ground and streaked round the corner of the cottage. "Sweep allays knows afore I do. Tom'll be here in a moment, you'll see."

Sure enough, the boy came up almost at once with Sweep on his shoulders and a bundle of wood under one arm. He was small for his age but with a big head, and his large ears standing out from it made it look even bigger. His arms seemed too long for his body. His hair was straw-coloured, coarse and thick, he had a snub nose, freckles, greenish eyes set wide apart and a large cheerful mouth. Those eyes did not appear at all vacant, yet there was something not quite usual in the way they looked at you: they turned the same intent disinterested gaze on everything alike. It always reminded the vicar of the way babies he christened gazed at him – if they were not yelling, that is.

"What sort of wood have 'ee got there, then?" asked the old woman.

"A bit o'beech, Granny," said Tom. His voice was pleasantly pitched and he talked like his grandmother and not as they had tried to teach him at school.

The old woman looked pleased. "Good boy, I thought you'd have more sense than to bring any of they dead elm branches from yonder. Burning elm's no better than burning churchyard mould for the warmth."

The boy put down the bundle he was carrying without haste and held out his hand, which the vicar took and solemnly shook. He was, by now, used to Tom's ways.

"Well, Tom," he said, "I think I've found a good place for you and your Granny's willing for you to try it. You're to go and see about it this very evening."

"Where be it then?" asked Tom.

"It's at the Darnley Ladies' Home."

The boy looked puzzled. "There's many a lady's home at Darnley," he said, "there's Jenny's mother's, and Mary's, and Tim's and old Mrs Martin's and –"

"No, no," said the vicar, "not that kind of home, Tom, but a big house called 'The Haven', you must know it well – it stands by itself a little way out of town. A number of old ladies live there together – it's rather like one of my bee-hives, Tom," he went on, warming to his exposition. "They each have a room to themselves like a cell and there's one lady who looks after them all. Her name is Miss Blackett and you must ask for her when you go there."

"Be she like the queen bee, then?" asked Tom.

"Well, yes, something like that," said the vicar. "You are to go and see her at six o'clock and I've told her you are a very good boy and will do your best to help her."

"Aye, that he will," said the old woman. Tom nodded and held out his hand again as there seemed to him there was nothing more to be said on the subject.

Mrs Hobb got up stiffly to bid the vicar goodbye. She thanked him for coming but it was clear from her manner that she felt she was conferring a benefit and not receiving one. The vicar thought: "I hope she *will* be able to manage without the boy, but it's clear she's made up her mind to part with him and nothing will budge her. Well, anyway, his keep will be a saving for her. I hope, too, he'll make good at The Haven."

"You'll let me know how things go," he said to them both. "It'll be easier to start now summer's really come. We've waited long enough for it this year and it was a hard winter, too."

"Oh, well," said the old woman, "we've never died of a winter yet."

Tom presented himself at the correct hour that evening. He wore a clean darned pullover with sleeves that were too short for his long arms and his trousers were patched. His hair looked very bristly and he was smaller and more childish looking than Miss Blackett had expected, so altogether he did not make a favourable first impression when Gisela had pushed him disdainfully through the office door. The warden did not think it necessary to get up to receive him but Tom came forward at once and held out his hand in his usual way saying:

"Be you Queen Miss Blackett, lady?"

Miss Blackett mechanically shook his hand but was struck dumb by this unlooked-for greeting. She had expected some stupidity perhaps, certainly shyness and even becoming awe. Tom waited for her to speak and looked round him with his wide detached stare. He saw Lord Jim, asleep on his special cushion and immediately went up to him.

"Don't touch him," said Miss Blackett, "he doesn't like to be disturbed, especially by strangers." But neither Tom nor Lord Jim took any notice of her words. Tom stooped and stroked him and the big cat opened his eyes, rolled over on his back and began to purr loudly.

"What be his name?" asked Tom.

"Lord Jim," said Miss Blackett, once more taken aback. Tom nodded his head in approval. Lords, he knew, were very fine people and this was a very fine cat.

"He's bigger nor our Sweep. Do 'ee know why we calls him Sweep? It was one day, Gran and I be sitting by our fire and right through our window he came a-leaping, and across the room and up the chimney afore we could stop him. Gran says a fox must a bin after him. We got a pail o' water quick and threw it on the fire, so as it wouldn't burn him, and after a long while down he comes and all the soot with him. We never found out where he comes from and he's bin with us ever since. So we called him Sweep – it's a good name 'cause he's black as soot anyways."

"This must stop," thought Miss Blackett; the interview

(which could scarcely yet have been called an interview) was getting out of hand and she decided to ignore all that Tom had said or done since he had come into the room.

"You're small for your age," she said disapprovingly. "I hope you'll be able to manage what I shall need you to do, if I decide whether to give you a trial. I shall want you to rake out the boiler and stoke it every morning and evening and fill the fuel pails and keep the boiler room clean."

Tom nodded.

"And you must sweep the stairs every day and help Gisela to carry the trays up and down and clean the ladies' rooms."

Tom nodded again.

"Well," said Miss Blackett, "we shall see. I am willing to try you because the vicar says you are a good, hard-working boy, but you must prove to me to be so here as he tells me you have been to him at the vicarage."

"Yes, Queen, Lady Miss Blackett," said Tom and he held out his hand again.

"You mustn't be a silly boy," said Miss Blackett and this time, being more prepared, she took no notice of his hand but continued: "And you must call me Miss Blackett and nothing else." What could have made him bestow royalty upon her? Nevertheless, a faint absurd flicker of gratification stirred within her. He had spoken in such a natural sort of way, not at all impertinently, though what he said was so ridiculous, and yet he was not exactly polite either. She could not describe it.

"Be I to come tomorrow then?"

Miss Blackett considered. She did not like doing anything in too much of a hurry, but if the boy was to come at all, there seemed no point in putting it off. "You can come tomorrow afternoon," she said.

After he had gone she sat for a while thinking. "I don't know quite what to make of him," she said to herself, "and I doubt if he'll be of much use. Oh, well, I didn't hope for

52

much after all. I'll just have to see."

Tom was to sleep in the little attic next to Mrs Thornton. To say that the warden had planned this with a view to reducing Mrs Thornton's contentment with her room would be untrue, for there was no other place to put the boy. Brenda had shared a room with Gisela. But it certainly crossed her mind. She was sure that Mrs Thornton would see reason eventually but it would be all to the good if the process could be speeded up, and she thought it likely that Mrs Thornton would not welcome Tom's advent, banging his door morning and night, as likely as not, and probably making his presence felt in other undesirable ways. She went up to the attic floor the next morning to inspect the little room and to tell Mrs Thornton about the boy.

The small attic had retained more of its original appearance than any other part of the house. It still contained the iron bedstead which had been used by the last of the family cooks, and hanging above it was a framed text – "Thou, God, seest me", illustrated by a huge eye whose black lashes rayed out like beams from a dark sun. There was a scratched deal chest of drawers painted green. Miss Blackett pulled out the drawers, which stuck badly. They were quite empty except for a black-headed hatpin. There was a high bent-wood chair of the kind that used once to be found at every shop counter and a corner washstand, also painted green, holding a chipped white basin and jug. The floor was bare except for a rag rug by the bed. These were all original furnishings but piled along one end of the room were a number of incongruous articles put there to be out of the way – a dressmaker's dummy topped with a torn red silk lampshade, an old knife-cleaning machine, a pile of bound copies of *Sunday at Home* and an umbrella.

Miss Blackett decided that Tom's first job would be to clean the room. She had no intention of doing it for him – he was coming to reduce work, not to add to it. She must look out some bedding for him, however. As for the junk, it would have to stay there. She did not think it would do for jumble even and the dustmen were very choosey about what they consented to take away. If only people wouldn't collect so many articles round themselves; the old ladies' rooms were a constant source of irritation to her, cluttered up as they nearly all were, and everything having to be dealt with somehow when the poor old things died, and meanwhile having to be kept clean. She always returned to her own sparsely furnished quarters with a sense of relief. There was Mrs Thornton's room, for instance, smothered in books, and books of all things attracted dust. She knocked at the door.

Mrs Thornton was sitting by the window in her turret watching for the mid-morning train. She liked to see it punctually on its way.

"Oh, Mrs Thornton," said Miss Blackett, "there is a boy, recommended by the vicar, coming to help till we can fill Brenda's place more adequately. He's to sleep in the little attic. I hope he won't be a nuisance to you."

"She doesn't really hope anything of the sort," thought Mrs Thornton, well aware by now of the warden's wish to remove her downstairs.

"I certainly hope not, Miss Blackett," she said coldly.

There was a slight pause and then Miss Blackett went on: "I am sure there is nothing to worry about, but I think perhaps you should know that, though a nice enough boy – he came to see me yesterday – and highly spoken of by both his school and the vicar, he is rather simple." She would have preferred not to mention this and to have let Mrs Thornton discover Tom's deficiencies for herself, but although she was convinced that he was harmless, he certainly was odd and her conscience told her it was only fair to warn Mrs Thornton of this. Miss Blackett was in the habit of obeying her conscience.

Mrs Thornton grew more and more indignant and

54

apprehensive as she listened. "This is really too bad," she thought, "not only a boy, but a mentally defective boy on my doorstep. I shan't pretend not to mind." She didn't.

"I was afraid you might not like it," said Miss Blackett, "but it really can't be helped. I am sure you see that he is needed and there is nowhere else to put him. When Mrs Langley goes you can always move down there, you know, such a nice room."

She turned and walked briskly away.

"Oh, indeed I can, can I?" said Mrs Thornton grimly, not caring whether she was heard or not. She recognised that the warden had reason on her side but over this she herself could not be reasonable. She looked round her room with something like desperation: its charms and its privacy seemed all the more precious now that they were threatened. She thought of her lost home with a fierce nostalgia. Her attic represented the last little bit of personal choice left to her and she was determined not to be driven out of it by all the demented boys in Christendom.

Gisela had been crying again. Her letter from home was overdue and still hadn't come that morning. When she brought in Miss Blackett's eleven o'clock coffee she was sniffing.

"If you've caught a cold, it's your own fault, Gisela," said Miss Blackett. "In all this cold weather we've been having, you've been going about in short-sleeved flimsy dresses. We have a very sensible old English saying: 'Ne'er cast a clout till May be out.' That means, don't leave off your warm clothes till the end of the month. Some people think it refers to the blossom May, but I am sure the month is meant. The boy, Tom Hobb, is coming this afternoon. I want you to take him up to his room and tell him to give it a good sweep out. You must show him where everything is kept."

Gisela now felt aggrieved as well as unhappy. She hadn't got a cold and her clothes were the right ones for the time of

55

the year – it was a stupid saying, that! It didn't even know what it meant, if people had to guess at it – and she resented having to bother with a rough boy. She had not at all liked his clothes or his clumsy looks, so that when Tom arrived she would not shake hands but marched on ahead of him ordering him to follow her. Tom was carrying a small bundle.

"What's that for luggage!" said Gisela disdainfully as they reached the attic and he put it down. He was looking at her with his unblinking direct gaze. "Why do you look at me so, it is not good," she said.

"You be so pretty," said Tom.

Gisela knew she was not pretty. She was, in fact, used to being called the plain one of the family. She was tall and thin with straight string-like fair hair. She was too pale, even her eyes were too pale a blue and her nose was long and a little crooked.

"Like one o' they moon daisies," said Tom.

Gisela, in her turn, gazed at him. Just as Miss Blackett had done, she sensed at once that he was not being rude and she began to stop feeling cross and smiled at him unwillingly, for it was rather nice to be called pretty for once, even though it was only by a rough poor boy, and then something in the way his yellow hair stood up like a brush reminded her of her youngest brother, the one she liked the best.

"Come," she said, "you like that I help you with the room?"

Tom nodded and looked round the attic. When he saw the dummy with the lampshade hat, he pointed at it and crowed with laughter. Gisela laughed too and suddenly she felt happy. Even if he was a peasant boy, he was young and, since Brenda had left, she had felt so lonely among all the ladies and Miss Blackett and Mrs Mills and Fred – all so old.

They set to work together moving everything out on to

56

the landing so that they could clean and sweep properly. They pushed open the window, stiff with years of neglect, and Tom stuck his head out and crowed again with pleasure.

"I've never slept so near the sky afore," he said.

Mrs Thornton had heard all the noise and laughter with dismay. It was going to be just as bad as she had feared. She was too upset to tell herself that it was unreasonable to pass judgement so soon. In this mood she spent the rest of the afternoon and most of the evening, waiting for every fresh sound, until at last she realized she must take herself in hand, so she found her *Radio Times* and turned the pages anxiously. Yes, she was in luck, and soon the divine melody of Beethoven's Violin Concerto flooded the room, routing for the time being the world, the flesh and the devil.

At the end of the first movement she heard a slight scuffling noise outside the room and quickly opened the door. Someone, crouched against it outside, nearly fell in. It was a boy – *the* boy, she supposed. She switched off the radio and demanded angrily what he was doing there. Tom replied by humming, in time and in tune, the concerto's opening theme. Mrs Thornton stared down at him and he hummed the tune again and then, pointing beyond her into the room he said:

"Can you play a bit more o' that, Lady, please?"

Mrs Thornton was amazed. She said, "So you were listening to the music, were you? Have you ever heard that piece before?"

Tom shook his head vigorously.

"And you liked it, I can see. Do you like music?" Tom nodded as vigorously.

Mrs Thornton experienced a blessed sense of relief. She could put up with much from a boy who could hum a Beethoven theme correctly after a first hearing, and there was something else as well as relief. The boy obviously really loved what he had heard. She was as convinced of

57

that as Miss Blackett and Gisela had been of his admiration of them. There was no one at all at The Haven besides herself to whom music mattered. Mrs Perry enjoyed Gilbert & Sullivan and Strauss waltzes from early associations, Mrs Langley loved hymn tunes, and Gisela sometimes strummed "Ach du liebe Augustin" on the old piano in the sitting-room, but that was as far as it went, and now this boy, whose invasion on her attic floor she had so resented, was apparently a comrade in felicity. She felt profoundly grateful that, even in old age, life offered such surprises.

6

TOM AND THE LADIES

TOM'S PECULIAR crow of laughter became a familiar sound at
The Haven during the weeks that followed. To Gisela it
brought a sense of fellow feeling and made her giggle. Mrs
Thornton, too, liked to hear it. She became thoroughly
interested in Tom and quite often of an evening she would
invite him into her room to share a radio concert with him.
She found that he was always affected by the music, but
that she could not tell beforehand how he would react.
Sometimes he could not remain still but jumped about in a
queer clumsy dance, or clapped his hands and nodded his
head to the rhythm; sometimes he sat motionless as if
enchanted, sometimes he rocked to and fro with laughter
and sometimes he put his fingers to his ears and rushed
away out of the room. She made an attempt to teach him to
play on the sitting-room piano, but, though he could pick
up quite complicated tunes very quickly and hum them
correctly, the mysteries of the keyboard were obviously
beyond him, or else he simply wasn't interested.

Old Mrs Langley was always especially kind to Tom
because she got it into her head that he was her Susan's
love-child. "He always was happy from a baby," she told
everyone.

Mrs Perry said it was good to hear him laughing about
the house, it reminded her of her grandchildren. Dorothy
Brown only heard it faintly.

59

"You grow deafer every day," said Leila, aggrieved. Leila hated Tom. "I never could bear defectives," she said, "and that noise he makes gives me the creeps. I'm a very sensitive person, I'm afraid, but I don't think it's fair to employ a boy like that here. I shall complain."

As for Miss Blackett, she found the laughter disquieting, she did not know why, but it was part of her uncomfortable inability to place Tom in her scheme of things. She could not make him out and this annoyed her. At the end of the first week she had decided to keep him on for there was no doubt he was a good little worker, thorough and willing and much quicker and neater than she had expected from his looks. But he had odd habits. For one thing, as the summer advanced, he seemed to wake earlier and earlier and would come down and set about his work before anyone else was astir. At first she determined to put a stop to this, not that anyone complained, for he was a surprisingly quiet worker and the offices in the annexe were shut off from the rest of the house. But it was not what she was used to.

"You must not come downstairs so early, Tom," she told him, "there is no need – there is plenty of time for you to do your work later."

But the day after she had spoken and all the mornings that followed, it was just the same. She expostulated but she might as well have not spoken. It was most irritating, yet there was no denying that after all it was pleasant to find everything swept and tidy when she herself got downstairs, and the boiler fire giving no trouble, and the breakfast trays set out for Gisela, who on the other hand was apt to be late, and Miss Blackett often had had to see to these herself. And there were little extra jobs done without the asking, such as Lord Jim's breakfast Whiskas tin opened and his evening snack plate cleared up, and the kettle on for her early cup of tea. But then, there was the affair of the bats. A pair of them had taken up daylight residence in a corner of Tom's attic and Miss Blackett, who looked upon bats as vermin, told Tom to get the kitchen steps and get rid of them, but Tom had said, "Best let 'em bide and have their sleep out, Lady Miss Blackett," and when she went up the next day to inspect, they were still there. She had a horror of the creatures and could not bring herself to go near them, but she was unwilling to confess this or to own up to the fact that apparently she was powerless to get Tom to do as he was told – so the bats remained.

His disregard of her order in certain matters, though never rude or defiant, naturally upset her and it did not happen only to her. Fred Mills, the old gardener, complained that Tom picked flowers from the garden occasionally without asking leave, and Mrs Perry, with some unwillingness, confirmed this.

"I've told the lad they're not his flowers and he's no right to them," grumbled Fred, yet Tom continued to make up his little nosegays quite openly.

What he did with them Mrs Perry later discovered when one day she noticed Miss Brown with a bunch of her treasured clove-pinks pinned to her flat chest.

"What lovely flowers," Mrs Perry shouted pleasantly.

Miss Brown actually blushed. "Tom brought them to me," she said. "He brings me flowers now and again, and I like to wear some of them sometimes, just to show how I appreciate them."

Mrs Perry, who had always felt a little sorry for Miss Brown, said no more. "She obviously doesn't wonder where he gets them from. Poor thing, I wonder if anyone's ever bothered to give her flowers before," she thought.

As for old Fred, he was completely won over by what happened when, before the repairs to the fence had been completed, Mr Jackson's bullocks staged another marauding expedition. This time, however, Tom was on the scene. "I never seed the like. That lad just told 'em to go home, just went up to that little devil of a leader, he did, and stood right in his way and put out his hand to him, coaxing like, and talked to him, and he turned tail and home he went afore he'd done any harm, and the rest just followed him. How did 'e manage that then? I axed him and he said, 'I tells 'im he was a silly ole duffer to come wandering into a mucky wood, leaving his nice medder, and how every step he took lost him a bite of his own good grass, and he saw sense.' He do have a wonderful way with animals, that's for sure."

That was another thing: at first Miss Blackett had been pleased that Lord Jim and Tom had taken to one another. It was a credit mark for the boy. But, as time went on, she began to resent the cat's marked preference for his company, even above her own. She would not admit that she was so foolish as to be jealous, but what she was beginning to feel was undoubtedly very like jealousy.

When she learned about Tom's picking Mrs Perry's flowers (it was difficult not to hear about things at The Haven), Miss Blackett felt she must apologize to her but Mrs Perry secretly thought that far more harm was done to her treasures by Lord Jim than by Tom.

"I don't really mind, Miss Blackett," she said. 'I think he believes all the flowers in the garden belong to us all, himself included, as if we were all one family, I mean, and perhaps too it's because he's used to picking wild flowers wherever and whenever he likes. Anyway, I don't mind at all, so please don't say anything to the boy."

Miss Blackett sniffed. "Much good it would do if I did, with Tom," she thought.

The little incident of the nosegay of pinks, however, made Mrs Perry observe Dorothy Brown more closely.

"Don't you think Miss Brown's changed lately?" she

said to Miss Dawson. "In spite of her deafness, which seems to be getting worse, she's brighter somehow. I don't mean more cheerful exactly, but less of a shadow. One used scarcely to be aware of her. Now, if only it wasn't for that dreadful Miss Ford with her all the time, I believe she could be quite a nice friendly person."

"I can't think why you want everyone to be friendly," said Frances Dawson, though without rancour, adding "but I suppose you can't help it."

"Can it be just Tom's nosegays that have changed her?" mused Mrs Perry, taking no notice of Miss Dawson's remark.

But though Tom's offerings were not without their effect, the change in Dorothy Brown which Mrs Perry had noticed had come about through a completely chance event. Yet this too was connected with the boy. Leila Ford had managed to keep him out of her room by bribing Gisela to do extra cleaning with some of the chocolates she always kept near her, but she could not avoid him altogether. One day, when she and Dorothy were returning to their rooms after dinner, they saw him coming towards them down a passage. Pleased at the meeting and feeling that he had not yet managed to show that he wanted to be friends with Lady Miss Ford, Tom ran towards her with his hand held out in his usual greeting. To her horror Dorothy then saw Leila raise the stick which she now always used to support her great bulk and strike at his outstretched arm, so that it fell to his side.

"Get away – you!" she cried, but Tom stood still. Dorothy, as if impelled by an almost reflex action, immediately stepped up to him and kissed him. Then she went into her own room and shut the door.

At first she was overcome with rage at Leila and surprise at herself. Gradually both anger and surprise faded away. She sat down on her bed ignoring, indeed not even hearing, the imperious tapping on her wall, Leila's customary summons. She knew that something very important had happened to her and that she had to find out what it was. She sat on, and eventually certain facts presented themselves to her. First, that she hated Leila and had done so for years: secondly, that the Leila she had once loved had never existed; thirdly, that Leila had never cared for her and perhaps had never cared for anyone; and lastly, that she had been too cowardly at the beginning and latterly too tired to admit all this to herself. It was as if Leila's stick had struck down not just Tom's arm but the whole false defensive wall that Dorothy had built all these years out of her longing and her pride – a defence against reality. She sat on and felt an extraordinary lightening of spirit. "The truth shall make you free." She knew now something of what these words meant.

Suddenly she became conscious of Leila's insistent renewed angry tapping. She felt emptied of both love and hate and, instead, an immense pity filled her heart. She got up and went to attend to her friend.

Miss Dawson was not much aware of Tom at first. She did not usually care for boys, classing them with cats as the natural enemies of birds. Mary Perry had told her that Tom was a nice boy, but Mary was too apt to think everyone nice. Still, she admitted that as yet she had nothing against him. There had been a native boy on one of her Himalayan trips of whom she had once been quite fond and though he was all grace and this boy was uncouth, yet Tom reminded her of him somehow. They both had the same open, gentle look.

One day, sitting by her window, she heard a sound she hated. It was Lord Jim, yowling triumphantly to let the world know that he had successfully tracked down and caught his prey. The peculiar unmistakable tone of the cry was occasioned by his mouth being full of his wretched victim. Miss Dawson peered out. Yes, there the beast was, carrying what looked very much like another thrush, pitifully quiet and still. Thrushes were especially vulnerable, being slow and trusting birds, and this was the third that she had known Lord Jim take already this summer, and there might of course have been others. Then she saw Tom and so did Lord Jim. He swerved away from the shrubbery where he had intended to deal with his catch privately and at leisure, and instead laid the bird at the feet of Tom, who stooped and picked it up. Miss Dawson called out to him to bring it up to her – she knew that a cat will sometimes carry a bird unharmed until some cover is reached – but she was too far away to make him hear. She saw him holding the thrush quietly in his hands for a little while without moving, then he walked out of sight still holding it, accompanied by Lord Jim, prancing gaily along at his side and waving his tail. As soon as she could, Miss Dawson sent for Tom.

"What did you do with the poor thrush that that wretched cat caught this afternoon?" she asked.

"He be safe and sound, Lady Miss Dawson," said Tom. "He baint hurt at all, only dazed like. I knew where he belongs, down in the copse, there be four on 'em, all from one nest."

"That's a good boy," said Miss Dawson approvingly, "but what about the cat?"

"I'll keep an eye on him," said Tom, "he thought as how I'd be pleased, but he knows now I don't like it. He can't rightly reason it out but he knows. I tell him he gets plenty o' good food given him and there be no need for him to go after the birds at all, but my Gran says once he didn't."

"That's nonsense," said Miss Dawson, "whenever did your grandmother suppose that Miss Blackett didn't overfeed her cat?"

"Not Lady Miss Blackett," said Tom, "but ever so

long ago, afore any of us were born, he didn't get fed, so he still thinks he's in the right to catch all he can – but I'll see as he don't get them thrushes."

Miss Dawson was not optimistic all the same, but she felt assured that Tom would try his best to protect the birds and admitted to Mrs Perry that he was a thoroughly well-meaning boy, "Though what he meant about the cat I don't know."

Old Mrs Langley was giving a party. The only visible guest was Tom, but the unseen ones – unseen, that is to say, by all but herself – were the friends and relations she had invited nearly seventy years ago on the occasion of her son's first birthday. Through Tom, who every week took the warden's shopping list to her grocer's and brought back the goods, she had managed to acquire a large chocolate cake and a bottle of sherry. Mrs Langley had happened to meet him when the idea, or memory, or vision of the party had floated into her butterfly mind, and she had firmly added the cake and the sherry to Miss Blackett's list. She had instructed Tom to bring them straight to her. It was Tom, too, who had provided the flowers that filled every vase, and there were a good many of these in Mrs Langley's room. The wild honeysuckle he had found in the copse, but the red roses had come from Fred Mills's beds and the white lilies had been Mrs Perry's pride. The room smelt very sweet.

Mrs Thornton wondered anxiously about all this when she inadvertently also became a guest. She had been passing Mrs Langley's door that afternoon when she heard Tom's unmistakable laugh, and then the quavering sound of Mrs Langley's voice raised louder than usual in one of her favourite hymn tunes. Stopping to listen, Mrs Thornton was able to distinguish the words of "All things bright and beautiful" and then Tom joined in with his humming accompaniment.

"All creatures great and small," trilled out Mrs Langley.

It was really not a wholly inappropriate birthday song, but Mrs Thornton was ignorant of the celebration when first she opened the door and went in. Mrs Langley, looking flushed and joyful, had an empty glass in one hand and was beating time with the other. Tom, too, was waving an empty glass about and on all the little tables scattered round were more empty glasses and plates and the remains of the cake. The room was full of sunlight and flowers and happiness.

"Come in, come in, dear Jessie, but mind baby; he crawls around so fast now, he is always getting under people's feet. Come in and drink his health."

Mrs Thornton, however, could not drink his health for there was obviously no more sherry left. She sat down and, as usual, Mrs Langley's fantasies of the past began to affect her powerfully. Just as once she had thought that she heard the trotting of horses bringing Mrs Langley's young husband to the door of The Haven, so now she could almost visualize the guests to whom Tom was handing round the diminished cake, as grave and as absorbed as if he were a child in one of those universal games of playing at grown-ups. She could even imagine the lively one-year-old, the centre of the party, that baby who was now a frail old gentleman with a stomach ulcer living unhappily in Birmingham with his successful stockbroker son.

"Now, my precious," said Mrs Langley, bending down, "it's time for bath and bed, birthday or no birthday, and you, Dickie –" she called Tom Dickie because that had been the name of Susan's boy – "take these glasses down to the pantry and wash them very carefully, for they were a wedding present and a lovely present, too."

She went off to the bathroom and Tom disappeared with the glasses. Mrs Thornton knew these well, beautiful cut-glass ones, which lived on the top shelf of the corner cupboard above the Worcester teacups. Unfortunately, when Tom was bringing back the glasses after he had washed them, he met the warden.

"What are you doing with those?" she asked him.

"They're from Lady Mrs Langley's party," said Tom.

"Party, what party?"

"Lady Mrs Langley's been having a party," repeated Tom.

"Nonsense," said Miss Blackett, and followed him into Mrs Langley's room. Mrs Thornton had gone and Mrs Langley, having returned from the bathroom, had gone immediately and peacefully to sleep.

"I can smell alcohol," said Miss Blackett loudly and sharply. "You know alcohol, unless specially prescribed, is against the rules, Mrs Langley; how did you get it?"

Mrs Langley, so suddenly wakened, looked frightened and bewildered.

"Dickie got it for my party," she said.

"There was *no* party," said Miss Blackett, "and, Tom, you must never get anything for the ladies without asking me about it first, do you understand?"

Tom first nodded his head and then shook it.

Miss Blackett sighed and went straight away to write to Mrs Langley's grandson, which she had been meaning to do ever since the committee meeting. She wrote:

Dear Mr Langley,

I fear your grandmother's state has deteriorated so that we cannot any longer give her all the care she needs. We are anxious that she should be better looked after in the very efficient geriatric unit of the local hospital than she can be at The Haven. If you could make it convenient to come here as soon as possible you will be able to judge the situation for yourself and if, as I am sure will be the case, you concur with our proposal to move your grandmother, I hope you will arrange for the disposal of her property. I believe your father's state of health makes it impossible for him to act in this matter.

Yours sincerely,
Agnes Blackett.

Mr Langley, being one of those to whom time is money, did not find it convenient to visit his grandmother nor, for that matter, had he ever done so. But he saw the necessity now, so he came down to The Haven not too long after receiving this letter.

Mrs Langley greeted him politely but without enthusiasm as her Uncle James. "I am glad to see you looking so well, Uncle," she said, "though I don't know to what I owe the pleasure of this unexpected visit. Now that I am a married woman I can confess that I once overheard you telling my father that I was disgracefully indulged and you made no secret of the fact that you dislike my dear husband. Still," she added hopefully, "perhaps you have had a change of heart."

"I must agree with you, Miss Blackett," said Mr Langley after this uncomfortable interview, "my poor grandmother is quite senile. It will be much better for all concerned if she can be placed in a suitable institution. I will arrange for her things to be sold, there are some quite good pieces among them I noticed, but my wife does not care for antiques. I must thank you on behalf of my father and myself for all the care you have taken of her since she came to The Haven – and now, if you will forgive me, I must be off. Good day to you, Miss Blackett, you will hear from me again shortly."

During the weeks since Tom's arrival at The Haven, Miss Norton had been feeling increasingly depressed; her eyes had been failing more rapidly than had been predicted, and the doctor had told her there was nothing to be done. Up to now she had not faced the possibility of total loss of sight. She could still distinguish light and darkness and dimly see large shapes of people and furniture, and if she looked obliquely and closely at an object, it became sufficiently clear for her to discern its nature. For instance, peering sideways across the dining-room table, she could tell a sugar basin from a jug, though it was a hazardous job to pour the contents of the jug into a cup or sprinkle the sugar on a plate. She could not bring herself to accept dependence on others for personal intimate services. She felt that death would be more welcome than utter blindness and helplessness and, when the time came, she told herself, there were ways of putting an end to things. A plastic bag would be the easiest; she believed she had the courage for this, though not for long years of darkness and decline. She began to set herself tests over and above the ordinary daily tasks. If she passed these tests she went to bed reasonably content.

One morning, however, she woke with a headache and a feeling of oppression and fancied herself distinctly less able to deal with washing, dressing and breakfast. Spurred on by a sudden onslaught of fear, she decided to set herself a more severe and hazardous test that day. She would walk to the end of the garden and through the copse alone, something she had not done for weeks. She chose her time carefully. It must be after the midday meal when nearly everyone rested and there was little fear of interfering warnings or help. After she had made this decision she felt quite calm and she set off at the right time and aided by her stick, with which she struck at the little iron edging to the gravel path, she successfully negotiated the long lawn and came to the boundary between this and the wood. Originally this had been a ditch which by now was almost filled up, but the path into the copse still crossed it by an old rustic bridge. The invading bullocks had lately broken down the wooden handrail of the bridge and, as the ditch was now almost level and the rail was scarcely needed any more, and as Fred always had more jobs than he could cope with, it had not been replaced. Meg Norton reached the bridge and followed the path across, but midway her stick failed to find any guiding rail and she halted. She could just make out the shapes of the trees looming up before her, then they seemed to advance and engulf her and panic seized her. She could no longer pierce the darkness and she felt it would be a step into a void and that this void was endless. She had been too engrossed in carrying out her plan to heed the weather, but it had turned colder at midday, clouds had gathered and it now began to rain. A plane roared overhead and to Meg it sounded like thunder and added to her distress. She had always hated thunder. She felt as terrified as if she were a child again, caught up in a nightmare and trying to call aloud for her mother, only no call would come. She forced herself to take a step, caught her foot on a little stump and fell. Then she must have cried out, she supposed, for there came a voice shouting her name and out of the blackness a pair of small, strong hands took hold of her and pulled her to her feet. Tom had been in the wood spying on his family of thrushes and had heard her. She clung to him.

"Why, Lady Miss Norton dear, be you hurt? he asked.

The warmth of his arm about her and the sound of his voice brought immediate comfort and relief. She was so glad it was Tom who had found her, she somehow did not mind *him* seeing her so helpless and frightened.

"It was silly," she said, "I came for a walk and fell. I'm going blind, Tom, you see. I *am* blind," she added loudly and firmly.

"Like my bats," said Tom cheerfully. He began to tell her about the bats as he led her back to the house. It was still raining.

71

"'Tis a good bit o' rain," said Tom. "Don't our flowers smell happy?"

Meg became aware of the summer scents jostling each other for her attention and a fresh warm tide of life seemed to flow through her. When she got to her room she asked Tom if he could bring her a cup of tea, and she lay down on the bed for, though not hurt, she was shaken by the fall and her fear. But when evening was come, she was quite able to go into supper and then she asked Mrs Perry, her neighbour, for the first time, to help her with her food and to pour out her drink, and Mrs Perry, who had been longing to do this for weeks past but had not dared to offer, did so without comment. It was one of Mrs Thornton's days for reading to Meg, and she went to her room as soon as supper was over. Shakespeare took his turn as usual after *The Times*. They were in the middle of *As You Like It* but this evening Meg said: "Would you mind if instead we had that bit near the end of *King Lear* about Edgar as poor mad Tom, with Gloucester." So Mrs Thornton found the place and came at length to Gloucester's speech.

> "Alack, I have no eyes,
> Is wretchedness deprived that benefit
> To end itself by death?

Edgar: Give me your arm.
> Up! so, How is't feel your legs? You stand
> alone?

Glouc.: I do remember, now henceforth I'll bear
> Affliction, till it do cry out itself
> Enough, enough and die.

Edgar: Bear free and patient thoughts."

Mrs Thornton read on and Meg lay back in her chair and listened.

Glouc.: "You ever gentle gods, take my breath from me,
> Let not my worser spirit tempt me again
> To die before you please."

And so at last she came to Edgar's final words to his father:

> "Men must endure
>   Their going hence, even as their coming hither,
>   Ripeness is all."

Here Mrs Thornton paused as she thought she heard Meg speak. "Did you say something?" she asked.

"Only what comes next, I think," said Meg: "'And that's true too.'"

"Shall I finish the play?" asked Mrs Thornton.

"No, thank you, dear," said Meg, "I'm rather tired this evening, so I think I'll go up to bed now, but thank you very much and goodnight."

7

PREPARATIONS FOR THE FETE

MISS BLACKETT was anxious to move Mrs Langley to the geriatric department at the hospital before the day of the summer fête and was pleased when she heard, soon after Mr Langley's visit, that a bed was vacant. The matron rang her up to tell her this and Miss Blackett expressed relief.

"I shall be very busy soon," she said, "for our great day is coming along and I really cannot supervise the old thing, day in and day out, and yet I feel responsible, of course."

"I quite understand," said Matron crisply, "right, well, I daresay I can save you the trouble of bringing her along. We don't use an ambulance unless it's necessary, but I have to come your way in my own car the day after tomorrow and could pick her up about noon, if you can have her ready by then."

Miss Blackett agreed to this.

"I suppose she'll come without trouble?"

"Oh, yes," said Miss Blackett, "she's quite an amenable old soul."

"Right," said Matron, "it's as well to know – we have our obstinate little ways sometimes. About noon, then, Miss Blackett. Goodbye."

It was not quite as easy as Miss Blackett had hoped.

"Come along now, my dearie," said Matron, "we're going to take you for a nice drive."

"But I don't know you," said Mrs Langley, drawing

74

back. "My name is Mrs Marian Langley," she added with dignity.

"That's right, dear," said Matron, "and we're going for a lovely drive together."

Miss Blackett was busy fastening down a suitcase which was difficult to shut and just then Tom came in with a message for her. Mrs Langley caught at his hand.

"Can Dickie come too?" she asked.

The matron looked over his head at Miss Blackett and gave a little nod. "Very well," said Miss Blackett.

"Right," said Matron, "let's be moving then, shall we?"

But when they got downstairs and out into the drive, she propelled Mrs Langley into the car and shut the door, leaving Tom on the steps. Mrs Langley's attention was distracted by the bright red cushions on her seat and by a mascot of a toy panda tied to the windscreen, and she forgot about Tom until the engine started. Then she leaned out of the window and called to him.

"Never mind, Dickie, you must come next time, tell your mother, please, to have tea ready, I'll be back very soon." She waved and Tom waved too till she was out of sight.

But she was not back soon. Instead, Mr Langley's secretary came down with a man from a Birmingham firm of auctioneers and took away all the furniture, pictures, china and glass, packing the last very carefully and with respect.

"Where be Lady Mrs Langley gone? Tom asked Mrs Thornton. "And when be she coming home again?"

"She won't be coming home," said Mrs Thornton, "she's had to go into hospital, Tom."

"She weren't in bed," said Tom, "she were going for a ride."

"I know, Tom," said Mrs Thornton, "but she had to go to hospital all the same, the doctor said so, and you see all her things are gone – she wouldn't want to come back to an empty room, would she?"

Tom looked puzzled but shook his head in agreement. He went away humming Mrs Langley's favourite hymn tune, which didn't now seem so appropriate as at the party. He was heard humming it several times in the days that followed, though he did not speak of her again. But Mrs Thornton noticed a curious thing: whenever he passed Mrs Langley's door in future, he always went on tiptoe.

Mrs Thornton asked the vicar on his next visit if he had been to see Mrs Langley yet, and how she was.

"Matron says she's fine, she's put on weight and she gives no trouble at all, but I found her very quite, very quite indeed. I'm sorry," he added, "but the committee and the warden all thought it was the right and sensible thing to do."

Mrs Thornton said nothing.

With Mrs Langley off her hands, Miss Blackett was free to concentrate on arrangements for the fête. She had decided that the deodar tree could not come down until this was over. It would make too much of a mess. A sub-committee consisting of herself, Mrs Mitchell, the vicar's wife, and Col. Bradshaw was due to meet to discuss all arrangements. The weather seemed settled at last.

"It's bound to be fine now we've decided on the marquee instead of a band," Miss Blackett said to Mrs Perry and Miss Dawson, who were sitting on one of the garden seats watching Tom watering the rosebeds. Watering was one of the few gardening jobs Fred could give him to do when he could be spared by Miss Blackett. Weeding was out of the question for he obstinately refused to pull up anything.

"They be all as good as one another to him – dandelions and daisies, just as vallible as roses and lilies," grumbled Fred. But he loved watering. When he had finished the rosebeds he came over to give Mrs Perry's border its turn. He was humming loudly and happily a Schubert song he had heard on Mrs Thornton's radio the evening before.

"That boy's a band in himself," said Miss Dawson. It was then Mrs Perry had her bright idea.

76

"I don't see why we shouldn't have a band of sorts at the fête," she said. "My grandson and his sister play in a music group, I know they went all over the place playing last summer. I believe they would come and play for us here if they were asked. Tom could help, too, I'm sure. It would be lovely to have them, and much more fun than a hired band."

Miss Blackett looked doubtful.

"We wouldn't want pop music, you know, Mrs Perry, and would they really want to give up the time, we couldn't pay them."

"Oh, I'm sure they'd come if they were free," said Mrs Perry confidently. "Austen is always ready for anything, and Nell's boyfriend Jake is very musical, properly musical, I mean, so it wouldn't have to be pop. I'm certain they wouldn't mind giving up the time. Why, you know Nell and Austen, Miss Blackett, you know they wouldn't."

No one at The Haven could help knowing about Mrs Perry's grandchildren, not to speak of her great-grandchildren. What space in her room that could be spared from her plants was taken up with photographs of them at many different stages. She had five altogether, and now three greats, but Nell and Austen were familiar in person to everyone as they quite frequently came to see her. Austen was in his second year at Oxford and Nell, who had taken an art course and painted flowers really well, had a job in an art gallery in Warwick. She shared a flat with Jake, who was doing a postgraduate course at Warwick University. They talked vaguely of marriage at some distant date.

"I don't approve, of course," said Mrs Perry cheerfuly, "but it doesn't really matter."

"If you don't approve, I don't see how you can say it doesn't matter," said Miss Dawson.

Mrs Perry ignored this; she often found it better to take no notice of Frances's remarks when they seemed irrelevant.

Miss Blackett liked Austen Perry, who always made a point of seeing her when he came. Nell she thought aloof and superior. After some consideration she agreed to put Mrs Perry's suggestion before the sub-committee and they reacted favourably.

Mrs Mitchell said it was really very sweet of Mrs Perry to think of it.

Col. Bradshaw said: "I've met those grandchildren of hers, an attractive pair. If they will come, I think we can trust them to provide a suitable programme, though perhaps we'd better vet it. It's good to involve young people in charitable affairs whenever possible."

Miss Blackett said: "Well, it would certainly be nice to have some music after all, but I shan't be surprised if it doesn't come off. You can't rely on the young nowadays, so I don't think we should count on it."

Mrs Perry, however, certainly did count on it, and so it was that when Austen Perry looked through his mail one morning, he picked out from the customary bills and circulars an envelope addressed in his grandmother's distinctive pointed script. He enjoyed her letters, she wrote just as if she were chatting away to him about her plants, and the family news, and amiable gossip concerning The Haven. This was a fatter letter than usual. It gave an account of Tom's rout of the bullocks, which amused him, and then came to the fête and the real purpose of the epistle.

I know you and Nell will help if you can. There won't be any money in it for you, I'm afraid, because, as I've explained, we can't afford a band this year; you had better make this clear to your friends, but I'm sure as they are your friends and bound to be nice, they won't mind, but they'll get a good tea with strawberries and cream, and they might win a raffle prize – I think we ought to let you have tickets free. If you can come, would you mind sending a list of what you are going to play, I know it will all be delightful, but they seem to want to know beforehand, at least Col. Bradshaw and Miss Blackett do, or better than sending it, perhaps you could run over here one day soon. It seems a long while since I saw you, but you've been hard at work, I expect.

And she remained his "very loving Gran".

Austen smiled and pondered a little and then went to his phone and dialled Nell.

"I've had a letter."

"From Gran?" interrupted his sister. "So have I, about playing at their fête."

"Just so, what do you think?"

"I'll have to ask Jake and he's asleep at the moment, but I don't really see why not. I've got nothing on that weekend, what about you?"

"I can make it, who else can we get hold of?"

"We simply must have Elizabeth, is she up still?"

The vac. had begun, but there were always undergraduates still around for one purpose or another, among whom was Austen himself, who liked to get a little work done after the hurly burly of the term was ended.

"In between her conferences and protest marches and meetings, she is,' he answered Nell.

"Well, even if we can't get hold of anyone else, the four of us ought to manage something, but we must get together pretty soon if we're to do it. What about bringing Elizabeth here for a night? You've been promising to come for ages."

"Good thought. I'll make a point of seeing Liz at once and ring you. Love to Jake – goodbye for now." Austen replaced the receiver, finished his breakfast and decided to stroll across the Parks to Elizabeth's lodgings then and there. Early morning was the safest time to find people at home, even if still in bed.

However, Elizabeth came to the door at once in a particularly fine dressing-gown, though her hair was hanging in wet strands over her face. She ws a handsome, dark-complexioned girl, with large prominent brown eyes and a determined mouth and chin. Her bed-sitting-room was untidy by any standards; everything, clothes, cooking utensils, food, were all mixed up with piles of books, and cascades of paper appeared to be spilling themselves over the whole collection. The only object that seemed to have a proper place was a fiddle on a shelf to itself. Elizabeth was an able violinist. Austen cleared a space on the floor and sat down. Elizabeth remained standing and, seizing up a towel from a heap of mixed garments, started to rub her hair with extreme vigour. Austen gave her the gist of his grandmother's letter and his talk with Nell.

"No, I'm afraid I'm booked for an anti-nuclear demonstration that day. Sorry."

"Oh, come off it, Liz, it can't really affect the peace of the world all that much if you are there or not, and you're indispensable to us.'

"He who would do good, must do it in minute particulars," quoted Elizabeth.

"Don't be sententious, besides, come to that, I bet Blake would be on our side; think of all the certain good you can do in the minute particulars waiting for us to perform at The Haven – whereas!' he shrugged his shoulders.

"But I promised," said Liz.

"Well, will you come if I find you a sub.?" asked Austen.

Elizabeth felt herself weakening. She was dismayed to find how unpleasant it was to hold out against him – it would be inconveniently hampering to fall for him in a serious way, and she feared she might be going to. "I suppose so," she said unwillingly, "but you ought to be demonstrating yourself."

"We'll ague that out on our way to Nell and Jake," said Austen cheerfully. "Thanks a lot, Liz, I'm sure I can find someone. Be seeing you – goodbye, then."

Austen possessed a wide and devoted circle of friends

and it was not too difficult to persuade one of them to take Elizabeth's place at the demonstration. "It's lucky it's for a respectable cause," he thought, "and not one of her way-out crazes."

So, her conscience more or less appeased, Elizabeth packed herself and her violin into Austen's shabby little car the following weekend, and immediately embarked on an argument on unilateral disarmament. They were still arguing when they drew up outside Nell and Jake's flat in Warwick. Nell received them joyfully. The flat possessed a fair-sized living-room, a tiny kitchen and bathroom, a double bedroom and one small spare room containing a large mattress that was scarcely ever vacant.

"Oh, by the way," said Nell to her brother at supper, "I hope you won't mind sharing your bed with a nice Irish roadsweeper – we're putting him up till he can find a lodging."

"That's all right," said Austen. "He won't be drunk, I hope?"

There were limits beyond which he was not prepared to go. "Where's Liz to sleep then?"

"She'll have Jake's side of my bed and he'll be quite OK on the living-room floor, won't you, Jake?"

"Of course," said Jake.

The flat was a pleasant place, tidy and clean and decorated with some of Nell's flower paintings. Her appearance was deceptive, she was very slim and small, with delicate features and a cloud of silvery fair hair. She looked like a cross between a Botticelli angel and a character from a de la Mare poem. But, in reality, both she and Austen were more efficient and practical than either Elizabeth, the idealist, or Jake, the mathematical mystic. Neither Nell or Jake were great talkers, but the other pair made up for this. At supper they started a vigorous debate on the ethics of space travel. Nell listened a little anxiously. Austen, she knew, argued for entertainment and was quite capable of changing sides at any moment, but Liz was always in deadly earnest and Nell felt, rather than consciously thought, that at least where Austen was concerned, she was emotionally involved. She was glad that she and Jake seldom felt the need to argue, but went their own ways in peace and comfort. She went out to fetch a jug of coffee and when she came back the argument had somehow shifted to Wagner.

"You're prejudiced against him, just because of his politics," Austen was saying. "Genius has nothing to do with politics."

"It jolly well had with Wagner," said Elizabeth, "and you're not fair either; it isn't just his politics, I hate the way he forces me to respond to his beastly genius, for I can't help responding. It makes me feel I'm being raped."

"I understand what Liz means," said Jake, "Wagner always wants total control, that's the great difference between him and Bach, his opposite. Bach is content to accept divine control."

Elizabeth looked at him with gratitude, and Nell said, "We've got a new cassette of Tortelier playing Bach's cello suite. Let's get down to business and then we'll play it to you. Now what shall we choose out of our repertoire for the fête?"

"The old will want something nostalgic, I should think," said Elizabeth.

"Don't talk about 'the old' like that," said Austen, "as though they were all alike and some sort of different species. They're as different from one another as can be, as we are, for instance – we're not just 'the young'. Generalizations are always stupid."

"You've just made one," said Elizabeth, "and a stupid one, too. Of course I know they can be wrong, even dangerous sometimes, but one can't do without them all the same."

"Why not?" said Austen.

"Oh, stop it, you two," said Nell, "and let's get on. It isn't only old ladies we've got to please, Liz, this fête tries to attract everyone it can."

She was sorting through a pile of music she had taken from a drawer and arranging it in neat piles. Their group had gone busking last summer vacation and besides had performed at weekends in pubs and sometimes at parties during the winter, and Jake had orchestrated a fair amount of material for them. The piles represented Old Time, pop and classical. After a good deal of discussion, they decided on Highlights from Gilbert & Sullivan, and Selections from Strauss Waltzes. "That's for Gran," said Austen. Then Gershwin's "Summertime", the Beatles. "Eight Days a Week", and "Yesterday".

"We're not allowed pop, I know," said Nell, "but the Beatles don't count as pop, do they?"

"That's for 'the young', I suppose," said Liz.

"Selections from *Fledermaus* – that ought to be for everyone," said Nell.

"We must have something from the classical heap," said Jake. "What about Mozart's 'Eine Kleine Nachtmuzik', or Handel's 'Water Music'?"

"We do the Mozart best," said Austen, "and we ought to have a rousing number to start off with."

They decided on the "Toreador's Song" from *Carmen*.

"That ought to do all right," said Nell, "but I wish we had a singer. Sarah's gone off to her beloved Austria; what's happened to Andrew?"

"He's taken a job as a dustman," said Austen. "He says it's horribly exhausting, but very good money. I vote for some Bach now, it's too late to start practising tonight. We'll get down to it tomorrow morning."

They relaxed comfortably while Tortelier did his best for them and then, full of content, they sought their beds.

Austen found Mike, the sweeper, already snoring but considerately squeezed into as narrow a space as possible on the far side of the mattress. He slipped in beside him and Mike was up and away before he woke the next day. The morning was spent in hard but pleasurable playing. Besides Elizabeth's fiddle, there was Jake's double bass, Nell provided the wind with her clarinet, and Austin performed quite creditably on the guitar, but there was no doubt that a vocal accompaniment to some of the numbers would have been an improvement.

"Can't be helped, unless we can pick up someone between now and the day – we must just do the best we can without," said Nell.

Mrs Perry proudly told everyone that her grandchilden had undertaken to provide music for the fête instead of the Boy's Brigade Band, and that Austen was paying her a visit soon to discuss it all. Austen was popular at The Haven. He possessed the art, or rather the gift (for it came naturally) of talking to children, his parents' contemporaries, and the old, as if they were all the same age as himself. Then, because he was interested in people, he remembered the old ladies' names, and often, too, bits of information about them that Mrs Perry had told him. He arrived at The Haven one Sunday with a miniature rose-tree in a pot for his grandmother, and a box of chocolates with a picture of a ginger cat on it, for Miss Blackett. She was more pleased with this than even Mrs Perry with her plant, though no one would have guessed it, for she had never learned to accept gifts graciously. She liked chocolates, but never bought them for herself, and she liked the picture of the cat, even though it was not handsome enough for Lord Jim, but best of all she liked the attention and the box was kept long after its contents had been consumed.

Austen had arrived in time for the midday meal and afterwards he tried to persuade his grandmother to take her usual nap.

"I can go for a walk, or talk to Miss Blackett."

"What, snooze away an hour of your company, I should

84

think not indeed! We'll sit outside in the garden and you can admire my border while you tell me all your news. Oh, and I want to hear what nice tunes you have all decided on, though I don't suppose I'll know any of them."

"You will two of them, anyway, for we've put them in specially for you, Gran. Here's the list."

Mrs Perry put on her spectacles.

"Hurrah! Gilbert and Sullivan, and the Vienna Waltzes – good boy, and I like the names of the songs, 'Summertime' and 'Yesterday', they sound like those that were sung when I was young."

"I'm afraid they're not much like that really, and they won't be sung, you know, only played, because we've lost both our singers, and haven't been able to find any replacement. I say, Gran, your pinks and stocks are fine this year, but what's happened to your famous tiger lilies?'

"Tom's happened to them," said Mrs Perry ruefully, "he borrowed every single one of them for a party dear old Mrs Langley thought she was giving and it has left rather a gap."

"Tom, Tom, the piper's son, stole your flowers and away did run," sang Austen. "Only he's not a piper's son, but a bullock boy, according to your letter. Tell me more about him – he sounds quite a one."

"He's really a very nice boy," said Mrs Perry, "and clever at a lot of things, though he's never been able to read or write. Mrs Thornton says he's exceptionally musical."

"Oh, ho!" said Austen, "does he sing, I wonder?"

"Not sing, exactly," said Mrs Perry, "but he hums quite loudly and Mrs Thornton says he always keeps in time and in tune. Oh, do you think he might be of any use to you. Austen? I wondered if possibly he might, he would love it so."

"I'd better see Mrs Thornton about him," said Austen, "a champion hummer might be a novel draw."

"I do approve of you, Austen dear," said his grandmother affectionately, "you're always ready to try anything, and I love you so much better now you have your hair nice and short and tidy again. I couldn't bear it hanging down your back like a Cavalier, which is funny really, as I always liked Cavaliers better than Roundheads, but then you didn't wear a lace collar and a beautiful coat underneath, and perhaps that made the difference."

"Oh, Gran, you never said you hated it," said Austen.

"Well, that wouldn't have been any use, would it dear?"

"The parents thought it would, they were always on about it."

"Yes, and I believe you grew it an inch longer whenever the poor dears mentioned it. I told them they only had to wait a little and the fashion would pass, they always do, though sometimes they come back again."

Mrs Thornton guaranteed that Tom could pick up tunes wonderfully well, but that he might wander away in the middle if he felt like it.

"Of course we'd have to get him to practise with us first," said Austen, "is he shy?"

"Oh no, not in the least," said Mrs Thornton.

"We could get here early in the day and the fête's an afternoon affair, isn't it? We could practise him in the morning."

"But the warden will need him then, I'm afraid," said Mrs Thornton, "there will be plenty of jobs for him to do."

"I'll ask her anyway," said Austen, "where is he now? I'd like to see him."

"He always goes home on a Sunday and doesn't come back till Monday morning."

"Oh, well, I'll take your word for his musical powers, Mrs Thornton, and I bet I get Miss Blackett's permission to rehearse him, you'll see."

He sought out the warden then and there, and perhaps it was the effect of the chocolate box, but, to Mrs Thornton's surprise, permission was given by Miss Blackett for Tom to

86

give up at least part of the morning to practise with the group if they really wanted him, though she couldn't believe that he would be of any real use, but then she didn't pretend to understand anything about music and never had.

"That's marvellous of you, Miss Blackett," said Austen. "If he's as good as Mrs Thornton says he is, he'll be just what we need in some of the numbers, and I promise you we'll help all we can when we're not actually playing to make up for robbing you of Tom."

When they next met together the group approved of including Tom, but cautious Nell said it would be advisable if Jake, who had the most time to spare at present, could run over to The Haven on his bike as soon as possible to try him out.

Jake came back a bit worried. "Isn't he any good after all?" asked Nell.

"He's fine," said Jake.

"What's the problem, then?"

"Too keen," said Jake, "we can't have him humming every number, not the Mozart, for instance, and he will if he gets the chance."

"I see," said Nell, thoughtfully. "Well, can't we give him an instrument, cymbals or something, to keep him happy and unhumming?"

"It's more than likely he'd be too keen on those, too," said Jake. "Can you imagine trying to compete with clanging cymbals coming in with every beat?"

"What about a drum?" said Nell, "That wouldn't really matter if it went on rather a lot. I can borrow a little drum from Earl Street Primary School."

"Just the thing; he'd love it," said Jake with relief, "and I think we could make it clear to him when to hum and when to drum."

"What shall we wear?" mused Nell. "I think something pretty eye-catching. I saw some cheap red and white denim the other day in the town. I could run up dungarees for Liz and myself to wear with white blouses, and you've got your red shirt, and I think Austen's got one too, at least I know he's got a check one, and you can wear white flannels with them."

"What about Tom?" asked Jake.

"Oh, I can run him up something, too, or we could buy him something. How big is he?"

"About your size, I should think," said Jake, "but best lend him some of your things – don't you know it's dangerous to give new clothes to elemental creatures such as Tom."

Nell laughed. "Is he a changeling then, d'you think, or a sort of Brownie, or Lob?"

"I don't know," said Jake, suddenly becoming half serious, "all I know is that I felt he was different, as if he knew things I didn't know and saw things I couldn't see, and was timeless somehow."

Nell smiled at him affectionately. She loved Jake when he talked nonsense.

Other matters connected with the fête were not going quite so well. There were the coconut shies, for instance. Mr Jackson always took charge of these. The site had to be far enough away from the house and the stalls to avoid damage, but this meant that balls were often mislaid in the rough patch between the lawn and the copse, or even in the copse itself, unless the nets were sound. This year, it was found that, though the stands stored in the old barn were all right, the nets had been used by Fred for some purpose of his own and had several holes in them. This led to a few words between him and the farmer, their relationship never being very warm on account of the bullocks. Then the coconuts, provided by the local greengrocer, had proved unsatisfactory the previous summer – almost a quarter were bad and there had been loud complaints, so this year Jackson had gone elsewhere for his coconuts. This gave offence and the greengrocer, who last year had sold the strawberries for the fête at a discount, quitely increased his price without notification.

There was always some bickering and jealousy between the old ladies' stall and a similar fancy goods stall run by the Women's Institute, who donated a part of their takings to The Haven in return for the privilege of selling their articles at the fête, and the competition for the best sites was not too amiable either sometimes. This summer the sudden spell of hot weather made the shady places in the garden especially sought after.

The sub-committee resigned themselves to the inevitable annoyances and frets and trusted that, as usual, everything would work out pretty well in the end. The stallholders were traditional and seldom changed from year to year. However, this time Col. Bradshaw, still mindful of Miss Hughes's financial assets, suggested that it might be as well to involve her yet further in The Haven's affairs by allotting to her the privilege and pleasure of one of the stalls. The other members of the sub-committee looked doubtful. How could this be done without causing trouble?

Someone suggested an extra stall. "What about a White Elephant Stall? We've never had one before."

Someone else said there would be enough white elephants already on the other stalls and that Miss Hughes was proving a bit of a one herself. It was a long, hot meeting and in order to bring it to an end, objections faded out and it was decided to adopt the idea of a White Elephant Stall to be presided over by Miss Hughes.

As the day approached, all the talk at The Haven was about the fête and, among other matters, the White Elephant Stall was discussed.

"I can't rightly see as there'll be room for them on our lawn," said Tom to Gisela, anxiously. 'I've seed elephants once in a picture Teacher showed us at school and they do be bigger nor any other animal, and they be grey and not white."

"It must be that you heard wrong about the Stall, Tom, certainly there will be no room and the elephants, they *are* grey and not white at all, but the English are strange about colour, I find," said Gisela.

But Tom was sure he had heard right, and asked Mrs Thornton, who was his oracle, and she explained, as best she could, the genius and purpose of a White Elephant Stall. The following day she was a little puzzled at a sudden cross-examination from Tom about her furniture.

"Lady Mrs Thornton, be all these things yourn?"

"Why, yes, Tom."

"All the tables and chairs and the pictures and all they books? Be they yourn as you can do whatever you like with 'em?"

"Certainly."

"Be all the ladies' things as are in their rooms theirs?"

"Yes, just the same as mine are."

Mrs Thornton thought of Tom's behaviour with regard to the flowers in the garden and that perhaps he had been getting into trouble with Fred or the warden again. Perhaps a word or two at this moment as regards personal property might be opportune.

"At The Haven, in the garden and in the dining- and sitting-room and the hall and the kitchen, Tom, everything is for us all to use and enjoy, and no one of us must take any of the things that are in these places away for their own use. But in our separate rooms, it is different, everything there belongs to the owner of the room as my things belong to me to do what I like with – do you understand now?"

Tom nodded and then crowed his sudden happy laugh and disappeared.

8

THE FETE

EARLY ON the morning of the fête a thick, white mist blotted out the landscape, then, gradually, the sun forced its way through. The black August tree tops appeared first and soon the swathes of vapour cleared off, leaving the lawn and the field beyond the copse sparkling and fresh. Everything was extraordinarily still and silent. Through Meg Norton's open window came the gentle scent of mown grass. Fred had been busy with the mower all the day before. Time was arbitrary at The Haven; often it ceased to be regulated by clocks and watches and took its cue from scents and sounds. So now, Meg, half-awake and half-dozing, smelt the summer of seventy years ago. It was the day of the annual cricket match against Widford. Harry and Paul were both playing and her father captaining the village team. She would help at the scoring board and with the tea. Of course they would win and afterwards there would be a party at the Hall. Oh, it was going to be a lovely, lovely day.

Only why was it so dark on an August morning? Even if she had forgotten to draw back the curtains last night (which she never did, for she liked to see the night sky), but even if she had, it ought not to be so dark as this. She sat up, still only half-awake, and then time swung on again and she remembered. Still, that day had been lived, that perfect day – nothing could alter that now – it was as real as this one

91

and hers for ever. She went on thinking about it and smiling as she thought. It all happened as she had expected. Harry had carried his bat and Paul had made one marvellous catch, and though poor father had been out for a duck, he didn't mind, for they won by 46 runs. She remembered the exact number and at the party she had worn her new Shantung silk dress and her greeny-blue Venetian beads, and Mummy had let her do her pigtail up in a doorknocker for the first time, with a big bow to match the beads – though she wasn't "out" yet, of course. Monica, her cousin, was staying with them. She married a doctor, he joined the RAMC and they went out to India afterwards and Monica died there. Yes, Monica was with them and after supper, they had rolled up the carpet and Mummy had played waltzes – "the Valse Triste", she could hear it now. She had danced a lot with Paul and he had told her she had the most wonderful eyes, which made her feel silly, but she knew Harry was pleased that she and Paul got on well together. It must have been three years before the War. Here her musings were interrupted by Gisela bringing in her breakfast – Gisela, who was German, and whose grandfather and father had both been killed in the Wars.

"It is the day of the fête, Miss Norton," said Gisela, "and it will be a very fine day, I think."

"I'm glad, Gisela," said Meg. "Be happy and enjoy it."

Mrs Perry ate her breakfast by her open window, the moisture from the mist was drying off quickly from the ground now and all the later summer colours were solid and thick, like oil paint. Beyond the dark copse was the bright cornfield. Soon the proud upstanding wheat would be reduced to square lifeless packets.

"You never see a lovely wheatsheaf now," mourned Mrs Perry, "unless it's made of bread and propped against the chancel screen at Harvest Festival."

But Fred admired the packets. He was busy tidying up the mess the men had made erecting the marquee.

"And then those hateful stubble fires," thought Mrs Perry. She leaned out of the window and called to Fred: "Is Mr Jackson going to burn his stubble this summer, Fred? One summer he didn't."

Fred straightened himself up to answer her. "That'd be by reason o' the drought, in case o' fire," he said. "I reckon he'll be burning this year, same as usual."

"Such a waste," sighed Mrs Perry, "when I was a girl we went gleaning."

"Depends how you looks at it, ma'am," said Fred. "It saves work and it saves time."

"And then the flowers," went on Mrs Perry, "the flowers that sprang up immediately after the harvesting, corn-flowers, and poppies, and mayweed, and scarlet pimpernel, and yellow bedstraw and speedwell – a perfect carpet."

"Nobbut weeds," muttered Fred. "Well, I'd best be getting on – them marquee men've mucked up my edges a caution."

At ten o'clock Fred's brother's wife arrived to help in the kitchen. Fred's wife called her "Old Misery". She was cockney born and bred. As she unpacked the china, lent for the teas, she held Gisela with her "glittering eye" like the Ancient Mariner, while she regaled her with intimate details about her family (though actually her eye was glassy rather than glittering).

"My grandfather 'ad eighteen children, 'e 'ad, and only reared four. My father, 'e was 'is only son and 'es niver bin right since 'e married, the doctors 'ave niver bin able to do nothing for 'im. My mother, she was five weeks late wiv me and the old cat died the very day I was born, the very same day, she did, and they say she was a lovely cat, too. My mother she went sudden like. It was my washing day, if I'd a' known she was going I'd 'ave got the washing done before."

Then the warden came in. "You shouldn't be standing

93

here talking when there's so much to do," she said crossly to Gisela. "Go and help Tom put up the tables in the marquee"

Gisela went off aggrieved – it wasn't her that was doing the talking, but Miss Blackett was not in a state to be fair.

Now the stallholders were beginning to arrive to stake out their territory, erect their stalls and assemble their goods. Honor Bredon, who was in charge of the old ladies' stall, went round to collect their offerings. Mrs Thornton's patchwork was beautiful and she admired it warmly.

"It ought to bring in a lot, especially the little cushions," she said, "they are so pretty and so much in request. I shall price them highly – it's a great mistake to let the nice things go too cheaply on these occasions."

Mrs Thornton felt flattered, for she valued Miss Bredon's praise. Mrs Perry wistfully delivered over two splendid white geraniums and a dwarf begonia and even more sadly two charming little streptocarchus. Miss Norton's distant cousin had responded quite generously; considering he was about the only relative she had left, he felt guiltily grateful to her for making so few demands on him and sent his annual box of foreign souvenirs (for he was a frequent traveller) with a good grace. Leila Ford suggested that what she called "my modest contribution", which was a large coverlet of knitted squares, would brighten up the stall if hung prominently in the front, "Not upon the stall, Miss Bredon, where it would be hidden and wasted, don't you think?"

Miss Brown apologetically said she had not been able to finish her crochet jacket in time, but it had been bespoke by the kind vicar for an old lady he knew, and would be paid for in advance. Honor guessed that more than half Leila's coverlet and all the dull matching and sewing together of its squares would have fallen to her lot.

Miss Hughes had been pleased when she was called upon to take charge of the White Elephant Stall. She decided that she must have a new oufit for the occasion. It would not do to let The Haven down, especially as she was now a committee member. So she made a special trip to London to a little shop she knew just off Bond Street and bought a summer suit of an expensively subtle shade of lilac. She was lucky enough, too, to find a hat to go with it, a fine soft straw, not easy to get nowadays and really quite reasonable considering. She returned home well satisfied. But beyond that her imagination did not reach, so now, suitably dressed as she was to preside over her stall, she found it was empty except for a small hand-propelled mowing machine from the vicarage and a pair of hideous vases, a wedding present long ago to Mrs Bradshaw from an aunt, now deceased. Miss Hughes was unperturbed, she had not had any idea of what had been expected from her, nor had she now, but with the calm assurance induced by the cushioning of wealth, she assumed that all would be arranged satisfactorily somehow. As of course it was. A hasty round-up was called for; articles, however potentially unsaleable, could not be removed from other stalls without causing offence, but Col. Bradshaw took his car forthwith and set out for a house to house rally, thinking as he did so that he had almost given up Miss Hughes. He returned with an assortment which had mostly been intended for the Guides' jumble sale the following week. The White Elephant Stall, however, still looked rather thin on the ground, and then he and Mrs Martin, who had the next site for her produce, saw Tom lugging the old knife-cleaning machine across the lawn towards his ladies' stall. He was intercepted by Miss Blackett.

"Whatever are you doing, Tom?" she cried.

Tom grinned up at her joyfully. "This be for our ladies, Lady Miss Blackett. "I'm a-giving of it."

"What nonsense," said Miss Blackett, "It's not yours to give – besides no one will buy a thing like that – take it back to the house at once."

"It be from my room, Lady Miss Blackett, and so it be mine to do what I like with. Lady Mrs Thornton, she tell me so."

"You must have mistaken her – now take it away, there's a good boy, and go and help Mr Jackson put up the coconut shies."

"Wait a moment, Miss Blackett," called out Col. Bradshaw, "I believe Miss Hughes could do with it – it's a curiosity and might catch someone's fancy. We want a few more things here if you can spare it, that is."

"I can't believe it's worth the space it'll take up," said Miss Blackett, "but you're welcome to it," and she hurried off.

Tom was reluctant to deprive his ladies of his gift, but was persuaded that it was more likely to sell if in the company of the mowing machine than surrounded by pieces of embroidery and babies' woollies. He went off to help Mr Jackson, but in the course of the morning, the dressmaker's dummy, the chipped jug and basin, the volumes of *Sunday at Home*, the lampshade and the umbrella, all found their way to Miss Hughes's stall, where they certainly helped to fill up the gaps.

The sun was now at its height and it was very hot, everywhere but in Miss Dawson's room. She had decided to spend the day there. She had never liked parties and liked them even less now. It was pleasant to look down through the slats of the flat black branches of her tree and see everyone else running to and fro in the heat like frenzied ants.

"It's no use, Mary," she said to Mrs Perry who was trying to persuade her to come down for a little while later on and listen to the music, "I don't wish to come, and that's that. I've nothing against your grandchildren and you can come and tell me how wonderful they've been afterwards. Now, go along and enjoy yourself and leave me to do so quietly here in my own fashion."

Lord Jim was of Miss Dawson's way of thinking. As soon as he realized that the usual civilized order of the day was to be upset by strangers and unseemly bustle, he decided to spend it in a sensible place immune from disturbance. He chose Tom's attic, and after inspecting the unfamiliar spaces left by the removal of the knife-cleaning machine and other articles, he settled down to a comfortable oblivion. It was fortunate that he had been out hunting the previous night and that a fat mouse had preceded his usual ample breakfast, so that it was unnecessary to bother about a midday meal.

At noon Lady Merivale, coming in from the garden where she had been lifting daffodil bulbs, found her husband in his study, which was a cool room, and sank gratefully into a chair.

"Do you think we should plant a border of narcissi along the west border this year?" she said.

After he had given the matter due thought and pronounced upon it (they were both keen gardeners), she remained there lying back with her head resting on the cushion. This was so unlike her usual habits that he was moved to ask her if anything was wrong.

"The heat's given me a headache and I was wishing I hadn't to go and open The Haven fête this afternoon, that's all."

"You drive yourself too hard sometimes, my dear. Wasn't it rather foolish to lift bulbs in this weather? We're not so young as we once were, you know."

"I suppose not; it's curious, isn't it, that now it does sometimes strike one that one isn't. I mean, for years and years one regards one's present state as static, and then suddenly old age looms up as a sea change in the not too distant future – and of course one tends to think of the old as static, too, I mean as if they have always been as they are now. It needs quite an effort of imagination to picture The Haven residents as young, for instance, or even as middle-aged like us. I wonder sometimes – don't you? – what we'll be like at their age, if we're still here at all, that is."

"No," said her husband, "the present's enough for me and a bit more than enough for you today it seems. You'd better go and have a bit of a rest before luncheon."

"Oh, I'm all right, and I don't need to stay long this afternoon, only make my little speech and do the rounds of the stalls, what are you doing?"

"I shall go to sleep," said her husband firmly, and with a sigh of envy she left him.

Lunch was served early at The Haven that day, but either owing to the heat or to the general excitement, no one but Leila Ford and Old Misery ate very much. Talking, on the other hand, flowed more easily than usual.

"How it livens us up when anything other than the daily routine is happening," thought Mrs Thornton.

Meg Norton, usually so silent, was speaking with some animation about the county cricket club results to Mrs Perry, and Leila was holding forth to the table at large upon a charity performance of *A Midsummer Night's Dream* given long ago in the grounds of Warwick Castle in which she had played Titania.

"Or wished you were playing her," silently commented Dorothy Brown, "you were really only one of the fairies."

"It was just before I left the stage for ever," said Leila. "Ben Greet happened to be in the audience and he congratulated me afterwards. He said I had a bright future before me, but, alas! I was infatuated at the time – my heart has always led me astray."

"It must have been a wonderful experience," said Mrs Thornton politely, "and what a lovely setting the grounds of Warwick Castle would have provided for The Dream."

"Indeed, yes! said Leila. "I always feel that the spirit of the Bard haunts our Warwickshire in a very special way, don't you?"

Mrs Thornton gave an inward shudder. It is terrible

when false tongues speak truth, or what one would like to think is true.

In the kitchen Old Misery was passing up her plate for second helps with relish. "Always partial to a bit o' fat, myself," she said, eyeing Gisela's plate, the rim of which was decorated with discarded bacon rind. "Waste not, want not, we was brought up on, not as 'ow, that's always true neither. My mum, she never wasted a mite, but there was plenty o' want about all the same. It ain't 'alf 'ot now, reckon we'll 'ave a storm afore the day's out."

The musicians, having arrived early enough to rehearse Tom, were picnicking in the copse. They had found a sizeable oak to give them shade.

"He does love his drum," said Nell. "I thought he would. I wish he could keep it. It's a pity about his clothes."

Tom after all had not fitted at all well into the shirt and jeans she had brought along for him. He was shorter than Nell and a good deal broader, so the jeans had been far too long and tight and he couldn't squeeze himself into the T-shirt at all.

"Whatever made you think he was my size, Jake?"

"Oh," said Elizabeth, "all men are utterly hopeless about people's appearances, especially their clothes. If you ask them they say vaguely, 'Oh, he's not all that big,' or: 'Well, she was wearing a sort of blue thing.'"

"You're absolutely right," said Nell, "it was silly of me to trust to Jake. Tom's own clothes are pretty shabby, but it can't be helped now, *he* doesn't mind. Doesn't he hum beautifully? And he is so happy."

"I think we might borrow a begging-bowl from Gran and collect contributions for The Haven; every little helps, we'll just have it in front of us so people won't feel they've got to give," said Austen.

"This wood must be pretty old," said Jake, "look at that ancient thorn."

"Gran says there was an old farmhouse here, possibly

Tudor, before The Haven was built. Tom's great-great-grandmother used to work there," said Nell.

"I expect the wood is older than that – reaching back to mediaeval times or further, some ancient boundary, perhaps."

"I wonder if Tom's ancestors planted any of it," said Nell. "I love the ancientness of it, it makes me feel bigger than I am, somehow."

"I should have thought it would have made you feel smaller," said Elizabeth. "I haven't much use for the past myself. We can't really progress unless we cut clear of tradition."

"Can't be done," said Austen, "and what d'you mean by progress, anyway? Cutting down this oak and the rest of the wood and building council flats here, I suppose?"

"Yes, if needed."

"Look," said Nell hastily, "there's Gisela and Tom going across the lawn to the marquee – their meal must be over – we'd better pack up and go and see if we can lend a hand."

She was right, the old ladies were all back in their own rooms getting ready for the afternoon. Dorothy Brown was trying to compress Leila into her best summer dress. Until recently the weather had been so unseasonable that she had had no occasion to wear it; it had been tight for her last summer and now was impossibly so.

"It's no use, Leila," said Dorothy, "it simply can't be done."

"You're not trying," Leila shouted, "it was perfectly all right when I last wore it."

"No, it wasn't," said Dorothy, "don't you remember, I had to let it out and now there's no more that I can let out."

"But what can I do?" wailed Leila. "I haven't anything else thin enough that's fit to be seen."

"We must use safety pins," said Dorothy. She disappeared into her own room and came back with two large

100

safety pins which she fastened firmly where it was most necessary, and a skilful arrangement of a silk scarf hid the gaps through which Leila bulged.

"It isn't as if you'll be moving around," said Dorothy. "We'll go down early enough to get you a seat in the shade and there's absolutely no wind."

Leila continued to moan but Dorothy paid no attention. She found her increasing deafness actually an asset now in dealing with Leila – she need not hear what it was unnecessary to hear.

At 2.30 p.m. punctually, Lady Merivale declared the fête open, the young musicians struck up the "Toreador's Song" and people began to move round the stalls. Everywhere throughout the country can be found a band of splendid women whose unfailing contributions of homemade jams and marmalade, chutneys and sweets, cakes and flans appear at all the innumerable charity coffee morning, sales and fêtes. These faithful willing workers are taken for granted, but they provide an indispensable service to the community. Their goods disappear quickly, too, for they are always excellent value. Indeed, it is not unknown for the donors to buy back their own gifts themselves, at the fixed price, of course, rightly judging them to be of excellent quality. For instance, Mrs Martin, knowing exactly how many eggs and lemons had gone into her lemon curd, secured it for her married daughter, and there was always competition for Mrs Brewer's delicious fudge and Miss Anderson's coffee cake. Thus the produce stall had little or no difficulty in disposing of its wares. Friends and relatives saw to it that the old ladies' work also sold well. Mrs Thornton's patchwork was snapped up at once and so were Mrs Perry's plants. Lady Merivale, dutifully doing her rounds, bought Leila's coverlet, thinking it would do nicely for one of her "Help the Aged" parcels. She often managed to kill two birds with one stone in this fashion. She left the coverlet to be delivered to her later.

"Lady Merivale has such good taste," said Leila, as she moved the SOLD ticket to a more prominent position. "Of course, she saw it would ruin the appearance of the whole stall if she took away my coverlet now – so thoughtful."

The White Elephant Stall was not doing so well. Miss Hughes sat between Mrs Bradshaw's great vases beaming with benevolence and handing out the wrong change to the few buyers who came her way. The vicar's wife, who was selling tea tickets nearby, looked with envy at Miss Hughes's beautiful outfit. She herself had not had a new summer dress for some time, in fact, now that her little girls were growing so fast and seemed to need new shoes at such short intervals, she got most of her clothes at the Oxfam shop in Darnley. She looked round now for Becky and Sue and saw them flitting about among the crowd, with their little trays of posies which they were very busy selling. The flowers were wilting already in the heat but everyone was buying them. "They can't resist the darlings," she thought fondly, "they look like flowers themselves; how pretty their frocks are – I'm so glad I chose those patterns and managed to finish them in time," and all envy of Miss Hughes melted away.

The musicians were hard at work and their begging bowl was filling up nicely. Down by the coconut shies, though, matters were not going too well. Bert Warren, the greengrocer's son, was too good a shot and was amassing coconuts with disconcerting speed. His father, still angry at Mr Jackson withdrawing his order, had forbidden Bert to go to the fête, but Bert did not mean to have his afternoon's sport spoiled; he could sell his coconuts at a profit at school the next day. But Jackson, seeing his stock disappearing too fast and all to the same customer, and that customer Bert, felt that this would cause trouble, and declared that from henceforth no one was to have more than three turns of three shots each. Bert, who was enjoying his sixth turn and had the ball in his hand, was annoyed by this and hurled it hard and recklessly in consequence. It flew through one of those neglected holes in the net straight at Lenny, Old Misery's youngest, for "old" was figurative rather than accurate and Lenny had only just turned six. He had drawn nearer and nearer the shies, fascinated by Bert's skill, and now loud shrieks rent the air, drowning the sweet strains of "Summer Dreams".

Lenny was borne off to the house – "All over bloo 'e is," said his sister Doreen with relish to the somewhat abashed Bert.

"It's knocked out two of his front teeth," said Mrs Mills later to an anxiously enquiring Mr Jackson at the kitchen door, "but the bleedin's mostly from his nose. Fred's putting a key down his back at this moment. The teeth were loose anyways, milk teeth they was, but it'll make his mother's day."

When most people had finished their tea, the draw for the raffle prizes took place. Sue, the vicar's younger little girl, tremendously solemn, picked the tickets from the brass bowl which usually stood in the hall, and handed them to Col. Bradshaw, who shouted numbers out through a megaphone. It had always been understood that should any of the committee or the donors of prizes draw a number they should hand back their ticket, but Miss Hughes had not grasped this, so when she was drawn she went up to choose her prize. By that time there were only the architect's drawing and her own clock left. She was pleased to get the clock back again – it had been inconveient to let it go as she had intended it in the first place for her housekeeper's Christmas present. It was at this point that Col. Bradshaw finally gave her up.

And now it became noticeable that clouds were darkening the hitherto bright sky and that they looked remarkably like thunder clouds. It was extraordinary how rapidly they blotted out the blue; without further warning lightening flashed, a great clap of thunder sounded almost overhead, and a few large drops of rain splashed down. Immediately people began feverishly to pack up what remained on the stalls and to hurry into the marquee, the rain then poured down in earnest and there was general confusion and dismay. Jim Bailey, the village postman who was a wit, seized the megaphone and shouted through it: "The rain is free, but we charge extra for the thunder." This made everyone laugh and feel better. The unsold goods were collected carefully in a corner and it was suggested that they should be auctioned. Mr Jackson, who had plenty of experience of auctions, was put in charge. There were not a great many articles, most were from Miss Hughes's stall, but of Tom's contributions only the knife-cleaner was left; the china and the volumes of *Sunday at Home* had gone quickly, Austen had bought the dressmaker's dummy, he said clothed or unclothed it would add distinction to his room, and Nell had got the lampshade for 10p. "The frame is sound and I shall cover it with parchment and some pressed leaves." What had happened to the umbrella was not known. Tom felt sorry for his knife machine. He went up to it and patted it.

"Don't often see one of them about nowadays," said Mr Martin to Austen, who was standing nearby. Mr Martin had arrived late from a meeting of the Darnley Preservation Society, and had not had time to go the rounds of the stalls before the storm.

"I suppose not," said Austen.

"Might catch the eye of an American," went on Mr Martin. "Edwardian relic, you know, quite the thing now. I'm a bit of a collector myself, not showpieces, can't afford them, just odd bits here and there, rubbish the wife calls them, but I find them quite an investment, you'd be surprised." Austen smiled at him and wandered away to find Jake.

The turn of the knife machine was not long in coming. "Now," shouted Jackson, "who'll be in luck and acquire this valuable piece of equipment, still in full working order – what shall I start it at – say 50p.?"

Mr Martin put up his hand; he did not expect any competition but Jake, who was standing at the opening of the marquee watching the storm, turned and waved.

"That gentleman there," said Jackson. "Yes, sir?"

"One pound," said Jake.

"And fifty," said Mr Martin.

"Two pounds," said Jake.

"Three," said Mr Martin, whose desire for the knife machine was growing with competition. Everyone became interested, the bids steadily mounted, but at twelve pounds, Jake thought it wise to withdraw. The knife machine gave place to a stuffed owl that had lost half his feathers, but it had made by far the top price.

The storm had moved off, though it was still raining. Austen, Elizabeth, Jake and Nell slipped away as soon as the auction was over and set their faces towards Stratford. They had decided beforehand to make a night of it, and Jake had booked seats for the evening performance. They bundled into his car, which was larger than Austen's, and had an open top.

"Where are you going to put that thing?" said Elizabeth to Austen, who was clasping his dummy to his breast. "It won't go in the boot. Whatever possessed you to buy it?"

"Answer number one: I shall carry her on my lap. Answer number two: to please Tom."

"He did well, I must say," said Elizabeth. "What a pity he isn't at a special school, I'm sure they could teach him to read and write. Perhaps I could get him a place in one."

"That's right, shut him up in an institution. Will reading and writing make him any better off than he is already? He's free and useful and happy and himself as he is."

"All the same, I think people like him do need specialized care."

"What do you mean by 'people like him'? I don't see that

105

Tom's any different from us except that he's got perfect pitch, which none of us have."

"Jake thinks he's different, don't you, Jake?" said Nell, teasing, but he did not answer. He was driving them through the lanes, avoiding the motorway, a habit of his that distressed Austen, who liked to get to places as quickly as possible. The rain had almost stopped and the air was deliciously fresh and cool.

"I feel just in the mood for Shakespeare," said Nell, "only not tragedy."

"It's all right, I think it's *Twelfth Night* or *Much Ado* tonight. I can't remember which," said Elizabeth.

"Neither," said Jake, "it's *The Tempest*."

"That's better still," said Austen, "that's got everything, men and gods."

"Gods?" queried Nell.

"Juno and Co.," said Austen.

"Every kind of magic," said Jake.

"And music," said Elizabeth. "Remember 'sounds and sweet airs that give delight and hurt not'?"

"Like we've been making," said Nell, "it's really got all today in it, old age and us."

"And Tom," said Jake.

Nell laughed at him again. "You and Tom," she teased.

"And it's got the wood with that oak tree," said Austen, "and the vicar's bees and Tom's bats."

They lapsed into silence. The lanes got narrower and turned about so that Jake had to go slowly and the branches of trees and bushes brushed against them. Summer scents invaded the car. The sky had cleared and a few stars were beginning to glimmer faintly in the dark.

"I'm so sleepy," said Elizabeth.

"Have a shoulder," said Austen. He disengaged an arm from his dummy and slipped it round her, drawing her gently towards him.

"Well, that's over," said Miss Blackett to herself as night

106

fell and peace descended on The Haven once more. It had gone well on the whole, she thought; the storm had not really mattered and it had meant that the marquee had been most useful after all. She hated waste. The Lenny child had not been badly hurt, thank goodness it was only his nose and a couple of milk teeth and not his eye, but they must not use those nets another year without a careful mend. She hoped that they might have made a bit more than last year, the attendance had been good. Col. Bradshaw would let her know soon, she knew; he was very reliable. Her door opened gently and Tom appeared with Lord Jim. In spite of constant injunctions, he did not often remember to knock.

"He was on my bed, Lady Miss Blackett. I think he be hungry."

Lord Jim knew very well that he was, who wouldn't be after such a well spent day, slightly disturbed by the thunder, but on the whole, satisfactory. He rubbed against Miss Blackett's legs purring loudly in anticipation of his supper, which she immediately produced for him from his holy fridge. She did not thank Tom; she would have preferred Lord Jim to have sought sanctuary on her own bed, which he had always done before whenever the need arose. Tom stood there smiling.

"It's bin a grand day, Lady Miss Blackett, weren't they tunes lovely?"

"I hope you thanked Mr Perry for letting you join with his party, it was extremely kind of him, and Tom, I hope you are grateful for being allowed the time off to do so," said Miss Blackett.

"That little old drum fair played hisself, he did," said Tom and hopped out of the room.

"Such an irritating boy," thought Miss Blackett. "I do wish I could hear of a really reliable girl or woman instead."

9

SOME GOODBYES

A PERIOD of calm succeeded the fête. Mrs Nicholson, the new resident, moved in and seemed to Miss Blackett as though she was settling nicely and likely to give little trouble. Of course she brought too much furniture with her, they alawys did, but she was quiet and very cheerful. Her cheerfulness sprang from the fact that she looked upon the home as a real haven and not, like many of the past and present residents, as a depressing necessity. She had given up her own house some time before, owing to heart trouble. It was impossible to get enough domestic help and the garden had got beyond her long ago, so she had gone to live with a married son. But it had not answered. Not that they had been unkind to her, quite the reverse. Her daughter-in-law Carol was dreadfully kind.

"Bob and I have moved out of our room into the guest room, Mother; we thought you should have the sunny one. No, really, we *like* the room and it doesn't matter a bit not having a guest room. After all, blood's thicker than water, isn't it?"

"No Kevin, you can't have 'Top of the Pops' on now, dear; I am sure Granny doesn't want it – no, Granny, please – he must learn to think of you before himself."

"Amanda, take your dressmaking things up to your bedroom, dear – no, it isn't too cold. Remember this is Granny's sitting-room now as well as your children's den,

108

and you see you are taking up the whole table *and* most of the floor as well. Oh, Granny, if you insist, you spoil her, you know, but I'm sure she's very grateful."

"No, certainly you mustn't walk to your church, Mother. No. I'm afraid none of the neighbours do seem to go, it's rather shocking, isn't it, but Bob can easily run you there and call for you again later; he only potters about on Sunday mornings and he can fit those two short journeys in nicely." And Bob, who had been such a downright outspoken boy, now seemed unable to say anything but "Of course," though in all sorts of ways she felt she was unwillingly adding to the burden of his already too busy days. She could not have borne it had she not put her name down for The Haven, unknown to Carol and Bob. Perhaps if she could have gone to her daughter's it would have been different. "A son's a son till he gets him a wife, a daughter's a daughter all her life." Yes, but only as far as her circumstances will permit, and Peggy had her plate full, what with her job and three children and, she feared, a rather difficult and exacting husband, let alone that there really wasn't an inch to spare in their flat. So she had been overjoyed when she heard that there was a vacancy at The Haven and that she could move in at the end of August. Carol and Bob were hurt at her insistence on leaving but, all the same, she could almost feel the relief blowing through the whole household like a freshening breeze. Now, when they came to see her, which she was sure they would do, they could enjoy each other.

Mrs Nicholson liked the warden's brisk businesslike manner, she liked the little notices stuck up in her room about times of meals, baths, etc. How dreadful it had been when Carol had served the evening meal an hour earlier to suit her. She knew that it suited nobody else and it had even been changed from dinner to a light supper for her sake. ("I know it is much better for you, Granny dear, and I expect it is better for all of us, the children get a good

109

wholesome midday feed at school, and they do serve cooked dishes as well as sandwiches at Bob's office canteen.")

Then Miss Blackett told her that the vicar came regularly to celebrate Holy Communion for those who could not get to church. Depending on Bob and his car for her services on Sunday had worried her so much, as she knew how it cut into his one well-earned leisure morning, and yet they meant so much to her. She loved, too, the solidity of her room with its Victorian sash windows and handsome fireplace, though this of course was filled in now. It reminded her of the rooms she used to know in her childhood. Bob and Carol's house, with its open-style rooms and great picture windows, had hardly seemd like a house at all. The greater part of her furniture had been sold when she gave up her home, but a few precious pieces and pictures she had put in store as there was really no room for them at Carol and Bob's. Seeing them all round her again now was like a reunion with old friends. As she hung her carved wooden crucifix over her bed and her print of Raphael's Madonna over the mantelpiece where she had found two convenient nails, Mrs Nicholson gave "humble and hearty thanks for all God's goodness and loving-kindness" to her in bringing her to The Haven.

"That Mrs Nicholson, she is Catholic, I think," said Gisela to Tom. "She has a cross upon the wall and a picture of the Virgin and some lady saints painted on her bookcase also."

Miss Blackett overheard her. "You shouldn't gossip about the residents, Gisela," she said, "and in England such things do not necessarily mean that you are a Roman Catholic; you might well find them in our vicar's study, for instance."

Gisela sighed; here was another of those English muddles. In Germany, if you had crucifixes and Virgins and Saints in your room, you were Catholic, if you did not,

110

you were good Lutherans, like her parents.

Tom had not seen Mrs Nicholson's room yet. He was pleased that she had come; he did not like rooms to be empty. He decided it was time to pay her a call. Mrs Nicholson was sitting by a small round table which held her work basket and a row of well-worn devotional books between two painted bookends. They were rather poor reproductions of pre-Raphaelite ladies and not saints, as Gisela had supposed, but they held lilies in their hands and looked holy. Mrs Nicholson was knitting and thinking how lovely it was that no one was being kind to her any more, but she had reckoned without Tom. He, together with Lord Jim, who had also decided to call, entered the room without warning. Tom came forward for his handshake.

"You be the first new lady since I comes here," he announced.

Mrs Nicholson, though she had already heard something about him, was a little startled. She laid down her knitting to respond, her ball of wool rolled on to the floor and Lord Jim decided to put on a juvenile act. He pounced on the ball and rolled on his back, clasping it with his front paws. Tom crowed his funny laugh and Mrs Nicholson began to feel at ease. Tom tickled Lord Jim, who let go the ball to bite his fingers and pretend to claw him, and he retrieved it and rewound it neatly. Lord Jim turned his back on them and began an inspection of all Mrs Nicholson's furniture and Tom, too, began to look about him. He turned quickly away from the crucifix, but stared up intently at the Raphael Madonna.

"Are you thinking how beautiful that picture is?" asked Mrs Nicholson.

"No," said Tom, "I do be thinking he be a monster little 'un. I reckon as his Mum's arms must be aching summat terrible."

Mrs Nicholson was taken aback; she had never viewed her picture in this light before and there was no denying it, the divine Child was certainly rather large, but she was quite sure that Tom was wrong about His mother, Raphael's Virgin had never felt weariness or strain; perhaps her arms were miraculously strengthened to bear the baby's weight. She suddenly realized that she was thinking of the picture as representing reality rather than the artist's vision. Did that matter? She thought it might. Ought she to explain to Tom that it wasn't like a photograph? But his attention had wandered to her two precious Ruskin pottery vases.

"Flowers," he was saying, "flowers for Lady Mrs Nicholson; which be your favourite flower?"

She could not think, it seemed a long time since anyone had asked her that sort of question really wanting to know the answer.

"I like snapdragons," said Tom. "Vicar's bees, they get tricked by 'em sometimes, they be too heavy for 'em."

"Snapdragons, yes," said Mrs Nicholson gratefully, "such lovely colours."

Tom beamed and vanished, leaving the door open behind him, and Lord Jim, having satisfied himself that Mrs Nicholson's furniture was respectable and bore no traces of undesirable acquaintances, followed him. He was back again in no time with a big bunch of antirrhinums, orange and lemon and pink and crimson; there were plenty to fill the two vases. Mrs Nicholson did not ask where he had got them, though she did wonder about it a little, but he was so extremely pleased and happy she felt it must be all right. The flowers made the room look very bright and pretty, and when they had finished arranging them, they both surveyed the effect with satisfaction. Mrs Nicholson thought it perfect, only one thing worried her a little. The removal men had placed her chest of drawers across one corner, instead of flat against the wall. It looked better that way but she hadn't thought of the space it would leave behind which could not be reached and where dust would

112

collect. She found herself explaining this to Tom, who looked strong enough to shift it, which indeed he managed easily. Mrs Nichlson then opened the bottom drawer and took out a tin of fancy biscuits. She did not much like fancy biscuits but Carol thought that all old ladies did and bought it for the childen to give their grandmother as a parting present.

"Thank you for helping me, Tom," said Mrs Nicholson, "and thank you for the flowers, it was very kind of you. Now, would you like one of these biscuits?"

"I be kind to you and now you be kind to me," Tom said, looking with pleasure at the biscuits, and Mrs Nicholson found that the distasteful word had somehow lost its sting.

Tom took a long while selecting his biscuit. At last he gravely chose out three and laid them before him on the table and then, after another pause, he replaced one of the three in the tin. Mrs Nicholson smiled at him as she used to smile at her small Bob.

"Keep both of those, if you like," she said, "and I'll have the one you put back to keep you company."

They ate together in silence and the fat Holy Babe looked down on them benevolently.

The weather had been so fine since the fête that harvest was over early and Col. Bradshaw delivered some of the spoils of Harvest Thanksgiving to The Haven for the old ladies in the first week in October. The scent of autumn was already in the air and some leaves were turned. Mrs Perry's border was a tangle of marigolds and larkspurs and dwarf dahlias. She did not care for the big showy ones, which were Fred's pride. "Like blowsy barmaids, I always think, though Austen tells me these don't exist any more, they are all university students earning a bit of extra money to pay for their cars, or even graduates, he says." She had had also a fine show of antirrhinums. She recognized them when she paid a welcoming call on Mrs Nicholson one day and guessed of course how they had got there. She did not

113

mind, there would be a second blooming and besides, she was happily looking forward to a visit to her eldest married granddaughter. Austen was fetching her for the christening of her third great-grandchild and she was staying on for at least a week.

The warden had decided that it would be a good thing to get the deodar tree cut down before the autumn damp set in. Mr Martin had supplied her with the name of a firm of tree surgeons and she wrote to them. After some time they phoned saying they would be round one day the following week. Miss Blackett sighed at the typical vagueness of the present day and she had further cause for sighing when the week passed without a sign. A return phone call produced regrets that, owing to unforeseen pressure of work, her job might have to be postponed until November. "How tiresome," thought Miss Blackett, "and they can't even say when in November." Then, without warning, the day after Mrs Perry had left for her visit, two men and a lorry with ladders, ropes and saws, turned up before breakfast and started to take off the top branches of the tree.

Miss Blackett had not felt it necessary to say anything to Miss Dawson about the tree coming down. She thought it better for the news to come as a nice surprise when the day for the felling had actually been fixed. Uncertainty of any kind always made old people fuss. Still, she certainly would have told her the night before had she herself known and, fearing that the old lady might, not unnaturally, be upset by the sight of a man suddenly appearing on a ladder or astride a branch close to her window, she thought she ought to go up to her at once.

Miss Dawson had been dozing after a broken night of arthritic pain – she fancied she was watching a native dance to the beat of drums when it changed to the rhythmic noise of sawing, and she was back in childhood and John, her grandfather's gardener, was cutting the hazels in the nut-walk. "Doesn't it hurt them, oh doesn't it hurt?" "No, Miss

114

Fanny, they'll shoot out again fast enough and twice as strong." But the sawing got louder and louder; John and the hazel trees vanished as she opened her eyes, yet the sawing still went on. She looked towards the window and saw the dark shape of a man impossibly silhouetted against the sky and heard the sudden snap and crash of a branch. At the same moment Miss Blackett knocked and came in without waiting for an answer.

"I'm afraid you may have been startled, Miss Dawson," she said. "I meant to tell you but the men arrived this morning quite without warning. The old deodar tree is coming down; the committee agreed with me, I am glad to say, that your room would be much brighter and warmer and drier without it, altogether healthier, you won't know yourself, your rheumatism will feel the benefit this winter, I'm sure."

Miss Dawson felt she was choking – she had to force the words out: "S'stop them, s'stop them," she stuttered, "they mustn't – they must stop, they must stop!"

"It's quite all right, Miss Dawson, you need not be frightened, they are skilled men who know their job – there is no danger that the tree will fall the wrong way or any of the branches come crashing through your window. It's all quite safe. They'll soon finish clearing the top part, they say, and they won't bring the machine saw for the main trunk till tomorrow, so just don't worry yourself. I'll pull your curtains across and Gisela will be here with your breakfast very soon."

She left the room and Miss Dawson turned her face to the wall, she knew she was defeated. She had fought authority several times in her life, and with some success, but now she knew without any doubt that it would be of no use. She was too old, too alone and too helpless, and it was too late. The sound of the sawing, malignant and relentless, filled the whole room.

After an aeon it stopped and she was able to think again.

"What had the woman said – 'The committee agreed with *me*'." It was her idea then, well, she should pay for it. If the murder could not be prevented, it could be revenged. Then her breakfast came in and afterwards the sawing began again.

The thought of revenge helped Miss Dawson to endure the horror of the next day, when the devilish petrol saw whined and screeched through the hours until her proud, beautiful tree crashed to the ground. She pondered long on what form this could take, but found nothing that satisfied her. All that time she never left her room.

Miss Blackett said, "Don't you find the noise disturbing? Why not stay downstairs in the sitting-room till they have finished?"

Miss Dawson did not answer. Miss Blackett found her silence a little disturbing, but Miss Dawson had always been a moody one, and really it was best not to worry too much about any of the old dears, but just to do what one knew to be right for them and, if she didn't mind the noise and preferred to stay upstairs, let her have her own way. It was certainly interesting to watch the men at work, she would have liked more time to see them herself.

It was on the day after the tree had fallen that Miss Dawson knew what was to be her revenge. Held prisoner by a sort of baleful spell, she had spent hours at the window watching the final stages of destruction. Lord Jim was equally, though very differently, fascinated. He had never experienced a horizontal tree before and much enjoyed stalking along it, sharpening his claws on its trunk, and pouncing on stray small twigs and dismembered branches. Frances Dawson looked down at his lithe golden body, so full of life, desecrating her dying tree, and hated him. Then it flashed upon her that of course her revenge on the warden must be to destroy her cat. It was so obvious and so just a solution that she wondered it had not occurred to her at once. She thought of the dead thrushes and the other

116

poor little corpses; this would be an act of revenge for them too. She remembered a talk with Mary Perry. She had said the only way to deal with cats was to get rid of them and Mary had said it would be difficult to get rid of Lord Jim, and she had answered, but not seriously, "Where there's a will, there's a way." Well, she was serious enough now, and a way must be found. She believed Mary was a little shocked at her then. She had been wishing that Mary had not been away during this dreadful time, for she alone would have guessed a little of what she was suffering. But now she thought it was just as well. She would certainly be of no help – too soft, and she might have proved a hindrance. "Where there's a will there's a way" – but what way?

Poison was the only possible answer, but how on earth was she to get hold of any? The problem occupied her all the rest of the day and by evening she was no nearer a solution, and she felt exhausted and frustrated by the time that the warden came in with her painkillers for the night. As her two regulation pills were shaken out, she stared at the bottle, because she did not want to look at Miss Blackett, and her eye caught the inscription at the base of the label. She did not have to read it, she knew it said: "Keep away from children and animals." That was it – that was the answer: hoard her pills, mix them with a tempting meal – fish, they always had fish for Friday suppers, that would do. Today was Tuesday, eight pills would surely be more than enough.

Miss Blackett said goodnight and left, and Frances grimly put away her pills. To forego her dose would mean long hours of pain, but she could endure more than that to achieve her end. During the next three days she kept a close watch on Lord Jim's movements. Like most cats, he was a creature of habit and addicted to a peaceful snooze after his meals. Since Tom's arrival he liked to take his morning nap on his bed, which smelt pleasantly of its

117

owner and was safe from disturbance. Frances Dawson noted that he passed her room on his way up to Tom's attic each morning at about the same time. On Friday evening she asked to have her supper served to her in her own room, a not unusual request with her. It was pilchards, and unluckily for Lord Jim, not in tomato sauce which he would not have touched, but pilchards in their natural state were exceedingly tasty. Frances pounded up her pills with the handle of a knife, mixed them with the pilchards on one of her own saucers and hid it in the bottom of her cupboard. She left a morsel of the fish on her tray.

"Miss Dawson, she has eaten nearly all her supper tonight," observed Gisela, "that is good, she has not eaten enough these days."

On that Sunday morning Frances, who had scarcely slept at all, struggled out of bed at the right moment, opened her door and put down the saucer of pilchards upon the threshold. Her fumbling arthritic fingers, shaking with excitement, nearly dropped it and she spilt some of the mixture, which worried her, but there was no time to clear it up. She sat down on the nearest chair and began to talk to herself.

"I'll have to take my chance of anyone noticing, but it isn't likely, they're all either in their rooms or busy downstairs now. If anyone does happen to pass, I'll say I wanted to give the cat a treat. I don't care what they think. I wish he'd come. The pills are almost tasteless, I know, and all cats are greedy."

Here she was wrong, all cats are not greedy any more than all people, but only an abnormal cat refuses fish. Lord Jim was not particularly greedy, but neither was he abnormal. This morning he was punctual as usual and was most agreeably surprised to find a saucer of pilchards on Miss Dawson's threshold. He cleared it up with relish and even attended to the spilt fragments. Then he went on his way rejoicing. Miss Dawson picked up the saucer and washed it thoroughly.

Miss Blackett missed Lord Jim first at his lunch hour. She was a little worried as his habits were usually so regular. When he did not turn up for his teatime saucer of milk she began to be anxious, but when he was still missing for his chief and most enjoyable meal of the day, the one he took after the residents' supper was over, she was seriously concerned. She went round asking everyone if they had seen him that day, but only Leila Ford remembered to have done so.

"I saw him early in the morning, Miss Blackett, he was going up to the attics, on his way to that boy's room I expect – he's always after him nowadays." Leila spoke with relish; she saw Miss Blackett's face harden into a stony mask and she sensed drama in the air.

Miss Blackett turned and marched upstairs; as she passed Miss Dawson's room the door opened slightly but she went on past it, straight on and up to Tom's attic. "He must have shut up Lord Jim there," she told herself angrily, "he would never have kept away from me for so long of his own free will."

She burst into the room. There was no Lord Jim there and no Tom either. She looked all round, on the bed and on the chair. But at a second glance the bed did not look quite right, there was a slight hump down the centre. Miss Blackett threw back the coverlet and revealed Lord Jim lying underneath. He looked far too shrunk and too still. She stood there motionless looking down at him.

Then Tom, who was coming to bed early as was usual with him, bounded past her with a queer cry and took up Lord Jim's limp body in his arms. Miss Blackett shrieked out at him:

"He's dead, you've killed him, its some hateful thing you've done like idiots do do to animals. He was quite, quite well – you've killed him, you wicked, wicked boy!" She rushed at him and struck at his head again and again.

"Stop that," said Miss Dawson's voice at the door. She

had heard the cries and had pulled herself up the stairs. "It wasn't Tom who killed your cat, I did."

Miss Blackett stared at her. "You!" she gasped. "You!"

"You killed my tree," said Miss Dawson, "so I killed your cat, a life for a life."

"But," said Miss Blackett, "a tree's not alive, not a *person*, I mean."

Miss Dawson simply looked at her, smiling a little. All of a sudden the silence between the two women was broken by sobs. Tom, still holding Lord Jim's lifeless body, had made no sound when Miss Blackett had attacked him, but now he burst out crying. His unrestrained tears, following each other down his cheeks, fell on the cat's fur which began to stick together as if he had been out in the rain. Miss Blackett snatched him from Tom's arms and put her face down against his wet coat. Immediately she was a child again, back on the night before her kitten had been taken away. He had jumped in at her bedroom window all wet and had leapt on to her bed and had dried himself by rubbing against her face, and this had tickled her so that she had laughed out loud in the dark. By the next night he had gone. Standing now with Lord Jim, so light and thin in her arms, she felt the darkness of destruction and loss envelop her. But also for the first and perhaps the only time in her life she experienced a moment of revelation. Looking up at Miss Dawson who was still calmly watching her, she suddenly seemed to see herself mirrored in the other woman's eyes. She and Miss Dawson were both, in some extraordinary way, one. She turned and went out of the room carrying the cat, and Tom followed her.

Miss Dawson dragged herself very slowly back downstairs in their wake. The unusual exertion and excitement had exhausted her and the consummation of her cherished revenge had left her empty. The pain, too, which she had had to endure while saving up her pills for

120

Lord Jim, had taken its toll. She sat in her chair and stared out at the hateful open sky. After she had stared for a little while, she could not see the sky so clearly; there seemed to be branches stretching across it, and then more and more of them, waving softly as they used to do, and the room became full of bird song. Miss Dawson left her chair and flew through the window and up into the branches of her tree – up and up her bird's soul flew and at last, beyond all vision.

"I'm sorry, Tom," said Miss Blackett when they reached her room, "don't cry any more." She laid Lord Jim down on his cushion and got a clean handkerchief from a drawer and gave it to Tom – it was a specially large one that she kept for the specially heavy head colds from which she suffered. Then she sat down quickly. She was still trembling.

Tom blew his nose loudly, then his eye fell on Miss Blackett's teapot on the shelf. "Tea," he said, "tea for Lady Miss Blackett." He filled the electric kettle and switched it on and made the tea.

They drank it together without saying anything more, and afterwards Miss Blackett felt a little less shaky. Tom washed up the tea things, shook hands with Miss Blackett and stroked Lord Jim very gently and went off to bed. He woke at his usual early hour and got to work and, when it was time, went into the kitchen to set out the breakfast trays.

Gisela appeared and Tom shook hands with her and began to take the trays round. The ground-floor ones were done and he went upstairs with Miss Dawson's. Then Gisela heard him drop the tray – there was a crash and a sound of broken china, then she heard him run across the landing, and going to the door, she saw him sliding down the balustrade. He was laughing.

"She's gone, she's gone away, Lady Miss Dawson's gone," he shouted joyfully. "Come, Gisela, come Lady

Miss Blackett, come and see."

Miss Blackett came slowly and heavily out of her room and followed Gisela upstairs. Gisela stopped outside Miss Dawson's room, afraid to go in, but Miss Blackett walked past her and Tom followed, still laughing. The breakfast tray lay on the floor with a broken cup and plate and the milk spilt all over the carpet. Miss Dawson's body was slumped forward in her chair. Miss Blackett could see at once what had happened.

"What a mess on the floor, they aren't supoosed to die here, she's done it just for spite. This is my fault. I should never have left her to come down those stairs alone. I should have seen she was ill, it's my fault, I shall resign." All these thoughts shouted at her at once and she did not know what to do with them. But Tom's laughter, that had to be stopped immediately.

"Be quiet," she said sharply, "can't you see the poor old thing is dead? Be quiet at once."

10

TOM'S DEPARTURE

THERE WAS much for the warden to do that day – phone calls and interviews with the doctor, the undertaker, the vicar and Miss Dawson's "next of kin" (a cousin in Cornwall) and all the time she felt a heavy weight of oppression and weariness. It made things worse that her emotions were not clearly defined, but all mixed up and muddy. She could not find relief in anger against Miss Dawson, for she was dead, and the liberating moment of vision vouchsafed to her in the attic was already banished from her conscious thought. She had decided by now that Miss Dawson had been too ill to know what she was doing or saying.

She felt guilty at having accused Tom so harshly and violently, yet this did not prevent her still suffering from the jealousy that had occasioned the violence. It hurt that Lord Jim had died on Tom's bed, and that these last weeks he had seemed to prefer his company to her own. Then there was the question of how far she was responsible for Miss Dawson's collapse. She felt she ought to have noticed that she had not been eating properly for some days past and had been more than usually withdrawn; and, knowing how crippled and frail she was, should she not have seen her safely back to her own room? That she had not fallen on the stairs, seeing the state she was in that night, had been almost a miracle. Had she failed in her duty as warden and should she offer to resign? She felt it might be a relief to do so. These thoughts and emotions chased each other round her tired brain all that day, and underlying everything was the ache for Lord Jim, which she knew would be even worse when everything had settled down again.

She had no time to see to him before the late afternoon; then she found a good strong shoebox and lined it with a silk headscarf, a favourite one, and laid Lord Jim in it and, looking carefully to see that no one was about, she carried the box to the further side of the copse where the old thorn tree grew. Lord Jim had loved to climb that particular tree, it had a comfortable branch along which he liked to stretch out on hot summer days when Mrs Perry's border was too warm for him. Miss Blackett laid down the box while she went to fetch a spade. The ground was hard underneath the tree and she found it difficult to dig a big enough hole but she did not want to ask Fred to help her and certainly not Tom. At last it was finished, but she had been too tired to dig very deep and there was a mound which she tried to hide with moss and leaves. She did not want anyone but herself to know where Lord Jim was. When she got back to her room she felt utterly exhausted, but before she sat down to rest she put away Lord Jim's saucer and cushion where they could not be seen.

That evening everyone but Leila Ford was subdued for, though no one but Mrs Perry had known Miss Dawson at all well, the presence of death in the house made itself felt. The residents of The Haven were too old not to be aware of its inescapable reality, and its dark mystery, seeming now so close and intimate, blotted out their customary and comforting trivialities. Only Leila's rudimentary soul still believed that such a thing could never happen to *her*, and she was pleasantly roused and excited by the unusual drama of the day. Rumours were flying round about Lord Jim.

"Of course that boy is at the bottom of it. I saw the cat, you know, Dorothy, going up to his room yesterday morning. It was the last time he was seen alive. It was I who told

Miss Blackett he was up there. No one else saw him, *and* I heard the row in the evening too. Mrs Thornton was with Miss Norton, *she* heard nothing. Well, what I say is that it only serves Miss Blackett right for employing such a boy here."

"You shouldn't say such a thing, Leila," said Dorothy Brown. "Miss Blackett says Lord Jim must have picked up some poison somewhere, probably rat poison, people aren't careful enough, and cats *will* wander."

"I wonder when Miss Dawson's funeral will be," said Leila. "I hope soon, I don't like the feeling of a corpse in the house. I hope we'll get somebody a bit livelier in her place. It'll make a change – she kept herself to herself, if anyone did. Funny, the tree and the cat and her all disappearing at once. My bottle's not hot enough, Dorothy; Gisela never does them properly."

"Give it to me," said Dorothy, "I'll heat it up for you."

After a night when she had slept from sheer exhaustion, Miss Blackett felt less inclined to offer her resignation. She decided to consult the vicar who was calling to see her about arrangements for the funeral service, she could not of course say anything about what had happened in Tom's attic, that was impossible, but she would try not to excuse herself in any way.

"I should have noticed that Miss Dawson had not been herself for some days," she began. "Gisela, our German girl, did say she was eating very little, but I did not take this seriously. Then, the night she died, for some reason she climbed the stairs to the attic floor. I should have prevented this, and certainly I should have seen that once there she should not have been left to come down those stairs alone, for I was aware that she was there. I ought to have seen that she was not fit to be left alone that night. In fact," she ended, "I feel I have been remiss and that perhaps I should offer to resign."

"You are being too conscientious, if you don't mind my

125

saying so, my dear Miss Blackett," exclaimed the vicar. "Miss Dawson was, I know, very reserved and she certainly did not invite questioning or sympathy. You must not blame yourself for what probably made no difference. After all she did *not* fall on the stairs. Perhaps the lack of appetite might have been a pointer, but it is easy to be wise after the event. I am quite sure the committee would not consider any offer of resignation from you for such a cause, and you must not think of such a thing. Now, about the funeral, don't let that worry you. I understand Miss Dawson left clear instructions that she wished to be cremated, and with no ceremony, but I think a short service at the cremation would be fitting, which I will arrange. Anyone who would care to be present from The Haven will be welcome of course –" he hesitated.

Miss Blackett said that she would like to come and Mrs Perry, if she were back in time, and she would enquire as to anyone else. She was relieved at the vicar's decisive reassurance. She really felt too old to start a new job and knew that she would not now easily obtain another post so good, and she could not afford to be unemployed.

"Goodbye, then," said the vicar, "and take care of yourself; you have had quite a shock, I can see. I shall send you along a pot of my honey, it is better than any tonic."

After Miss Blackett had thanked the vicar and seen him out, she felt her nagging sense of guilt partly assuaged, and more free to mourn her cat. Instinctively she found herself walking towards the copse, but when she got there she saw, to her dismay and indignation, that Tom was underneath the old thorn tree busily hammering away at some object on the ground, and that the little mound that covered Lord Jim had been carefully ringed round with roughly matching stones.

"What are you doing, Tom?" she asked.

Tom looked up. "I guessed as you might've laid him here, Lady Miss Blackett," he said. "The stones look right

126

pretty, don't they? And I'm making him a cross all proper like, the wood it be from chips off that big old tree as is cut down."

Miss Blackett felt the usual uncomfortable conflict which Tom always seemed to arouse in her. She could not help being touched, yet she resented him thus trespassing on her private emotions, and as to the cross, that she considered really ought not to be allowed.

"Yes, the stones are nice," she said, "but not the cross, Tom, the vicar wouldn't like it."

"Oh, yes, Lady Miss Blackett," said Tom. "Vicar, he loves 'em, churchyard be full of 'em, and so be church."

Miss Blackett turned away. She knew that, in spite of anything she could say, the cross would be finished and if she removed it, another would be made to take its place. She supposed that now the little grave would be bound to be discovered and pointed out and talked about, and this she would hate, and yet, at the same time she felt an absurd childish gleam of comfort as if Tom's cross might ensure for Lord Jim a minute corner of heaven.

Mrs Perry managed to return to The Haven in time for Miss Dawson's funeral. She was very troubled and sad about her old friend's death. She alone guessed something of what the felling of the deodar tree must have meant to her. "Perhaps," she thought, "if I had not been away, I might have helped." It seemed heartless, too, that she had been enjoying her visit so much and especially her delicious new great-grandchild while this was happening to Frances. She sincerely grieved, too, for Miss Blackett's loss of Lord Jim, and she could not entirely suppress a very unwelcome query as to his death, which she would not put into words, even to herself. It was just there, like a little cloud which would not go away – but no, she simply would not think about it any more, it would have been impossible anyway. But perhaps this made her express her sympathy with the warden more openly and warmly than anybody else had dared to do in the face of grim discouragement.

"Dear Miss Blackett," she said, "we had a retriever once who was such a darling, he was a most beloved member of the family. He got run over. I know what it feels like, one misses such a pet at every turn – you must get another cat, it's the only way. We got a puppy directly. Of course it wasn't the same as dear Rab, but it healed and helped. My daughter's tabby has lovely kittens and I'm sure she would gladly give you one."

Miss Blackett felt her lonely unhappiness melt a little, but she shook her head. She was not going to lay herself open to the perilous arrow of love a third time. "No, thank you, Mrs Perry, I don't mean ever to have another cat, but I appreciate your kindness all the same."

Mrs Perry missed Frances Dawson very much. She had admired her for her courage and her knowledge, though she was always a little in awe of her. Now she began to cultivate Mrs Nicholson's company; it was Tom's raids on her flower border that first brought them together. He kept Mrs Nicholson's vases regularly supplied with snapdragons, which were now enjoying their second flowering, and when she learned that the only border where they grew belonged to Mrs Perry, she thought an apology was called for. But Mrs Perry just laughed.

"You're welcome," she said, "and nobody really minds what Tom does, bless him."

A bit later she wrote to Nell: "I find that our new resident, Mrs Nicholson, plays Scrabble well and we have a game together most evenings. We are about equal. She is a pleasant person, though very religious. She had an uncle who was a bishop, but this doesn't matter for Scrabble. Tom has made a cross for poor Lord Jim's grave and she thinks this is sacrilegious, I fear, but, as you know, I always say I shan't be happy in heaven if dear Rab isn't there, and really, I think that dolphins and seals and whales and poor dear gorillas and some, though not all, dogs and cats, have much nicer natures and are better behaved than many humans, and I shouldn't wonder if God doesn't think so too, so we'd better look out. But of course I can't say that to a bishop's niece. It is nice to have another grandmother here, poor Mrs Thornton had no grandchildren, you know – though I can tell that Mrs Nicholson's are nothing like so nice or clever as mine. Your loving Gran."

The evenings were now definitely drawing in, as the residents remarked to each other, and an early frost had blackened the giant dahlias, though Mrs Perry's little ones in their warm bed were still unscathed, when Miss Blackett received a letter from Mrs Bradshaw. It said that her own invaluable "help" possessed a lately widowed and childless sister who was anxious to find work and a home near herself. "She sounds a treasure and I thought of you at once, for I was sorry to hear from the vicar you had had the shock of the sudden death of one of your charges lately, and I am glad to think that more adequate help than the boy, whom you kindly took in as a stopgap, may now be available. She is giving up her home but would like to keep some of her furniture, and I hope it may be possible for her to have a room for herself and that she can make it into a bedsitter. If all goes smoothly, she should be free in two or three weeks' time."

Miss Blackett immediately determined that nothing should prevent her acquiring this treasure. Mrs Thornton really must now see the necessity of moving down to Mrs Langley or Miss Dawson's room – there was already another applicant but Mrs Thornton could take her choice first, leaving the big attic, so unsuitable for her but just right as a bedsitter for a resident help. As for Tom, she could not pretend that it would not be a relief to get rid of him. He was a good little worker, but his behaviour was so unpredictable, so unreliable that sometimes, she admitted to herself, it thoroughly upset her. It had always been understood that his job was a temporary one, and she was

129

willing to give him a good reference. She wrote a grateful letter to Mrs Bradshaw and resolved to tackle Mrs Thornton as soon as possible.

Fate played into her hands for once. Mrs Thornton stumbled on the stairs on the way down from her attic one evening and fell. She did not break any bones, but she was badly bruised and shaken. Miss Blackett took the opportunity to press home the advantage of a room accessible by the lift and which would be warmer in the coming winter months. Stairs were apt to be dangerous after a certain age, well, she had proved that already, hadn't she? Then she told her about "the Treasure" who must have a room of her own for a bed-sitting-room. Mrs Thornton lay and listened with an aching head and bones, and the fight went out of her. It would be selfish, too, she thought, to cling to the attic in the circumstances. She agreed to move as soon as she had recoverd from her fall and she chose Mrs Langley's room, perhaps she would feel her gentle, merry spirit lingering there.

Next Miss Blackett summoned Tom to her. "Tom," she said, "you know when you came first, you were told it would probably only be for the summer, as I always intended to find someone older and more experienced when I could. Well, now I have found someone. She is a widow lady who wants a home, and she is coming quite soon, but you can stay your month out. You have been a good boy on the whole and worked well, and you can tell your grandmother I said so."

"He can make himself useful till Mrs Smith settles in," she thought.

Tom showed neither dismay nor pleasure at the news. He looked at her with his wide impersonal stare and said nothing. He could stand still and silent sometimes for quite long periods, as an animal will do, without any need to make himself felt, yet felt he inescapably always was.

"Do you understand what I am saying, Tom?" said Miss Blackett sharply.

"Farmer Jackson's Clover, she calved last night, Lady Miss Blackett, 'tis a fine little heifer, as like Clover as can be," said Tom, and went out of the room.

Everyone except Miss Blackett and Leila Ford were sorry to hear that Tom was going. "But he doesn't seem to mind at all," said Miss Brown to Mrs Thornton, "I don't understand it, he has always seemed so fond of us and so happy."

"I think it's just because he doesn't look before and after and pine for what is not."

Dorothy Brown looked blank. She had taken to a hearing aid but it was not always very helpful.

"I mean," said Mrs Thornton hastily, "that he just lives in the present moment. When it comes to the point I expect he'll show he's sorry; but I shouldn't count on it. He probably just accepts that things happen to him, some of them good, some of them bad, and that's that, as we used to do, didn't we, when we were children?"

"Did we?" said Dorothy vaguely. "Well, anyway, I was wondering if we could give Tom a parting present before he goes. It's nice when one leaves a job to be given a present, don't you think?"

"What a good idea," said Mrs Thornton warmly. "Had you thought of anything in particular?"

"I wondered if a new pullover might be welcome," said Dorothy, "the weather's getting colder and he's still got only his old patched thin one."

Miss Brown's proposal caught on; the pullover, a nice bright green one, was bought at Darnley's wool shop, and The Haven's champion knitters, Mrs Perry and Mrs Nicholson, worked hard at producing a pair of socks and scarf to go with it. In the end everyone except Leila contributed towards a whole new outfit. Miss Blackett's feelings were again confused. She could hardly do less than fall in with the old ladies' charitable plan, she thought, nor did she grudge Tom the clothes exactly, but she felt too much fuss was being made of the boy. She decided it would be best to give the things to him as quietly as possible, and although he was staying on till the end of the month, to give them before the Treasure arrived. So, the evening before this arrival, which she was keenly anticipating, Miss Blackett called Tom into the sitting-room after supper where the ladies were all assembled and where, laid out on the table, were the pullover, socks, scarf and, besides, a pair of stout jeans and some strong shoes, also a large glaring check handkerchief contributed by Gisela.

Mrs Thornton was feeling a little nervous. It occurred to her that Tom might resent being given clothes. She wished it had been a drum, yet it was certain that he needed them.

"Tom, said Mrs Blackett, "the ladies and I are giving you a present, or rather several presents, because you are to leave us soon and you have done your work here well. I hope you will take care of these nice clothes, for you are a very lucky boy to have them given to you, you know."

"Oh, dear," thought Mrs Thornton, "why need she have put it like that? And she sounds as if she were scolding him instead of giving him a present, yet I know that it was she who bought him these very good shoes."

Tom simply stood and stared – motionless he stood, and Mrs Thornton held her breath until at last he stretched out a hand and very gently touched the soft wool of the jersey, but otherwise he still did not move or speak.

"Go off and put them on and let us see you in them," said Mrs Perry, and gave him a little push.

At that he hooted with delight, gathered up everything and bounded out of the room, Mrs Thornton gave a sigh of relief.

"He might have said 'Thank you'," said Miss Blackett.

"Oh, he will," said Mrs Perry, "dear Miss Blackett, he was so excited – that was really his thank you."

When he came back, it was seen to the ladies' satisfaction that the clothes fitted well. He had tied the scarf crossways over his chest and knotted Gisela's hideous handkerchief round his neck. He moved as in a trance and, going up to Mrs Thornton, took her by the hand and led her to the old piano. She thought she knew what it was that he wanted and, after a little hesitation, she struck up the opening bars of the Mazurka from *The Gondoliers*.

And then Tom began to dance round the room, lifting his feet in their new shoes high in the air, clumsily but always in time. At this point Leila Ford got up noisily and stumped over to the television.

"It's time for 'Dallas'," she said loudly, and switched on, not waiting for the warden's permission.

Miss Blackett, however, took no notice of this infringement of her rules. She felt she had had enough of the evening, and of Tom in particular, and, leaving the room, she sought the solitude of her office and shut the door upon everyone and everything.

In the sitting-room the double entertainment continued – Leila squatting huge and central before the horrific goings on across the ocean, and Tom, wrapt in his grotesque yet somehow rather beautiful dance, circling round her. The idea suddenly occurred to Mrs Thornton that he and Leila were the only two completely unselfconscious people in the room, and that this constituted a sort of bond between them. Leila, with her dreadful perverted innocence, was a caricature of Tom. This thought disturbed her and she brought the dance to an end with a final chord, and closed the piano.

Then Tom shook hands twice all round, except of course for Leila who, ignorning him, continued to glare at "Dallas". When he came to Gisela she said wistfully:

"The handkerchief, it is from me, is it not very, very pretty?"

"It be *lovely*!" said Tom with great feeling. It was the

first time he had spoken and Gisela felt satisfied. He turned towards the door and Mrs Thornton got up to go with him, but he rushed away without waiting for her, and she just caught a vanishing sight of him doing a handturn on the landing. It was the last she saw of him, for in the morning he was nowhere to be found.

Miss Blackett was angry. That Tom should take it into his head to disappear when he was still needed and after having had such kindness shown him appeared to her to be thoughtless, ungrateful and again most unreliable behaviour. She was not placated by Mrs Perry who said: "He'll have run home to show his Granny his new clothes, he'll be back before very long. I'm certain." She was right in the first supposition but not in the second.

As the day wore on and no Tom appeared, Miss Blackett grew angrier – Mrs Smith, the Treasure, was due to arrive in the late afternoon and the warden resented the fuss and distraction Tom's absence was causing.

Gisela was in tears. "That poor Tom," she cried, "he will have been over run and killed in the road, I think!"

"Nonsense, Gisela," said Miss Blackett, "stop being so foolish, if an accident had happened, we should have heard about it from the police." But she rang up the vicar and explained the situation.

"I am so sorry to trouble you, Vicar, but I think we should know what has happened to the boy, and I have no one else to turn to. We think he has most probably run home. If so, perhaps you could make him see how irresponsibly he has behaved and that unless he comes back at once and apologizes, it may affect the reference I can give him – that is, of course, if you should have any time to spare and can get over to Sturton."

The vicar, who still felt some responsibility for Tom, promised to investigate. He himself had no doubt but that Tom had gone home; as to the efficacy of Miss Blackett's threats and reproaches, he was much more doubtful. He found old Mrs Hobb sitting close to her little log fire with her hands, usually so busy, folded placidly in her lap.

Yes, Tom had come home, but was now off again on an errand for herslf, she informed him quietly. She offered no further details.

"But he should not have run off like that, Mrs Hobb, Miss Blackett is very cross about it. He had caused anxiety and everyone is so surprised that he should have disappeared without warning and without saying good-bye. He was supposed to be staying the month out, you know."

"I be sorry, sir, that the lady be put out, but 'tis a wonder to me that it should be so. Tom said as there was a party and music and handshaking and, beyond all, those good new clothes as a present for his leaving, and so, to be sure, he left."

There was a little silence, then the vicar said, "I see."

He felt he could not give Miss Blackett's message as she had worded it, but that it was only fair to suggest that Tom should come back for the stipulated time.

"Maybe yes, maybe no," said the old woman. "'Twas a saying when I was young that 'fine clothes foretell a flitting' – Tom had the fine clothes and the flitting's done, and happen can't be undone and, sir, I be thinking I be for a flitting myself soon, it'll be further afield than the lad's and the fine clothes for it be laid ready in the press yonder."

She looked up at the vicar and saw that he knew what she meant.

"I'll be glad to have Tom by me till the time comes for it won't be long now, but if the lady *truly* wants him, maybe he'll go."

"She seemed to know quite simply and certainly that death was coming to her and when it would come," said the vicar afterwards to his wife, "and I believed her, and I wish you could have heard the way she said, 'If the lady *truly* wanted him.' I couldn't really convey it to Miss Blackett, though I tried."

But the warden would only have Tom back on her own terms, and he did not come. She felt justifiably aggrieved, and resolved to think no more of him. Yet an aggravating wish to see him once again persisted, a sense of something unresolved that might have been straightened out to some unspecified advantage – though whether to him or to herself, was not clear. She put away such muddled unprofitable feelings, but in the days to come caught herself thinking of the boy with a sort of dull regret.

Tom's unconventional departure was viewed wistfully by Mrs Perry, Mrs Nicholson and Dorothy Brown, emotionally by Gisela and pleasurably by Leila. Mrs Thornton, thinking it all over, with the memory of his dance and that last handstand on the landing, acknowledged to herself that she was not at all astonished.

"There was nothing ordinary about Tom," she said to Meg Norton.

"No," assented Meg, "and yet nothing extraordinary either, he always reminded me of a character out of one of our plays." Mrs Thornton thought that Meg often said rather surprising things.

"'My gentle Puck,' are you thinking of him?"

"Oh, no, not Puck," Meg said and said no more. She had never told anyone of the time when Tom had rescued her from despair down by the copse.

"A mixture of Puck and Ariel, perhaps, together with a bit of one of the clowns or rustics to humanize him," laughed Mrs Thornton. "Anyway, a timeless natural being and therefore you're right, Meg – certainly to be found in Shakespeare, though, now I come to think of it, considering how he left us, I can't help remembering the tales my old nurse used to tell me about Brownies –

'Brownie has got a cowl and coat

And never more will work a jot.'
I wonder what will become of him."

"He'll be all right," said Meg with conviction, "we need not worry about Tom, but I shall miss him."

"I think we all shall in our different ways," said Mrs Thornton.

11

MRS THORNTON'S DREAM

MRS SMITH, the Treasure, was a small wisp of a woman with quick mouselike movements. She was everything that Tom had not been, completely predictable and amenable and anxious to do what was required, and Miss Blackett told herself that she was very pleased with her. She had, it must be admitted, one annoying habit. When spoken to she almost always repeated the last few words of the speaker like an irritating echo.

"I would like you to go to Darnley this morning to do the shopping."

"To do the shopping."

"You will remember that Miss Brown is decidedly deaf."

"Decidedly deaf."

This habit proved a barrier to any prolonged conversation and, besides, Mrs Smith was always on the move. If asked to sit down she was the sort of person who always sits on the edge of her chair, ready to pop off again. But undoubtedly she was a treasure and seemed only too eager to be ordered about by everyone from the warden downwards.

"That Mrs Smith, she is no better than a commuter," remarked Gisela gloomily to Mrs Perry who looked puzzled.

"What do you mean, Gisela?" she asked.

"You put in the words – so, and out come they again – so, and always she does what she is told."

"Oh, you mean a computer," said Mrs Perry, "well, computers are very useful, but I see they may not be very good company."

"Me, I am not staying," said Gisela, "now that I know my English so well, I go home. I go perhaps before Christmas comes."

"Oh, dear! said Mrs Perry. "That is some time before your year is up, do stay with us until the spring."

"Yes, yes, I go, Mrs Perry, it was OK while Tom was here, but with a commuter – NO."

The successor to Miss Dawson's room arrived soon after Mrs Smith, Miss Long was a protégé of Mr Martin's. She was only in her early seventies, a retired secretary and still active and there seemed no very good reason why she should have come to The Haven. Miss Blackett privately thought that it was because Mr Martin found it convenient to have her there since she sometimes helped him out when he was particularly busy. Indeed she was seldom actually in the Home for she appeared to have many acquaintances in the district and she was inclined to adopt a patronising air towards the other residents. Mrs Thornton had hopes of her at first, for she noticed a row of rather beautifully bound volumes of poetry on a shelf in her room. But Miss Long, seeing her eyeing them, laughed and pulled one out. It was merely a box with the lid made to open like a book cover.

'My last employer gave them to me when he took up a post abroad, for he knew I had always admired them. He used them like files; bills went into Browning, circulars into Chaucer, letters into Longfellow, and so on. I do the same and I find it most convenient."

Mrs Thornton went away intrigued but sorrowful.

Even St Luke's little summer was now over, the leaves were still mostly thick on the trees but autumn colours were rife. The first autumn gale had blown down Lord Jim's cross – the ground had been too hard for Tom to have fixed it in securely. Miss Blackett let it lie and soon the little yellow leaves from the thorn tree would cover it up.

"The warden seems to have aged lately, don't you think?" remarked Lady Merivale to Miss Bredon after the autumn committee meeting was over. "Really she looks older than some of her charges, certainly than Mrs Perry."

"Shrivelled up, rather than old," said Honor Bredon. "You'd have thought that now she has Mrs Smith to take a good share of the work off her shoulders, it would have been the opposite."

The same thought struck Dorothy Brown one evening. She had lately managed it that if there was a travel film on television she would cajole Leila into going to bed early, never actually a very difficult task. Then she would slip downstairs again to enjoy herself. This particular evening there was a lovely film about Petra, "the rose red city", and she had it to herself which she preferred, for then she could think herself right into the scenes before her without disturbing interruptions. She had discovered – alas, far too late – what she would have liked to have done with her life. She would have been a traveller, even perhaps an explorer or an archaeologist, for she gloried especially in the ruins of ancient cities. She secretly collected select travel brochures over which she pored with a wistful pleasure. She was lost in excitement over this film when Miss Blackett came in at the regulation time to turn it off. Luckily it was just about to finish. There was something about the way the warden plodded across the room, not even noticing that Dorothy was there, that caught her attention. On a sudden impulse, for she always had been and still was an impulsive creature, Dorothy Brown said:

"I've been watching such a wonderful travel film, Miss Blackett, don't you ever want to go abroad? I'm sure you deserve a good holiday, and now that Mrs Smith has come, once she is thoroughly settled in, couldn't you take one?" She really felt full of pleasure at the idea. "Do, do think about it," she added.

Miss Blackett was quite startled. "How very odd of Miss Brown to spring this upon me so eagerly," she thought. "Could she want to get rid of me for any reason?" The suggestion that The Haven could get on perfectly well without her she found particularly displeasing.

"It's quite out of the question, Miss Brown," she said, "besides I've never liked foreign places." Actually she had never been out of England except for a day trip across the Channel years ago.

"But their faces are so interesting," said Dorothy, "so different from ours, at least they were in Greece, I remember."

"I said *places* not *faces*," shouted Miss Blackett.

Really, it was too tiring to have to talk to Miss Brown at the end of a long day. But Dorothy continued, for she could hardly bear it that anyone who could travel should not do so. "I'm sure it could be managed," she said, "why not just send for some brochures – there are marvellous tours to be had nowadays and really quite reasonable." But Miss Blackett shook her head and left the room, shutting the door behind her with what was almost a slam, so that Dorothy felt the vibrations, which affected her disagreeably. She sighed with pity. This vehement negation of a possible joy depressed her.

As for Miss Blackett, the gust of annoyance aroused by Dorothy Brown's proposal soon died down. She dismissed her suggestion as she had dismissed the memory of Miss Dawson, Mrs Perry's offer of a kitten and any further encounter with Tom. She thought instead that it was time to prepare for winter and winter at The Haven presented problems, as to how to keep the old ladies warm and the bills down, with lofty Victorian rooms built for large coal fires, long passages, wide landings and outside pipes that easily froze.

"Don't forget to put your watches back," she announced on the last Saturday in October. "Christmas will be here before we know where we are."

"Before we know where we are," echoed Mrs Smith. Gisela snorted. She knew where *she* would be by Christmas.

The announcement was received gloomily by all the ladies except Leila and Mrs Nicholson. Leila alone welcomed an extra hour of night and the difference between summer and winter really meant little to her now – she could sleep and eat during both, but perhaps rather more so when the days were short and cold. But the others disliked the prospect of the long dark evenings and penetrating winds and damp, and cruel frosts and snow. Only Mrs Nicholson did not really mind much, for the prospect of winter at The Haven had its compensations. She could go to bed early if she liked, with her lovely hot water bottle and her books. Carol and Bob had given her an electric blanket, of which she was much afraid, and had said: "Now, Granny, you'll be beautifully warm all over and you won't need a bottle, in fact it's not quite safe to have one with the blanket." But you can't cuddle a blanket. And now she could read as late as she liked without Carol bustling in with exclamations and offers of a hot drink. She usually had two books on hand, a good story and a holy book, that was besides her Bible, of course, Nevil Shute, Georgette Heyer and Monica Dickens were among her favourite storytellers. But she was always faced with a dilemma. If she left her Bible reading and her holy book to the last, she was apt to fall asleep over them, yet, on the other hand, to end the day with a novel did not seem either quite reverent or comfortable. This night, which was a little solemn because it was the last night of summer time, she read her story first, but resolutely laid it aside before she had even begun to feel drowsy.

Mrs Perry had been planting her bulb bowls that day and

now, before she went to bed, she patted down the fibre once again lovingly. "Sleep well for the next two or three weeks," she said to them, "and then get on with your growing." She did not like to think of the cold damp weather ahead, for she knew it was certain to bring her those tiresome bronchial attacks which got a little worse every year and, unlike her bulbs, she could not at her age look forward to much of a renewal of life in the spring. But, she told herself, the less she thought about that the better, and she was planning a winter knitting marathon for her family.

Mrs Thornton had by now reached *The Tempest* in her Shakepeare reading to Meg Norton and, like Austen, Elizabeth, Nell and Jake, she was filled anew with amazement at its all-embracing richness. She had just read Prospero's most famous speech and paused to look up and share the wonder of it with her friend, but saw that she was asleep. She looked frailer and older when her eyes were shut. There was no colour in her face, and this emphasized the still beautiful bone structure. She looked like a carved figure on a tomb, and at the thought Mrs Thornton felt a sudden pang. Mrs Langley and Miss Dawson had gone from their little company so recently – was Meg to be the next? "We are such stuff as dreams are made on, And our little life is rounded with a sleep." She repeated the lines to herself but the lovely words had lost their power to please. They now seemed menacing and dreary and she closed the book and gently left the room.

Behind her own door a deep depression engulfed her. She made no effort tonight to count her blessings. She did not feel at home yet in Mrs Langley's room but missed her attic with its sense of seclusion, and yet with the pleasant feeling of Tom just across the landing. Yes, she missed Tom curiously much and pervasively. Here, in this room, she was not immune from Mrs Nicholson's radio next door, and their tastes did not coincide. She could even hear Miss

Brown's too, for this was always turned up loudly because of her deafness, and Mrs Thornton did not like to complain. Not that this was distracting her now, for both radios were silent as it was growing very late, yet she did not feel in the least like bed. She looked from the window after a little while and saw that Meg's light had been extinguished. Had it not been, she would have gone to her again. She felt anxious about her, or rather she supposed it was for herself, as if death should come to Meg soon she knew that she would not grieve for *her* as she was almost sure that she would welcome it. No, it was for herself she feared. She could not afford to lose Meg whom she had come to love. The years had robbed her of too much. It seemed another life, a different, incredibly rich world in which she had once lived among so many friends and, above all, where she had been supported and enlivened day in, day out, by the love, companionship and need of her husband. Compared to that lost solid world, existence at The Haven was poverty-stricken and flickering – here, where this little group of premature ghosts shuffled round waiting for the end. There was no comfort at all in the realisation that this slow dissolution was natural and to be expected by the majority. What sentimental rubbish was sometimes talked about old age – at its best it could only be called a bad job.

She had been standing by the window where she had gone to look for Meg's light and now she turned away but without drawing the curtain. A chill late autumnal fog had risen and it seemed so in tune with her present mood that she almost welcomed it. She switched on the radio for the World Service to distract her thoughts, but this only made her fearful and miserble on a wider scale. She had longed for children once, but now she felt glad she had no close personal ties with the future. She often wondered how people like Mrs Perry and Mrs Nicholson, with grandchildren, were not more anxious and alarmed at what appeared to be in store for them. But she supposed that the temperamental optimism of the one and the simple faith of the other supported them. Mrs Thornton, who possessed neither, gave herself up to black despondency. She began to get ready for bed.

By now everyone else was asleep and it must be confessed that the inhabitants of The Haven did not look their best at such a time. Had one been able to see them, only Meg Norton and Mrs Perry could have been viewed with pleasure. Meg, in her spotless plain white nightgown, lying very straight and still beneath a similarly spotless white coverlet, was more than ever like a medieval effigy. Mrs Perry, propped up with fat pillows to help her breathe more easily, was comely still, her cheeks faintly tinged with pink that matched her fluffy bedjacket. Leila Ford had replaced her wig with a mustard-coloured knitted cap, which had slipped sideways, exposing part of her shining bald pate. She lay on her back and snored with her thick lips hanging loosely open revealing two or three old fangs of teeth. Her skin was wrinkled, leathery and grey, from the constant application of heavy make-up. She looked grotesquely ugly and pitiful, like some mythical monster.

Dorothy Brown next door was smiling in her sleep, the frowning strain of deafness gone from her neat pale face. Actually she was wandering among great red cliffs beneath a brilliant sky. Her thin grey hair lay across her flat chest in a childish plait, her cheeks were hollow and, with her teeth removed, her mouth was pinched and sunk. No one would have guessed that she was, almost every night, engaged in intrepid exploration.

Mrs Nicholson, too, appeared older now that look of placid content that beamed out from behind her spectacles during the day was absent. Her face had a bluish tinge and her breathing was a little uneven, but she seemed comfortable nonetheless, clasping her beloved bottle to her and with her shoulders snuggled into a beautiful lacy shawl knitted by herself.

Night had breached the brisk anonymity of Miss Long. She had taken from the book box named "Pope" a photograph of a handsome middle-aged man, her one-time employer – the one who had bequeathed her the boxes. This she had slipped beneath her pillow as was her wont. He would have been surprised to know that she frequently slept in his arms.

Mrs Smith had moved her bed out of the turret alcove, which to her had appeared spooky. Truth to tell, though she would never tell it, she found the attic room with no one near a bit frightening altogether. Her bed was now pushed against the wall furthest from the turret and she lay in it curled up tightly. Every now and then she twitched in her sleep. Tucked into the small of her back was a very old hairless Teddy Bear.

While all the ladies looked more ancient in sleep, Gisela looked younger. She sprawled across the mattress, abandoning herself to the deep motionless oblivion of youth. The fair hair which Tom admired so much strayed all about the pillow – one arm was flung across the coverlet; emerging from a flounce of bright red and green cotton sleeve, it looked thin and defenceless like a child's. There was a smear of chocolate about her mouth and chocolate wrappings on the foor.

Miss Blackett went to bed early these days. She began the night lying in the centre of the bed, but as soon as she was asleep she instinctively moved to the edge to leave room for Lord Jim. At midnight she half woke, stretched out her hand to stroke him and met nothingness.

One o'clock struck. Mrs Thornton, who was still awake, thought she would try to read herself into drowsiness, and took down the nearest book from her bedside shelf. It was an illustrated copy of Blake's poems, but her old eyes were too tired for reading, so she gazed dully at his pictures

146

instead – the piping boy, the dancing figures beneath the tree, the tiger, till at last she began to doze and dream, though at first it was more of a vivid memory than a dream which took over.

She was a child, or rather she was watching herself as a child, one day when her darling mother had said, "It's really too lovely a morning for school, we'll take the train to Brighton and picnic on the beach." And they had done just this, and there they were at Black Rock with the cliffpath to Rottingdean and the old man with his "Happy Families" box and cap for pennies behind them. Her mother was sitting by a breakwater and she herself, dressed in her favourite white and navy sailor suit, was standing facing the sea at the end of the little stone jetty. Only it wasn't a jetty now but Sir Francis Drake's *Golden Hind* sighting America, and she was, of course, Drake. Mrs Thornton watched the little girl who was herself and Drake, and knew that she was feeling very, very happy. Then her mother called, "Come along, Milly, I've unpacked the basket and there's Gentleman's Relish sandwiches and squashed-fly biscuits," and the child turned round, and though it was still the child she had known so well, the face Mrs Thornton saw was Tom's. But her mother had now changed into old Mrs Langley, who was pouring tea into her beautiful cups beneath the deodar tree. Mrs Thornton, deep in the dream by now, saw that everyone from The Haven was gathered round. She was pleased to see Mrs Langley again and Miss Dawson, too, and Lord Jim prancing about Miss Blackett's feet, but as she looked at Lord Jim, he began to grow. He grew huge, almost as large as a tiger, and his fiery coat flamed in the shade of the great dark branches. Mrs Thornton tried to call out to warn everybody, but she could not make a sound. Lord Jim, still rapidly growing, stepping delicately among Mrs Langley's teacups, was now definitely stalking Leila Ford, who, as he gained in golden power, began, as rapidly, to shrink until she was no more than a pitiful little creature, the size of a wizened child. Mrs Thornton exerted all her strength to move towards her but was quite unable to lift a foot. She was infinitely relieved then when her own Nanny appeared round the tree. "I'll see that the beastie doesna get beyond himself," she said, "and as for Miss Leila, it'll do her a power of good, so dinna fash yourself, Miss Milly." Mrs Thornton could not see what happened next, for a cloud of little birds flew down from the deodar branches and obscured her sight, but with Nanny there she knew all would be in order. The birds were singing loudly, but soon their song turned to instrumental music and there, out in the sunshine on the lawn, were Austen, Elizabeth, Nell and Jake, playing away as hard as they could go. Mrs Thornton was momentarily troubled because she could not recognize the music. Was it Schubert? Was it Mozart? Whatever it was, it was divinely inevitable and, delighted, she drew nearer to the players, and now they glanced round at her and each of them had Tom's wide untroubled stare. At the same time she was aware that the lawn was as crowded as on a fête day. All the village were there and, besides, here and there on the outskirts she thought she caught glimpses of figures in fancy dress, some splendid and some rustic, even a fairy or two – actors, she supposed, come over from Stratford. She looked round for Meg and saw her dancing with one of these, for now everyone was dancing and Mrs Thornton was overjoyed to see about her old friends and relatives, some of whom she had not thought of for years and some she remembered constantly with longing. She was not surprised then when her husband appeared close beside her but she could not help exclaiming, "You will laugh at me I know, but I thought you were dead!" He smiled his old amused affectionate smile and took her hand to lead her into the dance, and, as they whirled round, Tom was everywhere and nowhere, in a glance, in a gesture, in the rhythm of the music.

But then Austen, Elizabeth, Nell and Jake stopped as suddenly as they had begun and a way opened up before Mrs Thornton and saw that "set in the midst of them" was Tom himself. Lord Jim, now his proper size, was draped round his shoulders and he had a pipe in his hands. Mrs Thornton caught herself thinking: "But it was a drum, not a pipe, that he had." But this was only a momentary flashback, for Tom began to play on his pipe and she was caught up by that piping into unalloyed joy. All consciousness of time, place and self ceased, for she was inside the Kingdom.

Then she half woke. She knew she was in bed in her own room but her mind was perfectly blank. She was aware only of peace. She opened her eyes – a wind had risen and dispersed the fog and through the uncurtained window she could see stars. The thought of their multitude, distance and immensity filled her with pleasure and she turned over and went to sleep again.

When she woke the second time, it was full morning and her dream came flooding back. What did it mean? Did it matter what it meant? She remembered that this dream had contained glory, and how could one analyse glory? Through the wall of her room she could now hear Mrs Nicholson's radio broadcasting the first Sunday service of winter time. The resentment she usually felt at any aural invasion of her own territory seemed not to trouble her this morning. She knew that when Mrs Nicholson turned off, as she always did the moment the blessing was pronounced, not waiting for the voluntary, it would be time for her to tune in to her own music programme. The service meant little to her and the music less than nothing to Mrs Nicholson and yet, she supposed, they both really meant the same thing. This unity in variety she now welcomed. What the meaning was she believed she had known for a moment in her dream. The glory had now departed and probably would never come again, but she knew that what it had left her with was a sense of her own blessed irrelevance.

THE LOTUS HOUSE

To Polly Dyne Steel

CHAPTER ONE

OLD MRS SANDERSON stared down at a house agent's photograph of "a most desirable period property, ripe for modernization and offered at a bargain price for a quick sale, the owner now living abroad". As she looked it ceased to be a rather blurred picture of a square, gaunt, blind building and became alive, each window crowded with familiar faces; trees grew up on either side of the gate and, on the front lawn, a spaniel waltzed around a pony with bags on his feet drawing an antiquated mowing machine. "Why, it's the Lotus House, and I haven't set eyes on it for more than fifty years. Oh, dear, oh, dear, oh, dear," sighed old Mrs Sanderson. It was a house she had known intimately as a child and had loved as deeply, as momentously and as unconsciously as only a child can.

The house had been built in the year of Waterloo. There was a tradition that the first owner had been an East Indian merchant, who had established a lovely dusky harem there, and that it was he who had planted the giant cedar tree that dominated the upper back garden. This tradition was probably quite untrue, owing its origin perhaps to the name by which the house had always been known — the emblem of a lotus flower, the Indian lily, was carved over the entrance — but it was romantically cherished by the large cheerful family living there in the early part of this century.

It was a house well-suited for family life, being neither too large or grand, nor cramped or insignificant. It had a graceful fanlight flanked by Ionic pillars, and there were pediments over the long windows that looked northwards across the heath to the distant trees of the park. The ground on which it was built sloped south, so that the basement was on the garden level on that side, and curving iron stairs led up to a narrow balcony flush with the drawing-room. Twisted up the stairway and along the balcony was an ancient wisteria and, leaning against the south-west end, a large conservatory housed a prolific vine and two great camellias, one white and one red. Every house of character possesses its own subtle blend of scents — from the wood of floor and stairs and panelling, the polish used on these and on the furniture, the faint exhalations from curtains and covers, and all these blending with other scents drifting in from without. The Lotus House in early summer was pervaded by the wisteria blossom and all through the years that particular scent never failed to bring to the mind of Letty Sanderson the visits she had spent there as a child. One whiff and she was back again in that enchanted place which had been for her both a refuge and a revelation. Perhaps this was because on her very first visit the wisteria was in full bloom.

She must have been just eight years old. Her father had been in the Indian Civil Service, and Letty, an only child, had been sent home to England the previous year to be taken immense care of by a couple of spinster great-aunts. The aunts were as kind as possible and she was not unhappy with them or with the governess who came every day to the small sedate house in South Kensington. She did not know she was lonely, for she had been lonely in India; her mother was delicate and withdrawn and her father busy and seldom at home. Letty had been left to her ayah, from whom she had had the same sort of loving protective care as she later experienced from the aunts, but no real companionship. Then, one day, nearly a year after she had come to England, an invitation arrived from the family at the Lotus House, who were some sort of distant relations of her father's. Little girls were not kept strictly to their lessons in those days and so, although the spring holidays were almost over, she was allowed to pay a visit which seemed to her to extend throughout the whole summer, although afterwards she realized it could not have lasted as long as that. Memories of later visits merged with the first, so that there seemed to have been a continual renewal of joyous experience throughout the four years of her relationship with the house and family.

She remembered her first momentous arrival, though, distinctly enough. She had drawn back into the shelter of the musty old cab that had brought her and Miss Marchant, her governess, from the station, overcome by shyness at the sight of what appeared to be a large crowd of people of all ages and sizes waiting to receive her. Then a plump smiling lady opened the door and helped her down the step and said, "So this is Letty — Mary and Selina have been so looking forward to your coming. Now children, take Letty up to your room so that she can make herself tidy, and then come down to tea. The children have their tea together in the schoolroom, Miss Marchant, you must let me give you yours in peace before you have to return." Blissful words — *"the children"* — suddenly Letty felt a warmth she had never before experienced. Yes, definitely and immediately as she heard those two words pronounced she became a citizen of a new world, the world of her contemporaries to which she properly belonged.

In age she was equal to Mary and one year older than Selina, and she slept with them at the top of the house in a large attic room which used to be the night nursery. It still had bars across the windows through which came the scent of the wisteria. The days began with Minnie, the housemaid, bringing in the big brass jug of hot water and setting it on the washstand with a towel over it to keep it warm, though often they had been awake long before that, chattering to each other. Yet it always seemed a scramble to get downstairs in time for family prayers. The father of the family was, on the whole, an easy-going man but he was a stickler for pious punctuality. No one was allowed to be late for family prayers or for church services. The children sat in a row each morning with their backs to the windows so that their attention should not wander; the maids filed in and sat opposite. The mother closed the door after them and took her place before the coffee urn at one end of the table, the father was at the other end with the big family Bible open in front of him. Somehow, the day starting thus with the double sanction of two masculine deities, one above, the other below, gave it a structural security lacking in the visiting child's life elsewhere — then only dimly felt but important if only that it enhanced the sense of freedom that followed.

Set lessons disappeared with Miss Marchant and each day always seemed an adventure, but yet contained within an ordered pattern. With the wealth of companionship available there was bound to be some plan or other afoot. The eldest boy, Edward, must have been about sixteen at the time of Letty's first visit but to her he appeared practically grown up, capable of being wonderfully kind and condescending and at times exquisitely funny. His condescension occasionally stretched to shepherding the three little girls across the heath and through the park and on down to the Thames, to watch the great barges with their red and brown sails come sweeping along with the tide. The child Letty had believed for years that the East Indian merchant's fortune had been conveyed by night to that very same little pier upon which she loved to stand.

156

Edward had told her it had to be by night because it was all wicked gains got by looting temples and palaces, and probably his Indian wives were all hidden in the barges, too. She always believed every word Edward said, so she pictured a cavalcade crossing the heath in the darkness at peril of their lives from highwaymen, to arrive at the chosen site where eventually the sacks of gold were turned into the Lotus House.

On red-letter days they would even take the little steamer and travel as far as the Tower. But really most days were red-letter days at the Lotus House. If Edward was busy on his own affairs, the twins, Bob and Jack, were at hand, though it was often Selina who invented their games. There was the thrilling roof game. It was possible to get out on to the roof through a trapdoor, and then to creep all round the house along a deep gully and even to wriggle up and down the tiles into the valley that lay between the back and the front. In this game you were either a burglar or a policeman. Letty preferred being a burglar because it gave her time to look about her while she was hiding. It was a strange particular world up there — the tiles, hot in the summer sun which seemed much nearer than usual, burnt the backs of her legs, sparrows flew up, chirping crossly, she was level with the tops of the chestnut trees by the front gates. She would have liked to have stayed up there for much longer but the policemen were on her trail. The boys would not allow Selina to get out on the roof so she had always to be on guard by the trapdoor. They were always very careful of Selina because she was the youngest and delicate, but they let her climb the cedar for the Monkeys' Party game, though it was understood that the safe broad fork between the lowest branches was reserved for her particular use.

The garden at the Lotus House was, for the child Letty, the Garden of Eden, the standard by which she judged all subsequent gardens. Its especial glories were the cedar, the wisteria, the two camellia trees and all the fruit — the bunches and bunches of sweet little black grapes from the vine, the figs and peaches and greengages that grew along the south wall between the upper and the lower garden, where apple, pear, plum and damson trees all vied with each other in delicious abundance. The boundary of the lower garden was the railway and, though their elders might complain of the smoke and the noise (there was shunting on a side track that sometimes kept up a symphony of banging and puffing well into the small hours), to the children the railway was a source of both interest and pride. The boys especially pitied anyone who hadn't a railway at the bottom of their garden and Letty, who at first was a little frightened of the engines, soon learned to look upon them as powerful and benevolent friends.

A stable block housed the old grey pony who mowed the lawns, the carriage horse Kitchener, Bimbo the black and white spaniel and the children's rabbits. Fred the coachman and Chittenden the gardener were good-natured and long-suffering, and let the children do much as they liked as long as they kept a few well-defined rules faithfully. The three worlds of servants, children and parents each had their own rules. They were interdependent within clearly marked boundaries and the citizens of each world knew exactly where they stood. Even when Rosamund, who was the eldest of the family, passed from one world to another at her coming out, there was no uncomfortable undefined period. On Letty's first visit Rosamund still inhabited the children's world, then, almost in a flash it seemed, her hair went up and her skirts came down, and she belonged there no longer.

Rosamund was Letty's first romance; she was built on generous lines like her mother, and everything about her was warm and glowing. Mary and Selina were slim little creatures, rather pale, with straight fair hair and grey eyes, but Rosamund's hair was a rich red brown and her eyes were hazel, and she had cheeks that really were the colour of pink roses. She played the violin but her real passion was for acting. Those were the days of private theatricals and she was much in demand (but she knew it was out of the question to consider anything professional). She was very kind to the younger ones and invented charades for them and contrived wonderful costumes. "A duke is in love with her," Edward told Letty, "he will come and carry her off soon to live with him in his mansion and be his duchess." Letty was not surprised, though she wished the duke had been a prince and the mansion a palace, but she did not want even a prince to carry off Rosamund anywhere. She did not want anything to change ever at the Lotus House. When at night she lay in her bed between Mary and Selina, smelling the wisteria (for in her memory there it was, always in bloom and always scenting the whole house) and listening to far-off hooting of ships from the river and the nearby trumpeting and panting of the railway engines at the bottom of the garden, she felt so happy and so safe that she knew then for certain that the world was a kind place. Yes, she felt the house wrap her round with such assurance that she could look forward to the years with excited trust.

It was not altogether a trick of memory that made old Mrs Sanderson think of her visits to the Lotus House as being always in warmth and sunshine. Winter visits had been rare, as the aunts thought she needed their own special cosseting then. She would so much have liked to have spent a Christmas there, but this had never been allowed and, like most children in those days, she accepted as inevitable the decisions made for her.

She must have been granted one February visit once though, for Selina's birthday. She remembered clearly the drifts of snowdrops under the black branches of the cedar and the dancing shadows on the ceiling from the bedroom fire the little girls were allowed for a treat. She supposed on looking back that the three of them got on so well together because she, Letty, had fulfilled a need in both sisters. Mary and she shared the same birth year. "Why, you're twins," Selina had said on that first visit, and Letty's heart had given a little jump for pleasure and though the real twins, Bob and Jack, had pointed out the inaccuracy of this statement, still the notion that she and Mary had a special bond persisted. They were actually more alike in temperament than the sisters. "I like you because you are ordinary, like me," Mary once said to her, and Letty knew just what she meant. Selina was un-ordinary — set apart by being the only delicate member of the family, subject to alarming fits of asthma, but more so by the possession of a compelling imagination which often left Mary disconcerted. "You never know what Selina is going to be," she complained. Once for a whole tract of time she was a cat, and insisted gently but firmly on eating most of her meals from a saucer on the floor, and at another time, after Edward had been romancing about the East Indian merchant, she was one of his wives and coaxed Rosamund into making her a sari out of an old sheet, and pretended she did not understand what was said to her. But in spite of the inconveniences caused by such behaviour, she was such a sweet-tempered cheerful child, and so patient when ill, that everyone petted her and Letty, charmed by the delicious experience of mothering someone younger and weaker than herself, became the most willing attendant of all Selina's subjects.

This particular birthday was momentous because of one special birthday present — the doll's house. Letty herself had not possessed many treasures as a child; in India they had travelled too often from place to place, and at Kensington there was too little space. Like so much else at the Lotus House, the family toys and games became archetypal for her. There was the rocking-horse, off which she often had to be dragged protesting; there was the huge box of wooden bricks; there was the musical box with its magical brass discs; there was the boys' sacrosanct model railway with its trains, carriages and trucks, its signals and points and home-made stations, with which the little girls were only allowed to play as a special mark of favour and under strict supervision; and, best of all, there was Selina's doll's house. It was a family present: the twins had been working at it in secret for weeks, cleverly constructing it from old orange-boxes. Edward had painted it, the parents had given the furniture and Rosamund the inhabitants. But the peculiar charm of this particular doll's house, for Letty at any rate, was that as far as it was possible the amateur craftsmen had made it a small replica of the Lotus House itself.

On that birthday morning the three children stood in a row and gazed at the little house. There was the door with its pillars either side and the three windows of the dining-room and study, and above them the correct number of bedroom windows and the dormer attic ones in the roof. Old Mrs Sanderson remembered that she had continued to look at it silently while Mary danced about and clapped her hands, and Selina knelt down in front to open it and look inside. Edward had painted the rooms the right colours, white and green for the drawing-room and dark red for the dining-room, but the boys were quite apologetic that the back of the house was just a blank wall and that there was no balcony and no rooms behind the dormer windows in the roof. But there was quite enough reality to satisfy Letty and she remembered how Selina kept on saying, "But I don't want it any realler," and when Rosamund offered to dress the mother and father and little girl dolls like the parents and herself (for she had not had time to dress them properly and they just had their tiny arms and legs thrust through bits of material to make them decent), Selina had frowned: "No, no, Ros, they are Mr and Mrs Golightly and their little girl is called Wilhelmina Rose."

"Where on earth did you get those names from?" laughed Rosamund, and she had hugged Selina hard so that her hair, that still wasn't very used to staying up, tumbled all over her shoulders (old Mrs Sanderson seemed to see her more clearly now than the child Letty had done). So Mr and Mrs Golightly and Wilhelmina Rose became the focus of a whole series of adventures. In due course a cook arrived, a Dutch doll, affectionately known as "Cooksie", whose bark was worse than her bite, and an old gentleman in a black velvet suit who was Mr Golightly's father. He had been an engine-driver until Bimbo bit off his legs one day — an accident transformed into a terrible railway disaster — after which he had to spend all his time in bed.

There was no end to the Golightly adventures that Selina invented, each one wilder than the others. How they laughed at them! Old Mrs Sanderson smiled and sighed. Was that birthday visit the only winter one, then? No, of course not, there was that later one when the ponds on the heath were all frozen and Edward had taught her to skate. She remembered how proud she had been because he praised her for learning so quickly — all in one day — and how, intoxicated by the magic of it, she had gone on and on gliding faster and faster, until the extraordinary orange sun had set and the brilliant winter stars had appeared. Oh, yes, she remembered that winter visit too, but still it was the earlier one she remembered best, and how she had stood there in front of the doll's house "surprised by joy".

When Letty was twelve her parents came home to England and claimed her, and actually she had never gone to the Lotus House again nor seen any of the family. It now seemed incredible to old Mrs Sanderson that this

should have been so, but it had come about quite naturally and inevitably. First, she was sent to boarding-school
and her father and mother expected her to spend her
holidays with them, though neither parents or daughter
were particularly happy or at ease with each other. Sadly,
though they loved each other, they were not capable of
bridging the gap left by four crucial years of separation.
As for the Lotus House, Letty wondered sometimes if her
mother had not been jealous at her constant references to
her visits there. At any rate she sensed a total lack of
interest and soon gave up talking of them. She and Mary
wrote for some time but new interests crowded in, and
then just before the 1914 war broke out her father had
died after a riding accident, and the original link between
the two families was severed.

Her father's death and the cataclysm of the war
marked the end of the world of Letty's childhood. Her
friends dispersed, the girls to join the V.A.D. or to take
up other forms of war work, the young men to the front.
She herself was left with an ailing and bewildered mother
and a much reduced income. They moved to a tiny flat in
Bournemouth, recommended for her mother's health.
She heard from her old governess, Miss Marchant, with
whom she still exchanged an annual letter, that Edward
and Bob had both been killed, and that when peace came
Jack had emigrated to Australia. Rosamund, who had
joined an amateur acting group entertaining the troops,
had made a runaway marriage with a Canadian soldier.
Beyond that — a blank. She had thought of writing
again to Mary but the interval from childhood to maturity
had been too long, and with the war in between besides,
what could she say? Perhaps if she had written, thought
old Mrs Sanderson looking down on the dim picture of the
Lotus House in her paper, the memory of those early
times would not have remained so clear. Perhaps indeed
she had not really wanted to write, lest it might blur that

bright image with the stark realization of change.

Her mother lingered on year after year, as lifelong invalids often do, and after she had died Letty made a late unromantic marriage with the doctor who had attended her. He was a widower who needed a housekeeper and a congenial companion, and she wanted financial security. Both liked and respected each other and this had ripened into affection, but she could not pretend that his sudden death shortly before retirement had left her shattered. She missed him but, for the first time in her life, she felt free and independent. She decided she would leave Bournemouth, which she had never liked. London drew her and she began in a desultory way, for there was no hurry, to look at house agents' advertisements. Thus it came about that she was staring down at the picture of the Lotus House, which, in its turn, seemed to be staring reproachfully up at her. How long she had been looking at it she did not know, but now she made a careful note of the agent's address.

"I might do worse than find a flat somewhere in that neighbourhood," she said to herself. "It would be better than settling right in London itself, I think, and while I am about it, I might at least go and see the old place again — not of course with any thought of buying it, but I needn't tell the agents that. Perhaps they can give me news of the family, obviously none of them can be living there now. Oh, dear, how long ago it all seems."

A week later she was asking for the key of the Lotus House at the agents. "No, I do not wish to be accompanied there, thank you," she said firmly as she put the key into her bag, "I know the way quite well."

CHAPTER TWO

MRS SANDERSON WENT resolutely along streets that were familiar by fits and starts. The memories of childhood were patchy and of course there were many changes, though the chief landmarks — the station, the church, the concert hall ˙ — remained the same and she had no difficulty in finding her way. A general smartening and sophistication was apparent, two or three big ugly self-service stores had sprung up, and squeezed between them were numerous rather pathetic little boutiques, far too many, she thought, to be profitable. Here and there, though, like a vivid flashback, an old friendly shop-front appeared — the fish shop where the little girls had been half frightened and wholly fascinated by the fish-monger, who looked exactly like a giant fish himself, white and flabby, with pale protruding eyes and large sticking-out ears like fins. There was the confectioners, too, of blessed memory, now called the Honey Pot, where she and Mary and Selina used to spend their pennies and where one day they had actually each been presented with a whole bar of Fry's chocolate cream from a damaged package. Such unlooked-for benevolence could never be forgotten. And, yes! there was the tiny corner shop which, for some unknown reason, sold an extraordinary mixture of greengrocery and Japanese vases and toys. This was the child Letty's favourite shop of all. You went in through a bead curtain, in itself a beautiful and exotic attraction, and there were the piles of cheerful oranges and apples and blue-and-white china ginger jars, and Japenese dolls with round black heads and pretty kimonos and gaily painted parasols and, hanging down from the low ceiling, circles of painted glass pendants that tinkled softly in the draught from the open door. The children bought magic packets of floating flowers here that looked like shrivelled bits of paper, but when you got them home and shook them out into a tumbler of water, they turned into lovely tinted blossoms — "lotus flowers", they always firmly called them.

Mrs Sanderson crossed the road to reach the little shop; the traffic was frightening — it was like crossing a deafening tumultuous river, the ceaseless roar and rush of the roads was the greatest change of all from her childhood memories. But she got across in safety and peered into the bow windows of the shop. It still sold fruit and vegetables and the name over the door, Joseph Budgeon, was still the same, though of course the old man who had kept it must have died long ago, and there was no sign of any Japanese goods as far as she could see. She decided to go in and buy some apples and find out who kept the shop now. The thought occurred to her, too, that she might possibly discover more of the recent history of the Lotus House and of what had happened to the family than the agents had been able to tell her, which had been very little indeed — only that the sale was in the hands of a solicitor acting for the present owner, who lived in Australia. The property had only lately come into his hands on the death of his father, so the agents believed. She supposed that this must be Jack's son. She went up the two steps into the shop that she remembered so well. The bead curtain had vanished and everything seemed tidier, and there was a very neat small middle-aged woman behind the counter. Letty made her purchase and then said, "I used to come into this shop when I was a little girl, a long time ago now, but the name over the door is the same." There was a question in her voice and the woman answered it at once.

"That's my old uncle's name. Fancy that now, there aren't many left that remember him. You were living in these parts then?"

"No," said Letty, "but I often visited here. I've not been here since I used to stay at the Lotus House."

"Well, I never," said the woman, "to think of that. It's up for sale now, is the Lotus House, but who'll buy it I can't think; it's in a bad state. You see, after the two ladies left it, it was empty for a long while and it was damaged a bit from the blitz too; not badly, but neglected, that's what it was, and then it was let for offices. But if you're a friend of the family, you'll know all this, I expect."

"No," said Letty, "I lost touch. When did the ladies leave? Did you know them?"

"Not to say well," said the woman, "but after I came here to look after my old uncle and the shop, I remember them coming in sometimes, and when they were leaving for Australia (their brother sent for them, you see), they came in to say goodbye to Uncle. 'We'll be coming back again to the Lotus House,' said Miss Selina, she was the delicate one, you know. I remember her saying it well; 'Oh, we'll be coming back quite soon,' but they never did."

Letty took up her bag of apples. There seemed nothing else to say, but she looked round the shop rather sadly.

"Your uncle used to sell Japanese curios," she said, "I don't suppose you have any left?"

"We stopped that during the war," said the woman, "but I kept a few, not for sale but my uncle being so fond of them — they're in this cupboard." She opened the door of a little corner cupboard, and Letty saw a doll and

167

a ginger jar and a black and gold box and some faded paper packets.

"Oh!" she exclaimed, "Are these the magic flower packets?"

The woman laughed. "Did you love them too? Here, would you like a packet for old time's sake?"

"Of course I would," said Letty, "it's sweet of you." She slipped the little packet into her handbag and, cheered and touched, she faced the hazards of the road again. She went up a little side street she remembered, to escape from the noise. The houses here had all been drab cheap little Victorian dwellings, but they were now much smartened up with pink, yellow, and blue doors and window-boxes, and cars parked outside the minute front gardens. Old Mrs Sanderson hurried past them for she suddenly felt acutely apprehensive. At the end of the little by-way, she turned a corner, and there facing her was the Lotus House.

It looked even more grim and desolate than it had done in the advertisement. A large FOR SALE board was fixed to the broken-down fence which she read painstakingly through from beginning to end, though she knew it all before.

"Why have I come?" she said to herself. "Whyever have I come? It was a stupid thing to do, but all the same, now I'm here it seems foolish to go away without having a look round."

She decided to explore outside first, and crossing the shaggy brown turf of the neglected lawn she crept along the overgrown side path. The first shock was that the vegetable and fruit garden had turned into a council house development, beyond the ragged winter hedge and a dividing fence. Then the cedar tree had gone, or almost gone, for a great stump remained, but round this the snowdrops were all out, not in drifts where the sun had penetrated the dark branches as she had remembered them, but in a huge open carpet. Then with a wave of relief she saw that the wisteria was still clinging to the stairway and the balcony. The conservatory had gone with its vine and camellias, and in its place was a hideous garage, and all the rest of the garden that remained was a wilderness of rough growth, but the snowdrops and the wisteria had given her resolution to turn the key in the front door and enter the house itself. She needed then all the courage she could muster. Rooms had been divided by matchboard partitions, woodwork now scratched and defaced was painted a dark, dull green, window panes were cracked, boards were loose, old newspapers and wrappers strewn about the floor. Grimly, Mrs Sanderson looked into every room, and climbed the echoing stairs to the attics. These were less desecrated than the rest, they had probably never been used by the firm which had rented the house. The bars still protected the windows of the old night nursery and the faded Mother Goose frieze actually remained beneath the ceiling. It seemed to Letty Sanderson that she had been walking and standing and climbing stairs for a long while, so she sat down on an empty wooden box in the corner, and stared through the nursery bars at the fading February sky until it was too cold and dark to stay there any longer — much too cold and dark and dismal.

She returned the key to the agents just before they closed. "I will look at the flats you have recommended tomorrow," she said, "I shall not need this key again." The agent was not surprised. But when on the third day of Mrs Sanderson's property viewing (she was staying at a small guest-house in the neighbourhood), she asked for the Lotus House key once more, his eyebrows went up quite noticeably. "He obviously thinks me a little mad," said Letty Sanderson to herself, "well, I suppose I am, but I just feel I can't go away without seeing the old place again. I expect by the time I move here it will either have been sold or demolished." She had found the flat she wanted the previous day, quiet, sunny and very convenient.

As on the earlier visit she wandered round the garden of the Lotus House first. There were pale buds showing on the old lilac bushes by the stables, now converted into more garages; she picked a bunch of snowdrops and braced herself to enter the house again. She remembered that last time she had not penetrated to the basement. This, of course, had belonged to the servants' world, and as they reigned there supreme, the children had only visited that particular region as guests or invaders. There was a huge lift in the passage worked by a pulley for conveying the substantial meals and massive crockery to the dining-room, and the boys would sometimes be coaxed into working this with one or more of the little girls inside. But it was a game frowned upon by Cook — "It'll break one of these days, Master Bob, and then who'll get the blame?"

Old Mrs Sanderson crept down the basement stairs. The fixed dresser with its empty hooks and drawers and the old-fashioned grate, rusted over, were the only objects left in the big empty kitchen — the scullery, which she never remembered seeing before, had a vast stone sink and a copper for boiling clothes in one corner—beyond was a huge larder with slated shelves and a tiled floor. It all looked terribly dusty and deserted but there were no signs of alien office occupation here, and in the butler's pantry along the passage were two iron bedsteads, a rug, a basketwork chair and a calendar for 1941 hanging on the wall. *It must have been used as an air-raid shelter*, thought Letty Sanderson. *Perhaps Mary and Selina slept here on those two beds*. She could not imagine it — two middle-aged spinster ladies huddling beneath the bedclothes with the bombs dropping all round. No,

170

Mary and Selina were safe upstairs in the night nursery, with the friendly trains puffing and blowing at the end of the garden. She left the pantry and went out into the passage again and there was the old lift still there. She peered into it and saw at its further end a square object done up in sacking. There was plenty of light coming in from the window on the garden side of the passage, and she bent down to look more closely. A corner of the sacking was torn, and what looked like a painted minia-ture chimney was sticking out sideways. Letty caught her breath and stared, then dragged the object towards her and pulled hard at the sacking; it tore a great rent and revealed a tiled roof and a tiny dormer window. There was no doubt about it — it was Selina's doll's house.

Her first thought was *How could they have left it here?* Then she remembered that of course they expected to come back and thought it was quite safe 'ill they returned. "And so it has been and so it is," saiu Letty Sanderson. When all the rest of the furniture had been sold up and the office staff had moved in, nobody had bothered about the old lift, indeed it was obvious they had not bothered with the basement at all. With a good deal of effort Letty dragged the doll's house into the open and pulled off more of the sacking. To her joy it seemed quite undam-aged. She managed to open it and found even Mr and Mrs Golightly and Wilhelmina Rose and the grandfather and the Dutch doll cook still at home among their furniture, disarranged but otherwise not showing much signs of wear. Mr Golightly's father had fallen out of bed but seemed pink-cheeked and well. Absurdly old Mrs Sander-son could have cried for joy. She knelt down on the cold dirty stone floor and began to put everything to rights until it grew too dark to see clearly. Then she carefully covered up the doll's house with the sacking again and went home. It was too late to return the key that evening,

171

and when she got back to her hotel room she had a sudden panic that she had left it in the door of the house. She dived in her handbag and it was there all right, but in feeling for it her hand closed on the packet of Japanese flowers that the kind little woman had given her from the corner shop and which, until now, she had forgotten. "They won't be any good I expect, after all these years," she said, but she filled her toothglass with water and emptied the packet into it and, lo and behold! the magic still worked, the wrinkled paper expanded into pretty shapes and floated gaily in their small pond. Letty stared down at them. "Lotus flowers," she murmured to herself, "they must be a portent," but she had known all the way back that the sunny convenient flat would after all never be hers. She was going to buy the Lotus House and make it blossom into a home again.

But Mr Donovan, her family solicitor, was horrified at the idea. "An old neglected property, much too large, really Mrs Sanderson, I don't advise it, I don't advise it at all."

Mr Donovan's father had managed all Letty's parents' business, and he had had charge of hers now for many years, and she had the greatest respect for him, but she had expected disapproval and was not too cast down by it. "I intend to convert it into flats, Mr Donavan," she said, "and to live in one of them myself. It is going cheaply, you know; don't you think it would ultimately pay me?"

"It's going cheaply because it needs so much spent on it," said the solicitor. "You will find it is not at all cheap in the end. It would be a hazardous speculation at the best, but for anyone your age, if you will forgive me, it is a great responsibility — I don't like it, I don't like it at all."

"I'm in very good health," said Mrs Sanderson, "and people of my age aren't really old nowadays. You said yourself that I did well out of selling John's practice and

172

that the Bournemouth house should bring in a good sum."

Mr Donovan was silent. He was, as a matter of fact, very surprised. He had looked upon Mrs Sanderson as a sensible woman, a little shy and reserved, rather repressed he had thought, but decidedly intelligent, and now she appeared as rash and romantic and not sensible at all. She had explained that the property had a special sentimental appeal for her, but it was Mr Donovan's opinion that sentiment could easily be carried too far where house property was concerned. However, if she was absolutely determined on so rash a purchase, he could not stop her, and possibly the flats might be made to yield a reasonable return; the house was certainly in a good neighbourhood.

"Well, we mustn't do anything in a hurry, must we?" he said at last. "We'll get a good surveyor first. I know of a thoroughly reliable firm and we'll abide by their decision." Letty went away with the surveyor's name and address but was secretly determined not to abide by any decision but her own compelling urge.

The surveyor's report when it came was neither damning nor particularly reassuring. There was at present no sign of dry rot, but of course with houses of this date this was no assurance that it might not occur at any time. The roof, though needing some repair, was in fairly good condition, but a valley roof was never very satisfactory. Mr Donovan shook his head but reluctantly agreed to forward an offer to the owner's solicitor after a rough estimate had been made of the cost of conversion.

"Planning permission for the necessary alterations should offer no difficulty, I think, as your aim is to restore the outward appearance of the house as much as possible to its original condition."

"Certainly," replied Letty, "and the inside too."

Mr Donovan was not aware of the implications of this remark until they came to discuss the planning of the flats

173

with the architect and Letty refused to allow the spacious living-rooms on the ground floor to be divided.

"It will ruin their proportions," she said, "and the hall must remain as it is too, with that pretty archway and staircase."

"But, my dear Mrs Sanderson," said Mr Donovan, and the architect chimed in for he was proud of his plans, "that is really impracticable — how are you to get the necessary bedrooms and offices? And, besides, no one nowadays wants such big rooms to heat."

"Then I shall have to have the ground-floor flat for myself," said Letty. She had been undecided as to which of the four projected flats she should choose. At first she thought lovingly of the night nursery for her bedroom, but the rest of the top-floor rooms which had been the servants' were decidedly poky and the stairs, too, might prove a disadvantage with increasing age. Then she favoured the basement for its direct access to the garden, but much of this was rather dark and had fewer friendly associations so, although Mr Donovan again sadly shook his head and said she was sacrificing the most financially promising return of the whole project, it seemed that the dining-room and drawing-room (grand and august as she still held them in memory) would become her living-room and bedroom, and she would squeeze both a bathroom and kitchen and a second little bedroom out of the old cloakroom and the study, to the poor architect's distress.

Meanwhile communications were crossing and recrossing oceans and continents. Letty wrote a personal letter and got a friendly reply from Jack's son. He and his boys worked a profitable ranch and had no intention of coming back to the old country. His father, too, he felt sure, had not contemplated returning, but had never brought himself to sell the Lotus House for purely sentimental reasons. Now, however, he himself was anxious to be rid of the property. It would have been different if his aunts

174

had lived, but the younger had not long survived the transplanting from England, he did not even remember her, and his Aunt Mary had died some years before his father. Of his Aunt Rosamund he knew nothing but believed she was living somewhere in the wilds of Canada. He was glad that the house should go to an old friend of the family as he felt sure this would have pleased his father and aunts.

So that is that, thought Letty. She was not sure whether she was glad or sorry that she was to know so little about those unreal characters — the Lotus House children grown up. She had had some qualms about whether she ought to have mentioned the discovery of the doll's house, but now she decided she could count it in with "the articles contained within the house and the garden at the time of the sale". Six months later, after having disposed of her Bournemouth house satisfactorily, old Mrs Sanderson moved herself into the ground-floor flat of the Lotus House and set about looking for tenants.

CHAPTER THREE

MRS SANDERSON DID not admit to herself that she was influenced in Mrs Royce's favour by the colour of her hair, which was of that warm auburn hue that she had admired above all others ever since she had fallen in love with Rosamund long ago. Nor indeed was it necessary, for there was much else to be said in favour of this, her earliest applicant for the first floor flat. She had a charming smile, was beautifully dressed and was suitably enthusiastic about the whole house.

"I'm always very sensitive to houses, Mrs Sanderson," said Margot Royce, "and yours has such character. You're an answer to prayer, you know. I've been feeling I simply couldn't stand our poky little cottage any longer and this is perfect — two good living-rooms, one quite big enough to take Andrew's piano, it's only a baby grand but it's crowded out our present sitting-room. I must warn you he plays on it quite a lot, I do hope you don't object."

"No," said Letty, hoping the other tenants, when they had materialized, would not do so either, but the walls and ceilings were pretty soundproof, not like modern houses, and anyway, nowadays people were so used to background music of all kinds. So she added that she was fond of music, though she was afraid she did not know much about it.

"Just the same with me," said Margot Royce, "and

three bedrooms too, it will be such a comfort to have a spare room, we've had to put up our guests in our sitting-room, such a bore, and the little room at the end of the passage will do nicely for my small daughter. You don't mind children, do you, Mrs Sanderson? Harriet is a very harmless one."

Mrs Sanderson was really pleased at this. She very much wanted children at the Lotus House again, in fact it turned the scales decisively in Mrs Royce's favour, but she felt a little doubtful about the room at the end of the passage. It had been used as a box-room in the old days, though it did possess a tiny window. Letty could not help thinking it was a pity not to allot one of the proper bedrooms to Harriet, but of course it was not her business.

"It's all just what I might have dreamed of, but never thought to find, and to discover you, too, Mrs Sanderson," said Margot, turning to Letty with that entrancing smile and opening her large very blue eyes wide — "you too, how lucky we shall be to have *you* as our landlady and friend." She drew a silvery scarf round her neck, which was of just the right proportions, not too long and thin, nor too short, like Letty's own. Her thick little neck and, worse still, her double chin, had always been a grief to her. "I must fly," said Margot, "Andrew comes home for lunch and I always like to have something ready for him, and I'm simply longing to tell him all about you and this wonderful flat. We shall certainly want to take it and to move in as soon as possible."

She swept gracefully out of the house and into her rather shabby little Mini, leant forward to wave through the window and was off, leaving Letty, quite delighted, on the doorstep.

"I don't think I could do better," she said to herself contentedly, and it was only later that she remembered that she had not said anything about references.

177

"One thing I must impress upon you, my dear Mrs Sanderson," Mr Donovan had said, "don't agree to anything without taking up references, and be sure you don't trust to written ones only; I will gladly investigate personally myself if you would like me to do so."

So kind of him, thought Letty, *and now I have practically agreed to let the best flat without even mentioning the matter. Still, I'm sure it's all right. He is a Doctor of Science, she said, and she is so delightful, such lovely hair and obviously a good wife too, and with a little girl nearly eight years old.* She confessed her lapse to Mr Donovan but there was such a gleam in her eye as she did so that, though he intended to look into the matter himself, he was convinced that nothing less than a proven record for crime could shake her determination to allow Dr and Mrs Royce and Harriet to move in as soon as possible.

If she had slipped up over references for the Royces, Mrs Sanderson was able to produce impeccable ones for Aubrey Stacey, the would-be tenant of the top-floor flat. He was a schoolmaster, a bachelor with a brother who was a barrister. Moreover he and his brother had both been educated at Westminster. *Such a coincidence*, thought Letty with pleasure, for Westminster had been Edward's public school. She remembered this because he had once impressed her with its superiority over all other public schools. "It is the only one left up in London, the only one that counts, and London is the greatest city in the world." Yes, of course, he had told her this at George V's coronation. Edward had been in the upper school then and had a seat in the Abbey with the Westminster boys. This proved his point. Of course this had been long before Aubrey Stacey's time. He had read English at Oxford and was on the staff of a neighbouring large comprehensive school. He was not very communicative about his career but she got the impression that besides teaching he also wrote a little.

178

"Aubrey Stacey, an attractive name, don't you think? And he looks like Shelley," Letty said to Mr Donovan. "At least," she added honestly, "he has a brow like Shelley's." His receding chin beneath a straggling beard were less impressive, but he was an old Westminster boy with a poetic forehead and had a barrister for a brother.

"I don't consider that Shelley would have been a very desirable tenant," said Mr Donovan. Really, there was no satisfying him! "Still," he admitted, "he is certainly respectably connected. I think I have heard of that brother of his and he has a secure job."

Letty discovered another point in Mr Stacey's favour — he seemed to take especially to the old night nursery. No one had happened to tell the workmen to remove the bars from the windows and Letty apologized for this.

"I remember peering through such bars with my brother," he said smiling. "We used to play that we were monkeys in the zoo. I think I should like them left, so don't trouble about them. I shall make this my bedroom, Mrs Sanderson, if I am lucky enough to be allowed to take your attractive flat. It is on the quiet side of the house and I am a poor sleeper."

"Do you know," said Letty, "I often used to sleep here myself as a child and I remember the shadow of those very same bars falling across the whole room in a pattern. You'll think me fanciful, I expect, but I still feel this room is the safest place in all the world."

The basement flat took the longest to be settled for there were several applicants before a really satisfactory one materialized. There was the young couple, unmarried, uninhibited and very untidy. Old Mrs Sanderson was not yet acclimatized to the permissive society and although she found the couple interesting, she was bewildered by them. The girl announced that she was an artist, "entirely committed". What the young man did she never discovered — he remained speechless throughout the interview. "We want to find somewhere to leave our things while we tramp around Europe for the next month or so," explained the girl. "You see, I am not sure yet whether Jason is quite sound on the baroque and it makes a difference to our future. I may not wish to remain with him, but in any case if we take the flat, it will be in my name and I shall be responsible." But to Letty this did not appear a promising enough proposition for the Lotus House, whatever Jason might think of the baroque.

Then there was the anxious lady with the cats. Not that she was physically accompanied by them but they were very much with her in spirit.

"I am having to give up my home, alas, since my friend with whom I have shared it hitherto has moved away. There was a little difference between us about the pussies. It is quite a large house and what with the rates and the repairs and the heating, I cannot keep it on alone and must find somewhere smaller. But the pussies — I had ten of them and I've managed to find homes for Don and Titus and Sammy and Bogey. It's the girls who are the problem, though they are not really so, the dears, they are so good and I should hate to lose any of them. Susie is a wonderful mother and Di, she's the huntress, why she even caught a swallow once, and Plush is so affectionate, and of course it's out of the question to part with Clytemnestra, the largest black Persian that ever was seen I assure you, Mrs Sanderson, and Yum Yum and Peep Bo are Siamese and were given me by a dear, dear friend. So you see I must have a flat with an access to a nice garden and this would suit me perfectly. You've no idea how hard it has been to find just the right place for my little family."

Letty felt she did indeed know just how hard it had been and was still going to be, for she wondered how long the nice garden would remain nice with six cats dividing it between them — and would they even stay at six with

Susie being such a good mother? Besides, she loved birds as well as flowers, so she screwed up her courage to say "No" and to send the poor cat lady reproachfully and sorrowfully on her way.

At last, after one or two more unsatisfactory aspirants, a Miss Cook arrived from the agents one day. She was a retired Post Office official. Letty gathered that she had inherited a little money lately and wanted to settle in a place of her own.

"My brother is selling my parents' house with my full consent. I think I would prefer a flat if it is entirely self-contained."

"Oh yes," said Letty, "this is the most self-contained flat in the whole house because it is the only one with a separate entrance, as you see."

The basement, having practically no associations with the child Letty, and needing more radical conversion than any other part of the building, had been turned over to the architect without restrictions. As a result it was the most convenient of the flats with really modern offices, all shining with tiles and white paint and stainless steel. The big old kitchen had been divided into a very pleasant small sitting-room and a bedroom — the sitting-room with a door opening into the garden.

Miss Cook had a singularly inexpressive countenance. Her black hair was cut close in a tight fringed cap. She had the type of face that one cannot imagine as ever having looked young. It had a small buttoned-up mouth and round black eyes, and her cheeks, innocent of face powder, were reddened with a network of roughened veins. Letty wondered why she looked vaguely familiar. Later it suddenly came to her — Miss Cook reminded her of a Dutch doll — indeed of one particular Dutch doll, the one that had been Mr and Mrs Golightly's cook in Selina's doll's house, and who had been selected at the toy shop for this purpose because of Jane, the cook, in

Beatrix Potter's *Two Bad Mice*, but Selina had not called her Jane, she had always just been 'Cooksie'.

"Of course," Letty said to herself, very amused at the thought, "the resemblance is striking and her name actually *is* Cook. How very right and proper to have a cook in the basement of the Lotus House again, only unfortunately she's not a real one. How convenient if she were." She had yet to cope with the problem of domestic help for herself — the lodgers would see to their own rooms, of course, but she felt she herself would like some help if she could get it.

Miss Cook, or 'Cooksie' as Letty could not help secretly calling her, provided a watertight reference from the Post Office and was accepted for the basement flat, and so the problem of tenants was settled to Mrs Sanderson's satisfaction.

Meanwhile they in their turn were summing up their future landlady and the Lotus House. Margot Royce, as she drove away, not actually to prepare a meal for a husband but to keep an appointment with her hairdresser, congratulated herself on a good morning's work. She had left a note for Andrew about his lunch, she herself would have a sandwich and a cup of coffee while her hair was being re-tinted. She got back to the cottage a couple of hours later to find, as she expected, that he had not bothered with eating, but was busy working out some problem in his head while playing accurately and endlessly one of Bach's Fugues.

"I think it will do very nicely," she said switching on the cooker.

"What will?" enquired Andrew politely at the end of the next bar.

"That flat I told you I was going to see this morning, nice rooms, good outlook, good garage and convenient for shops."

"Good," said Andrew again, and then, more attentive-

182

ly, "you sound like a house agent. What about the rent?" Though he admitted that Margot had quite a flair for business, yet she was apt to be oblivious of costs once she had set her heart on something.

She named the rent and Andrew lifted his eyebrows. "You can't get anything decent for much less in that neighbourhood, really, Andrew."

"We can't afford that *and* Harriet's school," he said.

"Oh well," said Margot, "she'll have to leave, then. Anyway it's about time she got away from Queensmead now, she's had long enough there."

"You said the other day she was so happy that it would be a mistake to move her for another year at least."

"It wasn't the other day, it was last term. Mrs Campbell's over-protective, I consider, and it's time Harriet learned to rough it a bit at an ordinary school. There's a good one within easy reach I believe — I'll make enquiries."

Andrew said no more. He did not particularly want to move from the cottage, but he was not unprepared. He had noticed apprehensively when it had turned from being "an adorable find, so easy to heat and look at the garden, a dream, and really plenty of room for your piano," into "a poky little hole with your piano taking up the whole sitting-room, and the garden! Neither of us have time to cope with it, it's absurd."

Before the cottage there had been the seaside maisonette: "so good for all our healths, the air like wine and a marvellous train service . . . " but this in its turn had become "too inaccessible and really a little vulgar, don't you think?"

The frequent moves were expensive but Andrew's motto was "anything for a quiet life".

"At last there will be plenty of room for your piano and it's nearer both our jobs."

"Good," said Andrew for the third time. He had slight

qualms about Harriet, but she was not his child and therefore not his responsibility, he told himself.

"Mrs Sanderson said she wouldn't mind how much you played."

"Who's Mrs Sanderson?"

"Our prospective landlady."

"What's she like?" asked Andrew without much interest.

"Oh, I don't know, just ordinary I think, the kind of person who adores Betjeman's poetry and goes to the Academy and shops at Marks & Sparks. Well, I'm not sure about the last. She's got some really good rugs in her room, though not much else. She's rather sweet really and likes children. She'll be good for some baby-sitting I should think when we want an evening out."

"I should think so too," said Andrew, "if you want it that way she hasn't much choice."

"Eat your lunch," said Margot, "it's disgracefully late."

Aubrey Stacey walked away from the Lotus House across the heath with a sense of relief which was the nearest thing he got to happiness nowadays. The flat had an atmosphere of peace about it — that old nursery with the bars had taken him right back in time to his own nursery days which he had shared with his twin, his boon playmate and companion, before the years had separated them. The view towards London was transformed by the autumn mist into an ethereal and lovely city. Even the highrise flats and offices looked like fairytale towers. Aubrey, always sensitive to beauty, felt his heart lightened and the hope sprang up that this move would prove a fresh start for him. At the other side of the heath he boarded a bus which landed him near his present noisy lodgings, a shabby house shared with three other members of the school staff. How glad he would be to be free of them, and they, too, of him, he conceded wryly. What a mistake it always was to live with colleagues. He ardently hoped that Mrs Sanderson would not go back on her word, but the old school tie seemed to have done the trick. It was lucky that Westminster had happened to crop up in the conversation and that she had had some connection with the place.

Miss Cook was also pleased with the Lotus House. That kitchen and that bathroom — really nice they were! Of course, everything needed a good clean up, one could see that, in spite of the workmen pretending they'd done it already, and the rooms would look much better still when she'd finished with them. The sitting-room got a bit too much sun for her covers and carpet, but she would get some really substantial curtains to keep it off. Of course there would be drawbacks, there always were to everything. Still, Mrs Sanderson seemed a pleasant sort of person; a bit untidy-looking and the front hall and stairs might have looked cleaner there was no denying, but these wouldn't be her province. She had her own entrance, that was really a good point; her's was much the most private of all the flats, and she needn't meet the other tenants at all really unless she wished, and she couldn't see herself wishing it. She thought her furniture would all fit in well. She'd see about those curtains as soon as possible.

Everyone was settled in before Christmas and Letty Sanderson woke one morning in her new bedroom which had been the old dining-room and felt the house once again full of life around her. She sighed with satisfaction. She was getting used to sleeping in her august surroundings, for the room still kept for her something of its original dignity. It had been the most formal in the house, but she had replaced the dark red paper of her memories with a pale grey distemper and the heavy red curtains by striped blue and green linen. She lay and looked up at the ceiling, admiring its graceful mouldings which she had

185

certainly never noticed as a child. They were too far away she supposed or, more probably, she had always been too pleasantly busy to spend time staring upwards. In one corner of the room the doll's house now stood on a special stand she had had made for it. She looked forward to showing it to Harriet who, she thought with satisfaction, must soon be home for the Christmas holidays.

She heard a thump on the floor above, the opening and shutting of doors and later someone running down the stairs. She wondered if that was Mr Stacey or Dr Royce. Then a happy idea occurred to her. She would give a party at Christmas so that everyone could meet each other properly. It would be a party for the Lotus House too, to celebrate its starting to become a home once more, for she cherished the dream that they all might settle down so comfortably together that they would form a really happy, friendly community. It would be repaying a sort of debt to the past.

CHAPTER FOUR

WHILE MRS SANDERSON, in her bedroom on the first floor, was lying at ease planning her party, Miss Cook in the basement was sitting down to a well-earned cup of coffee and piece of toast after a good hour's work at further unpacking and cleaning and tidying up. She felt tired but appeased. It really did begin to look nice, she thought. She had carried her tray from the kitchen into the sitting-room where the wintry sun was just beginning to send slanting rays through her new curtains. "In summer I shall have to draw them," she said to herself, "can't have my new covers fading — they say these new materials are guaranteed, but you can't trust them, that's the worst of a south-facing room and the carpet, it can't afford to look worse than it does now, either." She gave it a resentful little kick.

She would have loved to have got everything new, she would have kept her grandfather's chair, of course, and her mother's best china, but that was all. She had been left the furniture and quite right too, but Henry would have been welcome to it if she could have afforded to replace it. Oh well, it had fitted in quite well here — the glass-fronted cupboard, you couldn't see a smear on it now and the china showed up well inside. She was glad she'd had grandfather's chair re-covered, pricey though it was. It looked handsome now, nobody could say it didn't, and the curtains were pretty though, looking at them from where she sat, she thought they could have done with a bit more length to them. This worried her, had she spoiled the ship for a ha'p'orth of tar? But she was really glad she had chosen that colour — she'd always favoured pink. Henry's Doris had wanted her to have green, quite cross she'd been about it, always had to be right, had Doris, came of being a schoolmistress she supposed. "There's plenty of green outside," she'd said to her — it was different at home with nothing but pavements and houses, but here there would be always something green to look at, even in winter. She could see some sort of evergreen bush now in a corner over by the fence. She had been told that the strip of garden below her windows belonged to her. "Well, I don't know that I want it," she had said to Mrs Sanderson. "I've never had anything to do with gardening." But on thinking it over she rather liked the idea, she could learn, she supposed. *Better than having someone else poking about so close any old time*, she thought. They hadn't had a garden at home, just a square of coloured pavement in front and a yard at the back for dustbins and washing. The house was in one of those utterly characterless suburbs of London, a district which was neither going up nor down. Its streets gave away nothing about their inhabitants — far less than did the neighbouring large cemetery about its graves.

No doubt Albert Street, where Miss Cook's home had been, contained some happy lively families but the Cooks' was not one of these. The dominating factor in all their lives was that Mrs Cook had married beneath her. Her father had been a country clergyman, without any private income and therefore of straitened means, but undeniably, by reason of his profession, a gentleman. She had been romantically inclined towards a young Air Force flight sub-lieutenant quartered in a nearby camp during the latter part of the first world war. But after the marriage, and Armistice Day when the uniform was laid by, there was found to have been nothing much inside it. Untrained for any civilian post and without influence and not very intelligent, Sydney Cook had failed in one job after another and had ended up driving a laundry van. Disappointed and resentful, his wife had concentrated on bringing up her two children — Henry, named for her father and Janet for her mother. She taught them to keep themselves to themselves and to despise their father. The neighbours in Albert Street where they were forced to live were potentially threatening to Mrs Cook's self-respect and her son and daughter were strictly forbidden to play with the other children in the street. She starved her family of all indulgences so that she might send Henry and Janet to second-rate private schools where they made no real friends — the right sort in Mrs Cook's eyes could not well be asked home, and the wrong sort were frowned upon. On the whole both children, she considered, had justified the care bestowed on them. They each qualified for respectable white-collar jobs and their mother died happy in the thought that she could now meet her Maker and her father (she had never really distinguished between them) with a clear conscience. By then Henry had made an entirely suitable marriage — his Doris was a schoolteacher and kept on her job. Janet had tried nursing but had found the paper-work difficult and had also had trouble with her back, so had given it up and entered the ranks of the Civil Service instead. She had qualified as a Post Office assistant. As for their father, he had driven his van and brought back his wages and eaten his meals, and bestowed a few furtive caresses on Janet when she was little, and gradually became invisible, and one day he had a stroke and died. His daughter could scarcely recall either his face or his voice. The voice of her mother, on the other hand, she remembered very well as an ever-admonishing wail — "do this, do that", or more often, "don't do this, don't do that". When she actually heard it no more in the flesh, she felt at first stunned by the silence and even yet, especially whenever she sat down to rest, as she was doing at this moment, sipping her coffee and warming her toes by her now gleaming electric fire, she heard it echoing in her mind and felt it unwise to be too pleased with her new quarters.

"There's sure to be snags," she reminded herself, almost with a sense of satisfaction. There were the other lodgers, for instance, "not nosey, that's all I ask," and she congratulated herself once again on having a separate entrance. "You can't be too careful."

The sounds of departure Mrs Sanderson had heard that morning were neither Andrew Royce nor Aubrey Stacey, but Margot setting out for her art gallery. Physics research laboratories keeping later hours, Andrew was still finishing a leisurely breakfast. The move had been accomplished with Margot's usual efficiency and though he did not care for these upheavals, he had to admit that each was managed with as little inconvenience to himself as possible. All that was left to him was the unpacking and arranging of his books, music and records and there was certainly more room for these here than there had been in the cottage. It was always a source of amused wonder to him that anyone so pretty and feminine as Margot could be so businesslike, but he did not think about this for long. People did not interest him very much. An only child, his relationship with his parents was amiable but distant. They were both always very occupied — his father as a GP and his mother as a practising physiotherapist. A capable nanny, prep school from the age of seven, followed by his public school, Cambridge and a year in the United States had not provided much opportunity for cultivating home ties.

At school he was sufficiently good at games to be allowed to go his own way without interference and this

190

way was that of a natural loner, increasingly absorbed in music and science. At college these had continued his main interests, and self-sufficiency had grown to be a habit. He had not mixed much with women but when he happened to meet Margot, older and more experienced than himself, he quickly fell under her spell. He had never seen anyone who charmed his senses so completely. They neither of them wanted marriage. She had fairly recently broken up a first unsatisfactory one, and was firmly set against a second, and Andrew was unwilling to undertake any definite commitment that might threaten his work in any possible direction. He was not unduly worried when he learned of the existence of Harriet.

"She's at a home school at present," said Margot, "I promise you she won't be a nuisance."

"That's all right," said Andrew. He knew very little about children and anyway it was Margot who mattered. He discovered quite soon that she was untruthful, self-centred, a snob and amazingly restless, but none of this troubled him overmuch. He had always accepted people as he found them with the same detached lucidity that he brought to his work. Physically, she enchanted him — it was like living with a rose. He sometimes wondered how long this state of affairs would last, but in spite of Margot's love of change, it seemed to have become a habit with both of them.

As for Harriet, he found somewhat to his surprise that he quite liked having her about. She reminded him of a small mongrel dog he had had as a boy and been very fond of, but he was glad that she was unlike the dog in that she showed no special liking for himself, which would have bothered him, but it was obvious even to the unobservant Andrew that she had no devotion to spare for anyone but her mother. This was unfortunate for Margot was not cut out for motherhood. He wondered why she had ever had a child — he could not suppose her husband had wanted it, he had shown absolutely no interest in Harriet as far as Andrew knew since the marriage had broken up, and besides, he did not think that Dick's wishes would rank very high as a factor in the case. He supposed it was consistent with her inclination to try everything once. These ruminations of his were aroused by Margot's decision not to bring Harriet home for Christmas. "We shan't be settled in properly before all the rush is over and it'll simply be a nuisance having her around. I'll fetch her in plenty of time for the new school term," she had said.

Margot herself considered Harriet her second big mistake, worse of course because the child was lacking in attraction, which she could not have foreseen. Still, it had been foolish to risk so much merely because she hoped that a baby would bring her the sort of fulfilment that it was said to supply to most women. The first mistake was, of course, her marriage, which she rushed into to escape from a home which was simply a wearisome battlefield.

Her father came from humble origins but possessed a good business head and had raised himself to the position of land agent on a large estate in the West Country — "my father's place in Dorset" as Margot was wont to refer casually to it. He had married a town-bred wife whom he had admired for her delicate prettiness, but this soon withered from boredom and indulgence, and she had developed a waspish neurotic temperament. They kept together, Margot supposed on looking back, partly because divorce then was both more difficult and more expensive — her father was always mean about money — and partly because mutual dislike seemed to have habituated them to a habit of scoring off each other, which brought a certain spice into their relationship. Their daughter became a pawn in these unpleasant games. Her looks and her intelligence made her a valuable asset as a possession. Incessant forays took place over her education, clothes, friends, almost every possible debatable point. Her father, who held the purse strings, generally came off as the victor, but her mother scored points by running up large housekeeping and dress bills and by occasionally staging a bout of frightening hysteria. Margot learned from an early age to play off one parent against another and that, both from them and from most other people, she could get what she wanted by the exercise of her beguiling charm. But then, what did she want? Certainly not Dick Harper after the first year, nor motherhood apparently. Lovers? Too easy to subjugate and too tiresome when enslaved. Success in her business? Yes, because she despised failures, but somehow this wasn't enough. Meanwhile there was Andrew whose demands were so simple, whose detachment intrigued her, and whose brains commanded her respect.

Aubrey Stacey was busy hanging pictures. Over the fireplace in the room which had been the old night nursery, he hung a college group. He had gone up to Oxford because his twin brother had been a Trinity scholar at Cambridge, where he had taken a double first. Almost as soon as they outgrew their babyhood, Aubrey had realized that he was fated to play second fiddle to Michael — if indeed he counted at all in his mother's eyes. "Is that you, darling?" he heard her cry sometimes when he had come home from school and he knew enough to answer: "No, it's me, Mother."

His father, on the other hand, had always been painfully determined to play fair. "It's rough luck on the boy," he would say to his friends, "that Michael happens to be rather a brilliant fellow all-round, though I say it myself. Aubrey should have been a girl, he'd have made a good one — he'd not have felt the competition then and it would have been natural the way his mother feels — mothers and sons, you know, and I would have liked a daughter myself too, but we've got to take what comes haven't we, till the scientist chaps have changed all that for us. Anyway, Aubrey will make it, I always say."

What "making it" meant exactly had never been quite clear. A minor exhibition in English to one of the less distinguished colleges at Oxford, a respectable second-class degree, one need not be ashamed of these, but they were perhaps not exactly "making it". Nonetheless, he had been happier at Oxford than at any other period of his life. He had been adopted by a set aspiring to the creative arts, had contributed several poems to a university magazine and had initiated a private resolve to "make it" in an entirely different but unmistakably as equally a successful manner as his brother, by writing a magnum opus. After much heart-searching he had decided on a subject. Actually this had been suggested to him by a sympathetic tutor — "I had thought of working him up myself one day but I don't suppose I shall ever get down to it, so I make you a present of him, Stacey."

The "him" in question was the 17th century bibliophile Sir Robert Cotton, who had devoted his life to collecting books, but who, in 1629, had been accused of sedition and whose beloved library was taken from him, which had broken his heart. The tutor had envisaged a scholarly monograph, but Aubrey was after fame and as wide a public as possible. He thought in terms of an historical novel — of a high literary standard, of course, serious in intent, with leanings towards mysticism and tragedy. Sitting in the Bodleian, whose founder, Sir Thomas Bodley, had been Cotton's friend, it was easy to envisage such a splendid achievement, but after he had gone down from Oxford the initial impulse had waned a little. Still, a sizeable pile of manuscript now lay in a drawer of the bureau which was his most prized piece of furniture, a present from his brother, who had always treated him with the greatest affection and generosity and for whom he felt a blend of devotion and envy but never of

194

resentment — *that* he kept for his parents.

A great literary work in the making could not support him so he had taken a teacher-training course and then a post as English master in a small sedate grammar school, where he had spent two uneventful years until it had been swallowed up by the neighbouring comprehensive. From that time on his troubles had begun. It was a completely different world demanding a robust self-confidence and the gift of establishing an easy relationship with the young. Aubrey possessed neither. Most of his pupils now came from a different background than his own, and he felt them alien to him, especially the girls, with their nonchalance and flaunting jokes and latent contempt, which grew in proportion to his own nervousness and inadequacy with them. Certain classes took on a nightmarish quality. He turned to his great work for comfort, but it was easier to plan it and to dream of it rather than to get down to the actual writing. He told himself that he must allow it to well up from his inner being — the sub-conscious, where all works of genius were conceived. But increasingly he seemed to need a stimulus to switch on: a glass or two of alcohol helped considerably. Now however, with this move, he hoped somehow that everything would take a turn for the better.

It was from this material that the innocent old Mrs Sanderson hoped to fashion a happy family group. There was indeed a common link between them, but this happened to be that none of them had experienced what it really meant to be a member of a family at all.

Letty was disappointed to learn that Harriet was not coming to the Lotus House for Christmas. She had planned her party to contain a Christmas tree with a child in mind. She could not help wondering at that delightful Mrs Royce apparently not longing for her little daughter to come home at once, as soon as the flat was habitable, especially for Christmas. Margot sensed this slight disapproval and reacted to it immediately.

"You see, Mrs Sanderson, Harriet has all her little friends at Queensmead, which isn't at all like an ordinary school, and they have a perfectly splendid time at Christmas, much better than she could have here, except for your lovely party, of course." She also managed delicately to hint that it was Andrew who was not too anxious for Harriet's company. It was now for the first time that Letty learned that Harriet was the child of a former marriage, though Margot did not think it necessary to divulge the fact that she was not legally Mrs Royce at all. She always found it better to adapt facts to her audience.

"Andrew is terribly good with her, of course, but he doesn't like to be put out in the way children can't help doing; you know what men are!"

Letty went away thinking that of course as Harriet was not Dr Royce's child, it must make it difficult sometimes for poor Mrs Royce. She had not taken to Andrew much, a bit superior and standoffish, she thought him. She decided to have the tree all the same. She felt sure that there had always been a Christmas tree at the Lotus House in the old days, though she had never been privileged to see it, and she was determined that the house should have its tree once more, and that it should have real candles on it and not the dead garish brilliance of those horrid coloured electric bulbs. It took her a long while to track down clip-on holders for the candles, but she found some at last. She also bought crackers and presents and ordered a special Christmas cake from the Honey Pot who were doing the catering for her. The cake was to have "Welcome to the Lotus House" written on it in silver balls. "Everyone is a child at heart at Christmas," Letty told herself delusively. She had worked hard and while she sat awaiting her guests, she looked round with satisfied delight. The room, she thought, looked charming — a well-shaped tree all ready to be lit up, her father's silver branched candlesticks on either side of the cake in the centre of the table which was decorated with the prettiest candles she had been able to find, a bowl of white chrysanthemums and scarlet-berried holly on the mantelpiece above the lively fragrant log fire and a fine piece of mistletoe suspended above the door. Everything, like herself, was waiting expectantly for the curtain to go up and the fun to begin.

There is nothing quite so flat and dreary as a party that never takes off and it is even more distressing when this happens at times that demand a specially festive spirit.

"Laugh, damn you, laugh," swore Mr Donovan inwardly, as the guests pulled their crackers and donned their paper hats almost in silence. He had just read out one of those sublimely silly cracker jokes, but it had perished in mid-air.

Mr Donovan had been invited to the party by his old client and had come purely out of the kindness of his heart, but he did not like parties. That was the trouble, they none of them did. Aubrey and Andrew thought them a tiresome waste of time, Miss Cook distrusted them because her mother had, especially the parties in Albert Street. "You never know who you might meet there," she used to say. Of course Miss Cook did know who she was going to meet at this particular party, but she did not particularly want to meet any of them. In Margot's eyes this boring childish gathering hardly qualified as a party at all. Nonetheless, she could not help saving it from total failure. She sparkled at Mr Donovan, admired Miss Cook's unbecoming dress and to Letty she cried, "Mrs Sanderson, you're a magician, I haven't seen a tree with candles since Christmas at my old country home, my father's place in Dorset, where *did* you find them?"

The candles, indeed, provided the only real glory of Letty's party, and as she extinguished them she acknowledged ruefully that it certainly had not achieved its purpose. The mistletoe mocked her. "How stupid of me to put it up." The scarcely-touched cake reproached her. "Nobody really wanted me," it seemed to say, and indeed no one but Andrew had eaten much of the lavish meal. He had set about it with his usual whole-hearted concentration on the business in hand.

"How you could eat at that ungodly hour I can't imagine," said Margot (the party had been fixed early to suit Mr Donovan, who did not wish to be late home). She tossed the embroidered linen handkerchiefs that Letty had chosen for her into her "bring and buy" drawer — she never used anything but tissues. Miss Cook was taking one of her digestive pills which she usually did as a precaution after a meal out, and eyeing with malevolence the gorgeous bottle of bath salts which she had received. "I am *sure* she never buys herself little luxuries," Letty had thought, "it's expensive but Cooksie shall have a treat for once." But Janet Cook had never used bath salts in her life and never meant to. "Just waste, stinks the place out and muddies up nice clear water." Whatever was she to do with it? She might give it to Henry's Doris, only as she never gave her presents like that, it would seem queer, it was a real worry!

"A party in a parlour, all silent and all damned," quoted Aubrey Stacey to himself as he thankfully ran up the stairs to his attic fastness.

But old Mrs Sanderson firmly put away disheartening thoughts together with all the remains of the food, the candle-holders and the present-wrappings. She must not be in a hurry, she told herself, it was early days yet, give them time and they would all be friends, she felt sure. Meanwhile there was Harriet's arrival to look forward to.

CHAPTER FIVE

HARRIET WAS USED to changes; she did not much like them, though. She did not really want to leave Queensmead because she had been at school there since she was five and a half and she was now nearly eight, and that was a long time. She had almost got a best friend now, too. When you were little, it didn't matter not having one so much, but later it began to matter. The friend had not been at Queensmead very long, and she had been glad of Harriet because she had a squint and they called her 'Squinty' — her real name was Mandy. They called Harriet 'Fatty', not being very inventive at Queensmead, and the two got left out of things together which was better than being left out of them alone, though Harriet secretly didn't like Squinty all that much.

But Margot arrived after Christmas was over and told her that she was to go to a more grown-up school. This was frightening but exciting and, what was more important even, she was to live at home with Margot and Andrew and go every day to this school from a new house. Margot had told Harriet to call them Margot and Andrew when she was six. She had never called Andrew "Daddy" anyway because he wasn't her real father, so she hadn't called him anything, and secretly she still called Margot "Mummy" to herself. She thought her the most beautiful and wonderful mother that anyone could have.

She knew the other children at Queensmead thought so too. When Margot came to visit Harriet she talked to them all and Harriet could see them liking it because she was so pretty and wore such lovely clothes. This was Harriet's one claim to fame, but though she gloried in her mother, she had also felt sorry and ashamed for some time now, ever since one of the children had said to her "You're not a bit like your mother, are you?" Once she had firmly believed she would grow like her when she was older, then she hoped desperately that she might — "O God, let me be, O God, let me be!" — but now she knew she wouldn't ever be. She felt it deep down inside.

When her mother came to Queensmead this time and explained that Harriet was to leave, she brought a big box of chocolates for her to give to all her friends and though, except for Squinty, she knew they weren't really her friends, she enjoyed handing them round and hearing everyone say how lucky she was to be going away from horrid old school with such a lovely mother. Mrs Campbell, the headmistress, was sorry to lose Harriet who was a quiet, if unresponsive, child and gave little trouble, unlike some of her other charges for whom Queensmead was a substitute home "especially designed to meet the needs of those children whose parents were, for reasons of all sorts, unable to provide a home for themselves".

"I can't thank you enough, Mrs Campbell, for all you have done for Harriet," said Margot and her upward gaze, for Mrs Campbell was tall and thin, was so expressive of deep gratitude that Mrs Campbell thought that she must somehow have had more effect on the child than she had supposed.

As they drove away Harriet's mild feeling of regret at leaving and her anxiety as to the future were temporarily swamped by delight as she realized that this was one of Margot's good times. Except for one complaint that she grew out of her clothes faster than anyone would think possible, there seemed nothing wrong with her at present, and Margot had called her "darling" twice — once in front of Mrs Campbell, which hardly counted, but once when they were alone together and when they stopped halfway for refreshment, she was allowed to have a chocolate éclair. "It won't matter for once," said Margot, looking at the stout square child opposite her with resignation. *Really, she grows more like Dick every day*, she thought.

Harriet was very pleased to hear that she was going to have a bedroom of her own in the new house. This had never happened to her before as long as she could remember. At school she had slept with Lucy and Rebecca who had secrets and ignored her and, at the cottage, when she was there which wasn't very often, she slept on a folding-bed in a sort of alcove between the bathroom and Andrew's room.

"Has it got a window?" she enquired anxiously. A bedroom wasn't a proper one with no window, and she had always wanted to be able to lie in bed and look out of one. Lucy and Rebecca could do this but she had had to look at a blank wall.

"Yes, of course," said Margot.

When they got to the Lotus House it was getting dark and Harriet was tired. Being with Margot was marvellous but it always made her feel as if she had run a long way rather fast, as if there was a clock ticking inside her that wouldn't stop.

"Don't leave me to carry all the things in," said Margot, "you're quite old enough now to try and be helpful. You can manage that case — why, your arms are almost as long and big as mine."

Harriet picked up the case, she knew her arms ought not to be so long and big at her age. She followed her mother into the hall, blinking at the bright light. An old

201

lady came bustling out of a door to greet them.

"Well, here we are, Mrs Sanderson," said her mother, "all safe and sound, and this is my little Harriet. Harriet, this is our very kind landlady. She's been longing to meet you. Say 'How do you do', Harriet." But Harriet, who had not until this moment heard anything of Mrs Sanderson, just stared, and Mrs Sanderson's smile of welcome grew a little fixed.

"How could Mrs Royce have produced such a very plain daughter?" she thought and then, feeling at once remorseful for such an idea, she bent down and kissed her. She felt Harriet stiffen and said to herself, "This child isn't used to being kissed."

If Mrs Sanderson was disappointed at her first sight of Harriet, Harriet was as disappointed in her bedroom. It was hardly bigger than the cottage alcove.

"It *hasn't* got a window," she said crossly, "Margot said it had." Margot had gone straight to her own room and it didn't matter what she said to Andrew.

"Yes, it has," said Andrew, "look, the roof slopes out here and it is just above the bed." Harriet looked up and saw a small square of glass that opened with a pulley.

"But you can't see out of it," she said.

Andrew switched off the light. "Now look," he said. In the frosty January sky the stars were brilliant.

"You are the only person who can lie in bed and see the sky properly," said Andrew, "and it's always changing." He switched on the light again.

"The bathroom's along there next to my room — you'd better have a wash and then supper will be ready. I bet you're hungry."

Left alone, Harriet switched off the light once more and gazed up at the stars. She thought she had never really seen them before. Her room was a proper bedroom after all, and it was the only one in which you could lie in your bed and see the sky above you. Andrew had said so.

"Hurry up, Harriet," came Margot's voice down the passage, "supper's ready," and Harriet hurried.

The next few days were a rush of getting ready for the new school. A uniform had to be bought. Harriet had looked forward to this, it seemed grand and important for there had been no school uniform at Queensmead.

"I'm afraid she's at least two sizes larger than the average for her age," said Margot, smiling apologetically at the young shop assistant. "It's a quite hideous brown, don't you think?" she went on, "Why, do you suppose, any school should want to choose anything so unbecoming? *You* could carry it off with that nice fair colouring, but for anyone sallow it's abominable."

Harriet, listening, knew without any doubt from the way the shop assistant then looked at her that she must be the "anyone sallow". "Sallow", she hadn't met the word before and it sounded horrid. The day's shopping with her mother to which she had eagerly looked forward became as dust and ashes.

"Really, dragging that child about London got me down," complained Margot that night.

"What does sallow mean?" Harriet asked Andrew next time they were alone together. You could ask Andrew things safely because he never wanted to know why you asked them.

"Sallow," he said, not bothering to look up from the paper he was reading, "it either means a kind of willow-tree or a sort of greyish, yellow colour - rather a nasty colour really." That was that then. She knew she wasn't a tree so she must have a sort of greyish yellow face. Perhaps that was the reason she hadn't ever had a proper friend — no one would want to have a person of that sort who was also called 'Fatty' for a best friend. She examined her face closely in the bathroom mirror, she hadn't one of her own, and it was true, though she had never noticed it before, her face wasn't pink and white

203

like her mother's or red and brown like Andrew's, it was sallow, sallow, sallow. And soon she would have to take it to the new school in the now hated uniform, but perhaps she would die first."Oh, God, let me die now." But she didn't die, and at first school was so noisy and crowded and altogether bewildering that she was too stunned to think of anything at all. She was always getting lost in endless passages and bells rang suddenly, which meant you had to be in another classroom, or in the cloakroom, or in the hall, or in the playground, and she was hardly ever in the right place or knew how to get there.

After some time, though, it got easier and there were so many people at this school that they didn't seem to notice her much as long as she kept quiet, and by the second term, though she hadn't found a friend, she *had* found a hero. He was a boy in the same class and he had found her on one of those early days when she had got hopelessly lost, and had told her where she ought to be and had taken her there. He had freckles and a nice grin and hair like a yellow bush, and she had found out that his name was Ben. He could do handstands longer than any one else and keep two balls going up in the air for ages, too, and he actually lived in the housing estate at the back of the Lotus House. After she knew that she used to watch for him, over the fence, hidden in the old lilac bushes. Margot had said the garden didn't really belong to them at all — the bit by the basement flat belonged to Miss Cook and the rest to Mrs Sanderson, who had kindly said that Harriet could play there whenever she wanted to. She didn't want to play there. There was nothing to play at and no one to play with, but she spent quite a long while watching the children playing on the estate. There were two distinct groups of these — one she called "the Terribles" who were mostly the older ones. Harriet did not dare to be seen by any of these. They fought and shouted and threw things about; once they were throwing things at a poor cat, but it escaped, and scrambling over the fence in its desperation, rushed into Miss Cook's part of the garden and then disappeared. The boys continued to throw a few stones after it over the fence — one nearly hit Harriet and so she dared not go in search of the cat until they had all gone away, but she could not find it. Instead Miss Cook found her and was cross with her for "trespassing", as she called it.

Of the other younger group Ben was the leader. Harriet, worshipping from afar, saw with approval that it was he who arranged all the games and that the others did what he told them. He was nearly always the centre of a crowd, but sometimes he would come out later, just before the "Terribles", and practise by himself with a ball. One never-to-be-forgotten day he was there alone when Harriet came out and he actually looked over the fence and hailed her.

"Hullo, kid, I've sent my ball over by mistake. Can I come and look for it?"

Harriet nodded, she was speechless with shyness and emotion. She stood stock still until Ben appeared again on her side of the fence.

"There's an awful lot of long grass and bushes," he said, "I didn't see where it went. Can you help? You look along here and I'll start further off."

Harriet began to look but without hope, her mother always said she could never find anything. And then she saw it, something red, half-hidden in the undergrowth and almost at her feet. But no, it couldn't be, such a thing could never happen, it couldn't actually be Ben's ball. Transfixed with excitement and disbelief, she couldn't move, she simply couldn't stoop down and see for certain, and then Ben came up and saw it too.

"Why, there it is, staring at you. You are a blind bat!" he said kindly but contemptuously. He picked it up and ran away tossing it in the air.

"I might have found it for him, I could have been the girl who found Ben's ball. It'll never, never happen again, Why didn't I, oh, why?"

She ran blindly into the house, on the way nearly knocking over Mrs Sanderson who, seeing the look on the child's face, was troubled. She had not made much headway with Harriet as yet, although summer was now at hand. On several occasions Margot, with many pretty apologies and expressions of gratitude, had asked her if she would give an eye to Harriet when she and Andrew were going out for the evening. At first Letty had suggested stories and games, but Harriet had so obviously preferred any and every television programme and taking herself off to bed without help at the stipulated time, that she had not persevered. There was no denying that she found Harriet unattractive and unresponsive, a definite disappointment, but, displeased with herself for feeling like this towards the child, she had determined to make a more positive approach one day. Now she decided she would not put this off any longer. The doll's house would be her trump card of course, and yet it was something of an effort to play it. It would be good to rescue it from being a mere museum piece, to witness again a child's delight in the previous object, yet she was conscious of a wish to keep it sacrosanct, secure in the past.

But with the impression of Harriet's stricken look as she had rushed past her, Letty dealt firmly with this sentimental weakness and wrote a note to Margot which she pushed into the Royces' letterbox.

"Harriet," said Margot the next morning. "Mrs Sanderson has kindly invited you to tea today to see her doll's house."

"Doll's houses are for babies," said Harriet indignantly. "The Queensmead one was kept in the nursery and I never played with it even when I was only five."

"Well, it's very kind of Mrs Sanderson anyhow," said

Margot, "and it wouldn't be polite or nice not to go."

"You'll probably get a splendid tea," said Andrew, "Mrs S. did us proud at her party."

Harriet did not reply.

"Don't sulk," said Margot, "it's not as if you get that many invitations to tea. It's about time that you made some little friends at school, isn't it, then you could ask them here and get asked back in return. Meanwhile, of course you must go to Mrs Sanderson's, and when you go, please try and look as though you want to see her doll's house."

So soon after four o'clock, having come back from school and changed from her brown jersey and skirt into her blue velveteen, Harriet knocked on Mrs Sanderson's sitting-room door.

"We'll see the doll's house first, I think," said Mrs Sanderson. "I keep it in my bedroom."

Mrs Sanderson's bedroom looked immense to Harriet — it would have held six of her own little room easily, and at first she didn't see the doll's house, which stood in an alcove which had once held a carving table.

"Here it is," said Mrs Sanderson and stood aside.

"Oh!" exclaimed Harriet, "Oh, but it isn't a doll's house, it's a real house. Why, it's *this* house got little."

"Yes," said Letty, "it's a little Lotus House, and it was made like that cleverly by two nice boys who used to live here once. I'll open it for you so that you can see inside."

Harriet eagerly knelt down in front of it, just as Selina had done long ago on that memorable birthday.

"It's got real furniture in it," she said, "real proper furniture, and pictures on the walls and pots and pans in the kitchen and bedclothes and curtains and little books, and there's people in it!"

"Of course," said Letty, "what did you expect?"

Harriet certainly had not expected anything like this.

The silly tiny toy doll's house at Queensmead hadn't any people in it, and only broken bits of plastic tables and chairs. She looked up at Letty and her small dark eyes, so extremely unlike her mother's, were unusually bright and shining.

"May I take the people out and look at them?"

"Yes, if you're careful," said Letty.

"There's a father and a mother and a little girl!" cried Harriet.

"That's Mr and Mrs Golightly and their daughter Wilhelmina Rose — aren't those nice names?"

"No," said Harriet, "they're silly names, I think."

Letty was taken aback and would have felt ridiculously annoyed had she not immediately told herself that this was absurd. It was, of course, for that other child that she felt momentarily hurt, the child who long ago had invented those odd, old, dear names — yet nothing now could touch that child, so why worry?

"What ought they to be called then, do you think?" she asked.

"*I* know," said Harriet. She had known at once but she was not going to tell. "I can see more people, there's an old man in bed — what's he in bed for?"

So then Letty recounted Selina's story of the famous railway disaster. "It happened at the bottom of this very garden," she said.

"It couldn't have," said Harriet, "there's houses there."

Letty explained patiently that the garden used to go right down to the railway; "There was an orchard and a vegetable garden where all the houses are now."

"Oh," said Harriet, not very interested, "well, I don't think there was a railway accident, *I* think he just didn't have any legs ever. Who's that lady in the kitchen? What funny clothes!"

"She's the cook, she's got a cap and an apron on, all cooks used to wear them."

208

But Harriet didn't know about cooks. "Is Miss Cook a relation? She's very like her."

"So she is," agreed Letty. "Now shall we go and have our tea, perhaps you could toast some buns?"

"Yes, I could," said Harriet, getting up slowly from her knees, "but may I come back afterwards?"

"Indeed you may," said Letty, "and if you promise me always to be very careful, you can come and play with the little house by yourself sometimes. I expect Saturdays would be best, when you don't go to school."

"Thank you," said Harriet, "thank you very much."

When the afternoon was over and Harriet had gone, Letty felt pleased on the whole, for Harriet, in spite of her rejection of the whole Golightly saga, had responded satisfactorily to the doll's house in every other way and she felt herself warmed towards the child.

From then onwards Harriet spent most Saturday mornings playing with the little house. She had begun, as every child will do, by rearranging all the furniture, and then settled down to her own particular inventions. The inhabitants led very humdrum lives compared to those they had enjoyed in the past. Letty, though she took care never to interfere or to stay in the room for long, caught snatches from time to time and soon learnt the new names of the late Golightlys: "And how are you this morning, my dear Mrs Royce, and how is your dear husband, Mr Royce, and your darling little daughter Harriet?"

Selina, thought Letty, had been a child who could afford fantasy, the wilder the better: "Oh, no, no, no, Ros, I don't *want* them real."

But now there were no more burglaries or elopements or fires or accidents.

"You shall have this big wardrobe in your bedroom, Harriet, for all the lovely dresses I have bought you. No, of course you need not go to school tomorrow, it's my birthday. Your Mummy couldn't have a birthday with her

209

darling little daughter at school. We'll ask Daddy to come home early and all have a lovely party together . . . " Or, another time: "Look, Harriet darling, Cook has made this cake especially for you, your favourite chocolate icing — would you like to ask your best friend Ben to tea — we'll send a piece up to grandfather, shall we? He'll love to see you — he says you grow more and more like me every day . . . "

These and like snippets of doll's house conversation overheard on Saturday mornings often made Letty Sanderson feel a little uneasy.

Harriet's school took music seriously. This was because it had been lucky enough to find Miss Johnson, the head of the music department, who was an enthusiast and who believed that everyone, given the chance, could develop some measure of musical appreciation and ability. She started all the younger children as soon as they came with singing, recorders, cymbals, whistles and drums. Harriet looked forward to the music sessions and to her astonishment it wasn't long before she had found that she was singled out for praise. One day Miss Johnson told her to stay behind when the class was over and asked her if she would like to have special lessons besides playing in the band. Had she ever thought of learning to play a violin for instance? They wanted some more violin players in the junior orchestra.

Harriet did not speak but her tell-tale face gave Miss Johnson her answer.

"I think you *would* like it," she said.

"Yes," said Harriet, "yes, I would, but I would rather learn the piano, please." Since coming to live at the Lotus House she had often listened to Andrew playing his piano and sometimes it gave her a prickly feeling down her spine which was queer but splendid. Her favourite piece of furniture in the doll's house had always been the little piano and the doll, Harriet, could play it quite well.

"Very well, the piano it shall be," said Miss Johnson, who believed on the whole in putting a pupil's wishes before her own, "I'll write to your mother."

And a day or two later Margot had the letter.

"The school seem to think Harriet is musical," she said to Andrew that evening. "They suggest that she might have piano lessons."

"Good for Harriet," said Andrew.

"Well, I don't know so much, the fees are high enough as it is — I can't afford frills."

"Music isn't a frill," said Andrew.

"Sorry, darling, but you know how mean Dick is, and his wretched parents have never offered to help."

"He's got another family now to support, hasn't he?" said Andrew. "And weren't his parents pretty sick at your leaving him?"

"Why are you defending him suddenly?" said Margot crossly.

"I'm not particularly," said Andrew, "I'm only stating the facts."

"Well, anyway, I think learning the piano will only take her attention and time away from proper lessons and she's backward enough as it is."

"Can I see the letter?" asked Andrew. She tossed it over to him and he read it carefully.

"I'd teach her myself," he said thoughtfully, "only I'd find it difficult to be regular and besides, I'm sure I'm not a good teacher, I know nothing about it. I expect there are all sorts of new methods. Look here, Margot, if you can't manage the extra money, I can."

Margot looked at him curiously. "I suppose I ought to be grateful," she said, "but I rather think you're offering this just to annoy me."

"Don't be silly," said Andrew.

"Well, why this sudden concern for Harriet?"

"I don't think I'm doing it for Harriet exactly."

211

"Whatever for, then?"

"For music, I suppose," said Andrew slowly.

Margot experienced a dim glimpse at worlds unrealized. She acknowledged, of course, the value of the arts in general. She went to an occasional concert though she knew (but would never have admitted it) that she would not really have wanted a single record on her Desert Island, but would have plumped for eight luxuries instead. She attended picture exhibitions as part of her work assignment and prided herself on her judgement of the monetary value of works of art, and she strove to keep abreast of the most talked-of films, plays and novels. Her furnishings and decorations were always interesting and in fashion, and therefore contained few permanent objects. Andrew's piano was really the only recognizably stable feture in their successive sitting-rooms, also the only one that was there because it was loved. Margot saw, but did not feel, how beautiful things were. She did not understand what Andrew meant about music, but Harriet got her lessons.

"Are you going to let the child practise on your precious piano?" asked Margot incredulously, for it soon became clear that practising at school wasn't enough for either Miss Johnson or Harriet.

"Yes, I think so," said Andrew, "not when I'm working at home, of course, and never with sticky fingers." He smiled at Harriet, "But I'm sure you'll see to that, Harriet, won't you?"

"Yes, I will," said Harriet.

"Now darling," Mrs Doll's House Royce said to her little girl, "you must practise regularly every single day and you must never, never forget to wash your hands *most* properly first."

CHAPTER SIX

ALL THROUGH THE winter and spring Mrs Sanderson had difficulty in procuring any reliable domestic help. The Lotus House was not the type to attract these rare specimens, especially her own rooms with their wide expanses of floorboards needing polishing (she disliked fitted carpets) and actually with two antiquated open fireplaces. Helps arrived, drank a great deal of her tea or coffee according to taste, disapproved and disappeared. The latest had been a chain-smoker and had left trails of ash all over the place. Letty at last decided to tackle her, not because of the ash, nor for the smell of stale smoke which was unpleasantly difficult to get rid of, but about the dangers of lung cancer. She feared that any advice might be taken as interference but the girl was so young and it did seem a pity. Her gentle remonstrance however was not resented nor was it of any use.

"Well, what I say is, we've all got a date fixed." And she in her turn vanished without any warning.

"You're looking quite worn out, Mrs Sanderson," said Miss Budgeon at the little corner shop. Letty bought all her fruit and vegetables there now.

"Oh, it's nothing. I get rather tired sometimes, that's all. I haven't any help at present." Miss Budgeon looked thoughtful.

Three days later a smart slim car deposited an equally

smart slim passenger at the Lotus House who rang Letty's bell. She was heavily made-up and wore a black silk blouse, tight scarlet trousers and matching scarlet stiletto heeled shoes.

"Mrs Sanderson?" enquired this vision crisply. "I'm Dian — she said at the shop you needed help, dear, and I think I can fit you in Tuesdays."

Letty gazed at her in astonishment. How could Miss Budgeon have possibly thought this black and scarlet dragonfly suitable for cleaning floors and scrubbing woodwork? Still, there she stood waiting.

"Thank you very much," murmured Letty, "but you'd better have a look round first, I think."

The look round, however, did not apparently disconcert Dian.

"Righty ho, then," she said when it was finished. "I'll be here Tuesday next, ten sharp." The car drove off.

"*She* won't last long," commented Letty to herself, "if she ever turns up at all."

Tuesday morning however, brought Dian all right, and in the self-same clothes, the only concession she made to her morning's work was to change her stilettos into a pair of equally smart sandals tied on with velvet ribbon, and to envelop herself in an overall of shocking pink.

It did not take long however for Letty to discover that Miss Budgeon had provided her with a treasure. Never had floorboards shone so, never had rugs and carpets looked so trim, never had tiles and taps twinkled so brightly. Dian was both quick and thorough — floors were her passion. She seldom seemed to look above the skirting-board in the sitting-room and bedrooms, but as the dusting was Letty's business, this did not really matter. Objects didn't interest Dian but after her floors had been attended to, she had plenty of observation for the people who walked on them.

"That Mrs Royce — she's a peach, she is. I wouldn't

much want my Luke to set eyes on her."

"Your basement, she's a shy one — puts me in mind of a goldfish we've got, slips away behind his waterweed at a shadow."

"Who does for your third-floor then? Doesn't often do to let men do for themselves, dearie — regular messers, most of 'em."

There might be something in this, Letty thought, and after a word with Aubrey Stacey, who seemed grateful, it was arranged that Dian should see to his floor too. "And quite time I should say, thick with dust you could write yer name on, but that vacuum of his came out of the Ark, I shouldn't wonder." Letty had a pleasant momentary vision of Mrs Noah busily at work.

Doing for Aubrey meant that Dian brought her lunch now and stayed on for an extra hour afterwards. Letty and she had the meal together. Dian obviously had never entertained any other idea for a moment but she refused to share Letty's food.

"Must keep to me diet, dearie — it don't matter for you but my Luke likes me sheer." Letty felt uncomfortable consuming her quite substantial lunch, while Dian pecked at two slices of Ryvita spread with a non-fat cream cheese, and nibbled at an apple. She hoped Luke persuaded her to cook for two in the evenings. Luke was another shock when she met him. He was a huge coal-black Jamaican, a junior partner, so Dian proudly boasted, in a garage in Deptford — hence, Letty supposed, the succession of cars that brought Dian every Tuesday morning.

"I don't have to oblige," said Dian, "my Luke brings in good money, but staying at home all day gives me the creeps." Luke and Dian lived on the estate but though so near, Dian never walked if she could avoid it. Sometimes, even, Luke would call again for her and take her back home. He had other uses too.

The delivery of Miss Cook's post was a constant source of annoyance to her. The postman insisted on ignoring her prized separate entrance and delivered her letters with all the others at the main door. Not that she had much in the way of post, but when she had, it meant that she either had to fetch it or be beholden to Mrs Sanderson or one of the other lodgers for bringing it round and Miss Cook did not care for this. One Tuesday it was Dian who came to her door with a sales catalogue and a picture postcard of Hastings from her sister-in-law Doris, where she and Henry were having a little break. Miss Cook could not refrain from complaint.

"It's too bad, causing all this trouble, what's he paid for, I'd like to know?"

"Well, it's only natural really," said Dian, "it's the same name, 'The Lotus House'. Pretty, I call it."

"But it's got 'The Basement Flat' written perfectly clearly," said Miss Cook, "and I've told him again and again."

"Not to worry," said Dian, "I'll get my Luke to have a word with him — my Luke, he's known all round here. Mind if I have a look at your catalogue? What they get up to these days!" she added, "You're in luck, luv, see what it says here," and she started to read out very slowly: " 'You have been chosen to take part in our very special draw, limited to only a few customers, and I have some more exciting news for you, Miss Cook. You have been selected to receive one of the superb gifts pictured on page 5 of our catalogue. All you have to do is to return your lucky number with your order.' Oo, let's look at page 5."

"It's all nonsense," said Miss Cook, "it's just to make you buy their stuff which I never have. I don't know how they got hold of my name."

"But they aren't all cons," said Dian, "my Luke he knows a fellow, met him standing drinks all round at the

216

Green Man one night, he'd won a Metro with his lucky number, red it was Luke said, he saw it there outside in the car park, brand-new all right, 's truth. Mind you, it's your stars as does it and they don't oblige often, but you never know do you — that's what I like about life really, you never know. Which one of them superb gifts will you choose, then?"

"I don't want any of them," said Miss Cook, sniffing contemptuously, "thank you for bringing round my post," and she moved purposefully towards the door.

"Goldfish," sighed Dian to herself and retreated. But Janet Cook had no more trouble about her letters.

"Postman behaving himself?" enquired Dian, "I says as my Luke'd fix him," and it wasn't long after this that Janet had a further greater reason to be grateful to Dian's Luke.

All the estate children were a source of irritation to Janet. Their shouting and screaming and shrill laughter (of all noises except perhaps the barking of dogs, the ugliest and most disturbing), this she was prepared to put up with as the unenviable snag which she had expected to discover when first moving into this otherwise pleasant new home. But the behaviour of "the Terribles" went beyond this (that of course was only Harriet's private name for them, but it was one of which Janet would have approved). On one occasion it even menaced her personal safety, or so she was convinced.

As winter had given place to spring, Janet Cook had begun to cultivate her strip of garden. Obsessively conscientious by upbringing, she took her responsibility for this seriously but also, unsuspected by herself, she happened to have inherited from her country clergyman grandfather something of more value than his armchair or the tradition of gentility so treasured by her mother. He had loved growing things and had possessed green fingers. Janet had always had a weakness for flowers and had not infrequently incurred her mother's rebukes for squandering her money on them. Now she purchased a paperback on gardening, several packets of seeds from Woolworth's, a trowel, a fork and a pair of gardening gloves. She had set herself to clear the ground so that she could sow her seeds, and they had grown splendidly — but so had the weeds. She was emptying her bucket of these on the compost heap among the old bushes by the fence one day just as 'the Terribles' rushed out in a body and started to use the fence as a target. *Pop, bang, pop* went their peashooters, making Janet jump so that she upset her weeds all over the place. One bullet came over and nearly hit her.

"Stop that at once!" she called out. Immediately heads appeared above the fence.

"Get along, you old cow," shouted out one boy.

"Let's see if we can hit her bucket," shouted another, "if she gets peppered it's her own bloody fault."

Janet trembled with rage but just then Dian appeared, it being Tuesday, to shake out the ground-floor rugs.

"Look out," called out one of the boys, "it's big Luke's trout," and all the heads disappeared.

Janet picked up her basket, she was still trembling at the outrage.

"What's them boys bin up to?" said Dian. "They get above themselves sometimes. Mind you it's their Mums' and Dads' fault. You and me was brought up different."

"I should think so!" exclaimed Janet Cook. "I shall complain to the police."

"Oh, I wouldn't do that, really," said Dian, "My Luke'll see to them, they'll mind him better 'n any policemen." Janet, recollecting the postman and considering how rapidly the Terribles had disappeared, was inclined to believe her and, true enough, she was free of insults from that day. Feeling under an obligation to Dian, she actually decided to invite her in for a cup of tea

218

on one of her Tuesdays. Dian accepted with alacrity. She looked appreciatively round the flat.

"It's real cosy, I wonder Mrs Sanderson didn't take it for herself, instead of them great fancy rooms of hers."

Janet was gratified. "It isn't just as I want it yet though," she said. "I'm saving up for a new carpet." *Now why have I told her that*, she thought, *it's none of her business*.

But Dian nodded in quick sympathy. "I favour them as suck your feet in like, as if you were walking in a bog," she said, "Luke and me'll buy one of those when we win the pools. But this one's a nice colour though. Tell you what, mind if I bring along me new shampoo? Got it as a sample last week. What you can get nowadays! Free it was, 'cept for the stamps. It brought mine up lovely."

The shampoo certainly did make a difference and the two women shared the pleasure of achievement and another cup of tea together.

"In spite of her looks and the way she speaks, I believe she really has a heart of gold," Janet said to that persistently admonishing voice of her mother, undeterred apparently by the grave, "and her Luke has been most useful. Yes, Mother, I know he is black, but I can't help that and nor can he, and whatever grandfather would say, he's been a real help."

Miss Cook soon had another worry. A mouse actually ventured into the kitchen of the basement flat. "I never thought to have had mice *here*," she exclaimed outraged to Letty, who found herself apologizing humbly.

"I wouldn't have thought it either," she said, "especially in *your* kitchen, Miss Cook."

Janet abominated mice. They were dirty, destructive and noisy — "How anyone can say 'as quiet as a mouse', I can't imagine, and they dart about so, it unnerves me."

"It's primeval," said Dian darkly, "you can't do nothing

about what's primeval — except traps."

"I can't bear dealing with traps," said Janet. There had been mice and traps at intervals in Albert Street, but her mother or Henry had always dealt with them.

"Traps is cruel," agreed Dian, "well, there's cats, they're more natural, and leastways the cat gets some fun."

"I don't really want to be bothered with a cat," said Janet. "We never were a family for pets."

"Well," said Dian, "it's traps or cats or mice, 'cause it won't stop by itself. Cats is the most lasting and reliable I'd say."

They were talking at Miss Cook's door, and just at that moment the fugitive cat which Harriet had once seen escaping from the Terribles streaked across the lawn again. She had appeared several times before this and Miss Cook had always shooed her away. She started now to shoo once more but Dian stopped her. "It's sent all right, fancy that — it's milk, not shooing, you ought to be after."

"What do you mean," said Miss Cook affronted. "Who's sent it?"

"It's your stars as sent it, Miss Cook," replied Dian solemnly.

"Do you really think I should encourage it?" said Janet doubtfully.

"If you wants to get rid of that mouse," said Dian.

"But what about its owners?"

"Don't worry yourself about *them*," snorted Dian, "till they worries you, which'll be never, see? It's starving, that poor cat is, anyone can see with half an eye. A saucer or two of milk and it'll be yours for life. That poor kid upstairs'll be pleased, too, I bet."

Dian was right about Harriet, who met the cat in the garden the next day and recognized it at once. Miss Cook was busy gardening.

"Is she your cat, then?" asked Harriet, "I didn't think she was yours."

"She is now," said Miss Cook grudgingly, "she kept coming over from the estate to get away from those boys."

"Oh, I *know*,' said Harriet, "I am so glad she's your cat now, what are you going to call her?"

Janet hadn't thought of calling her anything but "Puss". "But 'Puss' is every cat's surname," objected Harriet, "I shall call her 'Maisie'." Maisie had been the name of a beautiful aristocratic white Persian with blue eyes who lived next door to Queensmead, and who had reminded Harriet of her mother.

"Do you mind if she is called Maisie?" she asked anxiously.

"You can call her what you like," answered Miss Cook rather shortly. She had no special objection to Harriet who had not shown herself to be a snag as yet, but she did not want to encourage her to come chattering, nor to have her bothering round after the cat, so she did not continue the conversation but picked up her trowel and went indoors and Maisie followed her. "She doesn't like me," thought Harriet, "but she's kind, she likes Maisie."

Letty Sanderson learned more about her tenants from her Tuesday lunch times with Dian than from her own observations. She told herself she ought to stop Dian from gossiping but this was next to impossible, and it was also, it must be confessed, very tempting to listen. What she heard was sometimes disquieting and she wished she need not believe it, but Dian was so transparently and objectively honest, she found she had to.

"That Aubrey, he's a queer, I'd say, but not one of them jolly ones, if you know what I mean — too many bottles about, but no one to share 'em with, is there?"

Mrs Sanderson confirmed that Mr Stacey seemed to

have few friends and Dian nodded. "I'd know if there'd been a party."

"Mr Stacey spends his leisure-time writing," said Letty firmly, "He's an author."

"I dessay," said Dian, "poor chap!"

Letty smiled but the thought of the bottles haunted her all the same.

In addition to doing the rough work for Mrs Sanderson and Aubrey, Dian had sometimes obliged Margot when she had an extra work-load.

"You can't resist her, can you," she said, "but I don't get satisfaction out of all that matting she has on the floors, it's not homely. But that Margot, she'd make a fortune on the telly, I tells her — she's got what it takes right enough. Funny her taking up with that Andrew, regular stick he is, might be one of they computers doing all the work for all he cares, he don't see me even if I'm right under his nose, which I have to be as often as not, for he don't move an inch for the vacuum to get out of me way."

"But he notices his wife, I hope," Letty couldn't help saying a little anxiously.

"You bet," said Dian, "but mind you, if it came to busting up, he'd get along without her better nor the other way round."

"Well, it won't come to that, I'm sure," said Letty decisively. She really mustn't let herself discuss such matters with Dian. But it was no use.

"You never know these days," said Dian cheerfully, "and especially when there's never been any wedding bells neither."

"But Dian," said Letty shocked, "what makes you say' that? I know Mrs Royce uses her first husband's name still for her business purposes, perhaps that has muddled you."

She was dreadfully afraid that she saw Dian wink.

222

"What does she want with a business, anyways?" she said, "Of course, if it was the telly, it would be different, but her's is just a shop. My mum now, she had to leave us, my Dad got hisself killed in the war, see, but she made it up to us when she was at home, like one of them old boilers she was, stoked up early mornings and evenings so that it warms you all day long."

"But you go out to work and you say you don't have to," said Letty.

"I haven't a kid to look after," said Dian, "that Harriet, she's no better than a latchkey child, I wouldn't oblige as I do if I'd had a little kid." She was silent for a moment. "My Luke, he'd've liked one too, but I guess I was too old when I took up with him. Anyways, time to clear them bottles out of that attic now — tootle-oo, luv," and she disappeared up the stairs.

CHAPTER SEVEN

A YEAR HAD passed since Letty Sanderson had moved into the Lotus House. Miss Cook's efforts had produced a flourishing row of sweetpeas and clumps of drowsy-smelling stocks. These had given place to marigolds and red dwarf dahlias — the latter were expensive but she had been assured that after the first frost, if she dug them up and stored them for replanting in May, they would last her for a long while. The first frosts were late that year and the garden was bright till the end of October.

To Harriet the time she lived in the Lotus House seemed very long. She was still at an age when the past scarcely exists in the conscious mind and the future is too vague to intrude on the all-important present. Childhood is a violent period — an hour of misery or of happiness has no conceivable end. Time has not yet learnt its confines, eternity lies in wait for us at every corner.

For Letty, of course, it was the other way round. The year had flown by and as she grew older, time went so fast that the present was hardly to be caught and pinned down. It was like trying to lay hold of a dream before it vanishes into the light of the real world. And which was the reality, she sometimes wondered?

It was All Hallows day.

"Do you believe in ghosts?" Dian enquired of Miss Cook.

"No," said Janet, "certainly not."

"Luke and me do," said Dian, "Luke, he's seen things hisself, in other countries mind, not here, and there's plenty of people on the telly that's seen them."

Janet sniffed.

"But I wonder," went on Dian, "why are they always sad or wicked? Aren't there any happy and good ones?"

"There aren't any at all," said Janet firmly, "but if there were, the good ones'd have something better to do, I should say, than to hang around here."

"Well, but you'd think they'd like to come and see how we was getting on. I know I would if it was Luke was left, and the places where I'd enjoyed myself, too. P'raps there *are* nice ghosts but they don't get talked about. People'd think them soft, I dessay, and they wouldn't make a good telly programme, see. That's it, I expect. I like 'em best wicked myself — the sort that lure you on."

"What nonsense," commented Janet Cook to herself. She had somehow fallen into the habit of inviting Dian in for a cup of tea quite frequently on her Tuesdays. After the rescue from 'the Terribles', it had seemed polite so to do, and then actually pleasant. She was surprised at herself but there it was. Having a place of your own was so different, and Dian was appreciative, no doubt of that.

"Looks lovely now your carpet does; funny how much bigger your lounge looks than Luke's and mine though I bet it's smaller really, we're so crowded up. My Luke's a collector, see, all sorts of things. I tell him he hasn't left space enough to swing a kitten, let alone a cat. Talk of the devil, here's that Maisie at the window now."

"She's not allowed in here," said Janet.

"Looks as if she's in the family way," said Dian.

"Oh dear, do you think so? I hope not," exclaimed Janet. "Isn't it just that she was so thin before and you're noticing the difference?"

Dian shook her head. "She's plumped out all right but

it's all in one place. You should have got her seen to."

"I never thought. I don't know much about these things," said Janet.

"Well, it's too late now," said Dian cheerfully, "and anyways, I expect it'd be shutting the stable door after that Mrs Bates' Blackie had got at her. She's never had *him* done and never will and he's a regular Donje."

"A what?" asked Janet.

"A Donje, a Spanisher he was, and a sugar daddy if ever there was one. They Spanishers are worse than any my Luke says, and he's travelled all over the place, used to be a stoker, see."

Maisie was pressed against the window pane glowering at them balefully. Janet was determined that she should remain strictly a working kitchen-cat, but Maisie was equally convinced that by rights she had now attained the status of a drawing-room pet. She had somehow become "Maisie" to everyone, though Janet disapproved of animals being given the names of human beings.

"Will it be soon?" she enquired.

"Not so long, I'd say," said Dian, eyeing Maisie speculatively, "but you'll know it's when she starts to look about the place, see."

"What will she be looking for?"

"Her maternity bed," said Dian, "and it'll be no sort of use your giving her a box or basket, never mind if it's got ever so nice a cushion in it or anything. Cats are that choosy, no National Health for them, see, private and special, just what takes their fancy. My mum's Rosy, she had her first lot in my sister's bottom drawer, nipped in when no one was looking, Sis not shutting it proper after she'd been showing off her wedding veil. For her next she fancied Gran's cardigan — the one she kept for best. Then it was my Dad's box of picture papers — hoards 'em up he does for rainy days, but Rosie, she tore 'em all to bits, so then Dad had her seen to and Mum said she wished it had been her, 'cause there was five of us already, see, and another on the way, no pill then there wasn't and Mum careless, but she didn't mean nothing, she loved us all every one she did, and no one was to know my Dad was going to get hisself killed."

"Well," said Janet, "I shall take good care this cat is shut out from now on. I shall continue to feed her, of course, but she must not be allowed in — after all she's only a stray."

Sometimes Dian rattled on in a way that re-awakened in Janet Cook that disapproving voice, grown somewhat fainter of late; "This is not at all the sort of person to invite into your home, not a fit acquaintance for you, Janet."

All the same, she heard herself actually accepting a return invitation to visit Dian that very next week.

"It's a terrible early supper, Luke comes home that hungry. You won't mind, will you, dear?" said Dian.

Afterwards Janet Cook wondered why she hadn't made up some excuse to refuse, but it was difficult with Dian somehow, the mistake, she feared, was having got on such terms in the first place, as her mother kept tiresomely reminding her. Yet she found herself looking forward to the visit. It must be confessed she was curious to see Dian's home and to meet Luke, for, what with the move to the Lotus House and the garden and getting to know Dian, a strange new sensation had recently invaded her — an urge, faint but persistent, towards adventure.

Dian and Luke lived in one of the estate houses and outside it looked no different from its neighbours, but when the front door opened Janet Cook was confronted with something disconcertingly different. Facing her was a large wooden plaque on which was emblazoned in ornamental poker work the words:

Welcome All

227

To Happy Hall.

On the reverse side it said:

> Don't miss your train
> But come again.

Surrounding this and decorating the passage were flags of many different nations. A door painted a brilliant blue led into quite a large room, but as Dian had said, it did not look its size. Its walls were covered from top to toe with matchboxes of all sizes, shapes and colours, strung together in long festoons. In front of each of the two windows were stands crowded with flourishing pot plants. Above the mantelpiece were two more pokerwork plaques — one declared that "East, West, home is best", and the other "Good food, good drink, good cheer, Good health to all folks here". Beneath, one of those electric fires of mock glowing coal was flanked each side by a gnome sitting on a large red and white toadstool. In the centre of the room was a round table covered with dishes; two fat red plush chairs and a conch found space for themselves somehow, and in one corner was an outsize television set crowned with framed family photographs. In the other a guitar propped itself against a goldfish bowl.

Janet Cook, staring about her with her sharp black eyes, was quite taken aback by all this odd miscellany.

"See what I mean?" said Dian, "I don't care so much for objects myself, but Luke, he's a collector like I said, and he's that good about dusting all his boxes hisself."

"You've got some lovely plants," said Janet politely.

"Not half bad," agreed Dian, "though I says it. I have to have 'em all in here, there's no sort of use trying to grow 'em in the garden, see."

Janet looked out of the window and indeed did see that the garden also was very full, but not of flowers or vegetables. A great many more gnomes made a bright border to a patch of grass which was populated by a number of large and small tortoises, perambulating slowly round in search of the lettuce leaves strewn about for their benefit.

"Luke, he loves them tortoises," explained Dian, "he can't bear for to see 'em in those pet shops, crawling all over each other, dying and sad. I tell him the more he buys 'em up, the more the dealers'll get others in, but it don't carry no weight with him. He says as it won't make no difference to speak of to the trade but it'll make all the difference in the world to these here tortoises now, but he'll have to stop soon, 'cause there won't be any more room for 'em. Same with the gnomes, he buys 'em plain and colours 'em hisself, he can't keep off 'em; they gnomes and they tortoises, they're like children to him, and he feels almost as much for Fred, that's the goldfish. I can't get up enthusiasm for 'im myself. Won 'im in a raffle, I did, for cancer research — well, you never know, do you? I wanted a mink coat and I got a goldfish. Still, he don't give us trouble. That's Luke now, it's his boxing night really, but he said he'd give it a miss so as to come back early to meet you. He's a super boxer, is Luke, that's why the boys mind him."

Luke was enormous. When Janet Cook saw him filling up the doorway, she wondered how on earth he could fit into the crowded sitting-room, but he moved around with a slow sureness. He extinguished Dian in a huge hug from which she extricated herself as if used to it. Then he turned to Janet and seized her limp unready hand and worked it up and down like a pump handle.

"What have you got for us to eat then, darling?" he asked Dian.

"He's always afraid I'm going to starve him," she said.

"She starves herself, not me," said Luke to Janet. "Looks like there's plenty on the table anyways. Why, that's my gal, she don' forget her ole man."

"You don't have to taste them, if you don't want," said

Dian to Janet, "sweet potatoes and kidney beans, that's what Luke likes, but I never touch 'em — it's what you're used to, isn't it?"

Janet Cook, sitting bolt upright on the edge of her chair, nibbled at a paste sandwich and a piece of chocolate roll, and watched Luke as if he were some strange animal as he worked his way steadily through plateful after plateful. But at last he finished and began to talk. He had a soft warm voice.

"You like my matchboxes, honey?" he enquired.

"It must have taken you a very long time to collect them all," Janet replied evasively.

"Ever since I was a little 'un," said Luke, "I used to ask the sailors for them when they put in at the harbour. I was raised in Old Spanish Town and I were mad after the sea, went as a cabin boy soon as I were old enough, then got to be stoker — trading in bananas, we were, and everywhere we went I got them matchboxes. But one day come and I'd enough of wandering, was that the day I met my darling? Near enough. Then it was 'East, West, home's best', wasn't it, honey? But I kept my matchboxes."

"Give us a song, now," said Dian, "he sings lovely, as good as one of they pop guys any day."

Luke took down his guitar and bent over it lovingly.

"Sing 'To my donkey'," ordered Dian, and he began crooning softly. It sounded like a foreign language to Janet. "Tie meh dongdey."

"Now 'Yellow bird'," said Dian. The low rich voice crooned on and Janet Cook's stiff little body relaxed. Then the song changed again.

"This is his favourite," whispered Dian, "it's 'This is my island in the sun' ". Janet had never been out of England and had scarcely ever even seen the sea, but, as she listened, she felt as if she were lying by it — a very blue sea, with scarlet blossoming trees growing close to

230

the shore and brilliant yellow and green birds darting among them.

When Luke stopped singing Janet stood up to leave and Luke said he would see her home. "There's no need for that, thank you," said Janet, but Luke took no notice. Crossing the street he put his arm round her to steer her through the traffic. This made her feel queer and uncomfortable, and she was glad when they reached the Lotus House. Left alone she suddenly realized that she was tired and sat still doing nothing for a little while.

"Well, it takes all sorts," said Janet Cook to herself. And then, "Perhaps I might take one of those coach trips down to the sea one day." And then "Wouldn't like all those matchboxes about, and the tortoises, rather her than me." And then "Wonder what it's like to be her, all the same." She didn't remember ever having been hugged and hardly kissed even, since those hurried embraces from poor old Dad years and years ago — you couldn't call those pecks she and her mother exchanged "kisses". "They say you don't miss what you've never had — I liked the singing, though."

She sat for a bit longer. Then, "Mustn't be fanciful," she said, and got up to take off her jacket and put away her bag.

The next morning brought a letter from her sister-in-law. *Wonder what she wants*, she thought. Contacts between them were usually confined to a picture postcard on holidays and birthdays and Christmas greetings. The letter said that Doris (now second mistress in the large primary school of the very respectable suburb where she and Henry had their home), had been asked to deputize for her headmistress at an important educational conference in the north where her parents lived, and she had obtained extra leave of absence to extend her stay for a week so as to visit them. "We thought it might make a nice change for you to keep Henry company while I am

231

away. You have never seen our new house," Doris wrote.

"No, because this is the first time you have asked me to visit you since Mother died and you moved," said Janet, "It's as plain as a pikestaff you want me just to cook and clean while you're not there. How do they know I want a nice change? I don't, as a matter of fact. Pretty sure of me, too, Doris is, gives me times of trains and bus connections, not going to get the car out for me, no fear. Still, blood is thicker than water and I shall go, I suppose."

She duly gave Mrs Sanderson her spare key, packed her small neat suitcase, and set off on the day and at the hour suggested by Doris, who opened the door to her.

"Quite a walk from the bus stop," observed Janet, "further than the other house."

"The Avenue's a much better neighbourhood," said Doris. "We owe it to Henry's promotion — you knew of that, of course?"

"Of course," said Janet. "A bit overdue, wasn't it?"

Doris eyed her sister-in-law sharply. She was a tall rather imposing woman, still handsome, with regular features and large brown protruding eyes behind her spectacles, but her face was lined and Janet thought she looked distinctly older than when she had last seen her.

"Where's Henry?" she enquired.

"He's washing down the car," said Doris, "it's a new one and he's very careful of it. I expect you got a cup of tea on the journey."

"No," said Janet, "there was no opportunity."

"Oh, well, it's a bit late now, isn't it, and we have supper early. Come into the lounge."

The lounge was a long narrow room with windows at both ends. It struck Janet as cold, for it was one of those days when rain is in the offing and there is too much wind about. If she had been at home she would have switched her fire full on. The pale grey walls, empty of pictures,

232

and the dark green covers and curtains gave her the shivers.

"I'm glad I stood out against Doris and got pink for mine," she thought. Then Henry appeared. He had the same small tight mouth as his sister and the same sharp black eyes, but his face was pale with a long chin and, whereas her hair was still black and thick, his was grey and brushed in careful thin strands across his head.

"'And he's three years younger than I am," said Janet to herself with satisfaction. He began to tell her about the new car in which she was not interested. Supper, when it came, consisted of a cheese soufflé that didn't allow of second helpings, salad and fruit.

"We find a light supper much healthier and I know you have trouble with your digestion," said Doris. "We don't take coffee in the evenings, we find it keeps us awake, but I can make some for you if you like."

"I'd like a cup of tea," said Janet. Doris did not move for a moment.

Henry said, "I'll make it dear, you've had a heavy day."

They spent the rest of the evening looking at the television news and then at a travel film of wild life at Spitsbergen, until Janet, who was getting colder and colder, said she would like to go to bed.

"Oh," said Doris, "I don't usually switch on the heater so early, so I'm afraid there's no hot water yet, but I'll heat a jug from the kitchen for you."

Janet took a long while to warm up in bed and even then she did not sleep well. The room smelt musty and unused and she had not opened the window because it was now raining outside, and moreover she had reached the age when a strange bed took getting used to. Also she was hungry. But she slept at last, and then of course did not wake when she should have done and was late down for breakfast. The coffee was tepid and the toast had gone limp and she had disapproving looks from Doris who said:

"Henry has had to leave, I'm afraid, I would have called you if you had asked, I've got to catch an early train too. I've left notes about the housekeeping by the phone; we have weekly accounts with the grocer and butcher and Mrs Binns, my help, comes on Wednesday morning to clean — there shouldn't be any difficulties. Henry's got a Conservative Association meeting tomorrow night. I expect you'd like to go with him." (*And I expect I wouldn't*, thought Janet.) "And there's a W.I. lecture on peasant embroidery on Thursday," continued Doris, "you'd be welcome there I know, and the park is nice and handy for walks."

Doris's habit of arranging other people's lives for them always irritated Janet; aloud she said "Oh, I'm used to amusing myself, you needn't worry."

As soon as Doris had left, Janet went into the lounge with the newspaper and switched on all the bars of the electric fire. When it stopped raining she went out shopping and bought herself a hot-water bottle. She also bought a nice piece of beefsteak at the butchers. "People get indigestion just as much from eating too little as too much, and Henry looks as though he could do with a good supper for once." There had been nothing to drink either, the previous evening, so she bought a bottle of sherry. She went to sleep, hugging her hot-water bottle for the whole of the afternoon.

When Henry came home that night she produced the sherry. His eyebrows went up when he saw it.

"Not to worry," said Janet, "it's a present, I noticed you were out."

"Well," said Henry, "actually we had a few friends in the night before you came and we don't usually treat ourselves, got to keep the housekeeping down for a bit."

"Why," said Janet, "I thought you and Doris were both getting more now."

"A little," conceded Henry, "but there's the mortgage,

234

houses in the Avenue are expensive you know; and the car — we had to have a decent one; and Doris thinks we should take our holiday abroad this year. Our neighbours — he's on the Stock Exchange, really nice people, Janet, you must meet them — they're going to Majorca, we rather thought we'd try there too."

Janet did not meet these desirable neighbours after all because Henry made no move towards the introduction, but she spent her time quite pleasantly not doing all the things her sister-in-law had suggested, and providing what she felt were really good meals, and roasting herself before the electric fire, for it remained cold.

"It won't matter for a week," she thought as she ordered a prime cut of lamb and bought a carton of cream to have with the chocolate mousse she had made. She also replenished the sherry, this time not at her own expense. "They'll be paying three times as much for trash at that hotel of theirs in Majorca without blinking an eyelid, I bet. Anyway, I think all this saving and scraping behind the scenes is silly — just to put on a show — that expensive car, don't tell me it's paid for yet. It's Doris — no, that's not fair, I can see it's Henry too — Mother always pushed him more than me and it's just taken this turn." Generations of hard-working honest forefathers stirred in her blood: "Well, I shan't get my new carpet till I can put down every penny's worth."

In the middle of the week Mrs Binns arrived to clean. She was a small, dim little woman with a stutter and seemed upset at being a little late.

"I'm s-sorry, Miss Cook, but this morning our old cat had kittens and I had to s-see to them."

"Oh," said Janet, "what did you do about them?"

"D-drowned them," said Mrs Binns, "that's why I'm late. You have to drown them quick — they don't feel nothing then."

Janet registered this useful piece of information. But

Mrs Binns was no Dian and they had no further conversation, though she seemed surprised and grateful for a bountiful elevenses.

Henry and Janet did not talk much in the evenings but then they never had. On the last night before Doris returned, they watched a travel film together because it was about Majorca, but you didn't see much of the country — it was mostly of the hotels and people eating and drinking and dancing, all of which looks much the same wherever it's done. Then there was the news and then a programme on immigrants, which Henry switched off almost at once.

"A great mistake ever to have let them in," he said.

"But they've got to live somewhere," said Janet.

"Not here, they haven't," said Henry, "all these blacks and gypsies, too, rascals and scroungers the lot. Do you know, Janet, they even talk of a gypsy site on a disused railway property within walking distance of the Avenue. It'll be the blacks next — you have to fight for a decent society all the time nowadays, I don't know what the country's coming to."

Janet looked at him. She had never noticed before how like their mother he was. The spirit of opposition which he and Doris often aroused in her flared up. For a moment or two she had a vision of the cold grey walls of Doris' lounge festooned with coloured matchboxes and flags, and it improved them.

"Well, I think it makes life more interesting not to be all the same," she said.

Henry frowned. "You've changed, Janet," he said accusingly, "I've been thinking so all the week. What's come over you? Don't think I haven't noticed how much the housekeeping books must have gone up with what you've spent, and now these notions. I don't know what our mother would say."

Yes, you do, thought Janet, *and it would be just the*

236

same as you. But she was a little shaken all the same. She went to bed that night wondering if she *had* changed and she felt uncomfortably sure that Henry was right — this was a bit frightening. She fell asleep with her mother's, or Henry's voice (it didn't matter which) chanting over and over again, softly but insistently, like an unpleasant lullaby, "You can't be too careful."

Meanwhile, at the Lotus House, Maisie had had her kittens. Being denied entry to her rightful territory, she had made do with the tool-shed which had a convenient window and a not too inadequate pile of sacking in a corner. There Letty found her, the proud mother of five as far as she could see. She wished Miss Cook had left instructions about what she wanted done with them. "I ought to have asked — I am getting forgetful — I've noticed it lately." For the moment however she did nothing but fetch Maisie a large saucer of milk. *Anyway she's due back tomorrow*, she thought, and forgot about it again.

But in the afternoon she was disturbed by a flushed and agitated Harriet bursting into her sitting-room without even knocking.

"Oh, Mrs Sanderson, come quickly," she cried, "poor, poor Maisie, she's in the tool-shed being bitten dreadfully by lots of horrid rats."

Letty stared at her and then began to laugh. "Oh, Harriet, they're not rats, they're her kittens, she's feeding them."

Harriet didn't believe her, she stamped her foot: "They're not kittens, they're horrible little rats."

"Come along," said Letty, "come and look again."

Maisie greeted them with a roaring purr. "Listen," said Letty, "don't you hear and see how pleased she is?"

Harriet could not deny the purr. "But kittens are pretty and fluffy little things, why should poor Maisie have such ugly kittens? And they've got no eyes," she added horrified.

"These will be pretty and fluffy very soon, and their eyes will open," said Letty. "All kittens are like this when they are born. I must say they are rather like rats; but look, this one is going to be a tabby like Maisie, you can see the markings, and three are black, and this one black and white."

Harriet bent over and Maisie gazed up at her proudly, still purring. Then Harriet put out a finger and touched one of the kittens very gently.

"I'm so sorry, Maisie," Letty heard her whisper, "I'm very sorry I thought your children were rats."

Janet Cook arrived home the following evening. She felt a new and definite pleasure as she walked up from the station to the Lotus House. For one thing, it was really a relief to have left Doris and Henry, especially as for the last twenty-four hours she had certainly been under a cloud. She had felt she could not go before Doris returned, that would have looked queer, and Doris had not arrived back until late in the evening.

She was very full of all her doings at the conference. "Might have been running it," commented Janet silently, "thought she was too, I bet, another Maggie Thatcher, that's what she thinks she is."

Then, after Doris and Henry had been alone together, while Janet was getting ready for supper, the cloud had come down, the cloud under which Janet had to finish the evening, pack her bag the next morning, eat a sparse last meal, bid her farewells and take herself off. "Never seen the inside of that car once and probably never will." But besides the shaking off of the cloud, there was the warm anticipation of her own little flat again and her own garden border. The house at Albert Street had simply been her parents' home and an unloved one at that. It had never welcomed anyone. Now she felt a definite welcome as she opened her door and there was even actually a "Welcome Home" card from Dian lying on her mat. *Nice of her*, thought Janet, *nice I'm sure*. But there was also a note from Mrs Sanderson, and when she had read this she was not so pleased. It enclosed her spare key and told her that Maisie had had her kittens and they were in the tool-shed.

Drat the animal, thought Janet, *I suppose I shall have to bother with her now, but I'm going to have a cup of tea first*. She was tired after her journey and had looked foward to a really relaxed evening; but she believed in doing what had to be done, even if tiresome, without delay, or at least only the delay of a cup of tea; and what had to be done now was to get rid of those kittens.

Janet knew very little about animals. She would never have been consciously cruel to one but she was almost totally ignorant of their habits and needs. They were not part of her world. Cows, sheep and the occasional horse she accepted as objects in a landscape. Dogs she disliked when she met them, as dirty, noisy and sometimes dangerous. They might keep burglars away but were almost as bad as burglars. Cats had their uses where mice were concerned, but in her view Maisie was not much more than an animated sort of mouse-trap. She remembered however, Mrs Binn's words about drowning kittens as soon as possible. Well, this was as soon as possible. After her tea she filled a bucket full of water and made her way to the shed. She found the business a more unpleasant job than she had anticipated. The little things were warm to her touch and struggled as she held them under the water. She had to keep telling herself that Mrs Binns had said they did not feel anything. An uncomfortable thought obtruded itself that Mrs Binns had drowned her lot sooner, but surely it didn't make all that difference. She had not expected either that Maisie would make such a fuss, in fact she hadn't thought about her at all. After the kittens had been disposed of she shut her up in the shed and closed the window. The cat was making a loud, continuous noise. When she got back to her room she felt exhausted; really it had been quite a day.

Harriet had got up early the morning of that same day and had paid Maisie and the kittens a visit before she went to school. Already she thought they were looking more like real kittens and she decided that the black and white one was going to be the prettiest, she could see his little shirt-front quite clearly. She was enraptured. She happened to be late home from school that day, it was her piano lesson afternoon and then, after she had had her tea and done her prep, Margot wouldn't let her go out again. "But I'll get up early so as to see Maisie and the kittens before school. I mean to go and see them every morning."

Janet too was up early. She had noticed that her michaelmas daisies wanted staking — they had grown so while she was away, and the wind was getting up. She was interrupted by Harriet.

"I can't find the kittens," she said, "and Maisie's miaowing dreadfully. Have you got them here, Miss Cook? I know they're lovely but Maisie wants them back."

Janet Cook felt uncomfortably embarrassed and this made her speak brusquely.

"There aren't any kittens any longer. Cats have far too many, you know; they have to be got rid of."

Harriet stared at her, then: "What do you mean, 'got rid of', you don't mean *killed*, do you?" she asked in a whisper — the words were too dreadful to say aloud.

"Now," said Janet, the more sharply for an irrepressible, though she considered a quite unwarranted, sense of guilt, "don't be silly, when people don't want kittens, they always drown them, you know; they are much too little to feel anything."

Harriet, after a shocked silence, shouted loudly: "I hate you, you're a wicked woman!"

The ingrained red of Janet Cook's cheeks became

redder. "And you're a very rude little girl," she rejoined, but Harriet had fled.

She had to see Mrs Sanderson at once. "You've got a murderess in your house, Mrs Sanderson," she cried when she had found her, "you won't let her stay, will you?"

"Is it the kittens?" asked Letty apprehensively. Harriet answered with a flood of tears.

Oh dear! thought Letty, *Oh dear, dear, dear!* Aloud she said, "Don't cry so, darling, they were too young to know anything about it." But Harriet did not believe her, nor really did Letty herself.

"But Maisie, *poor* Maisie," Harriet sobbed, "she's calling and calling for them."

"She'll forget about it in a day or two," said Letty, this time with more conviction, "she really will, Harriet."

Harriet stopped sobbing in consternation. "But she oughtn't to forget," she cried, "I don't want her to forget!"

"Do you want her to go on being miserable, then?" asked Letty.

Harriet was silent. She did and she didn't — all she really knew she wanted, and that passionately, was to have the kittens alive again.

It was a miserable day. That evening Harriet said to Andrew: "Do kittens go to heaven?"

"I don't know," said Andrew.

Harriet sighed; if Andrew didn't know, no one would know, but on the other hand, if he didn't know one way or other, there was still a hope that they did.

CHAPTER EIGHT

THE IMPROVEMENT IN his job that Aubrey Stacey had
hoped for after his move to the attic flat in the Lotus
House had not materialized. It was indeed a relief to
return to his peaceful rooms after the day's ordeal instead
of the incessant noise and permanent smell of stale smoke
of his old lodgings, but at school matters became even
worse. He had been allotted an older class of mixed
ability. The mixture was divided roughly into three
groups — the aggressive, the apathetic and a minority
who, with a possible GCE as a target, gravitated to the
front of the classroom where they were just able to hear
the teacher and, by ignoring what went on elsewhere,
managed with difficulty to accomplish a little work.

A ringleader amongst the first group was an overweight
black-browed girl called Marcia. She had quickly classi-
fied Aubrey as a creep and thenceforth as fair game. His
subsequent mortification was systematically planned.
There was first the straightforward crude "hubbub"
ordeal to which each of the staff in turn were subjected as
a matter of course. Aubrey, as Marcia expected, fell into
the trap and responded by shouts of, "Silence, stop that
row at once."

Silence immediately ensued but it was too complete,
too sudden, and soon the tapping began — tap, tap,
tap of ball-point pens on desks, and then of boxes and

transistors, anything handy, gradually mounting to a crescendo and then dying down, only to start again after a pause. Next there was the veiled insult, the innuendo that must not be noticed in case worse should follow, and the provocative personalities:

"Oh, Mister, I like your shirt — look at Mister's shirt. Cool, isn't it?"

"Did your wife choose it for you?"

"You boob, he hasn't got a wife."

"Hasn't he? Well, now's your chance then, Tracey."

"Why hasn't he?"

"Oh, Mister, Pete's *bent* my book!" (Hilarious laughter).

"Mister, tell Marcia not to take off her cardigan, I can see her big boobs and it's distracting me."

"Yes, what is it, Doreen?"

"What's what, Mister?"

"You had your hand up."

'Oh, I was only combing my hair."

Or, again, there was the stonewalling ordeal, and in this the apathetic group would often join.

"But it's so *boring*, it doesn't *mean* anything. What the hell's the guy after?"

"It's like difficult to do this, Mister."

"Why should we anyways? My Mum, she never had to bother with this dope and she's done all right."

Lastly there was the absolute defiance — "Pass us a fag, mate," or a chair hurled across the room, a window broken deliberately.

After each failure to cope with one or other of these challenges, Aubrey sought escape from humiliation in dreams of his true vocation as a writer; after all, no creative genius could be expected to succeed as a hack teacher — look at the Brontës, look at D.H. Lawrence. He would get out his manuscript and sit with it before him, his pick-me-up at hand which he felt to be not

243

only a necessity but a just compensation for what he had to endure during the day. Often the whole evening would slip away in a vague pleasant trance which he excused to himself as a period of gestation. True inspiration could only occur at the right time, when the subconscious had done the preparatory work, so this period of relaxation was not at all a waste of time.

But as he filled and refilled the glass beside him, his musings over his plot and characters were apt to merge into bright fantasies. The six presentation copies of the finished book lay there on his table, together with the reviews, all highly appreciative, or he heard his brother calling him up on the phone, or better still, appearing at the Lotus House with a bottle of champagne under each arm to celebrate, or he was receiving the congratulations of his headmaster and the staff. Best of all he pictured his mother and father overcome with pride and pleasure. After such an evening he would put away his manuscript in a euphoric haze. Then would follow the deep oblivion of the night; and next morning a hangover and the grim reality of another school day. He sometimes thought of giving in his notice but shrank from the confession of failure; also his parents were not rich and he could not see himself living on the dole, having no taste for economy, and it would not be easy to find another job, for he could not hope for an enthusiastic recommendation. Anyway, would another teaching post be any better, there were worse places, he knew, and he lacked the confidence to launch out into fresh fields. No, he must keep on until his novel was finished.

But the autumn term brought some improvement. In the holidays he had had two weeks' holiday in Greece, where he had been intoxicated by colour and warmth. He was among friendly, civilized people, and the world of sordid savagery in south-east London seemed thousands of miles away, tiny, unreal and of no importance.

Although, on his return, this impression naturally faded, he felt the benefit in health and spirits. Surely things must be better this term, and so, at first, they were. Marcia and her chief cronies were themselves in sight of freedom, being due to leave at Christmas, and therefore less aggressive. Besides, baiting the same creep for so long became boring, like everything else. And then there was Hassan. He was a new boy, a Pakistani with a mobile intelligent face and the large appealing dark eyes of his race. Aubrey immediately became aware of those eyes fixed upon him in eager anticipation. Here was someone actually anxious to learn. He felt as if, parched with thirst, he had been offered a drink of water. He soon discovered that the boy was responsive and sensitive even to the poor material he was handing out to him.

When he had first started at Brook Comprehensive he had intended, as had been his custom, to include some carefully selected classics into his general syllabus, but this hope was quickly dispelled.

"My dear Stacey, we keep in touch with reality here. Teach them, if you can, to speak and write grammatically and to spell, that's your priority; they'll need that to get jobs. As for any reading, go easy — there's quite a useful anthology on the staffroom shelves — Salinger and that *Lord of the Flies* man, and Wynham."

"Poetry?" Aubrey had asked tentatively.

"No go, my dear chap, they won't take it, I'm afraid, though if you're keen you might try to squeeze in a contemporary now and again. There was a fellow I heard on the radio the other day, a description of a decaying fish, very lifelike I thought it — you a fisherman?"

"No."

"Well, you wouldn't appreciate it then. But something like that might appeal."

Now, however, Aubrey found himself longing to try out on this boy some of his favourites, and this became compelling after he had had Hassan's first bit of written work. He had read the class a descriptive passage of D.H. Lawrence out of the staffroom anthology, about the Australian bush, and then told them to write what they remembered of it and what they liked or disliked about it — a routine exercise from which he expected little. Half the class would never attempt it, would not even have listened. "It doesn't mean anything anyway," "What right's he got to bother us!" The rest would vary in presentation but would be depressingly similar as to content. Then suddenly he came upon this:

"Words are magic things, sometimes they dance, sometimes they cry, sometimes they sing. Some are terrible, some take me travelling. This man's words make me feel alone, the only person left in the world, but I do not mind because I am changed into a magician by his words. I can do and see anything I wish."

Aubrey, staring at the round careful script, was silent upon his peak in Darien. His discovery filled him with excitement, almost with awe. From then on he taught for Hassan, waited in suspense for his response, contrived opportunities to see the boy alone that would appear accidental — excuses to retain him after class, or seemingly chance meetings out of school. He began to lend him books: poetry, Stevenson, Kipling, the short stories of Conrad; which the boy returned shyly, without much comment, but with such glowing looks of appreciation that expressed better than words that they had done their work. Aubrey experienced in all this the deepest satisfaction that life had yet offered him. He planned how he would continue to nourish Hassan's talent, how, as he grew older, Hassan would become a real friend as well as a pupil, yet would always keep that gratitude and admiration for himself that he now gave so innocently and openly. Too openly, too innocently, for after a time things began to go wrong.

246

Aubrey had been aware that he must be cautious about the relationship, but he was not conscious of how his face lit up whenever he spoke to the boy, nor that Hassan's response had been noted as beyond even that expected by the despised and ridiculed "snobs" in the front row. Hassan became all of a sudden withdrawn and silent during lessons and avoided all other possible encounters. Then one day, after the others had all gone, he did return to the classroom with Aubrey's copy of "The Ancient Mariner", which he hastily thrust at him with a quick glance over his shoulder and round the room.

"Thank you, sir," he half whispered, "but do not lend me any more just now, please — I am too busy." He was gone before Aubrey could detain him and as he started up to try and do so he thought he saw a face pressed against the window.

The next morning as he came into the room, there was a sudden unnatural hush. He opened his desk to get out his books and there, lying on the top of them, was a large bold drawing executed with a crude vigour in black and red. It was an obscene picture of himself and Hassan and beneath was scrawled "Mr Stacey is a bent." The drawing gave Aubrey an almost physical sensation of a violent blow between the eyes. It was probably for only a second or two that he gazed at it behind the shelter of the desk lid, though it seemed an age. Then he became conscious of the air of suppressed excitement in the classroom and with a tremendous effort he controlled his rage and disgust. Hassan . . . he must think of Hassan, and force himself to carry on the lesson as usual. Aware of rows of eyes fixed upon him in expectation, aware, alas, though how he did not know for he did not look at him, of the boy crouching down over his books, he heard himself saying quietly, "Get out your exercises and take down a dicta- tion." Mechanically he started reading out the passage — "Think of this sentence," he ordered him-

247

self, "now, the next and the next — now collect the books, now write up the difficult words on the board, now ask for their meanings — soon the bell will go and the lesson will be over. Nothing exists for you except the next necessary action."

"Not so hot after all," said Doreen at the end of the morning. "Looks as if old Creep Stacey's got no bloody eye for art."

"Oh, fuck it," said Marcia.

"Watcher doin' tonight? Goin' home?"

"You must be kidding, my Mum's got her new bloke there, or she'll be out with him and not back till morning."

"Where you goin' then?"

"What bloody business is it of yours?" said Marcia, pushing her way through the crowd.

"What the hell's got her?" asked Tracey.

"*She* won't be home till the morning either, if I know her," said Doreen.

"She got a Dad?" enquired one of the others. "My Dad'd bloody well murder me if I didn't show up."

"Never had none as far as I know," said Doreen.

Luckily it was a Friday, the day when the afternoon was supposed to be given over to organized games and crafts, so Aubrey was free. He had intended a visit to the British Museum to look up some fresh data on the lately neglected hero of his novel, but now his one wish was to get drunk as soon and as thoroughly as possible. He reached home, unaware of the journey or of anything but the goal ahead, but before he could start on his drinking bout there was one thing that had to be done. He took out of his pocket the crushed ball of paper that was Marcia's drawing. This must be destroyed at once. In feeling for some matches in another pocket to set it on fire, he came across the little volume of Coleridge where he had thrust it on the previous day, and recalled how he had looked forward to sharing its glory with Hassan. A wave of love and loss swept over him and he threw the book across the room. By late afternoon he was lying on his bed in the desired state.

Something wonderful had happened to Harriet that day at school. It wasn't that Miss Johnson had said "good" after her piano lesson which made her feel powerful and good, (she had been learning nearly a year now and Miss Johnson not infrequently praised her), but this time she had added; "I think you already manage the little Mozart piece almost well enough to be able to play it at the end of term Christmas concert."

"Do you mean the big one when everyone comes?" asked Harriet incredulously. She had heard this event talked about with awe.

"Yes, would you like that?" asked Miss Johnson.

"I don't know," said Harriet, "I think I *would*. Mothers and fathers come, don't they?"

"Oh yes," said Miss Johnson, "especially the ones whose children are playing, we keep special seats in front for them. It's great fun. Now, just run through the sonatina again."

This time the notes seemed to play themselves, Harriet's fingers didn't have to find them on the keyboard at all. She loved this piece, the little twinkles that Mozart had put in here and there always reminded her of the way the stars twinkled and flashed at her through her window on clear nights.

When she had finished Miss Johnson said "That is really very nice indeed, Harriet, you can tell your mother now that you will certainly be playing at the concert. Of course she'll get a proper invitation soon."

At the end of the afternoon Harriet ran all the way home. She was early. Mrs Sanderson let her in but was on the point of going out to visit a friend, Andrew was not at

home and Margot too was not yet back, and there was no
sound from the basement either; not that Harriet would
have felt like telling Miss Cook her great news, the
murder of the kittens was too recent a tragedy. The whole
big house seemed empty and silent. Well, there was
always the doll's house family. She knew she wasn't
supposed to go into Mrs Sanderson's room except on
Saturdays but now she had to. Harriet Royce, alias
Wilhelmina Rose, *must* tell her mother and father she was
playing in the school concert. They clapped their hands
for joy. Harriet thought she had better not stay long with
them in case Mrs Sanderson came back and found her
there and was cross. She gave every room in the little
Lotus House a loving happy glance before she shut it up,
and seeing the grandfather on his bed upstairs made her
wonder if perhaps the big house wasn't quite empty after
all, for Mr Stacey might be at home and she could tell her
news to him. She had never been up to the attic floor
before but the need to communicate was too great for
shyness.

When she reached the top landing she thought she
heard a noise coming from the back room and she
knocked on the door. No one answered so she opened the
door and looked in. The room smelt very queer. She took
a step inside and saw that Mr Stacey *was* there. He was
lying on his bed with his eyes shut. This did not surprise
her for, although part of her knew quite well that he was
not the doll's house grandfather on his bed in the top
room of the little house, any more than Miss Cook was
'Cooksie' in the kitchen; yet as she had felt a compelling
need to identify the doll's house parents with her own
parents, and their dolly daughter with herself, the others
had to follow suit: so it seemed somehow natural for the
top-floor gentleman to be on his bed in the day time. And
now, disturbed by her knocking and entry, Aubrey
opened his eyes and saw a girl in a school uniform

standing inside his room and gazing at him, and all at once the rage and disgust he had been suppressing for so long took over.

He stretched out his hand and beckoned to Harriet. "Come over here," he whispered. The whisper sounded hoarse and strange and his hand was trembling. This, and the fact that he did not ask her what she wanted but seemed to have been waiting for her, frightened Harriet, she did not know why. But all the same his eyes were so compelling that she took a step or two towards him.

Man and child both stared at each other as if mesmerized. It had been a grey, sultry day of low cloud, but now the setting sun suddenly blazed out, and threw the shadow of the old nursery bars across the white coverlet of Aubrey's bed — his gaze deflected on them for a minute, and at once, as if released, Harriet called out, "No, no!" Aubrey's arm dropped. "Go away," he shouted, "go away at once," and Harriet turned and went.

After she had gone Aubrey staggered over to his basin and was very sick, then he lay down again and fell into a series of half-waking nightmares. He was always conscious of being in his room and lying on his bed, but from a corner of the room came the sound of his own voice chanting relentlessly and monotonously the *Rime of the Ancient Mariner*. Presently there seemed to be a huge white bird flying round and round the ceiling and beating against the window, trying to escape. He knew at once it was the albatross and that soon he would be forced to kill it. More horrible still, as it flew it turned a child's face towards him — Hassan's, then Harriet's as she had looked at him from the door — but then, before he had even fired the inescapable shot, the body of the bird began to disintegrate and dissolve and the room was full of white feathers, cold feathers, snowflakes falling upon his bed and heaping themselves upon him. And now the voice from the corner changed to his mother's reading aloud from Hans Andersen. "In the midst of the empty endless hall of snow was a frozen lake and in the centre of this lake sat the Snow Queen when she was at home. Little Kay was quite blue with cold and his heart was already a lump of ice."

This can't be a dream, thought Aubrey, *or I could not remember the words*, yet he knew that it was his mother who was the Ice Queen and he was little Kay. He felt very cold — he was lying uncovered and it was now night and the room was full of a white light, so that the shadow of the nursery bars still showed. He pulled the bedclothes over himself and another verse of Coleridge's mighty poem quoted itself to him:

"The moving moon went up the sky and nowhere did abide,

Softly she was going up and a star or two beside."
Warmth began to steal over him and he drowsed off once more and again a voice was speaking. This time it was Mrs Sanderson showing him the room. "This was the old night nursery. I have slept here many a time long ago — it still seems to me the safest place in the world."

After this he awoke thoroughly, got up and undressed and washed. The little volume of Coleridge lay on the floor in the corner where he had tossed it. He picked it up and replaced it carefully on his shelves. Then, knowing himself for the first time capable of both crime and redemption, he lay down and slept, this time deeply and dreamlessly, till late morning.

CHAPTER NINE

ON THE MORNING of the concert, Harriet woke to see an unclouded square of pale wintry blue through her window. She was glad, not that it mattered all that much for a concert if the sun were shining, but grey skies and rain would not have felt right. She was too excited to eat her breakfast. Andrew, who was anxious over the outcome of an experiment, had gone off early to his laboratory and Margot was hastily looking over her post. She always felt slightly aggrieved when Andrew left the house first and she had everything to see to, including getting Harriet off for school.

"What's the matter with you?" she said, becoming aware of the untouched food. "You've just messed about with your egg — I hate waste."

"It's because of the concert," said Harriet.

"Oh, I'd forgotten, it's today, is it?"

"But you're coming?" said Harriet, suddenly consumed with anxiety.

"Yes, of course," said Margot, "what time is it?"

The time was engraved on Harriet's heart, it was also on the invitation card which she had proudly brought home some time ago and which now lay among the pile of papers which Margot kept in a fruit bowl on her desk, but she was glad her mother had asked so that she could tell her once again. "It begins at half-past two and performers' parents are having the first two rows kept for them."

"What a godless hour," said Margot. "Well, if you won't eat a proper breakfast you won't, I suppose, so hurry up now and be off."

"You won't be late?" Harriet couldn't help asking.

"Don't fuss, I'm not Andrew," said Margot.

During that morning she had a phone call from a young sculptor, Crispin Keylock, whose work they were showing at her shop.

"It's awfully short notice but could you possibly lunch with me today? I'm feeling good this morning — I've just finished a presentation portrait bust and want to celebrate, and I'm off tomorrow to France, which makes too long a gap before I see you again."

Margot hesitated. "That would be lovely, but I've got to be at my daughter's school concert by 2.30," she said.

"How ghastly for you, but how admirable. We'll make it early then, shall we? I'll fetch you at noon." The lunch *was* early but it was also absorbing and delightful, and when Margot thought to look at her watch it was already nearly 3 o'clock.

"You should have reminded me," she said.

"You could hardly expect that, I'm human after all," he replied, "and now, as I suppose you've got the afternoon off, what about that new film at the Curzon?"

While watching the film Margot managed to stifle any compunction as to the concert, but when she was driving home afterwards she felt the need to justify herself. "She'll soon get over it. I'll take her out at the weekend if I'm free, anyway she may even have been relieved, playing in front of one's family Andrew always said is an ordeal worse than playing to strangers, she's probably done much better without me."

Harriet had spent the morning in a daze but it did not seem to matter, for allowances were made. She played

254

her piece once through again to Miss Johnson, who said it went very well. At dinner time she found she was suddenly very hungry. Then there was an interminable period of doing nothing in particular, until at last it was time to watch for the parents and friends to arrive.

"Oh, there's Mummy and Dad," called out Susan Phillips, who was playing a recorder solo just before Harriet. Then more and more mums and dads arrived and were hailed with joy.

"My mother is more pretty and wonderful than any of them," said Harriet to herself. "When she comes everyone will look at her, they always do. Miss Johnson said I played well this morning and I shall play better this afternoon and everyone will clap me and Mummy will clap too."

Presently she began to be anxious, the front rows of reserved seats were filling up fast. They all had little tickets on them and Harriet knew where Margot's seat was, towards the centre of the second row. Soon it was the only empty one and she felt, inside her, something ticking away very quickly. Then Miss Johnson herded them all together into the little classroom at the back of the big hall and the concert began. There was Barbara and Tessa's duet, and next Susan's solo, and then it was Harriet's turn. As she crossed the stage to the piano she could see that there was still one empty seat where her mother should have been. She sat down and began to play, but her fingers felt like heavy lumps and she couldn't see the music properly, everything was blurred. She hadn't really needed the music either, because she could play the piece perfectly well without, but now she couldn't remember it at all. She stumbled on to the end and the audience clapped kindly and loudly, though she did not hear them.

"Why, Harriet," said Miss Johnson, "you must learn not to give way to stage fright so badly as that!" and then, looking at her more closely, she added: "Never mind, it

255

was a pity, but it can't be helped now."

Harriet said nothing. No one saw her slip away, they were all too busy. She did not ask for leave to go home and no one stopped her. When she got there she found Andrew in the sitting-room, immersed and frowning over his papers.

"Where's Margot?" said Harriet. Although when she had been playing she had had to blink and blink away her tears, now she did not want to cry any more.

"Hasn't come home yet," said Andrew, not looking up, "and look here, be a good Harriet and don't bother just now, will you?"

She went through the little kitchen that led to the landing. By the kitchen door Margot, with her usual efficiency, had put up a rack to hold all the household tools. Harriet took the hammer from its place and went downstairs again. Presently Mrs Sanderson, coming in from a visit, saw that her bedroom door was open and heard an odd sound of splintering wood.

Burglars, she thought at once, and went intrepidly to confront them. What she saw was Harriet hacking Selina's doll's house to pieces.

"Harriet!" she shouted.

Harriet dropped the hammer in the middle of the wreckage and turned to face her.

"It's the bomb!" she cried in a curious shrill voice, "it's the bomb and it's killed them all dead!" Then she burst into sobs and rushed past Letty out of the room.

Aubrey Stacey was coming home and just approaching the gate when he saw Harriet running towards him. On seeing him, she swerved away off the path into the road straight in front of an oncoming tradesman's van. The van pulled up with a screech of brakes but it had caught the child, who fell backwards against the curb. Aubrey ran forward as the driver of the van was getting out. He looked very pale.

"You saw it, sir," he said, "I hadn't a chance of missing her."

"Yes," said Aubrey, "it wasn't your fault."

"What happened to the other child?" asked the man.

"There wasn't another child that I could see," said Aubrey.

The man looked puzzled. "I saw her," he said, "she caught at this one to pull her back – if it hadn't been for her, I'd have gone right over her."

"Well, this isn't the time to argue," said Aubrey kneeling down by Harriet. "She's breathing all right, stay here. I must go and phone for a doctor and an ambulance," and he rushed into the house.

Mrs Sanderson was still standing in her room gazing at the wreck of the doll's house when she heard Aubrey calling for her. After that it was all hurry and confusion, phone calls and interviews with the doctor and the police. Aubrey bore witness to the fact that the van driver was not to blame. He stuck to his story of another little girl but she was never traced. Harriet lay in a coma at the hospital. She had a broken leg but that was not serious, the doctor, however, could not yet pronounce on the extent of injury to her head.

At the Lotus House where she had been so unobtrusive, so shadowy a little presence, she was now inescapably important. All, in various degrees felt guilty, though each kept this to themselves. Letty blamed herself for shirking the implications of those overheard doll's house conversations; could she have helped without appearing interfering in what was not her business? She did not know, but she had not tried; and how could she have not followed a desperate sobbing child out of the house! Aubrey Stacey believed that Harriet, whom he had scarcely seen since she had visited his room, had swerved into the road to avoid him. Janet Cook unwillingly recalled the scene in the garden about the kittens. *I suppose it wouldn't have hurt to have kept one*, she thought. Andrew cursed himself for not having remembered that it had been the day of the concert and that Harriet ought not have have been coming home at that hour, nor Margot to have been at work, and why did he have to tell the child to go away — she was never any real nuisance.

But what Margot felt was the absence of feeling. She had refused to discuss the concert with Andrew. "I had an expected engagement crop up," she said, "and when it was over it was too late."

Andrew, taking it for granted that it was a business matter she could not have avoided, or thought she could not, refrained from pressing her or reproaching her in any way. To judge others was almost pathologically alien to him; besides he imagined with sympathy that she must be remorselessly judging herself. They drove to the hospital every day and sat by Harriet for a short while. A week after the accident there was little or no change; she sometimes moaned and clutched her hands but did not open her eyes or show any consciousness of their presence. One day as they got up to go, Margot saw Andrew lean over and very gently put back a strand of the straight heavy hair from the child's forehead. A sudden strange pang of envy consumed her. "He knows how to love, but I don't, I never have."

During that troubled week everyone concerned knew a part, but not the whole truth about the accident. Miss Johnson, who assumed it had happened on the way back from the school, believed that upset by the fiasco of her performing at the concert, the child had been terribly heedless of the traffic. Aubrey, unaware of why she was rushing from the house, rightly guessed she had dashed into the road to avoid him, though he was wrong in her reasons for so doing — she would have done so whoever it had been.

Miss Cook's theory was that Harriet must have been escaping from an attack by one of those dreadful estate boys. Andrew and Margot both suspected that her mother's failure to turn up at the concert was somehow responsible, but they were ignorant as to the destruction of the doll's house. Letty, only too conscious of this, was anxious to keep it secret. Harriet's bomb had done its work thoroughly: there was no possibility of repair. Letty found a few little pots and pans and two bent fireplaces among the debris. The bodies of Mr and Mrs Golightly Royce, the grandfather and Cooksie looked as if they had been stamped upon: only Wilhelmina Rose Harriet had escaped all injury. She was found under a chair where she had fallen clear of the house. Letty had picked her up and laid her away in her handkerchief drawer. She had then consigned the wreckage to the dustbin sack, she could not bear to look at it. She trusted that Dian with her habitual lack of interest in objects above the floor level, would not comment on the doll's house's disappearance. Ignorant on her part of the fiasco of the concert, she wondered continually what could have caused this whole disastrous crisis.

In the days that followed she felt wretchedly depressed. Harriet's bomb seemed to have shattered not only the doll's house but much else. It was time to stop playing Happy Families, she thought, and to put away the useless cards. The beloved image of the Lotus House was itself menaced, it was after all no more now than a lodging for five unhappy people — no, six counting herself. The darker symbolism of its name struck her for the first time — the Lotus House — the house of delusive dreams. Were all the memories she had cherished only the bitter-sweet myth of childhood? *Stop telling your stories, Selina, stop, stop. Through what struggles and suffering may you and all your family have had to pass to the final defeat. "We'll be coming back," you said, but you never came back.*

She was alone in her sitting-room; the short winter daylight was fading and the fire had sunk to a dull glow, but she did not move, but sat on in the darkness. At last she got up to put on the light. "The past is gone now beyond recall," she said, speaking aloud as if addressing the great empty room. But the dark bulk of the house she felt all around her seemed to answer defiantly, "Yet the past is here now, beyond oblivion." As she drew the long curtains, a child's laugh sounded faintly from the dark garden. *The children are playing late on the estate,* she thought, *their mothers let them stay out in the cold and dark at all hours nowadays.*

Ten days after the accident Harriet opened her eyes for the first time. There was no one at hand but a nurse, who hearing a slight movement bent at once over the bed. Harriet was staring into space with an unmistakable look of horror, she murmured something almost indistinguishable and shut her eyes again.

"She spoke, you say — did you hear what she said?" asked the doctor.

"I'm not sure," said the nurse, "but it sounded like: 'I've killed them all dead'."

"A nightmare," said the doctor, "those wretched TV films all about murders, and children *will* watch them. We must get her mother here at once. Meanwhile, stop with her, nurse, hold her hand and talk to her, anything soothing that comes into your head."

It was lucky that this particular nurse had younger brothers and sisters and possessed a fund of nursery rhymes and songs, for she had gone through many before Margot arrived.

"Doctor says, hold her hand and comfort her by repeating anything she used to hear from you when she was a baby, but you'll know what is best to do better than I can tell you, Mrs Royce."

Margot took the small limp hand in hers but she

experienced nothing but the repulsion that any illness always produced in her and she could not think of anything at all to say. The nurse, passing and repassing, glanced at her in surprise and Margot, always acutely aware of others' reactions towards herself, felt both resentful and embarrassed.

Yet her touch seemed to reach through to Harriet after a little while, for she opened her eyes again and this time, seeing her mother sitting by her, she said quite clearly with a look of intense joy and relief, "Oh, I thought I had killed you dead."

"Darling, what nonsense," said Margot, "you've been having a horrid dream."

Then she drifted off once more, but presently she spoke again. "Where am I?" she asked.

"You're in hospital, there was an accident, you got knocked down by a van, but you'll soon be well again now, so don't worry and don't have any more silly dreams." Harriet gave her mother a long pleased look and then with a small sigh of contentment she dropped off into a natural sleep.

Andrew came in later and she woke again.

"I can't move my leg," Harriet confided to him in a whisper. She seemed puzzled rather than alarmed.

"You've broken it," said Andrew cheerfully. "Not to worry, legs mend again quite easily, especially when they are young ones."

But Harriet frowned. Something seemed to be troubling her again.

"I broke all their legs," she whispered. "I know it wasn't really you and Margot now, but I broke everything."

"Well, I shouldn't worry about that," said Andrew firmly. "She seems still to be bothered with bad dreams," he told the nurse.

"I expect it's the leg paining her, but she's doing fine.

Doctor's pleased with her."

"Harriet wants to see you, Mrs Sanderson," said Margot a few days later, "she seems to have something on her mind about your doll's house. We think it's from a nightmare she had when she was coming round from the coma. Do you think you could fit in a visit soon, it would be so kind?"

"Of course," said Letty, "I was only waiting till you thought it advisable for visitors other than you and Mr Royce."

Before leaving for the hospital, Letty took Wilhelmina Rose Harriet out of her drawer and slipped her into her bag.

"I remember properly now," said Harriet as soon as the nurse had left them alone together. "I didn't at first. I smashed the little house as well as the people. I'm so sorry." Tears began to roll down her cheeks. "Is *everyone* killed?"

"Not everyone," said Letty. She fished in her bag and brought out Wilhelmina Rose Harriet and laid her on the bed. Harriet clutched her with both hands but the tears came faster than ever.

"Why, whatever is the matter?" said Nurse Hutchinson appearing again. "We never cry, not even when our leg hurts." She turned a reproachful eye on poor Letty. "We're *such* a good girl *always*." She mopped away the tears. "I think she's had enough of visitors for today," she said rather severely.

Letty kissed Harriet's damp cheeks and went away as she was told but, in spite of the nurse, she suspected that those tears were not a bad thing.

"Where did that funny little doll come from?" asked Margot that same evening.

"Mrs Sanderson brought her," said Harriet.

"I should have thought she would have suspected you were too old to play with dolls," said Margot.

"I shan't play with her," said Harriet.

"Well, she'll do as a mascot, I suppose," said Margot.

"What's a mascot?" enquired Harriet the next day of her never-failing encyclopaedia.

"Something to bring you good luck," said Andrew.

Harriet smiled.

A time came when the doctor said "I think you can look forward to having Harriet at home soon, Mrs Royce. Of course she'll need nursing and careful treatment for some time yet, but we don't want to hospitalize her longer than necessary. She could come to you in about another week, I should think."

Margot responded after a very slight hesitation and not with quite the eagerness he had expected, but he thought her a delightful woman and sensible too, quite free from that neurotic fussiness he often met with in mothers.

"Andrew," said Margot that evening, "the doctor says Harriet can leave the hospital next week."

"Really!" exclaimed Andrew, "That's good."

"I suppose she'd better go to the guest-room."

"Of course, her own's much too small."

"She'll need a lot of care for some time," he said.

"Well, you'll be able to get leave, I'm sure," said Andrew, "you're too valuable for them to make any fuss, especially in these circumstances."

There was a silence, then Margot said, "It's no use, Andrew, I can't face it, I'm the world's worst nurse, I loathe it and it simply wouldn't work. She'd do better in a convalescent home somewhere."

This time it was Andrew's turn to be silent.

"I know what you're thinking," burst out Margot at last, "that I ought to have gone to that bloody concert and that at least now I ought to be able to look after my own child, but how was I to know she'd take it like that, and am I responsible for that van being there just at that moment?"

"You've never let yourself realize how she adores you," said Andrew.

"Yes, I have," exclaimed Margot, "and it always exasperates me, it did with Dick, too, and with others. Oh, Andrew," and suddenly she sounded humble and defenceless, "the truth is I don't know how to love or be loved."

Andrew got up and came over to her. He disliked emotional scenes and was certainly not used to them from Margot, and words seemed to him useless. He suspected that what she said was true and yet he had never liked her so much before. He put an arm round her and pressed her gently to him. After a while as they stood there he said "Harriet must come home here, you know that really, don't you? We'll manage all right somehow, you'll see."

But he did not quite see until astonishingly Miss Cook came to their rescue. She was astonished herself. She had been upset of course by the accident, well, that was natural, a child under the same roof, anyone would be. But unwarrantably, yes, she told herself, quite unwarrantably, she was still haunted by her last encounter with Harriet which would not have bothered her at all, she felt, had it not been for the accident, but there it was. Dian had told her that Harriet was coming home soon.

"Mrs Royce, she wanted to know if I could spare her some extra time; well, I'm that sorry but I can't, it would mean letting down my other ladies, see — not used to having the child on her hands all day and don't look forward to it, I can tell you."

Janet Cook thought about this for some time. She had had very little experience of children but she supposed she could help look after a little girl as well as anyone else if she gave her mind to it. So one afternoon that week Andrew answered a knock on the door and found Miss Cook on the threshold. He ushered her into the sitting-room; she had never been there before and looked around with interest.

Striking, she thought, *but not at all pretty — that picture, just squares of black and red, not worth framing, I'd say, and that huge silver lamp hanging on a chain like something out of a church, not proper in a room.* And then she saw Crispin Keylock's carved elongated female nude and decided she did not like the room at all. The thought darted into her mind, rather shocking her, that it, like Doris' lounge, might be improved by some of Luke's matchboxes.

"What can I do for you, Miss Cook?" enquired Andrew politely, for she had been so busy looking round that she had not spoken yet.

"Well, it's like this, Dr Royce," she said, "I hear that little Harriet is coming home soon, and if Mrs Royce wants a hand with looking after her, amusing her and so forth, and I've done a bit of nursing too in my time, I'd be glad to help. Neighbours should be neighbourly, you know." Could this be her mother's daughter speaking thus? Most unlikely, but so it was, and when all was said and done really it was those five little drowned kitten corpses that were responsible.

Miss Cook's offer was gratefully accepted and Letty also promised help, so Margot was able to keep her job going and Harriet, in due course, came home.

CHAPTER TEN

AT FIRST ALL went well. Harriet was happier now than at any period she could remember. She was a different Harriet, an important person, and yet at the same time someone for whom nothing was important. Time no longer mattered, nor lessons, nor what she said or what she didn't say. The past didn't matter, in fact she didn't seem to remember the events that led up to her accident at all clearly — it was like a bad dream, though it seemed somehow important to keep the little doll's house girl within reach. People sent this Harriet "Get Well" cards, which stood in a row on the mantelpiece opposite the spare-room bed in which she lay in splendour and gazed at them. There was one from Mrs Campbell and Lucy and Rebecca, and one from Squinty and one from Miss Johnson, and a large beautiful one of birds and flowers and rabbits signed by all her class, including Ben, in his big bold hand. Then there were presents, chocolates from Mr Stacey, a manicure set from Dian which gave her great satisfaction, it was the first really grown-up present she had ever had. Miss Cook brought her a pink geranium in a pot and Andrew a jigsaw called "Farmyard Friends". Mrs Sanderson read stories to her and Miss Cook played games with her. Letty had wondered how Harriet would receive the ministrations of a murderess, but the drowning of the kittens also was now part of the bad dream;

266

besides Harriet, who heard the Bible read at school assembly and sometimes listened, remembered that Jesus had said God loves sparrows, and if He loved them, they must go to Heaven, and if sparrows, surely kittens, where presumably they get on well together. Also, because she was now an important person, Maisie was allowed to stay on her bed where, with the unerring instinct of a cat for comfort, she had located Harriet the day after she had returned from hospital, and Maisie was obviously now thoroughly contented and prosperous. Best of all, her mother spent the last waking hours of every day with Harriet. These periods however, were an increasing strain on Margot. She felt both inadequate and bored.

"How can any adult communicate with children? We live in different worlds," and she marvelled irritably at the way others seemed to bridge this gap.

"How have you been today, darling? How is the leg feeling?"

"Better, thank you." Then, what else was there to say? She fell back upon continuing the stories that Mrs Sanderson had been reading. Like everything else about Margot, her voice was attractive, low and clear, but she read aloud to Harriet badly, partly because she was not in the least interested in what she was reading, often indeed thinking her own thoughts simultaneously, and partly, because as if by doing so she could shorten the hour, she read very fast. But none of this mattered to Harriet, she knew Mrs Sanderson would read it all over again the next day. She was quite content to lie there and look at her mother and listen to the sound of her voice. But sometimes she sensed the impatience behind the reading and, thinking Margot was tired after her day's work, she would pretend to be asleep. Her mother would shut the book and go quietly away. "She doesn't kiss me goodnight because she's afraid of waking me, and when I'm awake she doesn't because we don't, but when I'm fast asleep she does."

But this halcyon period came to an end and before the geranium flower had withered or the "Get Well" cards had begun to curl at the edges, the indulgent reactions to "our little invalid", as Miss Cook always called her, showed signs of strain. By the time that Harriet was well enough to be dressed and move around with the aid of crutches, the atmosphere had changed. She had reached that stage of convalesence which is apt to be more trying than actual illness.

What a pity we are not characters in the kind of book I was given to read by my aunts long ago, thought Letty Sanderson, 'What Katy did' *and* 'The Daisy Chain', *for instance. Then Harriet would be the little Angel in the House and all of us would be ennobled by her misfortune.* But it wasn't like that for, with returning health, Harriet felt frustrated and fretful and actually her leg hurt her more now she was trying to use it. At the same time the patience of the grown-ups was becoming frayed. Miss Cook caught her cheating at Ludo one afternoon and she could not explain that it was because she felt too tired to finish the game.

"I don't play with little girls who cheat," said Janet Cook.

Harriet would not say she was sorry, so Janet stumped away downstairs. She was sometimes left to herself now for what seemed a long time — while she was in bed the hours had melted into one another, for she had slept so much.

"Now you can be in the sitting-room, Harriet, you can look at TV again — isn't that nice?"

But she didn't want to, she didn't want to do anything that she could do, only the things she couldn't do. She tried playing the piano one day but it had turned into an enemy. Andrew found her crouched over it in tears.

"It hates me, it won't do a thing I want," she sobbed.

"It's too soon, Harriet, it's made your head bad, you

268

mustn't try yet a while, promise."

And Maisie was banished from the flat. "I can't have that cat about any longer," said Margot, "she leaves her hairs all over the place and she's clawed the chairs."

Margot felt she needed a holiday badly. The Christmas break had been ruined by Harriet's accident. Now spring was in the air, always a time of restlessness. Crispin Keylock, whom she had been seeing fairly frequently, had suggested that she and Andrew might join him and his wife for two weeks trip up the Nile in April. She was attracted to the idea for it was less ordinary than Spain or Italy or Greece, where everybody went nowadays. Crispin's wife, whom she had met once or twice, had seemed an unassuming little creature, unlikely to be a nuisance to Andrew. Had Harriet been quite well there would have been no problems. Mrs Campbell ran a holiday camp at Easter and in the summer in some suitable country or seaside resort where Queensmead's or other parents could park their young, but the child was still suffering from headaches and her leg was not yet fully serviceable.

"You go," said Andrew, "I'll take some leave at home and look after the infant. I'm not all that keen on Egypt, I prefer a cold climate."

"Oh no," exclaimed Margot, though eagerly, "I can't let you do that."

"Nonsense, I'm not under your orders, my girl!."

"Crispin will be disappointed if you don't come."

"You know he won't give a damn — come to think of it, I'm not sure I'd care for his company for two whole weeks."

"Why, don't you like him?" asked Margot curiously.

"I don't think he's a serious artist."

It wasn't the answer she had expected.

"What *do* you mean? His sculptures fetch very good prices."

"I dare say."

"Anyway, you're not qualified to judge."

"True enough. It doesn't matter anyway. You go and do your Cleopatra stuff and enjoy yourself, don't worry about me."

"You won't worry about *me*, I suppose," said Margot slowly, "I might have an affair with Crispin."

"Go ahead then," said Andrew, "God knows there's no value in our relationship, or any, that isn't free." He paused and then added, as if making a discovery —

"Come to think of it, God does know — of course that's why Adam had to fall."

"What *are* you talking about?" said Margot crossly, "Don't pretend you believe in God."

Andrew laughed. "Now I *have* shocked you!" He turned round on the piano stool upon which he was sitting and struck some bars of the Bach fugue that happened to be on the stand. Margot interrupted him.

"You never take me seriously. Why can't you answer me?"

"Don't I?" said Andrew, "I'm sorry, I meant this for an answer."

But Margot then and there decided that she certainly would go on the cruise and also amuse herself with Crispin if she felt like it. She needed a complete relaxation after all the strain of Harriet's illness.

One of Margot's charms was that she always looked so fresh with a crisp elegance that yet managed to seem perfectly natural. Letty Sanderson, coming in one morning from the garden where she had been picking the March daffodils, saw her standing in the hall with a letter which she had just taken from the postman and was obviously intent on reading immediately. She was wearing a pink and grey striped dress of some soft woollen material with a wide skirt gathered in at the waist by a matching pink belt, and she had a string of pale corals wound several times round her neck. The spring sunlight caught at the gold of the clasp and the buckle of the belt and at her shining hair. Letty found herself wishing she could keep her there, standing beside the curving white staircase beneath the graceful arch of the Lotus House hall. But then she looked up — her lovely eyes were sparkling and she was smiling to herself before she saw Letty, and though all she said then was a conventional greeting, it sounded like poetry.

"Really," said Letty to herself, "she's too delicious. How difficult life must be for her."

The letter Margot had been reading was from Crispin Keylock, giving details of the cruise and expressing extreme delight in the prospect of her company. She had been conscious lately of a longing to bask once again in the warmth and excitement of admiration and desire, not of course of the grovelling kind, but there was an undoubted austerity in living with Andrew. She was certainly due for a change.

When Harriet heard that her mother was going away and far away too, she was curiously upset, for although she saw little of her, she was yet the pivot upon which her world turned.

"Andrew will look after you," she was told.

"But what shall we do?" she asked Andrew disconsolately on the first evening after Margot's departure.

"Listen to things and go to places," he said, an answer which filled her with both curiosity and apprehension.

"What things and what places?" she asked.

"Wait and see," said Andrew, "I don't like talking while I'm eating" — they were at supper — "but we can begin now." He put on a record of Vivaldi which made a cheerful noise until they had finished.

"That low-down part that goes on and on the same is like Margot reading aloud," remarked Harriet thoughtfully.

Andrew laughed. "She wouldn't thank you for that," he

said, "but it's true enough."

Harriet looked shocked. "Oh, I didn't mean it wasn't nice," she said.

"It's nice in this bit of music, but it's not a nice way to read aloud. Don't think it's a crime to admit that Margot can't do everything perfectly or even very well. Music can be perfect, people can't."

Harriet frowned in the effort to absorb this.

"But it's people who make the music, that's funny!" Andrew looked at her appreciatively. "You're right, it's divinely funny. Actually there's a lot of funniness around, and don't forget your mother's part of it."

"*Is* she?" said Harriet frowning even harder.

In the days that followed Andrew quite often took her out somewhere in the car. Sometimes they even went as far as the sea. Once they went to a lunch-time concert in London and ate sandwiches afterards in St James' Park and fed the ducks. Except that he made her go to bed early and wash properly and do her exercises, Andrew treated Harriet as an equal, which was a new experience. She had never before felt herself the equal of anyone except perhaps Squinty. She did not always understand all the words he used nor exactly what he meant, but this did not matter. She had moved back to her own little bedroom now and she would lie and look up at her sky and think about what they had done and talked about during the day.

Sometimes in the evenings Andrew would say "Let's be silly," and they were — very silly. Letty Sanderson used to hear them laughing. She remarked on it once when she took a note up to Andrew which had been left for him.

"I like to hear it," she said. "In the old days there always seemed to be laughter about this house."

"I used to hear people laughing," said Harriet unexpectedly, "when I was in the guest-room before I could get up."

"You must have been dreaming," said Andrew.

"Yes," agreed Harriet, "I was rather mixed up but it was nice."

Meanwhile Margot was not feeling at all like laughing. She had supposed that the East would hold enchantment, the days beguiling her with exotic sights, sounds and scents, the velvet nights full of huge stars. Instead she found days of dust and dirt, and nights full of huge mosquitoes. The boat, boarded at Cairo, was the first disappointment. It was uncomfortably old-fashioned, no air-conditioning, verging on tawdriness, undeniably smelly and the few single cabins were the least supportable. Hers, she discovered, was the noisiest and had a broken fan, but it took Margot only one day to subjugate a fellow single-cabin passenger. This was a middle-aged, kind, dehydrated American lady, very vulnerable to charm.

"My little girl has been desperately ill," confided Margot to her as they lay beside each other in their deck chairs, "and I'm ashamed to say that I am completely worn out by nursing her, so my husband insisted on this trip — oh yes, she is quite recovered by now, thank you, but I'm afraid I'm not too good about heat. They said April would be all right — it's my cabin, you see, isn't yours quite terrible too?"

It proved much less so, bigger and with a fan that worked. "It's just too bad, your little girl having been so sick. I guess I'm first cousin to a salamander, heat never seems to trouble me. Now, Margot — I may call you Margot, mayn't I? and I'm Dimity — why shouldn't we change cabins? I've not properly unpacked — now don't say 'no'."

"Oh, but I must," said Margot, "I couldn't possibly let you." But she found it was possible after all.

It had been a relief to get away from Cairo, which

Margot thought hideous, noisy and full of beggars, but it seemed there was no more to be seen before Luxor, which would take five days to reach, during which time there was nothing to do but sit about on the deck watching the long endless river banks slip slowly by and eat the rather unappetizing food which apparently, nostalgically trying to ape the menus of a Victorian schoolroom, consisted of too much meat, too few vegetables, and milk puddings. "Don't touch the salads," warned Miss Benson, the experienced BBC producer who sat at their table.

The English-speaking party consisted of Dimity and her married sister and husband — the sister, Holly, was slightly larger and both wore enormous pale-rimmed spectacles which made them look like a pair of starved owls. There were, besides, an elderly retired Civil Servant closely resembling Alec Guinness, with a small waspish French wife, two knowledgeable school teachers, Crispin and his wife Prue. The rest of the tourists were Germans and Dutch who kept to themselves.

The weather was excessively hot, unusually so they were assured. The slow motion of the boat, the unvarying light and landscape, produced in Margot a sense of unreality as if she were viewing, or even herself part of, a monotonous film, and Crispin, who should have brought everything to life, was proving the second and more insidious disappointment. He had behaved as she had expected, the affair between them had developed as she had intended, but their love-making seemed disconcertingly irrelevant, as if he too were a degree removed from reality.

Then there was Prue — Margot had been disconcerted at first that Crispin, who had assured her that he could find someone to take Andrew's place to keep Prue amused, had apparently not bothered to do this, but she soon concluded that it had not really been necessary. Prue not only accepted the situation but seemed relieved by it.

"I bore him, you know, and it is so important for him not to be bored." Dimity took Prue under her wing and soon knew more about both her and Crispin than Margot had ever known or cared to know.

"She sure comes from one of your real old families, the kind that don't appreciate Art unless it's ancient and hung in their galleries, and they didn't care for her to take up with it. But she had money of her own and she quit, and she and he were studying together in London — but you sure know all this, Margot. Well, don't you agree it's a shame she's given it all up? She was doing fine, just loved painting flower pieces, I bet they were real pretty; he said so too, he said they were cute. That ought to obligate her to continue, shouldn't it? Because he must know. She could do some pretty views right now, I tell her."

What pretty views? thought Margot drearily. *Shaggy banana trees with bananas growing the wrong way up, repetitive palm trees and flat green strips of land backed by the ever-lasting sand.*

Prue didn't talk, she generally had a book for company. "It's too hot even to read, I think," said Margot. "What have you got there?"

"Nothing that matters," said Prue hastily.

"Prue enjoys Edwardian fiction," remarked Crispin. He made it sound like an addiction to dominoes. She was often inclined to be vague and unpunctual. "I can't think why you can't wear a watch like other people," said Crispin.

There was something in the way Prue used to look at him and the tone of his voice when he spoke to her that seemed familiar to Margot, but the train of thought was somehow distasteful and she did not pursue it. Her relationship with Crispin became less and less satisfactory. Her meetings with him in London had been accompanied by good food and drink, and generally diversified with some entertainment to follow, but now she found long stretches of talk with him more and more wearying. There was a central point in their conversation from which everything radiated and to which everything returned, and this was Crispin Keylock and not Margot Royce. She felt herself growing less charming and less charmed, and at length Crispin appeared to feel this too, for he turned more and more to others of their party and especially to Boone Cleveland, Dimity's brother-in-law. Boone was impressed to learn that Crispin Keylock was an avant-garde sculptor who had held successful exhibitions in London and Paris and whose portrait busts were beginning to be sought after.

"Tell me, Mr Keylock," he said one evening, "how can an ordinary guy like me get to appreciate what fellows like you are getting at? I just would like to support you but I want to know what I'm paying my money for."

Quick on the scent, Crispin braced himself to reply in his most professional vein.

"For myself," he said, "I feel I perform, as it were, a holding operation between the concept and the media. Don't you agree it is the job, to put it no higher, of 'fellows like myself', as you say, to establish the insightful on both points? Conceptually, you see, the public — if I may include you under that umbrella? but you have placed yourself there — "

"I sure did," agreed Boone Cleveland.

"Well, as you say, quite naturally and honestly, you do need us to mediate; after all, that's what the words imply when all's said and done."

Boone nodded.

"You have abstract emotion on the one hand," said Crispin warming up, "totally unacceptable, wouldn't you say? And yet utterly indispensable, and the ritual forms of aesthetic experience, including — one must absolutely these days strike out for the all-inclusive — the

276

Royal Academy for instance."

Boone clutched at the Royal Academy.

"A fine show," he said, "Holly and I visited it last time we were over."

"Well yes, the all-inclusive, as I was saying," continued Crispin, "and that does of course include both the Royal Academy and the public urinal via that vital participant, the *individual*. That's where portraiture comes in, so often a chat show these days as you must have noticed. But in my work, Mr Cleveland, I do see myself actually as an interviewer in what I consider as the great straight tradition on the box."

Boone Cleveland was visibly impressed, though not much elucidated.

"I'd sure like to see some of your work, Mr Keylock," he said.

"I think my wife has some photos with her some-where," said Crispin, "if you really would care to look at them."

The photographs were produced. Clipped to one of them was a laudatory review of an exhibition.

"Oh yes," said Crispin casually, "I'd forgotten that was there, unaccountably the critics this time did seem to see what I was after."

"Read it out, Boone," said Dimity, peering at the prints. "It's gotta help!"

Boone Cleveland read: " 'Crispin Keylock conveys the ominously indicative with a rare blend of nonchalance and holistic expertise suggesting that here at least we have an acceptable equivalent of Nouveau Beaujolais which has a lotta bottle and may well stand the test of time, specially in 'Portrait of a Taxpayer' and 'Mood No. twenty-one'. Eclecticism is by no means a pejorative phrase in the right hands. His skilful use of polystyrene and titanium to convey overtones of despair are especially successful.' "

"Well," exclaimed Dimity after a little pause, "isn't that fine!"

"Which is the Taxpayer, have you got one of him?" asked Holly.

"Yes," said Crispin, "you've got him there."

"Doesn't look too good to go to bed with," said Holly, "all that wire."

"Now, Holly!" reproved her husband. "We must have you over in the States, Mr Keylock," he continued, "I think I can promise you you'll be appreciated there, and I'd be proud to help you all I can."

"You know, I've a good mind to take him up on that," said Crispin to Margot afterwards, "it might not be at all a bad thing."

Margot agreed, but Andrew's dismissal of Crispin as "not a serious artist" recurred to her as his remarks often had a habit of doing, however irritating at the time. What was a serious artist anyway? Well, Boone Cleveland was willing to back Crispin, obviously differing from Andrew, and he was certainly beginning to make a name for himself, which was good for her art gallery, she supposed.

At last the boat reached Luxor and they disembarked and went by donkey carriages to the Temple of Karnak. Here Margot's sense of unreality intensified — the vast columns and statues diminished her almost to vanishing point. Awe invaded her like a dark cloud, blotting out all familiarities. She recovered a little at Tutankhamun's tomb, which was smaller and less impressive than she had expected, and where the garish paintings partially dispelled the awe. But the expeditions during the days that followed were filled with inexorable ruins. The Germans and Americans, bristling with note-books and cameras, asked endless questions of the incomprehensible Egyptian guides, and the dark steps, the subterranean tombs, affected Margot like a miasma. Before they reached Aswan she became ill. It was easy enough, Miss Benson had said, to pick up a bug, as everything unmentionable went into the river. She had bouts of sickness and diarrhoea. Cardboard figures of Crispin, Prue and Dimity hovered about her. Crispin brought a huge bunch of scarlet objects pretending to be flowers from which she tried to hide. She slept most of the time with a recurring nightmare that she saw herself at Karnak again, a minute figure running down an unending passage between the monotonous columns. Far away in front of her was a patch of mirage brightness, in the centre of which she seemed to glimpse the quivering image of a house — of the Lotus House — but she knew she would never reach it, and the pitch of horror came when she was forced to watch the tiny figure disintegrate into nothingness.

After two days the attack wore off and she struggled out very early in the morning to catch a breath of coolness and lay hidden in a corner on the deck. She had fallen half asleep again when the sound of her own name woke her immediately. She recognised the voices of the Civil Servant and his wife.

"I wonder how that pretty Mrs Royce is doing. They say she has been quite unwell. She should have a husband here to look after her."

"In more ways than one," said his wife.

"You mean that posturing sculptor fellow — yes, that's a pity, and there's the little wife too."

"You distress yourself unnecessarily, chérie — the wife was swallowed up long ago, she no longer exists, and as for the beautiful lady and the artist, that will not last long, they are too much of the same portmanteau, two beans in a row, how do you say it?"

"I say 'peas in a pod', my dear; but how do you make *that* out?"

"Both are *tout à fait égoistes*."

The voices faded away as they moved off, leaving

Margot surprised by the intensity of the anger that possessed her. She was not in the least like Crispin — the woman was a fool, not worth thinking about. But she continued to think about her furiously. It became absolutely necessary to refute her, and now she found herself unaccountably arguing the case with Andrew.

"All right, I give it to you about Crispin, but you must see that Frenchwoman's quite, quite wrong. I'm *always* aware of other people, you say too much so, *he's* only aware of himself, and look how he treats Prue." Suddenly the half-recognized familiarity in Crispin's tone as he spoke to his wife, and of her answering look, thrust itself once more into her consciousness — this time with greater clarity and she did not like the revelation at all. "That's utterly different," she said. But now the sun had crept round to her corner and she went back to her cabin.

They were nearing Aswan and it seemed hotter than ever, but at Aswan the cruise would be over. "My next holiday abroad will be among snow mountains," decided Margot. "Switzerland, I think, the cleanest and tidiest place I know."

At Aswan everybody else went to see more ruins in a felucca, but Margot drove through sandy poverty-stricken streets to a grotesquely grand hotel, where they were to spend the night and where, with a totally unexpected eagerness, she hoped to find some mail.

"I daresay you won't want letters and I daresay I shan't write," Andrew had said, "but you'd better leave an address in case." There was a letter but she saw with disappointment that it was addressed in Harriet's unformed script.

"Dear Margot," she read, "I can cook, Andrew says I do sossages and bacon very well. We put all the things back in the wrong places. Andrew says when the cat's away the mice do play. We went to a consert. Love and kisses, Harriet. P.T.O." Margot turned the page quickly, but there was only the briefest of postscripts. "Greetings, my serpent of old Nile, Harriet's fine. Andrew."

"Why does he call me a serpent?" said Margot, angry to find her eyes filling with tears of disappointment and self-pity, "The weakness still from that horrid attack, I suppose." She read Harriet's letter again, really, it was hardly worth sending. "He might at least have seen that she spelt it properly." But there was a new note in it quite unlike any letter she had had from Harriet before. *I hope the child's not being a bore*, she thought, *it sounds rather as if she is*.

Andrew, however, was not at all bored. Letty Sanderson thought the trouble he was taking over Harriet showed true kindness. Margot would have supposed him to be carrying out some kind of psychological experiment in his usual detached manner. It was neither of these. He was actually and unexpectedly simply enjoying himself, he was discovering the pleasure of communication. It was necessary to explain and to comment to Harriet on many things, which to him had become merely commonplaces, and this gave them fresh value. After Harriet had gone to bed, he sometimes found himself ruminating, not about her but about himself. He knew himself, both in temperament and experience, to be lacking in the practice of communication, he had not hitherto felt the need, in fact he considered it hazardous. The lunchtime concert he had taken Harriet to was in an eighteenth-century church. "It isn't a bit like a church," she had said. She was right, thought Andrew, it was too calm, too lucid, prayer here would be irrelevant, in a building that accomplished perfection by exclusion. Was it an analogy of his own aims and ideas? Hitherto he had gone his own way, with a fair amount of good humour admittedly — but that was just the luck of his genes. You couldn't go your way so completely with a child however, and though it was only for so short a time, the commitment necessary was a new experience. He was conditioned by training to pay attention to fresh phenomena and examined his reactions with interest. They were mixed — he saw with apprehension cracks appearing in his carefully constructed attitudes, but the cracks undeniably let in new light. After which musings he would play a little Bach and take himself off to bed. One evening he gave his parents a ring, realizing he had not made contact with them for months. They seemed pleased, if surprised, and he arranged for a meeting in the near future.

"You'd like this house," he said.

When Margot arrived back Harriet was out having tea with Miss Johnson.

"Hullo, darling," said Andrew, "I didn't expect you so early, the plane must have been punctual for once."

"You didn't think of meeting me, I suppose," said Margot.

"I never meet people unless they've been away for at least a year," said Andrew.

"It seems like a hundred years," said Margot, "but I don't suppose you'd have missed me however long I'd been. I expect if some Arab sheik had abducted me, you'd have merely said 'how interesting'."

"No," said Andrew, "I wouldn't, but it would have been all the same."

"Oh, you're hopeless," said Margot, with a sort of sob.

"Yes," said Andrew — but looking up at her quickly and with surprise, "I'm hopeless and so are you, and that's where the fun begins."

"Does it?" said Margot, "I don't call it fun."

"Try," said Andrew, "you and Harriet take life too seriously, and I'm beginning to think I've never taken it on at all."

"What *are* you talking about?" said Margot.

Andrew kissed her. "Let's get married," he said, "I'm sure this house is the sort that would appreciate a respectable married couple."

Margot turned away from him but Andrew crossed the room and put on a dance record, caught her to him and whirled her about the room.

With a sudden overwhelming sense of having reached home at last, Margot capitulated. They spun round ever more madly, yet, in her heart, there was an extraordinary stillness and peace.

It won't last, of course, thought her parents' daughter. *But it will come again*, thought Andrew's love, *and anyway, I've known it and I'll remember it for ever*, thought Margot.

As they were still dancing, Harriet came in. She stood astonished while the music slowed to a halt.

"Put on the other side, Harriet," shouted Andrew, "we don't want to stop yet and we'll have to without your help."

Harriet did as she was told and then Margot, by way of greeting, put out a hand and caught her up with the two of them in the dance.

CHAPTER ELEVEN

THAT SPRING PASSED in a grey mist as far as Aubrey Stacey's state of mind was concerned. Since Harriet's visit to his attic and the night that had followed, he had no longer hated nor feared his so-called pupils, he simply accepted the fact that he did not have either the personality or the skills needed to deal with them. Hassan had not appeared for his second term; his father had found a better job in another district. On learning this Aubrey felt a dull relief. He had reached a sort of compromise with his classes; perhaps they sensed that he was no longer antagonistic or even desirous of putting up a fight. At any rate, they ceased to torment him but merely stonewalled any attempt on his part to make them work. He went through the motions of teaching like an automaton and the front row "snobs" had to make the best of it.

During the Easter break he resolved to get down to his magnum opus in earnest and filled a notebook with period data. He was classifying and neatly copying out these for easy reference one afternoon, a job he enjoyed, when he was disturbed by a knock on his door and, opening it, was surprised to see his brother on the threshold.

"Michael!" he exclaimed, "What brings you here?"

"Bad news, I'm afraid, Mole." It was the old nickname, dating from childhood days when, under the spell of *The Wind in the Willows*, they had been Ratty and Mole to

284

each other. The names had outlived the nursery and even school and were still sometimes used, especially by Michael.

"Come in," said Aubrey, and he led the way to his sitting-room, pushed a chair forward and sat down himself by the open window, as if he needed air.

"It's Father and Mother," said Michael, "the police phoned me this morning. . . an accident with a lorry on the motorway."

"Serious?" asked Aubrey, but he knew the answer.

"Very, I'm afraid — it was instantaneous."

"Both?"

Michael nodded and the brothers remained silent for what seemed to Aubrey a long time as he looked from the window, noting meticulously the clouds drifting high in the pale sky, and the brilliant green of the new chestnut leaves.

Then Michael said: "There were no witnesses and the driver of the lorry escaped, but the evidence, such as it is, seems to confirm that it was not his fault, or at least not wholly so. Father shouldn't really have been still driving; his reactions had slowed up but he so hated any suggestion that he should give it up. It's hard to take it in, isn't it? They were both so active still. Mother was with us very recently and we were out and about a lot."

Aubrey said, "I haven't seen them for a good while."

"No, well, time goes by so quickly," said Michael, "and one is always so busy. Can I have a drink?"

"Yes, of course," said Aubrey, but he made no move to get it, and it was Michael who poured them both one and took Aubrey his.

"Nice place you've got here," he said, "a good view."

"Yes," said Aubrey. The detached remark had cleared the overcharged atmosphere a little and he got up. "My bedroom's really the better room. Come and see it."

"Facing south," said Michael approvingly, "I like a

south bedroom, but whyever the bars? I suppose it must have been a nursery once. Why didn't you have them taken down? They spoil the outlook." And then, not waiting for an answer, he went on: "Funny how old this makes you feel all of a sudden, isn't it? I suppose one's parents are always a sort of bulwark against old age and death and now the barrier's down. Well, there's a lot to see about, of course, and Julia and I hope you'll come back with us. It's holidays still, isn't it? If you've nothing special, on perhaps you could come straight away?"

Aubrey assented at once. He put away his papers and went to pack a bag. On his chest-of-drawers stood the photographs of his father and mother in a double frame. Looking at them, Aubrey felt the first real pang of emotion. They had already taken on that remote alien quality that always seemed to belong to the portraits of the dead, and it struck him that he would now never be able to prove his true worth to them. It was this sense of negation that substituted itself for any real grief. He had not encountered death on intimate terms before, and it was its monstrous impossibility that stunned him. This impression did not weaken in the days that followed. He behaved and spoke as he was expected to behave and speak, at the funeral, and at the gathering of friends and relatives afterwards but beneath this façade there was nothing but disbelief. How could anyone who was alive believe in death? Where *were* his parents? Their absence in their own home was extraordinary. Why did he not hear their voices or their footsteps? Everything expected them — all the household objects, their favourite chairs, their clothes, their shoes — his father's sticks in the hall, his mother's gardening gloves. There was dust on the mantelpiece where his mother had never allowed dust, that was an outrage. When no one was looking he took out his handkerchief and removed it. But he knew that the emotion he was feeling was different from his brother's — it was largely impersonal. The nearest he got to anything closer was the gratitude he felt towards his father when his will made it clear that no difference was to be made between himself and his brother, the elder by half an hour. But gratitude is not grief.

The house was to be put up for sale, and Michael and he met together there again later to settle what they wanted to keep of its contents. Aubrey only wished for some of his father's books and a fine chiming clock which he had always admired.

"Are you sure you won't reserve anything else?" asked Michael.

"Quite sure. I've not room in my flat, for one thing."

"But you may marry and want to set up a home," said Michael, but Aubrey shook his head.

"I shall never marry," he said decisively.

"Well, anyway, Julia and I have got plenty of storage space and it's a shame to let so much go to strangers; I shall take some extra pieces and you can draw on us if the time comes that you need them."

The brothers finished their last look round and went out together. The door clicked to behind them and Michael said, "Well, Mole, I suppose we may never come here again — how strange that is."

"Very strange," said Aubrey, "wonderfully strange," he repeated to himself. Gradually the enormity of death had receded and a feeling of profound ease had taken its place — an inapt ease and a lightness of spirit.

"I wish you'd come and pay us a proper visit soon," said Michael, "we don't manage to see enough of each other somehow."

"Thank you, Ratty," said Aubrey, "I will."

There were only a few days of the holidays left now and he had decided to give in his notice as soon as the term had begun, for there would be enough from his father's estate to enable him to devote himself to his writing, at least for some time to come. On the evening after he had got back to the Lotus House, he settled down to his manuscript once more.

"I'll go over the whole thing again first, to get into the right mood for tackling the next part. I've got enough notes I know, but in a big work one has to be careful to maintain consistency of plot and characters". So much had happened since he had begun the novel that he could hardly remember details of the early chapters, only the glow with which he had conceived the whole enterprise. But, as he read his neatly typed pages, the realization grew relentlessly upon him that their glory had departed. It had apparently only existed in his imagination. The book was a study in monochrome, lacking even the neon-lighting of melodrama; the characters, stuffed into their historical roles as if into fancy dress, had never come to life. There were long passages of guidebook description interspersed with sudden bursts of inconsistent action. It was lamentable! Well, no, now he was going to the other extreme — some of it wasn't so bad, but still it would not do, he saw very clearly that it would not do.

"I'm a failure as a creative writer as well as a teacher," he declared, but the declaration was almost triumphant. "It doesn't matter though, it simply doesn't matter any more." This discovery was extraordinarily exhilarating. On the top of his desk were arranged all his research notebooks — *It's a pity to waste all that I must say*, he thought, *perhaps I'll produce that monograph on old Cotton one of these days, yes, I think I might make quite a good job of that, but what on earth else shall I do?* His eyes wandered round the room as if for a clue, they dwelt lovingly as usual on his books. *I must put up some more shelves for Father's*, he thought. There were two packing-cases of these waiting on the landing.

Then inspiration came — "Of course, that's what drew me to Cotton, the great librarian, in the first place.

I'll take a librarian's course and live happy and humdrum ever after. In my spare time I'll write my monographs and edit texts. 'Nuns fret not at their convent's narrow room, and hermits are contented with their cells,' " he quoted, "and why not, I should like to know." He looked again at the magnum opus lying in confusion all over his desk and felt the need for some symbolic act. "I'd like to burn it and see the silly dream vanishing up the chimney in smoke, but that's the worst of an electric fire. I think I'll borrow a spade, yes, 'bury it certain fathoms in the earth' like Prospero's book, only I'm not a Prospero and never have been." For the present however, he shovelled all the chapters back into the drawer. The end of *The Tempest* was drifting through his mind as he did so. He had a less difficult task than Prospero, after all — it is easier to forgive the dead.

It was getting late, his father's clock chimed midnight and a new day was beginning as Aubrey went to his bed. *I'll get those bars taken down*, was his last thought before he went to sleep, *Michael was right about them, they do obscure the view*.

The bars were duly removed and one warm May afternoon Aubrey was able, by leaning out, to see the first wisteria blooms here and there between their pale patterned leaves. Further down beneath them he caught sight of Miss Cook bent over her border, assiduously weeding and planting.

It was not an uncommon sight, for Janet Cook's grandfather's genes had been ever more busily asserting themselves since she had taken over the strip of garden allotted to her by Mrs Sanderson. The box she had once labelled "Sitting-room new carpet fund" was not getting any heavier, for all her spare cash seemed now to go in providing herself with garden tools, sprays and fertilizers, not to speak of seeds, bulbs and plants. She was a regular listener to "Gardeners' Question Time" and viewer of

"Gardeners' World" and this did not, with her, result in envy or despondency but in inspiration and achievement. She was rewarded. All her plants behaved well and did what was required of them, making sturdy but not ill-mannered growth both outside and in the house for, emulating Dian, she soon had a row of healthy pot plants on the broad window-sills behind the pink curtains. Letty Sanderson, on the other hand, admitted sadly to herself that though she loved flowers, her plants didn't seem to like her much! "It's because I'm sentimental over them," she sighed; "sentimental", a dirty word nowadays, could, she feared, be applied to her in general. It was awful to be sentimental and know it: if one didn't know it, it could make one happy. Anyway she was afraid she really was very sentimental over flowers. She adored their beauty but often forgot to water them, and then to make up for it she watered them too much, and of course that made them bad-tempered. So bad-tempered that they died just to spite her, she thought, as she threw out what had once been a splendid cyclamen given to her by Margot in gratitude for her help with Harriet after the accident. Margot had made a similar presentation to Miss Cook — she had got them cheap from the firm that supplied decorative plants to her art gallery. Janet's cyclamen, of course, had flourished and the lovely but-terfly blossoms would probably renew themselves for years to come, thought Letty, and having seen how successfully the basement border had been cultivated, she had asked Janet to extend and broaden this, and there was now quite a sizeable little sunny flower-garden beneath and beyond the balcony. So, in this second summer, as Aubrey Stacey looked out from his window, he could smell, in addition to the wisteria, the warm late wallflowers and the early fragrant pinks. He could also see a neat edging of deep blue forget-me-nots and a clump of single white peonies just coming into flower. Later, there would be sweetpeas and roses and just now Janet was busy with her summer planting, snapdragons and petunias and stocks and, in the sunniest spot, a row of zinnias. She had raised all these from seed in what had once been the old scullery and here, too, she kept during the winter the cuttings she had taken from her geraniums and pelargoniums. She loved these. "Anyone's welcome to all that greenery," she had said derisively once to Dian, who was describing admiringly the fashionable trailing spider plant that Margot had lately established on the landing of the first floor flat — "a bit of colour for me!"

"Well, that there geranium with a '*p*' does you credit, I must say," admitted Dian. It was a splendid purple and white pelargonium, the queen of all her pot plants, and had actually been the first she had ever brought. Miss Budgeon of the little corner shop had embarked on a small stand of plants and flowers, squeezed between the fruit and vegetables. Influenced by Miss Sanderson, all the tenants of the Lotus House patronized the corner shop, and one day Janet Cook, after having purchased a nice little cauliflower, found herself transfixed by a vision of glory. It was the finest pelargonium she had ever encountered. She looked at the price and turned away. She was not yet a fully committed addict and the carpet box beckoned. But those extravagantly rich purple and white flowers danced before her eyes all day and were a trouble to her dreams by night. She resisted all the rest of the week, but on Saturday morning she gave in and, in a panic lest the plant should have been sold, she rifled the carpet-fund box and almost ran to the shop, returning guilty but triumphant.

"Wasting all that money on a flower," said her mother.

Of course the pelargonium flourished in superb health; and in the late summer she had taken two cuttings from it and cossetted them through the winter months and now they were putting forth strong shoots.

Afterwards Janet always felt annoyed that it was Dian and not herself who had first discovered something odd about one of the cuttings. She was showing them off and pointing out that each had two fat buds when Dian said, "I thought they were purple and white."

"So they are," said Janet.

"Well, this one's different," said Dian, "looks funny to me, a kind of grey, see?"

Janet saw — and it *was* distinctly different from the other cutting, the bud tips of which already showed the correct hue, yet it was just as healthy. Janet gave it a little extra feed and pushed it into the sunniest corner.

On Dian's next Tuesday she found Janet waiting to waylay her.

"She was really over the moon, she was," Dian told Luke that evening, "her eyes popping out — well they do pop a bit most times, but this time I thought they was just like my Monday lady's peke, so I went along with her as quick as I could, though I ought really to have been doing the drawing-room floor. 'It's my pel . . . ' whatever it's called, she said, 'it's going to be a blue one and I don't believe there's never been a blue one before.' Well, it wasn't what I'd call proper blue, more airforce, if you know what I mean, but you could stretch a point. 'Oo,' I says, 'it might be goin' to make your fortune, what did your stars say this week, did you look at them?' But she never does, careless I call it. What d'you think, Luke?"

"I dunno, honey, flowers is your concern, but you tell her to take advice, there'll be those who'll know."

By the time Dian saw Janet again she had already taken the pelargonium to Miss Budgeon to show her the blue flower. Miss Budgeon belonged to the local horticultural society and had tried to get Janet to join. "I don't join things," was all the response she had had hitherto. Lately, however, Janet had secretly been weakening. There were

292

lectures and shows and gardening stock to be had at a discount and it didn't seem fair to her flowers somehow to keep out of it. Now she felt the need both for information and encouragement. Miss Budgeon, for instance, was full of sympathetic interest in Janet's blue blossoms.

"You really should join our society, Miss Cook," she said, "there's our summer show coming off next month and there's a special class for last year's cuttings."

It'll mean mixing with a lot of strangers, thought Janet dubiously, *still it may be my duty in a manner of speaking.* Miss Budgeon produced the necessary forms for her to fill up and she decided that, besides entering her pelargonium, she would also compete for the best nosegay of annuals and for the sweetpea section as well. Roses were chancy, if you only had a few bushes, you couldn't count on any blooms being just at the right stage, whereas her sweetpeas promised very well.

"In for a penny, in for a pound," said Janet to herself, and it really turned out to be several points on her right side, for her posy of cornflowers and clarkia and larkspur and pansies was awarded a third prize, her sweetpeas a second, and a first with special distinction for her pelargonium, now proudly displaying no less than three blue blooms.

The judge, a BBC personality called Tom Austen, presented the prizes and when it came to Janet's turn he detained her.

"As a member of the Geranium and Pelargonium Society, Miss Cook, I am very intrigued by your blue flowering plant. You have grown it from a cutting, I see. Have you been experimenting with different varieties long?"

"Oh, no," said Janet, "I haven't experimented at all, it just came like that. As a matter of fact, I am not an experienced gardener, I had never grown anything till I retired two years ago."

"Really!" said Tom Austen. "And you've run away with three prizes, quite a record I should think. I congratulate you and if you will allow me, I would very much like to keep in touch on behalf of the society with regard to your interesting sport."

Janet gave a grudging consent. "Letting a strange man have your name and address like that," exclaimed her mother.

"You see," Miss Budgeon had explained afterwards, "they'll want to find out whether more blue pelargoniums can be grown from yours, and if they can, Miss Cook, you might become quite famous."

When Janet got home after the show she put all her prize money into the carpet-fund box which had been so neglected and even robbed. It was a kind of placation; she was determined not to spend any more on the garden, just at the present. It was as well not to tempt fortune, there were always snags about. All the same, she felt very proud, it had been an amazing day, perhaps the most exciting she could remember, and even more extraordinary things were to follow.

About two weeks later, her phone rang and a voice, a polite, pleasant, voice enquired if it could speak to Miss Janet Cook.

"Who is it?" asked Janet cautiously.

"My name is Cassie Kay," said the voice, "I'm from the BBC and I would very much like to speak to Miss Janet Cook."

"Speaking," said Janet.

"Oh, good morning, Miss Cook," said Cassie Kay, "we are doing a short series on BBC1 telivision called "Senior Starters", aimed as its name implies primarily at the active retired category, but of course we hope of interest to a wider circle. It comes on on Tuesdays at 7.10 p.m. Perhaps you have seen it? No — well, Tom Austen tells us you have taken up gardening since your retirement

294

and have produced a new species of geranium. It seems to us that you might make a valuable contribution to our series, if you would allow us to make a short film of you in your garden and with your wonderful plant."

There was a pause.

"Well, I don't know, I'm sure," said Janet at last, "I never thought of such a thing."

This was an understatement. "A bolt from the blue," she said afterwards, "that's what it was, a regular bolt from the blue."

There was another pause, but only a short one this time. "You would like to think it over, of course," said the beguiling voice of Cassie Kay, "perhaps I could ring you tomorrow. I do so hope you'll say 'yes', Miss Cook. I'll ring tomorrow evening if that is convenient. Goodbye for the present then."

Janet was flustered and apprehensive, but beneath this there burned a small flame of glory. She decided to consult Mrs Sanderson. It was right to do so anyway, she couldn't very well let photographers and who-knows-what descend on the Lotus House unbeknown to its owner.

"But how lovely!" exclaimed Letty. "I do congratulate you. Dian had told me about your geranium and I have been meaning to ask you if I could see it. Now tell me all about it, please, from the beginning."

"It's what they call a sport," said Janet, "the parent plant was purple and white, I got it from Miss Budgeon's shop."

"Oh," said Letty, "that explains it, that shop has always dealt in magic.'"

Janet thought, *How silly Mrs Sanderson is sometimes, but there, she's getting on after all.*

However, the conversation with Letty somehow settled it, and so it came about that one morning what seemed like a perfect army of strangers descended upon Miss Cook at the Lotus House basement flat and took over. It was this sensation of being taken over that was the strongest impression left with Janet when the day was done. She was posed standing in the middle of her garden, walking up the path, picking flowers and lastly in her sitting room holding her pelargonium.

"A fine house this," the photographer had commented, "it's a bonus as a background. May we just trouble you once more, from a little distance this time, so as to concentrate on a good picture of the whole building . . . That's splendid, thank you so much, Miss Cook, I think this will make a really rewarding film."

"I just wish it had been me," said Dian. "Didn't it make you feel like the Queen?"

"I don't know what the Queen feels like," said Janet tartly. "It made *me* feel silly."

"What did they say?" enquired Dian. "Some of them interviewers are lovely, but some can be horrible, only Luke says they don't mean no harm really."

"This one wasn't horrible," admitted Janet, "just stupid."

"How d'yer mean stupid?" asked Dian, shocked.

"Asking questions nobody could answer like, "How does it feel, Miss Cook, to have made the desert blossom like the rose?' " said Janet in a mincing voice.

"I call that pretty," said Dian, "like something out of a musical."

"It's out of the Bible," said Janet.

"What did you say?" persisted Dian.

"I said 'It's good loam soil, not at all sandy.' And then they asked me what I was going to call my new wonderful blue variety, and I said it might never do it again and I wasn't one to count my chickens before they were hatched."

"Well," said Dian reproachfully, "you weren't very kind to the poor chap, was you? He was only trying to get you to talk nice."

"It can't be helped now," said Janet. "I dare say I was a bit short. It's not what I'm used to, you see."

Janet was informed that the film would be shown in three weeks' time. She debated whether to let Henry and Doris know. She hadn't told them anything at all as yet, not even about the flower show and the pelargonium. She didn't want Doris interfering and she couldn't tell how Henry would take it. Finally she decided it would be mean not to say anything. Besides they'd be sure to get to know, though she didn't think they would look at the programme unless they were told. But people always did get to know things when you didn't want them to. So she sent them a picture postcard of Westminster Abbey just before the great day and wrote on it: "Don't miss 'Senior Starters' BBC1 Tuesday 7.10, love Janet." *I'm sure they'll be too curious not to look and when they do they'll get the shock of their lives*, she thought with satisfaction as she posted it. She could just see their faces.

Everyone else knew. "I can't wait!" said Dian. "Mind you come home in time, Luke. You ought to've heard her telling off that interviewer, ever so cheeky, she was."

"I expect they'll cut it, they mostly cuts half of what they make you say," said Luke.

"Seems funny when you comes to think of it," said Dian, "all those people all over, going to hear her and to see her and when I first knows her, there she was darting away behind her door, scared to show herself just to me. Not much of the goldfish left now."

CHAPTER TWELVE

IT IS A fact, and not a very admirable one, that a person or a building or a landscape that is familiar to oneself, if it is to be seen in a photograph or on the television screen, takes on a compelling interest. Although probably not one of the inhabitants of the Lotus House would have bothered to look at a travel film that might have enlarged their visual experience and added to their knowledge, all were glued to the box on that summer evening to see Miss Cook, her garden and her plant against the background of their own home, which they could have seen, and indeed did see, any and every day much better in reality.

Letty had thought it might have been pleasant if they could have watched the film together, but Janet Cook had said, "It's kind of you, Mrs Sanderson, but I don't fancy seeing myself in public somehow. I mean it's not natural, is it, if you see what I mean."

Letty thought she did see and did not press it. Then there was Aubrey Stacey, he too thanked her politely but said that he was afraid he really couldn't bear colour television — it was an idiosyncrasy for which he apologized, but there it was, and he really would prefer to see the film on his own set as he knew he was in a small minority and couldn't expect people to turn off their colour for him. After that Letty gave up. She knew the Royces had a bigger and better television than hers.

Janet Cook sat upright on the edge of her grandfather's chair gripping its arms. She could not have described her state of mind — "queer", that's all she could have said, "definitely queer." Wasn't there a story about someone meeting himself one day and getting quite a shock? She could believe it. Why had she let herself in for all this? *You've only yourself to blame, Janet*, but this never made things easier — one could often enjoy blaming others.

Well, now it was time and, pressing her thin little lips even more tightly together, she got up and switched on, and there she was already, coming straight down the garden path right at her, only it wasn't herself after all, it was her mother. She would have known her anywhere, but of course it couldn't be, it must be her. She supposed that through the years her own face had become too familiar to be seen any more, and because her hair at least was still black, she hadn't realized that now she looked quite old, a bit shrunk and bent and decidedly skinny. Why, she was more like her mother than Henry after all, because of course they were both women. But now that other Janet was stopping and looking down at her flowers — this was when they had asked her to pick some. She was stooping down to choose which to take, but you could still see her face, and, staring at it, the one Janet saw the face of the other change, it wasn't her mother's face any longer. Who did it remind her of? She couldn't think at first, then a long buried memory flashed upon her, her father looking down on her, a very little girl and saying: "Coming for a walk with me, little 'un?" "Who'd have thought it?" said Janet aloud to the empty room: "Poor old Dad."

But now the talking began. *Well, I've never heard that voice before in all my life*, thought Janet indignantly, *they must have done something to it*. She simply couldn't pay attention to what was being said — the squeaky, jerky tone of her own speech, like a ventriloquist's doll, horrified her. Then the scene changed again and there she was holding up her pelargonium in the sitting-room. Well, that at least was all right, splendid it looked, and the last pictures were really pretty. She suddenly decided she would ask Mrs Sanderson to let her have still a bit more ground this autumn — that piece by the garages, she'd plant it out with flowering shrubs to hide them, you could get lovely ones nowadays. And now came the last shot of all, the one taken at a little distance with the whole house in and all her flowers in front. A flood of pride and satisfaction invaded her. Perhaps hundreds and hundreds of people were seeing the garden she had made and were enjoying it. She felt her heart expand to take them all in.

Had it not been for Mrs Sanderson, Aubrey would not have even known about the programme, and but for Dian would probably have forgotten to look at it. Dian had written a note with the red felt pen he used for correcting his school exercise books and had left it for him, propped up by his clock. It said: "Mr Stacey, don't you forget, 7.10 this evening, Miss Cook on TV as ever is. Dian."

Dian had adopted a protective attitude towards him lately. "Poor chap," she had said to Letty, "losing his parents like that. I remember when Mum went, you feels all cold. I went on feeling cold, really, right on till I met my Luke, but it's sobered him up no end, nothing like the bottles to clear out nowadays. Funny isn't it? Took my brother Fred right the other way — well, it takes all sorts."

Aubrey seldom used his television set and had to clear away a pile of books that had accumulated in front of it. He considered watching a waste of time and really thought it so now, for he wasn't much interested either in flowers or Miss Cook, but he felt it would be discourteous to ignore both Mrs Sanderson and Dian's recommendation, and also even he was not immune from the strange fascination of seeing the familiar reproduced by the media. Afterwards he was glad he had done so, for he had noticed something about the house that he had not known was there before. Over his bedroom window was carved a second lotus flower similar to the one above the front entrance. He supposed the bars had obscured the view of it before. He began to wonder why the carvings were there. He had once asked Mrs Sanderson about it, but she could tell him little. She had some vague romantic story of a connection of the house with the East, but she did not seem to want to follow this up or to transform it into anything more substantial. He began to muse over the mythology connected with the Lotus. It seemed, as far as he could make out, ambiguous. There was the classical association through Homer of the sinister compelling magic that had inspired Tennyson's *Lotus Eaters* — the false dreams of a hollow land — but the Eastern Lotus of Vishnu and Buddha was life-giving, a vision of creative energy and truth, whose emblem was the white lily rising from the dark waters. Was this the house of fantasy or of vision, or perhaps of both? Aubrey Stacey continued to ponder for some time, then he got out his monograph on old Cotton and started to work on it.

To the Royces, if anyone had been able to trace it, the transition from the one realm to the other was perceptible, if precarious. Harriet had started school again fairly happily at half-term. Andrew and Margot had got married very quietly one weekend. When told of this, Harriet was pleased.

"This makes you a real relation to me, doesn't it?" she had said to Andrew. "And us into a proper family." She had confided the news to her mascot which she generally carted around in her pocket.

"I think we ought to have a honeymoon," Andrew said to Margot, "your trip to Egypt didn't do you much good, and I've still some leave left. Where would you like to go?"

"Switzerland," said Margot without hesitation.

"We could take Harriet with us as chaperone," said Andrew, "newly married couples always took a chaperone in Jane Austen's day."

"But this isn't Jane Austen's day," said Margot, "it *isn't*, Andrew."

"No, perhaps not," said Andrew, "I've always wondered what they did, the chaperones I mean. What can we do about her then?"

"Miss Johnson did say something about a music school away somewhere in Wales in the summer holidays, and would she be fit, did I think?"

"Just the thing," said Andrew, "she's really almost as fit as a fiddle now, isn't she?"

"Switzerland's expensive," said Margot, "and the music school won't be cheap, but we could sell the Crispin Keylock statue, he's fetching quite high prices now and it would help a bit."

Andrew had agreed enthusiastically. He had never cared for that annorexic nude, as he called it, and the thought of Crispin helping to pay for their honeymoon pleased him. Now he sat comfortably beside Margot and Harriet on the sofa in preparation for Miss Cook's programme. Harriet was in what Margot called a tizzy, afraid that they might miss the beginning since Andrew insisted on waiting until the exact time advertised in order not to have to see the preceding item, which he declared would turn his stomach.

"Don't fuss," said her mother.

Harriet stole a sidelong look at her. "Well, you fussed yesterday when you thought he would make you lose your train."

"How right you are, Harriet," said Andrew, "but then you women always fuss, I suppose you can't help it."

Harriet looked quickly at her mother again, but it was all right, she was smiling and the smile was for Harriet and was almost like a wink. She gave a contented giggle, but she was still anxious. At last Andrew stopped concentrating on the second hand of his watch and switched on just as the programme was being announced, and then they each saw the strip of flower garden and Miss Cook and the house.

Andrew noted once more with affectionate approval its fine proportions and classical grace. He hoped Margot would not want to move again for a long while. He was glad that the Lotus House was their first home as man and wife.

Margot, looking at the bright small image before her, was suddenly reminded of her nightmare in Egypt for, as bright and small had been the vision at the end of that dark avenue. She remembered but no longer felt the horror of her dream. It had been a horror of vacuity. Perhaps this had always haunted her, perhaps she had always been trying to escape from it ever since her empty childhood, and always in vain, for without love there is no identity. Since Harriet's accident she had sensed this dimly. The quest and the flight (for they were one) still harried her, but there had been that moment of peaceful radiance in the midst of Andrew's absurd dance, the influence of which had never entirely deserted her. She watched the picture of the Lotus House and garden before her change now to a close-up of Miss Cook holding her pelargonium proudly aloft for all to see. Her hands, clasping the pot, were out of focus and looked too large. They were untended hands with short stubby fingers. Margot looked down involuntarily at her own hands, beautifully smooth, the nails like small very pink shells. Then she glanced at Harriet's and noticed for the first time, and with surprise, that they were prettily shaped and very like her own. She did not need to look at Andrew's — those inordinately long, very sensitive fingers — she had an odd sensation that they were as much a part of her as her own.

"Who are those three little girls on the stairway hiding behind the wisteria?" Harriet was asking.

"I can't see any little girls," said Margot.

"It must be the shadows of the leaves," said Andrew.

"Oh, look!" cried out Harriet excitedly, "There's Maisie, I'm so glad she's there, she's walking all the way down the path. Wasn't she clever to know about it?"

"I expect they decoyed her with a bit of fish," said Andrew, "cats are TV personalities, the public loves them."

Underneath the Royces, Letty sat alone in her beautiful old green and white drawing-room, the least altered room in the house, and the one she liked the best. She regretted that she was alone but knew now it was only to be expected. The crisis of Harriet's accident had drawn them all together for a short while, but that was an artificial association with no basis of natural growth, and once over, they parted again into their four separate units and really seldom met. It was not at all what Letty had at one time dreamed of, but she had come to accept it almost with amusement. She knew herself to be sentimental, but she was relieved to find she was not a coward. She had come to terms with loneliness, to which after all she was no stranger. Lately a warning physical sympton had taken her to her doctor, who had told her there was no cause for alarm, but that the time had come for her to take care. The care she had taken was for the Lotus House. She had had a session with Mr Donovan.

"I do not want it to become an institution and as far as possible I want to ensure its being looked after properly. I have no close relatives still living," she said. "What do you advise?"

It was decided that the property should go to a favourite charity on condition that they fulfilled certain obligations as to its upkeep. "But if anything should

304

happen to me while the present tenants are still in residence, I want their interests safeguarded," said Letty earnestly, and Mr Donovan said he would prepare the necessary papers. She had gone away satisfied.

It struck her now as she sat there waiting, that it was curious that it should be Cooksie in the basement that was the one who was responsible for setting all this activity in motion, that had brought producer and researcher and cameramen and interviewer and designer, and who knows how many more, into contact with her Lotus House, while she herself remained passive, a mere onlooker. But she had perhaps been more of an onlooker than anything else throughout her life — the child who enjoyed watching the sparrows on the roof more than the game — the one who stood entranced, motionless, before the doll's house — the dutiful daughter, the useful wife at home. "They also serve who only stand and wait," she had learned the sonnet at school. Milton however could not have actually done much standing and waiting, she thought, with twelve books of *Paradise Lost* to be written. Really, the only important action she had ever taken on her own was to buy the Lotus House, and how much that mattered she could not tell. The house kept its secrets. Now she felt her part in its history was over and done with, sealed up in Mr Donovan's office. She was not needed any longer, even as an onlooker. But why should one always demand of life to be needed? It was not in the bond. She could still love her drawing-room as much as she liked.

Unlike Andrew, Letty had switched on early, but she had been paying no attention to what was going on. How breathless thought was. She had traversed labyrinths of the mind in a few moments, and now she collected her wits together. As "Senior Starters" was announced, her television set gave a flicker. Perhaps after all it was as well that none of her tenants were watching with her, it was an old set and she knew she ought to replace it. *It is typical*, she thought, *that I do nothing about it because I'm used to it and it was a wedding present.* Then she caught her breath — what she was looking at was the back view of Selina's doll's house, the part that had never been seen before. It was just the right size, only a little brighter, a little further removed from reality. Where, oh where, were the Golightlys? She could not see any of them anywhere, unless that was Cooksie standing among a lot of flowers that were pretty enough but had no business to be outside the kitchen window. No, of course, Selina's doll's house was destroyed and that was Miss Janet Cook who rented the basement flat. Well, she couldn't really be bothered at her age to keep the past and the present separate any more, though she remembered clearly enough now. It was all about a blue pelargonium, but they had liked the house so much, Janet Cook has said, that they had taken a special picture of it at the end to show the whole of it to the best advantage.

There it was now, very clear, with Maisie the cat just coming round the corner. But for Letty Maisie never finished her walk, for suddenly as she gazed the whole house quivered and then splintered into a thousand shimmering dancing peacock patterns and then disappeared.

MOVING HOUSE

To Anne Dickenson

Although some incidents and places in this story are drawn from life the characters emphatically are *not*, the relationship between the heroine and her son and grandchildren, for instance, being entirely fictitious.

Chapter 1

CLARE CURLING was writing a letter, sitting in her suburban garden in the spring sunshine. Her three children, wholly ignoring each other, were playing round her. Patrick, the eldest, aged eight, was systematically beheading the daffodils; Becky, aged five, was whirling aimlessly round and round the lawn; Bertram, aged three, clad according to his latest whim in a cast-off pink muslin dress of his sister's, was laboriously pushing a large toy car up and down in a straight line, up and down, "over hill, over dale", like a bulldozer.

Clare, looking up and seeing the destruction of the daffodils, called out, "Stop that, Patrick! The poor flowers!"

"They're enemy outposts – there's a war on, I can't reduce the invading force."

Clare sighed and folded up her letter. "It's lunchtime," she said. "It's so warm we'll have it outside, come and help carry the dishes out."

The two elder children came.

"And how have you been amusing yourself this morning, Mother?" enquired Patrick kindly.

"I've been writing to Granny. Bertram, come to lunch."

"No," said Bertram. It was the first time he had spoken to anyone that morning, but he could have been heard chanting to himself resolutely: "Two, twenty, three, ten."

"He's got to push his car one hundred times to and fro," explained Becky.

"But he doesn't know how to count up to a hundred," said Clare.

"No," agreed Becky, "he might go on for ever; we shall have to push food into his mouth as he goes along."

"You could stop him, Mother," suggested Patrick, but Clare only sighed again. She did not feel like a confrontation with Bertram that morning.

"You spoil that child," said Patrick, but the subject did not interest him. "Which do you like best," he continued, "Norsemen or Vikings? I like Vikings."

'Aren't they the same?" said Clare.

"I hate Romans best," said Becky, "I hate Romans much the best, don't you, Mummy?"

Her mother made no comment – she was thinking about Bertram. She didn't believe she spoiled him, she just couldn't do anything about him. That dress, for instance; he'd tripped over it twice already and got a nasty lump on his forehead. Besides, she didn't fancy having a transvestite in the family.

"What children have you got, Mrs Curling?"

"Oh, a boy, a girl and a transvestite."

Bertram was like his grandmother, she thought; you simply couldn't influence either of them once they had made up their minds, and they were both always making up their minds.

"Are we going to stay with Granny soon?" asked Patrick. "Will she let me wind up the grandfather clock, do you think? She said I could next time we came, but she might not remember."

"No, we can't go just yet," said Clare, "she's had a fall and hurt her leg."

"Well, I fell out of the pear tree and hurt mine, but I could see people while it was getting better."

"But she's old."

"Oh, very, very old," said Becky. "She'll die soon, won't she?"

310

"You shouldn't say things like that," said Patrick, who was fond of his grandmother when he had time to think of her. "There's lots of people older than Granny who aren't dead."

Becky nodded, "There's Mr Jackson – he's very old; he hasn't any teeth."

"He's only a toad in a book, silly," said Patrick. "Toads aren't people."

"I hate toads best," said Becky dreamily. "May I have Bertram's tomato, please? I've eaten mine."

But just then Bertram came up, silently climbed on to his chair and began to eat his peas one by one with his fingers. Clare pushed a spoon at him, but he disregarded it. It was surprising how quickly the peas disappeared.

Yes, thought Clare again, *he's just like Granny – contrasuggestive. And now it looks as though she's going to be a problem – she really ought not to go on living at that place on her own, but I doubt very much if she'll hear reason.*

Roberta Curling, the incipient problem, was in reality the children's great-grandmother, but this fact was all but forgotten. She had made an early marriage, and her only child had done the same. Her son and his wife had died tragically in a road accident, leaving twin babies to be brought up by their young grandparents who had, in every sense but the literal one, been Mother and Father to them. When Patrick was born, Roberta had refused to be labelled a "great" and as she was both firm and active no one thought of her as such.

On this particular day she was also writing a letter, propped up in bed and fighting against the drowsiness induced by her pain-killer. "You will soon be hearing from Clare," she wrote to her granddaughter in Austria, "perhaps you have already done so. This is just to say – don't be worried, I am quite all right. I had a little fall and have damaged my knee, entirely my own fault, slipped on the basement

311

stairs, too much in a hurry as usual, you will say, and you will be right, but it's hard to change the habits of a lifetime. Anyway, no bones broken, and Nurse Higgins and dear Mrs B. are taking good care of me. Clare is certain to fuss, so don't take any notice. She and Alex will be on at me more than ever to leave Rowanbank, but I don't mean to. The question is, will you back me up? I am not sure of this."

She lay back on her pillow, tired. No, she was not sure of Naomi. Alex she could fathom easily, but Naomi. . . . She thought of her with love, longing and irritation. Roberta shut her eyes and there she was before her, one of the many Naomis – this time a dryad disguised as a schoolgirl, absorbed and grave, and in her grandmother's eyes utterly charming, playing her flute under the walnut tree. Naomi was musically so talented, and after her school-days were over the way to a promising career had seemed to be opening out. But she had gone off to Salzburg, inspired by a suggestion of a fellow music student. And she had fallen in love with Salzburg. "There's a river," she wrote home, "a perfectly useless river running through the very middle of the town – you can lie on its banks under flowering chestnut trees – and, in a park, another river of white tulips, miles long, that winds away among the grass and the towers, all different shapes and colours and the mountains in a circle all round."

That was all very well; but next she fell in love with a young Austrian doctor, with a taste for music, though very much dedicated to his work, and they were married. Early and rather precipitate marriages did run in the family, Roberta grimly admitted. Then Naomi, without a struggle and apparently with complete content, had dwindled into nothing more than a wife. It was two years ago now since all this had happened and there were not yet even any children as an excuse for giving up her career. She still played, of course, but never professionally and she had only come

312

back to England twice since her marriage and then with Franz, who couldn't take much in the way of holidays, and Naomi would not leave him.

Still, thought Roberta resolutely, *I must not repine. She is happy and she might have died that time when she was so ill as a baby*.

A knock came at the door, it was Mrs Baxter from the cottage; it was always known simply as "the cottage" because it was the only one near and it had had Baxters in it ever since Roberta had known it. The current Mrs Baxter sailed into the room like a duchess. She had immense but comfortable dignity. She "did" for Roberta and obliged extra in emergencies.

"I'll boil you an egg for your tea and I'll leave you a thermos of coffee so you won't do so badly till Nurse comes," she said, "for I am that sorry I can't stay this afternoon, as William's not so well."

"Oh, dear," said Roberta, "you shouldn't have had to leave him. I'm sorry to be such a nuisance."

"Don't fret," said Mrs Baxter. "I'll be back before he comes in, only I wanted to be there and have his supper ready and the fire bright for him."

"I'll soon be about again," said Roberta. "I mean to hobble round the room tomorrow."

"You must be careful, though," said Mrs Baxter, "it's falls that lie in wait for many when they're getting on, and stairs especially. You ought to have asked me to fetch up those apples. I don't hold with you going down into the cellar, if you don't mind my saying so."

Roberta, when left alone again, lay looking out of her window, watching the late pale spring sunshine filter through the interlaced branches of the walnut tree. She was wondering if she herself ought to hold with going down into her cellar any longer. It was stupid to have continued to keep the store of apples there, but there they had always been kept and she had never thought about any other place for them. When you had lived a long while in the same house, it was difficult to adapt even in details to the exigences of age.

She reluctantly allowed that Alex and Clare might have some reason on their side, for it was true that the house was not really suitable for her any more, in fact had ceased to be so years ago – an inconvenient rambling, servant-planned building, not even very attractive to look at, with far too big a garden but an incomparable view. Here, in the middle of a field, long ago, her mother had sat herself down and said to her father: "This is where you must build me a house." He had gone straight off to bargain with the farmer who owned the field, leaving her sitting there in entranced contemplation, and in no time the house was built. *You could do those sort of things then*, thought Roberta. *How spoilt they were, those Edwardian middle classes, until their sons were taken away from them to be slaughtered*. Perhaps after all her parents had been glad then that she was Roberta and not Robert; for she was a disappointment: they would have preferred a son and there were no more children.

The home was named "Rowanbank" because its site was bordered by an old hedge containing a rowan tree greatly prized by her mother – "A magic tree," her mother had told Roberta, "full of power to keep evil away." It had been of reasonable size at first and used only as a country retreat from Highgate but, as the years passed, a study library was added here, an extra bedroom there, in preparation for her father's retirement.

Rowanbank became Roberta's at his death and, as things turned out, she continued to live there after her marriage. Charles did not mind where he lived as long as he could paint, bless him, and there was plenty of room for that and for her mother to live with them. Here her son was born, her she had brought up his children and there was plenty of space for them too. She had never thought about the appearance or convenience of the house, it was simply home to her. The view miraculously had remained unspoiled. Beyond the garden, so lovingly planned by her father, whose hobby it was, stretched Kent hop gardens and cherry orchards, flanked by gently sloping wooded hills, then a stretch of marsh and on clear days the blue line of the sea. No buildings were anywhere to be seen, except a cluster of hop kilns, their white cowls cocked up into the sky like some curious land-locked sailing craft. One of Roberta's bedroom windows looked out on this view, the other on to the walnut tree.

But it was too dark now to see out of either and her knee had started to ache quite badly. Willow, her large grey tom cat, who adored people in bed, had come in through the door left ajar by Mrs Baxter and, carefully searching out the injured leg, had settled himself heavily upon it. She was very glad to hear Nurse Higgins's car.

Having let herself in and come up the stairs, Nurse Higgins asked: "Well, and how are we feeling this evening?'

Roberta wondered why double vision so often afflicted Nurse Higgins, but she accepted this odd fact without irritation, for her touch was gentle and she brought with her the benefaction of cleanliness and order.

The next day Roberta felt distinctly better and more able to cope with life, which that morning contained Clare's letter, a succession of anxious chirps: "Do hope you are better, so unfortunate, knees are very tricky, wish so much I could come and look after you, but it is Patrick and Becky's holidays still and they are at home all day and, even if I could find someone to look after them, I should have to bring Bertram with me, I am afraid, as he is going through a difficult stage just at present, am so glad that you have dear Mrs B. and that you find Nurse Higgins so helpful and the neighbours too. That is the best of living in a village, though of course Rowanbank is not really in the village and Alex and I both wish you were not so isolated except for Mrs B., in fact we do wish you were nearer to us. It would be so nice if we could have you living here with us at No. 30."

May you be forgiven, Clare, you think no such thing, poor dear; and heaven knows I don't either. Roberta paused in her reading of the letter at this point and lost herself in memories of Alex and Clare's house. The recollection made her draw her bed-jacket close round her. Neither of them felt the cold, letting windows and doors stay perpetually open for the convenience of the children and Boffin the cat. She had long had a closed season from November to March for her visits there, but the English climate was no security for warmth at any time. Then the one small spare room had no space for clothes (the wardrobe and chest of drawers being filled with the family's overflow) except for one peg and, with luck, one little drawer. As for the children, she was very fond of their company in small doses, but they seemed omnipresent from early in the morning, when both Becky and Bertram loved to invade her narrow bed, till late at night; like most children nowadays, they kept the same hours as their elders. There was a show of getting Bertram off earlier, but he never failed to reappear in his night garments to be greeted with resigned indulgence. There was no children's room, so their games, toys and garments were everywhere. Roberta liked order and the haphazard ways of the household harassed her. Meals were at odd and arbitrary hours and very healthy, vegetarianism being one of the many "isms" Alex loved. He would soon have trouble with Patrick about that one though, thought Roberta, remembering an occasion when the boy had enquired suddenly: "Why is it wrong for me to eat meat but all right for Boffin to eat mice?"

Alex's job as in town planning but he also served assiduously on many local committees – UNA, CND, gipsy welfare and Friends of the Earth – in all of which he was supported by his wife. Both of them were ardent idealists; however, whereas Alex devoted himself to his causes with something of the same pleasurable ardour as his grandfather had for his painting, Clare's commitment was strained. She typed endless letters, arranged coffee mornings and put up in the little spare room various visitors, from respectable or near-respectable lecturers to down-and-outs.

The trouble was, thought Roberta, that she had been brought up from childhood to be too unselfish. This, unless you had a strong natural zest for life, was apt to get back on you. Clare had too low a level of personal enjoyment. Even with her family, although she undoubtedly loved Alex and the children deeply, she somehow seemed not to delight in them – or not often.

Roberta turned again to her letter:

But as our house is really too small to make you comfortable, Alex and I do hope, dear Granny, that you will think seriously whether you shouldn't leave Rowanbank, for since this fall we are anxious about this. You know Alex is on the committee of a very well run Home for the Elderly at Penge. You would be within easy reach of us there and Alex wants to know if at least you will let him put your name on the waiting list. It is so popular that there is quite a long list always.

Your affectionately, Clare.

P.S. Patrick is writing to you – it is his own idea and he will not agree to enclosing it in mine, so I do not quite know when you will get it as he is always busy about something or other.

Roberta slowly pushed the letter back into its envelope. What a fuss about a silly little fall! *No, no, my dears, not for*

317

me your Home, however popular; I shall stay on at Rowanbank until they carry me out in my coffin. But her irritation was tempered by a little pleasant warmth, aroused by the postscript. She was touched by the fact that Patrick had thought of writing to her, even if he never actually finished or posted it. He was her favourite of the children. She *liked* him as well as loved him. He already showed signs of possessing more practical ability and common sense than anyone else in that family, and these were qualities that she valued.

When Patrick's letter did arrive some days later it did not disappoint her. It said:

Dear Granny,

I am sorry you have hurt your leg. Is your grandfather clock keeping good time? I think I shall learn how to make clocks when I am older – they are most interesting. At present. I have invented a loom. I am making mats on it. I have made a green and red one and a blue and yellow, the fasteners off of them is not very good yet. When I get it right I will send you one and I think I will inclose a plan with instructions for making a loom like mine and if I were you I would try it yourself.

Yours faithfully, Patrick.

Roberta smiled and looked carefully at the plan for the primitive loom. She thought it neat and ingenious. *Perhaps he really was a turn for invention – much more useful than the arts these days. I suppose, considering his background, that he had to begin with looms, but it'll soon be computers and robots, I expect.*

She was downstairs again and getting about with two sticks, though the knee was still painful.

"I'm afraid it won't be all that reliable in future," said Dr Thompson. "Knees are tiresome. Still, you won't want to be seeing me any more for the present. I'll get the physiotherapist to look in and give you some exercises and Nurse will help you for a bit longer. But watch out on your stairs – it's a long way up to your bedroom, isn't it? Do you ever think you'd do better now in a flat or a bungalow?"

"No," said Roberta, "I hate flats and bungalows and don't intend to have another fall."

"Well, well," said Dr Thompson, assuming his best soothing manner, "I'm sure you'll be careful, though it gets less easy to avoid trouble with advancing years, Mrs Curling."

That makes three Jeremiahs, Roberta reflected to herself after he had gone, *four, if you count Alex and Clare as two. I wonder who will be the next.*

The next was her cousin Kitty who came down from London for the day to see her.

"Every time I come here the place looks larger and shabbier," Kitty said cheerfully over lunch. "All the carpets are wearing out; you'll trip over them next and they'll cost a fortune to replace – there's yards and yards of them. And as for the garden! Doesn't William Baxter work for you any longer?"

"He's been under the weather with his arthritis for quite a while now, poor fellow. It's as much as he can do to get through his work on the farm; but he'll do what he can for me once he's better. It's been such a wet spring. Yes – perhaps things are wearing out – what else would you expect? . . . But how can the house look larger?"

"Well, it does, I can't think why you stay on here, Berta – it would give me the creeps. Aren't you afraid at nights?"

"Why on earth should I be? What is there to be afraid of? Rowanbank isn't haunted, it's not old enough."

"I'm not thinking of ghosts, silly – don't you ever read the papers or listen to the news? Old ladies living alone are beaten up or murdered every night."

"No, I don't read the papers or listen to the news if I can

help it, at least not that sort of news, though if I did I bet they'd tell me that far more people are killed on the roads than murdered in their homes, yet it doesn't keep you out of your car."

"But I'm forced to take that risk or I'd never go anywhere. You're not forced to stay on here alone in this barracks of a place. Well, you always did know your own mind and I won't go on about it . . . I only meant to help. . . . Let's talk about something else – your view is as lovely as ever anyway."

Roberta, who had been thinking how tiresome Kitty could be, melted at once; besides, she felt she had had the best of the argument and she was really very fond of her cousin.

After Kitty had gone the phone rang. It was Naomi.

"Is anything wrong?" enquired her grandmother anxiously – it was not yet time for her usual monthly call.

"No, I'm fine, but I've had your letter and Clare's and really, dear, though I know she fusses, I do agree with her this time. Besides, it isn't only her, it's Alex too. Do think about it, don't just refuse because they're urging it."

So, clearly Naomi was *not* going to back her. The very idea of moving from Rowanbank! She might have considered it if the place was really like an old barracks, as Kitty had called it, and therefore bare; but it was more like a furniture depository stuffed from top to toe with the accumulation of years, and everything encrusted with memories and associations.

She looked at her husband's big oil paintings that covered the walls. They were workmanlike, very well painted, but old-fashioned in subject and treatment, faithfully representational; colour photography had really made them superfluous, she thought sadly. Still she loved them, not only because she, at any rate, thought them beautiful, but also because they reminded her of holidays they had spent together. Besides the landscapes that dominated the dining- and sitting-rooms, there were stacks of canvases in his studio – then there were all the books and her parents' solid large Victorian and Edwardian furniture and the few antiques that she and Charles had collected. . . .

Oh, no, it was hopeless, she and Mrs B. together could manage quite well, she felt sure, in spite of all this uncalled-for advice and admonition. Deciding not to bother any more, she went to sleep.

The real and decisive blow came some weeks later. Mrs B. was very late arriving – an unheard-of event – and, equally strange, she actually hurried as she came up the path to the kitchen door. As soon as she got in she sat down heavily on the nearest chair and began to weep. Roberta, who propped on one stick had been slowly stacking up the breakfast things at the sink, was struck with horrified amazement. There is something quite appalling in witnessing the breakdown of what has hitherto seemed an unassailable and blessed bulwark against misfortune.

"Oh, whatever is the matter?" she cried.

Mrs Baxter spoke between sobs: "It's my William, he's fell off a ladder almost as soon as he got to work. They came to tell me from the farm. His bad leg must've given way – it has been worse lately. They've brought him home."

"But," said Roberta stupidly, "you mustn't stay here then, you must go to him."

Mrs Baxter looked up at her, "Do you think I'd be here if he'd wanted me any more?" She was in command of herself now that the news was out and it was Roberta who was crying.

"You mustn't take on," she said. "It was God's will."

Roberta stifled a quick dissent; what was an outrage to her she saw was Mrs Baxter's one comfort.

The funeral was a week later. William Baxter had been widely loved and respected in the village and the new grave in the old churchyard was heaped with the bright flowers of spring.

"Grandpa's flowerbed is better than yours," said Mrs Baxter's youngest grandson, who had come with her to see Roberta the following day.

"You go and play with Willow, dearie," said Mrs Baxter. "You can give him his dinner if you're careful – it's all ready on the kitchen table. He asked me what a grave was," she explained when he had disappeared. "Someone had told him his grandpa was down in the grave now. I don't want him to think like that, I said it was grandpa's flowerbed and we'd come back and plant a rose tree on it later and now he's going round saying his grandpa's flowerbed's the best in the village."

The little boy's mother was Mrs Baxter's only daughter; she had two sons besides, one farming in Canada, the other in the navy. She was going to live with this daughter who kept a guest-house at Ramsgate and she had come to tell Roberta this.

"The cottage is tied, but you'll know that. Mr Chittenden wouldn't turn me out right now, don't think that, but I know he needs it and I can be of use to Betty: her husband's not up to much, though she won't admit it, and there's another baby on the way. I'm glad to go really, only I'm that worried about leaving you here all on your own, how will you manage?"

How indeed! thought Roberta. Then something seemed to snap in her brain and she heard herself saying: "You won't have to worry, Mrs B., for I'm going to make a move too – but that's between ourselves just for the present."

Mrs Baxter's face cleared. 'Oh, well, I *am* glad; fancy that now, it seems meant, doesn't it? No, no, of course I won't mention it to a soul and I'll not be going myself yet awhile. There's a deal to see to first, so I'll be coming along as usual for the time being. I dare say it'll be as long as you want me."

Chapter 2

THE DECISION seemed very sudden set off by Mrs Baxter's tragic news but Roberta realized that the skies had been gradually darkening since Kitty's visit. For instance, she had begun to notice things – stains and cracks, pieces of rotten woodwork, some patches of damp and a general air of dinginess. *You don't see wrinkles and lines on a loved familiar face until someone from outside remarks on them*, she thought, *and then you seem to see nothing else*.

She was now able to hobble round the garden. There, spring with its terrifying splendid growth had been this year left a free hand. Strong unpruned shrubs were thrusting aside the rarer timid plants, and the weeds! – not the pretty feathery wild flowers: cow parsley, campion, clover, sorrels and moon daisies that had in early summer once grown in the field before it became a garden, but huge fierce nettles, and thistles and docks in the corners; thick carpets of ground elder seemed to flourish everywhere while festoons of ivy spread across the paths and smothered the two lovely stone urns her father had brought from Greece long ages ago. Even the lilacs and the snowball trees had grown too large and straggly and failed to comfort her. She bent down in feeble protest to tug at some couch-grass rooting in the lily bed but found she couldn't straighten up again and would have fallen had she not clung to her stick. *Old age, really, why need it be so spiteful!* She had returned to the house a little shaken.

Now, after Mrs Baxter had gone, Roberta sat in the kitchen for a long while apparently doing nothing. Actually she was busy enough at the always unpleasant occupation of facing facts. Could the Baxters be replaced? Only by a miracle. There used to be no such problems, but now it seemed less and less possible to get anyone to do anything. No doubt she could be allowed a home help and "Meals on Wheels", but though that might keep her afloat it couldn't save Rowanbank. Could she or ought she to live on here with the place decaying all around her? Dry rot, wet rot, she saw them like little demons grimacing at her out of the shadows cast by the jungle outside that, growing and thrusting up and up, finally quite blocked out her view, while she herself, a cross between Miss Havisham and the old Queen in the Sleeping Beauty's Palace, dreamed and mumbled, covered with cobwebs, in a corner.

"No! If I can no longer cope with Rowanbank it must go to those who can," she said at last, and roused herself to finish the washing up.

But where could she go? Not to Alex's irreproachable Home, that was certain; nevertheless it would be nice to have some alternative before she let her family know that she was now prepared to leave. Barring the Home, probably everyone would expect her to find some convenient corner in the village. Actually she knew of three cottages that were or soon would be vacant, but to live so close to Rowanbank and not actually in it was somehow unthinkable. Besides, the cottages were too familiar. How could she ever feel that poor Alice Rose's little sitting-room, where she had often drunk tea from the best china that was kept in the alcove to the right of the fireplace with the portrait of Alice's mother over it, belonged to her? Could she presume to occupy John and Rachel Turner's marital bedroom after they had moved away to Folkestone, or invade Mrs Vincent's kitchen? It was impossible.

The more Roberta thought about it the more she felt that if she could not go on living at Rowanbank (and it seemed clear to her now that she couldn't) it would be better to make a clean break. It came to her in a flash that she would go back to Highgate, the only other place in the world where she had roots: had she not been born there and run about its streets as a child? It might do better than anywhere else to end there also.

She decided to consult Kitty. Kitty was the nearest to a sister that Roberta had known. She was six years younger, a gap wide when very young but narrowing with adolescence and negligible in middle age. Now, however, it was observable again, for Kitty was still mobile and energetic, running a shop and a library service for her local hospital and dashing about everywhere in her mini. She had lived in London all her life and had a flat in Islington.

"I'm glad you've seen sense at last," she barked briskly down the phone, "though very sorry about William, and I must say I think it very good sense, Berta, to come back to town. It'll be much easier to find the sort of thing you want – you're not going to be silly about flats, I hope?"

"Now don't bully me," said Roberta.

"As if I could, but if I did it's only what you deserve, my dear. Heavens! How you and Rollo used to boss me about in the old days; and you bossed Alex too, that's why he's so keen on the underdog now."

"Look here," said Roberta, "I'm not paying for this sort of talk, even if it is at the cheap rate. What I want to know is, will you find me somewhere to go as soon as possible? And I don't want Alex and Clare to know till I've burnt my boats."

"I'll do my best. It oughtn't to be too difficult. As soon as I've anything in view you'd better come up and stay for a night or two."

"Thank you," said Roberta. "I'd be very glad to do that."

325

Kitty's flat was much more comfortable than Alex's house, and Roberta always enjoyed her visits there. The curious thing was that Kitty herself seemed incapable of benefiting by its comforts. She had an odd way of kneeling on the floor instead of relaxing into one of her charmingly easy chairs. A favourite occupation was to play intricate games of Patience, kneeling there, talking volubly all the time, with the cards spread out before her on the carpet. She seldom bothered to take off her coat or change her shoes once she had put them on in the morning and this gave her an air of impermanence.

"You call in at your flat," said Roberta, "you don't live in it. And why don't you get a decent television? Everyone looks terribly ill on this one, and they all have green hair."

Kitty, kneeling in front of it, simply giggled. Roberta wondered why she found this endearing, while if Clare had so behaved it would have irritated her. *It's because I love Kitty, I suppose, and accept the whole of her, whereas I'm just fond of Clare and don't accept much of her at all.*

Not very long after she had consulted her, Roberta found herself at Kitty's in order to view a flat which she thought might do for her.

"If you should take to it, it would save a lot of trouble in the future and it really would be lucky to have found somewhere so soon."

It was one of a small complex planned for the elderly but not the incapable. Each flat had a fair sized sitting-room, a small bedroom and a still smaller kitchen and bathroom. The flats were perfectly private and independent of each other and there was a nice neutral warden who was only called upon in emergencies. The situation was quiet, facing a small, slightly dingy square garden for the common use of all the tenants.

'It's not a bad outlook from the front," said Kitty, "but the bedroom looks out on to a blank wall – do you think you could stand that after your view?"

"There was plenty of sky," said Roberta, "and do you know, I believe a blank wall might be better than ugliness."

"The kitchen's dreadfully small."

"I liked the kitchen; its fittings are so ingenious, like a ship's cabin, you couldn't be untidy in it, there wouldn't be room."

"So you really think you'll put in for it?" said Kitty.

The flat they had seen was still occupied but was to become available in the near future. Roberta optimistically hoped that she would have sold Rowanbank by then or at least that the dates would show a reasonable co-operation.

"Yes," she said decisively, "I want something settled in my mind and I don't see that I could do much better than this. I'd only be wasting your time; and I can't keep on coming up to town to look at places."

"What will you do about Willow?" asked Kitty. Sadly, but understandably, pets were not permitted at Coleridge Court.

"Willow wouldn't transplant to town life anyway," said Roberta. 'I'll have to find a home for him in the village." She would miss him but he had not proved one of her favourite cats. His mother had been both more intelligent and more affectionate. She considered Willow greedy – unless she were in bed he preferred the kitchen and Mrs Baxter to her company, but she could recommend him as an excellent mouser and he was undeniably handsome.

"Well, don't blame me if you don't like it when you get there," said Kitty. Whenever she succeeded in influencing her cousin she experienced a sort of fearful joy. Twelve years old had once declaimed to six years old: "I'm twice your age and therefore twice as clever." "You're not, you're not!" shouted affronted six years old, but secretly feared that twelve years old was right.

"Of course I shan't," said Roberta, "I'm truly grateful to you, Kitty."

327

As a matter of fact the whole business had taken on an air of unreality and it was as if in a dream that she asked the Warden to put down her name for No. 14 Coleridge Court and paid a deposit. This mood persisted when she wrote to tell Alex of her plans. It seemed as though she was inventing a passage of some imaginary autobiography. She enjoyed it. She decided to imply that it was largely owing to Alex and Clare's advice that she had made up her mind to leave Rowanbank, thus softening her absolute refusal to consider the wonderful Home for the Elderly. *And even if they don't swallow that*, she thought, *its a gesture.*

"Well!" exclaimed Alex on reading her letter. "It seems that Granny has decided on quitting at last."

"Really!" said Clare.

"She says she has come round to our way of thinking: I shouldn't wonder though if William Baxter's death hadn't something to do with it."

"Why, isn't Mrs Baxter staying on at the cottage?"

"She doesn't say."

"Is she going to take up a place at Fairlea?"

"No, she says she wants to go back to the Highgate district. Kitty's already found her a flat somewhere. Apparently it's all fixed up."

"I think she might have consulted you first," said Clare.

"Oh, I don't mind as long as she gets Rowanbank off her back. She wants me to run down and see her to talk it all over as soon as I can spare the time."

"And when will *that* be?" said Clare, frowning. "Your diary's absolutely full up for ages."

"I shall have to fit it in somehow," said Alex cheerfully. "I must say I'm relieved, I thought we'd have a regular tussle to move her and that she'd leave it too late. I'm sorry she's not going to Fairlea, though. She'll be no nearer us at Highgate than she is now."

"Oh, so am I," agreed Clare emphatically, and she really

did feel sorry because it was not going to happen. She even caught herself indulging in a sense of grievance because Roberta was turning to Kitty for help instead of to her. *Why do I want what I don't really want?* she asked herself anxiously.

It was only during Alex's visit that the reality and magnitude of her decision began seriously to dawn upon Roberta. She was about to break up her home, to destroy what was a living rich entity with which she had an immensely strong personal relationship and to replace it with an alien little box that had nothing whatever to do with her. Was this madness or was it sense? But William Baxter was dead, Mrs Baxter was leaving the village, Rowanbank was falling to bits, "change and decay in all around I see". It was not she who was committing this outrage, it was Time.

'Alex had put the house into agents' hands and was now suggesting an auction of its contents – "There's a lot of furniture to be got rid of and the books – some of those must be quite valuable. I think an auction is really necessary, Gran."

"Yes," said Roberta mournfully, "but you and Clare and Naomi will want some things, I hope. I should like Patrick to have the grandfather clock."

"That's good of you," said Alex. "Now don't worry about anything – I'll see to all the business side of things. I know it's a wrench for you but I'm absolutely sure you're doing the right thing."

But after he had departed Roberta looked round about her and despair once more seized her.

"I must make a list," she said to herself, "that will help me, several lists in fact." She had always been addicted to making lists. Almost as soon as Roberta could write, her nurse used to find, stuffed into secret corners of the nursery, lists of her toys (the dolls with their names and ages), lists of her pets, and later on she made lists of her teachers and schoolfellows, carefully graded as "very nice", "nice", "harmless" and "horrible". She continued through life to make lists, of books that she had read during the year, of those she meant to read, lists of Christmas and birthday cards; even making out shopping lists gave her a sort of satisfaction. She supposed she liked lists because they imposed order, which she liked, on confusion, which she feared. But now, faced with a more chaotic state of affairs than she had ever known or, she hoped, would ever have to face again, she found herself disinclined after all to begin on any of the required lists. Instead she thought she would write to Patrick about the clock. *No, I will phone him*, she decided, *I'd like to hear his response.*

Alex had not yet thought to mention the matter. He was enjoying a rare time of leisure with his family in the garden. It was a lovely day and everyone including Bertram was in a genial mood. Clare was sewing, Patrick reading, Becky drawing houses with beautiful bright red roofs and Bertram was again busy with his car, now filled with as many of Becky's dolls as could be squeezed into it. Then, suddenly deciding that he would prefer it to carry bricks, he called out:

"Becky, will I bring your children back to you, shall I?"

"Yes," said Becky.

It took him some time, since he was at the bottom of the garden and the car had to be carried up some steps, but he arrived panting and pleased and unloaded the dolls.

"They cried all the way up," he remarked complacently.

"What for did they cry?" asked Becky.

'Well, I doesn't like them and they doesn't like me," said Bertram.

"What for don't they like you?"

"Cos I think they've got silly-looking faces and *so* I doesn't like them and *so* they doesn't like me."

"But they likes me," said Becky.

"Oh, yes, they likes you," said Bertram.

"Why do they like her?" enquired Alex, who had been following the conversation with interest.

"Because *she* doesn't mind them having silly-looking faces," said Bertram, "and so they likes her."

"Yes, they likes me," said Becky, disregarding, however, the heap of dolls at her feet and adding another lovely red house to her drawing.

"I wonder if Bertram is going to be a philosopher," said his father, and Clare immediately had a vision of her younger son lecturing in a university hall to a crowd of enthusiastic students. Was it Oxford or Cambridge? She knew that ideologically she ought to have preferred one of the modern universities, but there were certainly towers about and the Hall was panelled. She was drawn back to the present by the telephone.

"I'll go," she said, "and then I'll see about tea."

But she came back almost at once. "It's Granny," she said, "she wants to speak to Patrick. Whatever for, I wonder?"

They soon knew. Patrick came flying out of the house shouting: "She's going to give me the grandfather clock, Granny's giving it to me for myself!"

"Good gracious," said Clare, "she can't."

"Why do you say she can't, Mother?" said Patrick. "She can, can't she, Dad? I think it's super of her."

"Oh," said Alex. "She did mention it to me, now I come to think of it. What's the problem?"

"Where on earth can we put it? There simply isn't room," said Clare.

"Sorry, dear," said Alex, "I never thought of that, but I'm sure we'll manage somewhere."

"We might build a tower for it in the garden," suggested Patrick, "or we could make a hole in the dining-room ceiling so that it could poke through into mine and Bertram's bedroom, then you'd never feel lonely when I wasn't there, Bertram, because it would go on talking to

331

you. I shall never forget to wind it up and so it will never stop talking."

"All through the night?" asked Bertram in sepulchral tones.

"Yes, all through the night. You'll like that, won't you?" said Patrick.

"No," said Bertram.

Clare agreed with him. She remembered that the clock, a handsome very large mahogany Victorian piece, had a particularly penetrating chime. Really, Alex might have had more sense; but then men hadn't, even the nicest of them. Now it was impossible for her to refuse to have the clock without mortally offending both Patrick and Roberta. The only place for it, she thought in despair, would be in the hall round the corner by the stairs, but that was also the only place to keep the family's coats and shoes and where a most useful row of pegs and a basin would need to be removed.

"*I* want a clock," remarked Becky, "I want a clock much the best."

Bequests are sometimes tricky, even more so perhaps when the donors are still alive. Roberta had not meant to embarrass Clare, she had thought only of pleasing Patrick and of keeping the clock in the family. It hadn't even looked particularly large to her in the lofty hall of Rowan-bank. Similarly, though far from unimaginative, she failed to envisage the suitability of Charles's paintings in different surroundings.

Dr Thompson had always particularly admired a menacingly dark mountain storm scene that hung above the wide fireplace in the dining-room.

"I'd so like you to have that," said Roberta when he came to give her a final check up. She wasn't to know of the conversation that would take place when Dr Thompson took it home.

332

"I couldn't say 'no'," he told his wife, 'she meant it so kindly and it is a good painting; after all it might be worth quite a lot one day. You never know with pictures."

"You'll have to hang it in the surgery," said his wife grimly, looking round her pretty pastel-coloured sitting-room, "and I only hope it doesn't frighten the patients as much as it does me."

Then Alex, who so seldom wanted anything for himself, expressed a strong feeling about a needlework stool, a golden gentle Venetian lion on a crimson background which he asserted he had loved from babyhood. But Kitty laid claim to it, as it had been worked by her mother. In the end, there was feeling on both sides which was unpleasant, though Alex gave in.

Naomi was simply vague. "You know what I'd like, Mother," she said, but Roberta didn't know, nor what she would be prepared to pay to take back with her to Austria.

Value, sentiment and utility were all complicating factors in the division of goods, which Roberta had supposed a simple matter. And she still had not begun on what Alex said should be her first concern, those articles she herself was going to take with her to Coleridge Court. The problem of Willow, the cat, also worried her. She had not yet found a home for him. All animal-lovers seemed already to possess a cat or dog or both, and Willow, she knew, would never take to sharing; he was a born indi-vidualist.

It was a thoroughly disagreeable time but Roberta supposed she would get through it somehow – the sense of unreality was still with her and was a help. Mercifully too Mrs Baxter was as good as her word and, stoutly refusing to leave the cottage until Rowanbank itself was vacated, came in to do for Roberta as usual. Since William's death there had been a growing bond between the two women. Roberta had begun to call her Ellen, a familiarity she had never presumed on before, and it seemed welcome. She looked forward to seeing her and to discussing their mutual problems.

One morning Mrs Baxter put down a saucer of milk for Willow, who sniffed at it as if it were poison and then walked away.

"He'll come back to it," said Mrs Baxter. "Have you placed him yet, Mrs Curling?"

"No," said Roberta, "and I *don't* want to have to take him to the vet."

"Well, now," said Mrs Baxter, "I was wondering, Betty's old Dinah has had to be put down; she had bronchitis, poor thing. I could ask if she'd mind me bringing Willow with me. It won't be what he's used to but the children are good with animals and there's a fair piece of garden."

"Oh, Ellen! That would be a relief," said Roberta. "I'm sure he'd be happy with you – he's always preferred you really."

Willow had returned to the milk, finished it, washed up and polished the plate and was now regarding them with a fixed intensity.

"He knows we're talking about him," said Mrs Baxter fondly. But it was really only a flea, which when located he dealt with proficiently.

"I wish I could do something for *you*, Ellen," said Roberta. "I suppose there's none of my things you'd fancy?"

Mrs Baxter shook her head. "I'll take the will for the deed, dear," she said. "I'll only have the one room and that I'm sharing with Lenny after the baby comes, so there'll be very little I can take."

"Oh, dear," said Roberta, "what are you doing with all your things then?"

"Will's brother's coming for them with his van – my niece, she's getting married and setting up a home and'll be glad of them so I haven't near so much bother as you have."

"But don't you mind parting with everything?" said Roberta.

Mrs Baxter stopped what she was doing to consider.

"I don't know that I hold much with minding," she said at last in her calm, curiously impressive way. "There's always something to be going on with. No, I'm not troubled. I've arranged with the vicar about keeping Will's grave nice; I'm sending something regular – not that I think of him as there of course, only he always liked to have things neat. It worried him lately about your garden."

"Yes, I know," said Roberta. "I'm sorry."

That day, after Mrs Baxter had left she sat for some time thinking. At length, "There's always somthing to be going on with," she quoted to herself. She took a sheet of paper from her writing desk, sat down and headed it:

List of articles to be taken with me to Coleridge Court.

She paused and looked round the room. Opposite her she saw a branch of the walnut tree and the portraits of her father and mother hanging above her bed. But it was not the actual tree nor the real portraits that she was looking at, rather their reflections.

No. 1, she wrote, *The Mirror*.

Chapter 3

"'How NICE it would be',"" read Roberta's mother from the Alice book, "'if we could only get through into Looking-Glass Land! I am sure it's got such beautiful things in it. . . . Why, the glass is turning into a sort of mist now, I declare. It'll be easy enough to get through,' and certainly the glass was beginning to melt away just like a bright silvery mist."

Roberta sat up straight on her mother's lap. "Is it true?" she asked.

"Of course, it's true," said her mother, "magic is always true." And then Nurse came for her to put her to bed and her mother closed the book.

"Oh, can't you go on and Nurse go away?" said Roberta.

"No, darling, you'll have to wait till tomorrow evening but I'll tell you now if you like that Alice *did* get through into Looking-Glass Land."

The next day when she was left alone and on one was in her mother's room where the mirror hung – the big oval mirror that Roberta admired so much – she stole in quietly. The mirror had two little gold boys on top of it, holding a crown of gold leaves between them. On the dressing-table below were two cut-glass scent bottles with silver stoppers and a silver-backed hairbrush and comb, and a beautiful little china tray on which a shepherd in a blue coat was bending over a shepherdess in pink, and looking as if he were just going to kiss her. Roberta loved this tray but now she had eyes only for the mirror. She pushed a chair up close to the dining table and climbed upon it, just as Alice had climbed on to the chimney piece, and she looked and looked and it did seem to her as if the room in the mirror must have something wonderful and exciting round the corner that you couldn't see. She began to press against the glass, feeling it all over, but it did not melt for her as it had done for Alice. She pressed and pressed; being an impatient child she began to get cross. Then it struck her that magic didn't always work the same way in stories; but if her mother said it was always true, it was only a question of finding the right way to go about it. Perhaps this looking-glass had to have a door made in it. She looked round for a tool and decided the back of the hairbrush would do. She lifted it up and with both hands hit the mirror a resounding crack. She was a strong child for her five years and there was a splinter of broken glass while the brush, rebounding from contact with the wooden back, flew out of her hands, fell on the china tray and broke it in two. Roberta, standing on the chair among splinters of china and glass, began to cry with disappointment and sorrow. There was no looking glass land after all and the beautiful tray was broken so that the poor shepherd and shepherdess were parted for ever.

But now the room became full of cross surprised scolding people, and rage was added to despair.

"What a wicked little girl!" said Nurse.

Roberta, climbing down from the chair, tried to hit her and burst into a passion of sobbing.

"Stop now, Roberta," said her father. "You've done enough to upset Mama already." He bore her away and his authoritative but calm tone of voice and his large pocket handkerchief reduced her sobs gradually to silence.

"Now tell me," said her father, "what made you go smashing up all Mama's pretty things of a sudden?"

"I was only trying to get through into Looking-Glass

Land like Alice. Mama said it was magic and magic was always true but it wasn't true," hiccupped Roberta.

"Now listen," said her father, "magic is true always for Mama, but for you and for me, Roberta, it is different, do you understand?"

She nodded. She did not understand, of course, but dimly she saw that there was something to be understood. She was also for the first time aware that, though a divinity to be worshipped still, Mama was not always to be depended on.

"But the poor shepherd and shepherdess," she cried.

"Who?" said her father. "Oh, Mama's tray – I expect that can be mended and the mirror too; if not, we must buy her another mirror and another tray."

"But they won't be the same," said Roberta.

And though the mirror had a new glass, which looked too bright and clear for its frame, and the tray was stuck together cleverly so that you could only see a tiny line dividing the two little figures, things were actually never quite the same again.

By the time Roberta had reached her tenth birthday she was tall enough to see over her mother's shoulders the reflection of her face as she sat before the mirror. Her father was clasping round her neck a new necklace. It was of greenish-blue turquoises to match her eyes. They were lovely eyes with dark curling lashes and finely arched eyebrows and the face was a classical oval like a Botticelli goddess. It was pale like a Botticelli too with a flowerlike clear pallor that added to its charm. Her father also was looking at the reflection and smiling.

"Why does Father always give you a present on my birthday?" asked Roberta of the face in the mirror.

"She's jealous," laughed her mother.

"Well, I give you one too," said her father. "Didn't you like it? I thought you wanted a watch."

"Oh, yes, of course," said Roberta, "I didn't mean that."

But they neither of them answered her.

Long ago, naturally, she had asked her mother the usual questions of how she had come to have a birthday at all.

Her mother's eyes shone perilously. "Well," she began, "well, darling, have I never told you? It was like this; one day I woke up early and I heard a great whirring and a beating of wings at the window. I jumped out of bed and looked and I couldn't see the sky at all for the rose-coloured feathers of a huge bird with eyes like emeralds and a golden beak outside my window. He swooped past once, twice, but the third time he perched upon the sill and I saw that on his back, nestling among those glorious feathers, was a tiny baby girl who stretched out her arms to me – and that was you!"

"Was it?" shouted Roberta. "And what did you do?"

"Of course, I leaned out of the window and caught you up and the bird flew off at once and vanished high up above the clouds."

This story had charmed Roberta until she grew too old to believe it, or possibly she had never really believed it, not at any rate after she had broken the mirror; and later, instead of pleasing her, it began to haunt her. *Perhaps I am adopted*, she thought, *perhaps this was just Mother's way of telling me I'm not really their child at all*.

At last, making her voice sound as matter-of-fact as possible, she said one day to her father: "By the way, I've been reading a story about a boy who was found as a baby and adopted. I'm not adopted by any chance, am I?"

Her father laughed. "My dear Roberta, come and look in Mama's mirror. Now don't you see, you and I have got just the same sort of eyes – cat's eyes my mother called them, a queer kind of yellowish colour that polite people call hazel; and I'm afraid you've got my big nose too and jutting-out chin. It's hard luck on you, my dear, to have taken after me so obviously but you've got your mother's

339

hair." He pulled Roberta's thick fair pigtail. "Well, now are you satisfied?"

By that tenth birthday, however, she knew that babies came out of their mothers but she did not know how they got there. Children were never then taught the facts of life, they just picked them up or didn't, as the case might be.

"Does it hurt getting the babies out?" she asked Rose, her best friend, who was a mine of information.

"Yes," said Rose, "and sometimes you die."

"But why don't men have babies?"

"I don't know, they just don't, and it's their fault too. I don't quite know how yet, but I don't think it's fair."

Roberta thought this conversation over. Perhaps it had something to do with the presents to her mother on her own birthday. Later, once when she was spending the day with Kitty, her aunt came in from a neighbour's and exclaimed to her uncle: "Thank goodness, Bessie's baby's come at last. It's a boy. I'm afraid she's had a bad time but it's all right now."

"Oh, what's he like? Did you see him?" asked Kitty, but Roberta said:

"Did Mother have a bad time when I was born, Aunt Margaret?"

Her aunt looked flustered. "Oh, girls, I didn't notice you. Whatever makes you ask that, Roberta?"

"I just wondered."

"Then you needn't wonder any more. You mustn't think all babies are difficult. You behaved very well I remember and gave your mother little trouble. Of course," she added, "your father made a fuss, perhaps you've heard something, but he makes a fuss if she pricks her little finger."

Roberta said nothing. She was aware, and not for the first time, of an edge in her aunt's voice when she spoke of her mother. It was not at all what she was used to, for everyone else seemed to adore her. Her mixture of beauty, gaiety and a sort of innocent silliness combined with that indefinable grace, which is called charm, was generally irresistible. Men of all ages were her slaves and her husband accepted this with pride, for he was confident in her absolute reliance on himself. As for love, there are infinite varieties of this. When she was old enough to observe such things, Roberta sometimes thought there was little difference between her mother's love for her father and her own, and that her relationship with other men was rather like a little girl's pretending to be grown up, pleased with admiration, expanding like a flower in its warmth but never in the least troubled.

The years passed, but her mother's face in the mirror hardly altered. Roberta, now in her mid-teens, was watching her sitting in front of it trying on hats. Beside her, thrust anyhow into an old blue and white pitcher, was a bouquet of flowers: pink roses, pale blue delphiniums and purple columbine. There was never anyone who took less trouble than her mother arranging flowers, Roberta thought, yet the effect was often unpredictably perfect.

"I look a fright, a perfect hag."

"Of course you don't, Mother."

"Yes, I do, none of these hats will do. Ever since I sold that little black one to my dear, dear friend Helen, I have wanted it desperately. I really must get it back from her."

"Why on earth did you sell it then?"

"I suppose I must have wanted the money terribly for something and your father must have been away. I thought I had too many hats but I was completely mistaken. Now what am I to do?"

"Why can't you wear that lovely one with the curling feather that makes you look like a Gainsborough?"

"Too big, especially in a storm."

"But it's perfectly fine."

'Not when I wear that hat, it always turns to thunder then – there must be something sinister about it. No, I shan't wear a hat at all, just a wrap, I think." She threw a rose-coloured scarf round her head. To Roberta it was as if the little shepherdess on the china tray had stepped out of her Virginian landscape into Looking-Glass Land. She said so.

"Darling, you are sweet," said her mother, "but where is my shepherd? Immured in London, poor fellow. Never mind, I'm going to meet my knight instead."

"Old Sir Joseph?" enquired Roberta. Sir Joseph Maxwell was the squire of the village and owned the woods around Rowanbank.

Her mother nodded. "Do you know, Roberta, I was walking in the woods one day and I sat down to rest under our special oak tree – the one you used to love to climb – and Sir Joseph came riding by on his great horse and he dismounted and bowed to me and said: 'Lady of the woods, you must not sit upon the ground. I shall have a seat put here for your own particular use.' Yesterday he sent the word that it was there ready for me and I am to meet him there this morning."

"Is this true?" asked Roberta. She never knew.

"True, true, true, as true as Una and the Red Cross Knight in the dark forest," her mother said, and left.

"It's a lovely seat," she told Roberta and her father that evening, "and actually inscribed with my name. Do, do both of you come now and see."

"I've got my preparation to do," said Roberta.

They were spending most of the year at Rowanbank by now and she had wanted to go with Rose to one of the new big public schools for girls, but her father had said: "We want our only child at home," so she attended classes in Hastings instead. She knew that if she had been a Robert, though still an only child, there would have been no question of staying at home.

"'O fret not after knowledge, I have none
And yet the evening listens.' . . . Remember Keat's thrush, Roberta," said her mother.

342

"But I'm not a thrush," said Roberta and would not go. Birds, for her mother, she reflected, were never themselves, always voices or spirits.

The years ticked away on the grandfather clock. Roberta was now so tall that if she wanted to look into the mirror she had to stoop or sit on her mother's chair, for she had inherited her father's height as well as his looks. Her mother seemed a sprite beside her. *So much change in me*, thought Roberta (she was nearly twenty-one), *and so little in her*. For there was not a grey hair in her mother's head, nor a wrinkle on her face. But her father, on the other hand, seemed suddenly to have aged and to be always tired. He had become very thin and his skin, instead of being tanned by the summer's warmth, was dry and sallow. He had been away for a few days, ostensibly on a visit to his brother's home, but Roberta anxiously suspected it was to consult their old family doctor in London. Her mother had noticed nothing wrong – or had she just shut her eyes to it? One could not tell. She did not seem at all troubled the evening he was expected back.

"Read me some poetry, Berta," she said.

"What shall I read?" asked Roberta obediently.

"Tennyson, I think. Yes, I feel like some Tennyson today, anything that comes."

Roberta took down the volume and it opened at "The Lady of Shalott".

"'And moving through the mirror clear
That hangs before her all the year,
Shadows of the world appear –'" She had got thus far when she heard her father's step on the stairs.

"Hallo, my dears," he said. "Reading poetry?"

He bent over Roberta and took the book from her; turning the leaves, he read out the last verse himself:

"'Who is this and what is here?
And in the lighted Palace near
Died the sounds of royal cheer.

343

But Lancelot paused a little space.
He said: "She has a lovely face.
God in his mercy grant her grace,
The Lady of Shalott.""

His voice broke and Roberta looked up quickly.

"You look very tired, Father," she said, "let me get you something to eat." She got up but he followed her out of the room.

"You mustn't worry your mother by saying things like that in front of her," he said. "I'm all right, only a bit washed out by the journey in this heat. I don't want any food. I think I'll go and have a swim, that always makes me feel better. Don't wait dinner for me – goodbye."

He sounded brusque and, a little hurt, something made her go to the door and wave him off. He waved back and that was the last she saw of him.

They found his clothes in his usual favourite bathing spot, folded up carefully – he was always neat – but they never found him, and Roberta was sure that that was what he would have wished. "He was such a good swimmer," they said, "it must have been a sudden attack of cramp."

The next day the letter came for her. Her father knew that she was always down first in the morning and collected the post. As soon as she saw the writing she took it up to her room. It was very short and said: "I have inoperable cancer. Your mother must not be subjected to the strain and ugliness that my probably drawn-out illness would cause her. This is the last thing I can do for her, for she will be able to bear it much better this way. You will keep my secret and there is no need to ask you to cherish her. You are my good daughter. I have left all my affairs in order. God bless you."

She sat with the letter in her lap for some time and then she found some matches and burnt it and went down to breakfast.

Her mother, thought Roberta, was one of the few people

who could cry without making herself look hideous, in fact her tears seemed only to add to her appeal, making her eyes look larger and more vivid in colour. She had wept quietly all the previous day but she was not crying any more now.

She looked up as Roberta came in and said, "It was such a beautiful way for your father to go, wasn't it, darling, at sunset, with the sea like a shimmering pearl? I noticed it especially that evening."

"Yes," replied Roberta, but to herself she was saying: *How can I bear this romanticizing? You can't romanticize death, it is too big. A beautiful way to go – to go where? To some island of Avalon I suppose. "A woman incapable of tragedy",* where had she heard that and about whom? Then she rebuked herself for this bitterness. Tennyson's poem still rang in her ears. Was not her mother another Lady of Shalott, sheltered behind the magic web of her father's protective love that had kept her away from reality, among "her space of flowers", in Looking-Glass Land to the end?

It was too late now for any change and, as far as Roberta could tell, the spell was never broken, for after her father's death, her mother withdrew further and further away into her dream world. She managed even to evade the reality of her own ageing and death. She never went grey, instead her hair became a moonlit instead of a golden halo round the smooth face and her eyes, lovely still, gradually grew vacant, the enchanting smile meaningless.

The grandfather clock struck the hour, but in what year? At first Roberta simply could not think and was it in her mother's room or her own that the mirror, which had ceased to reflect anything at all, was now just a dim oval shape in the darkness? Slowly the present imposed itself once more upon her consciousness and she pulled her ageing bones out of her chair and switched on the light.

345

Chapter 4

ROBERTA DECIDED that, what with the mirror and book-shelves and cupboards, there would not be room for many pictures on the walls of the little flat at Coleridge Court. The bedroom was really very small; she would keep her family photographs there and she must make her choice of only three or four paintings for the sitting-room. It was a difficult and distasteful problem, for Rowanbank was full of pictures, most of them Charles's, and she must decide which of these to keep, which were really her favourites among them. Only the smaller ones would be practical, she feared; the others, if they could not be disposed of among family and friends, she supposed must go into the auction. But there was one other picture that she must certainly keep beside her husband's – it had belonged to Rollo, her cousin, Kitty's brother and her first love. To part with this would hurt – yes, even after all these years.

Rollo was only two years older than Roberta and this is no barrier to a companionship if tastes are shared so, whereas Kitty was held to be too young for her brother's pursuits, Roberta, who was what her elders disapprovingly called a tom-boy, was his inseparable ally.

"I don't like your friend Dick," she had said to him when they were children.

"Why?" asked Rollo. "He's a nice boy."

"No, he isn't; he thinks I'm no good because I'm a girl, but you don't, do you? Because you know I'm really a boy."

Whatever Rollo did, Roberta had to do too. "They egg each other on," was the general complaint. Neither had any sense of physical fear, but Roberta, being the younger, often came off the worst in their scrapes. Rollo's passion was for climbing roofs, trees, rocks, the higher and more perilous the better. Both children seemed to have charmed lives, but several times Roberta fell and each time bore her bumps and bruises with nonchalance so as not to call down vengeance on Rollo, who had whispered: "Good for you, Bobs" – recompense enough. He was a nice-looking boy, with very blue wide-open eyes and freckles, about which he was sometimes teased.

"Well, I like them," declared Roberta, "and Mother says they show you are favoured by Apollo the sun-god, you know."

"She *would*," said Rollo but added, being no less under his aunt's spell than the rest of mankind: "She can if she likes, but I won't have anyone else talking such rot about me."

When tired of more active pursuits, he and Roberta would devise adventure stories and then act them out, with Kitty dragged in to be a squaw or a cabin-boy or a prisoner.

Childhood passed, the long days grew shorter and soon began to race past. Roberta, now in her teens, still knew and thought nothing of sex. She liked being with Rollo better than with anyone else, but she took him for granted. In that Freud-free world she remained utterly ignorant and unconcerned, though when she did give any such matter a thought it seemed as though it was rather fatally easy to find yourself having a baby. The Bible, an irreproachable if not very explicit source of information, spoke simply of "knowing each other", whatever that might mean, and in Shakespeare's *A Midsummer Night's Dream*, which they did one term at school, Hermia seemed mysteriously

347

anxious for Lysander to "lie further off". Then there was *Adam Bede*: Hetty and Arthur just met each other in that summerhouse and it seemed that neither of them thought anything special had happened; it was weeks later before poor Hetty knew about the baby.

Roberta had been reading the book one holiday when Rollo and Kitty were staying at Rowanbank; she was fifteen by then. She and Rollo had been for a long bicycle ride together and had flung themselves down on the sweet-smelling Downland by a dew pond to rest. They were lying so close together that she felt the warmth of his body and saw the little beads of perspiration on his forehead, and that night she lay awake worrying. She had certainly "lain with him" and she didn't want a baby at all. It would ruin her chances of being captain of hockey. Besides, she did at least know that it was considered terrible to have a baby without being married, *Adam Bede* had taught her that. Well, she couldn't help it – if it happened, it must. But it didn't, so that was all right. But as far as excitement went, Miss Godfrey, her darling games mistress, was a far greater source of thrills than Rollo.

The following year she was sent to a convent school in Bruges to improve her French and to learn not to be such a hoyden, and then she was brought home again in a hurry because of the War. What with all this, she and Rollo saw little of each other until she was seventeen and he had just left his public school. Then he came for another visit and things were changed; they were still good companions, but he looked at her in a different way and this made her look at herself differently too.

"I like that yellow dress you've got on," he said one day. "It matches your eyes. I don't know anyone else with little gold flecks in their eyes like yours, Bobs."

"Father has, he calls them cat's eyes," she said quickly, because she felt suddenly shy though pleased. Fancy Rollo making her feel shy!

348

But the last evening of his stay she took care to put on the yellow dress again and something made her pin a yellow rose at her neck. After dinner they were left alone, her parents having gone for an evening stroll. Rollo chose a record, a collection of songs, and put it on the gramophone – a new acquisition with a huge blue and gold horn. The songs were mostly old and sentimental, the last was her mother's favourite "Roaming in the gloaming with my sweetheart by my side".

"Well, let us go roaming, shall we, Bobs?" said Rollo when it was finished. "We may as well follow the example of our elders, but we'll take a different path, I think; they went to the woods so we'll go through the fields."

They went into the garden full of the evening scents of white jasmine and late-flowering honeysuckle and the heavy scent of elder flowers shining like multitudinous small moons in the dusk. As soon as they had gone through the gate with the meadow beyond, Rollo put his arm around her, turned her face to his and kissed her gently. It was the first kiss she had ever had that meant something special and, though it was so gentle, the memory of it was to remain with her – a part of her life always. But he soon took his arm away and began to talk eagerly.

"I'm going to join up of course now I'm eighteen. I shall join the RFC, I've quite decided on that and I can't help hoping the war won't be over before I've had a go. You'd like me to be in the RFC, wouldn't you – rather than the other services, I mean?"

"Oh, yes," said Roberta, thrilling to his enthusiasm, even though she could not help a little stab of fear.

"After the war I'll go to Oxford; the parents are set on that. But I mean when I've finished there to take up engineering, I think, because I really want to build bridges and railways and things in Africa or somewhere the other side of the world. You won't mind that, Bobs, will you? You'll marry me, won't you, and come with me?"

"Of course," assented Roberta. It seemed both beautiful and inevitable and her heart danced with joy, in spite of that small creeping shadow; the war couldn't go on much longer anyway.

He was off early the next day.

"Rollo and I are engaged," she announced to her parents after he had gone.

"How sweet, darling," said her mother.

But her father said: "You are much too young, both of you."

Rollo adored his training. He wrote Roberta letters that were full of the exhilaration of this new element he was exploring. "Every time I go up, there is this terrific feeling of power when the plane takes off, spurning the old earth, and in a few moments there I am higher than the highest mountains – amazing!"

There were his companions too – all marvellous, according to him, but especially his Squadron Leader – "not what you'd expect somehow, an amazing sort of chap, paints in his spare time and reads poetry. He's lost an arm and that's why he's trainng us now. He sells some of his pictures, sometimes in aid of the Red Cross. I've bought one, I'll bring it home on my next leave which, with any luck, will be my last before I'm off on active service."

But Roberta didn't see the painting until a good deal later on. It was spring when they heard that he had been shot down but had managed to make a forced landing behind the front line and was in hospital with a broken leg. Roberta was arranging daffodils in a bowl when her father told her the news, and suddenly she felt fully conscious of the fear that she had all this while refused to contemplate. "Now," she said to herself, "now there is a future."

The end of the war was at last in sight and, because of his leg, Rollo's demobilization came through quickly and he was able to enter his father's old college. Just before Armistice Day, Roberta was allowed to go up to Oxford with her aunt and Kitty to help settle him in. She always afterwards saw the city in her imagination as it was then – the trees golden against the grey stone walls, the misty faint luminous river, dahlias still smouldering in the college garden round which Rollo proudly limped as if he owned it all. He was simmering with high spirits. It was as though the horrors that had engulfed so many of his generation had passed him by and the whole of that visit seemed to Roberta to be blissfully and simply happy. A sort of unacknowledged capitulation had apparently taken place among their elders. She knew that they still considered her too young for a proper engagement and also that both sets of parents disapproved of first cousins marrying, but she and Rollo had no reservations. Rollo bought her a string of amber beads at a little shop in Ship Street and when he gave it to her they both became very serious.

"I'm saving up for a ring. I want to have something really nice; you shall have it by Christmas," said Rollo.

His rooms in college were, so his mother pronounced, both dark and poky, but Rollo was delighted with them. The painting he had written about had pride of place above the mantelshelf. It was an arresting picture that looked as if it had been hurled on to the canvas: it was nearly all of the sky, great clouds, thick and solid; below, darkness with the suggestion of roofs and chimneys, and then, in one corner, a break in the clouds and a bright patch, flying into the midst of which was a tiny plane.

"When I bought it, do you know what he said to me, Bobs?" said Rollo: "'I'm glad you're the one getting that picture, young Connolly, but look here, that plane's not a bomber, you can see that, can't you? It's a civilian plane.' Yes, he said that as if it were important."

"It's so small, I don't see how anyone could tell," said Roberta.

"Oh, I can tell all right and I can see the pilot too; bomber or no bomber, I bet he's happy."

351

"I wonder if I shall ever fly," said Roberta.

"Of *course* you will, everyone will be doing it soon. We'll fly together to wherever I'm going to build my bridges."

The letter she had after that visit was as buoyant as ever. Men were coming up now from the services and he had met an old RFC pal who greatly admired his picture, work was fine, everything was terrific, but people had begun to go down with that beastly Spanish flu germ that was going round everywhere, a fellow he coached with, a terrifically good chap, had it, he hoped it wouldn't reach Rowanbank. "Always your Rollo." There was a postscript about Armistice Day: "Glorious, wish you had been here, we painted the Caesars' heads red – the ones outside the Sheldonian you know, fine old bastards, they look as if they enjoyed it; brightens them up no end. Will tell you more next time."

But there was no next time. Aunt Nell was summoned to Oxford after Rollo had been found slumped over his books in the grip of the terrible post-war influenza.

"It is mostly the strongest who get it worst," said the doctor. "They won't give in until it is too late."

Rollo's temperature soared and after a few days' struggle his heart gave out. There was nothing to fight the germs with but aspirin. Whole colleges became hospitals, and the bells were tolling as if the great Plague had come to Oxford again.

"He never knew he was dying," her aunt told Roberta. "I'm so thankful for that, he loved life so, even in his delirium he seemed happy – he talked continually of flying and he spoke often of you. 'Bobs, Bobs,' he kept on saying, 'I must tell Bobs.' I want you to have that picture he was so fond of, I am sure he would wish you to have it."

Roberta, as she now looked at Rollo's picture, wondering where she would hang it at Coleridge Court, saw it again with attention for the first time for many years, while thoughts of Rollo came flooding back. With his death, something had also died in her. *Bits of us are always getting killed and other bits are born*, she thought. With Rollo had vanished her age of innocence – there was to be no more "piping down the valleys wild"; the joys that came later were no less, perhaps even greater, but they were certainly different. She wondered, not indeed for the first time, what her life would have been like had Rollo lived. It would probably have taken her away, far away from Rowanbank, it would at least outwardly have been more eventful and exciting and they would have been happy together, she was sure, as they had always been. But to what depth this happiness would have reached she was not certain. Their young love had grown between them as naturally as if it had been born with them – it had been like spring water rather than wine.

She decided she would hang Rollo's picture above the door in the new flat and the bookshelves would go against the wall facing the gas fire, free for at least two of her husband's paintings. Which should she choose?

Chapter 5

THERE WERE so many of Charles's pictures, he had been a prolific painter and during the latter part of his life his pictures had gone out of fashion and he had not sold many, so there they were on the walls of Rowanbank and stacked in his studio. He had never been, as he would ruefully agree, a very original or inspired artist.

"Well, I think it's lovely!" Roberta would say.

"No," said Charles firmly, "it's lost the spark – of course it was there to begin with or I never would have started, but it's got lost on the way. Never mind, I can always have another go."

Roberta was completely sincere in her admiration, for she never asked that a painting should do anything but faithfully recall a scene or an object that she thought beautiful and this her husband's pictures invariably did. She was not therefore, she was ashamed to admit, now concerned with which were Charles's *best* pictures but merely with what they represented. She also had to consider their size. Her first choice was a watercolour, subdued in tone, of a cluster of grey roofs in the foreground and, beyond, a wide stretch of moorland.

Charles Curling had literally jumped into Roberta's life. It was nearly a year after her father's death, her aunt had packed her mother and herself off for a holiday in Scotland. They were to stay at Dunfermline with Kitty's old governess,

Miss Jamieson, known as Jimes to all the family. Jimes now kept a small very select guest-house in that historic town and Aunt Nell had the satisfaction of killing two birds with one stone.

"You both need a holiday and Jimes needs guests now that the holiday season is over. You can have a few days in Edinburgh on the way, everyone should visit Edinburgh once at least."

They had both loved Edinburgh – Roberta for its architecture and grand views and her mother for its romantic associations: St Margaret and Robert Bruce and Mary Queen of Scots and Bonnie Prince Charlie, all mixed up together in her glancing butterfly mind. Roberta would have liked to have stayed longer but Jimes was expecting them and was not one to be kept waiting, so they caught the prescribed train. Just as it was leaving, the door of the carriage was flung open and a strange-looking young man flung himself and his bag into the corner opposite Roberta, who was first alarmed and then annoyed. *He might have hurt himself and perhaps he means no good*, she thought, for it was not a corridor train and she had always been warned to look out if a man invaded a carriage containing only one or two unprotected females. At first his looks did nothing to reassure her: he had a scar running down one cheek, his eyebrows were non-existent and, although he was young, his hair was quite white. He was no albino, however, for a pair of very alert grey eyes met hers and then crinkled at the corners as he smiled and apologized. She felt at once that there was no cause for alarm but she was still annoyed, especially as he began at once to make conversation. Roberta did not approve of people who talked to strangers in trains.

The young man had noticed the guide book on Roberta's lap. "This your first visit?" he enquired and then, as they drew free of the station, he began to point out places of interest.

"See that imposing building? Queen Victoria took a fancy to it. She asked the city to give it to her but they refused so she

355

never came here again. It's a hospital now."

"Really," said Roberta, and ostentatiously opened her book.

"I'm afraid I'm disturbing you," he said, "I'm sorry. Now there, the airport is on your right and then you need not look at anything more till you get to the Forth Bridge."

She could not help smiling.

"You know Scotland well, I see," said her mother graciously, "yet I think you are English like ourselves."

"And you are perfectly correct, I'm at the university, a failed medical student. I haven't failed quite enough yet to satisfy my father but soon I shall and then I mean to be an artist. I'm on a sketching weekend now – going to Loch Leven; but I won't talk any more, your daughter wants to read in peace. She is your daughter?" he added questioningly.

"Yes," said Roberta quickly, "but people hardly ever believe it." *I really rather like him*, she told herself, *though he is certainly tiresome – now I suppose I must read*. She bent her eyes on her book but found it hard to concentrate, feeling his glance annoyingly fasten on her instead of gazing at her mother – *Which he should be doing, especially if he's an artist*, she thought.

At Dunfermline, which they soon reached, he insisted on helping them out with their luggage and finding a porter for them and very nearly lost his train again.

"What a charming boy," said her mother. "Didn't you think he had a distinct likeness to that portrait of Bonnie Prince Charlie that we saw at Holyrood?"

"Oh, Mother, had Prince Charles white hair, no eyebrows and a scar? Besides, he's English."

"But I expect he's got Scottish blood in him, dear, we all have. And of course he got the scar in the War, and some terrible experience on the battlefield turned his hair white."

"Oh, well, we shall never know about *that*," said Roberta. "We are not likely to be seeing him again ever."

She was wrong on both counts; his appearance was due to a

356

careless experiment in the laboratory at school and this she learned because he turned up at Jimes's guest-house the very next afternoon.

"I decided that what I really wanted to sketch was not at Loch Leven after all, but Dunfermline Abbey; and by a coincidence I believe I am staying at the same guest-house as yourself. I saw the address on your labels."

Roberta did not know whether to be amused or irritated; she decided, or something decided for her, to be amused. The next day he asked if he could make a drawing of her.

"Of me?" she exclaimed, surprised. "Surely you mean my mother, artists always want to paint her."

"Yes, I know, the galleries are full of her, especially in Florence. I shall not add to their beautiful work. It is your face I happen to want."

He worked steadily on the study for a couple of sittings. "It's not bad yet," he then said, putting away his things. "Tomorrow I shall paint it and most probably ruin it. I am really no good at oil portraits. I always work them up too much."

"Then wouldn't it be better to leave it as a drawing?" said Roberta. "I'm no judge but Mother likes it very much."

"Oh, I can't keep off colour," said Charles, "so let's take the bull by the horns in the china shop, as my Uncle Ebenezer used to say."

"Oh," said Roberta, laughing, "have you got an Uncle Ebenezer?"

"Yes, haven't you?" said Charles.

It was at that moment, thought Roberta later, that she had fallen in love with him.

At the end of the first week the Minister of the Kirk which Jimes regularly attended invited the whole party to supper, Roberta, her mother and Charles Curling now being the sole remaining visitors.

"He thinks you are one of the family," said Roberta, "and I didn't undeceive him."

"Thank you," said Charles gravely.

It was an old house with unexpected little steps here and there, one of which led into the sitting-room. Charles, his eyes elsewhere, missed his footing on entering and fell headlong into the room.

"Och, then," exclaimed the Minister's wife, "the poor laddie!"

"Please don't worry," said Charles, picking himself up, "I always come into a room like that," and it was then that Roberta decided that this was the man she was going to marry.

As for Charles, he said he had known that from the moment he met her disapproving eyes in the railway carriage: "Funny eyes they are too," he had added, "yellow rather than brown."

Her engagement met with disapproval from her aunt and uncle, Rollo's parents, who after her father's death had assumed a position of parental care for her.

"You hardly know him, dear," said her aunt, "and you tell me that his parents used to keep a shop somewhere in Yorkshire. I don't know what your father would have said!"

Her uncle was gloomy over Charles's prospects.

"He's very talented," said Roberta, "he's sold some pictures already." (Actually two watercolour sketches to a college friend for £5 each.)

"I dare say," said her uncle.

"He means to teach," said Roberta, "and I have enough for both and we can live at Rowanbank with Mother, of course I don't intend to leave her."

"Well, you have turned twenty-one and are your own mistress, Roberta," said her uncle, "I can't stop you, but at least wait till your Charles has got a job; perhaps he may get his medical degree after all."

He didn't, and his father reluctantly agreed to his transference to an Art course, but his family welcomed Roberta. Her mother, who had taken to Charles from the first for his courtesy and kindness and the romance of his odd appearance, was delighted. They were married as soon as Charles had finished at his art school and a piece of luck had fallen their way in the shape of a teaching post at a school on the coast within easy reach of Rowanbank. The salary, though small, and the beginninng of a limited but steady demand for his landscapes, saved his face as a breadwinner in the eyes of their respective families.

"Your mother and I see God's will in this," wrote Charles's devout non-conformist father.

"So that's all right," Charles remarked.

On Roberta's first visit to Charles's home she found herself in a world different from any that she had previously come across, the centre of which was in another dimension.

"God is more real to my father than any of us," said Charles, "not that he doesn't love his children – and, by the way, he'll accept you at once as one of the family – but he feels he must present us spotless before his Maker and as we are far from spotless it is a fearful responsibility."

"And your mother?" asked Roberta.

"Oh, my mother," said Charles, "she's been known to giggle in Chapel. My father ought to have been in the Ministry," continued Charles, "but he was a miner's son. He left school at twelve determined not to go underground, took an errand boy's job, worked his way up and became the manager of the best ironmonger's shop in the whole district – that's my father."

It was said with pride but Roberta could see that the relationship between the two was not easy. Far worse than his failure to become a doctor was the knowledge that Charles no longer attended Chapel or even church – veiled allusions were made to this and other shortcomings in the extemporary family prayers which, with a reading from the Bible, began and ended the day, and heated theological discussions often followed. Roberta, who was quite unaccustomed to talk on such matters, was uncomfortable and embarrassed, especially when she found herself taken aside first by Charles's father and then by his mother and appealed to to lead Charles back into the fold; they would prefer a Chapel fold but an Anglican one would suffice. Altogether they seemed much more concerned over Charles's and her spiritual welfare than over their worldly prospects.

"If you and Charles make a point of sharing your devotions together as Mother and I have always done, all will go well with you. I shall pray constantly for this," said his father, and to Roberta it sounded almost like a threat.

But his mother said simply, "I shan't be happy in Heaven if Charles can't be there too."

"Why do you tell them what you believe or don't believe?" asked Roberta.

"I couldn't pretend to them," said Charles, "any more than I could to you; and besides I can't hold my tongue. You must know that by this time – why, I couldn't even in the railway carriage."

Roberta laughed. Charles could always make her laugh – that was why she had fallen for him, she supposed. She had needed to laugh so much. She thought probably that Charles's father, that hard-working little boy grown into the serious young man, had needed it too and had found the same relief in his marriage.

Meals with Charles's family were also a new experience, even the food and the times at which it was served were different – there was no alcohol, and lavish midday spreads and high teas replaced lunches and dinners. These were convivial affairs after the long grace was over. Charles was not the only member of the family to be loquacious: his two sisters, both teachers, but deprived of possible husbands by the War, were still based at home and bickered and argued amiably with their father and Charles, but the life and soul of the party was always the mother. After lovingly bustling about till all the cups and plates were filled to her satisfaction, she settled down to enjoy her family. She loved to tease her solemn husband.

"George, you must get your beard trimmed – it's much too long – it's a bad example for Charlie."

"But Charles hasn't got a beard," objected Charles's father, "and you used to like it long."

"Ah, but I loved you then," she exclaimed.

The glance between them, as everyone laughed, remained with Roberta. *That's rare*, she said to herself. *That's what I want with Charles.*

Well, she had had it; not always, of course. There had been times when, had the divorce laws been as they now are, she reflected wryly, she might even have walked out on his maddening inflexibility of conscience and tiresome unworldliness. He never took the least care over his clothes, was abnormally untidy, never bothered what he ate or drank and was dreadfully careless over his health. Equally, of course, he might have left her; heaven knows he had enough provocation at times. But she knew that if they had parted they would have missed a pearl of great price.

Now she looked again at the little watercolour she had chosen. Underneath one of those grey slated roofs she had slept on that first visit to Charles's family which had taught her much about the roots from which Charles had sprung. She had been bewildered and uncomfortable from growing pains, but she had also been deeply happy. Each day she had woken to see from her bed a view of the moors that dominated the picture – a beauty so strangely different from her own soft landscape at home but that related to some impregnable sense of security and strength which she knew she had found.

The school holidays had begun and Clare had reconciled herself to the grandfather clock and was pleased to receive a letter from Roberta suggesting that she might like to make a selection of china for herself and Alex: "I have far more than I need or can find room for in the flat and I expect you can do with some additions."

"I should say we could!" said Clare to Alex. "You and the

children aren't easy on breakages and chips, not to speak of our guests; but I wonder whenever I can go."

"I think Gran would like it if you took the children with you," said Alex. "It's quite a while since she saw them."

Clare began to look worried. "Wouldn't it be too much for her?"

"I don't think so, she's quite well again now – they probably won't be able to go to Rowanbank much more. If we make it a weekend I might arrange to come too."

Clare's face cleared. "Oh, yes, do," she said. She always felt more at ease with Roberta when Alex was around.

Roberta responded warmly to this suggestion. "Dear Mrs B. has offered extra help," she wrote, "and it will be a real family party – if only Naomi could come too but she has promised to come over later when I shall need her more." The house was now in agents' hands and the thought that this might be the last time the expanding flap of the table would be used, the last time she would get out the big tablecloth and the set of handpainted fruit plates that she meant Clare to have, the last time the old schoolroom would be opened up for the children to play in, did not depress her unduly. *Everything has a last time*, she told herself, *so I am not going to allow such thoughts to dampen my pleasure. I mean to enjoy this visit.*

"But what will Boffin do that weekend?" asked Patrick. When they went away for a holiday in the summer they always lent the house, together with Boffin, to one or other of the indigent families known to them through Alex's many involvements.

"Can't Mrs Dent see to him?" asked Alex. Mrs Dent was the latest hard-come-by "Help".

"I don't quite like to ask her," said Clare, "it might frighten her away. I don't think she's fond of cats."

"And she only comes for a little while," said Patrick. "Boffin would be dreadfully lonely, and he'd starve himself – you know he takes ages getting used to people and goes off his food when we're not here."

Bertram, who was either quite callous or deeply sentimental about Boffin, turned down the corners of his mouth, always a danger signal.

"Won't leave Boffin," said Becky gently but firmly.

"Can't he come with us?" asked Patrick.

"Willow hates all other cats," said Clare.

"But Rowanbank's huge," said Patrick, "it's got hundreds and hundreds of rooms – Willow needn't even see Boffin."

"Yes," agreed his father, his eye on Bertram. "I really think that's the best solution if Granny doesn't mind; Boffin can have the run of the attics and a tray."

Although a tray was an affront to his dignity Boffin accepted the situation and settled down comfortably in the Rowanbank attics, where he was visited regularly by Patrick and Becky but never by Bertram, who, however, was no trouble at all on the visit because of Roberta's television.

Clare and Alex had no television, mainly on principle but also because their lives were both so full that they had no time for it. They thought it bad for the children but Patrick had lately taken to paying very regular visits to a school friend. His innocent mother said, "Surely it's time you asked Martin here instead of always going to him," but Patrick had said the children were too much of a nuisance.

Roberta's television set, which she considered an ugly object, lived behind a curtain in an alcove off the sitting-room, an alcove that had once contained her mother's harp which her husband had bought at her request: "So lovely an instrument to look at and the most beautiful of sounds – I really must own one and learn to play it." But the first aspiration was easier to achieve than the second and, after a few not very satisfactory lessons, it was all given up; the harp, still decorative but forever silent, remained in its corner till after her mother's death. Roberta, whom it had always somehow annoyed, sold it to make a convenient space for her newly acquired TV.

The family arrived at tea-time. This was always a proper meal at Rowanbank, not the despicable snack it had often become elsewhere. After consuming paste sandwiches, fruit cake, chocolate buns and a second go of sandwiches Patrick pushed back his chair and sighed with satisfaction. It was good to begin a visit with eating, thought Roberta, especially with children. Now they could be left to themselves up in the old schoolroom to play with the traditional Rowanbank toys that they looked forward to seeing whenever they came – the dolls' house and the Noah's Ark for Becky and Bertram, the fort and the old bound copies of the *Boys' Own Paper* for Patrick. She must somehow find room for these at Coleridge Court – but could she? Well, they would all too soon grow out of them anyhow.

Peace reigned below as the elders chattered together until Roberta, a little maliciously, remarked: "I know you won't mind if I have on my *Gardener's World*; I really mind missing it and I think you'd both enjoy it too."

All eyes then were on "the Box" and no one noticed the door opening slowly or saw Bertram standing in the doorway transfixed. As soon as Roberta switched off he silently vanished. That evening Alex with unusual firmness insisted on Becky and Bertram going to bed at a reasonable hour.

"You *must*, or you'll only be overtired and a nuisance to Granny tomorrow and wear her out."

Bertram had made no objection and Clare said hopefully, "Worn out for once."

But this was not the case; on leaving the dining-room after supper everyone was startled to hear violent loud noises coming from the sitting-room, unmistakable gunshots and screams. Hurrying in, they saw Bertram in his pyjamas, sitting entranced before the television alcove, and heard him remark to himself loudly and complacently, "Wish I don't be there, do I!" Before him was depicted a scene of maniac crowds, bloodshed, fire and fury.

"How did he know how to turn it on, I wonder?" said Roberta. That was never divulged; the difficulty was to get him to turn it off throughout the visit.

"Leave him to it," advised Roberta.

"But Alex and I think television so bad for children, Granny," said Clare in her patient voice.

"I know you do," said Roberta, "but we're not talking about 'children', we're talking of Bertram and Becky and Patrick. I don't believe television will do them any harm. As a matter of fact I was going to ask you to take my set off my hands. I can't install that monster at Coleridge Court. I mean to get a little one."

Clare was silent and Roberta went on: "If you have television yourselves, at least you can keep an eye on what they see."

"But why should they see it at all?" said Alex.

"Don't be foolish, Alex, haven't you noticed how much Patrick seems to know about space-men lately? I really don't think it's quite fair on him and Becky. How do you suppose they feel at school among their friends? Either deprived or dreadfully priggish – it's unavoidable."

"Well," said Alex, after a little pause, "thank you very much anyway for the offer. You may be right; we'll think it over."

Clare knew what that meant: Bertram and Roberta had won again. But she was very pleased with the china. The fruit plates were really lovely and she was able to add to them a set of soup bowls, a good many useful cups and saucers and a big jug and dish of Italian ware in bright soft colours, which she had always admired.

"Isn't there anything you want for yourself, Alex?" asked Roberta. His lack of acquisitiveness always drove her to press him to accept gifts. But it was of no use, he simply smiled and shook his head.

They went off in a loaded car, Boffin glaring from his basket, perched precariously on the top of the television set. After they had gone, the house seemed very quiet and empty; they had had a festive farewell meal and, looking at the children's faces round the big table, Roberta thought of the old flower-sellers cry: "All a growing and a growing and a going and a going."

Well, it's not as if I were off to Australia; and, even if they don't come here again and I can't put them all up at Highgate, I can surely have them for the day – if I've kept enough china. She looked a little ruefully at her depleted shelves. Although she had thought them too large to take with her, she would certainly miss her Italian dish and jug and their loss decided her on the second of Charles's pictures, for if she couldn't have the real objects any longer, then at least she could have them on canvas.

Charles generally preferred to spend his holidays in his native Yorkshire or in Scotland, but his year a fellow artist had tempted him to Italy, to a certain villa a little way out of Siena. "September, that's the time to go, when the peaches and the grapes and the figs all ripen together in the garden here and you can wander among them and pick them at your will and, as you do so, glimpse the towers of celestial Siena from afar." So off they had gone with their baby George for a golden month.

They slept in a spacious stone-floored room with a high ceiling painted with a star surrounded by festoons of flowers; the furniture, pale green, was also painted with flowers and the view, wide and peaceful, extended over vineyards and olive groves to the bare brown Umbrian hills crowned by a white or an orange or a pink farmhouse. They took their breakfast on a loggia, where tiny cyclamen were thrusting up between the stone flags and from where you could indeed see the towers of the city.

Roberta, on her first morning, felt like a child opening a wonderful present. She had never been to Italy before and she had high expectations about art and architecture; in these she was not disappointed, but actually it was the unexpected casual encounters with beauty that delighted her most. No one had happened to tell her of the white oxen peacefully plodding through the centuries, nor of the dazzling blackness of the ilex trees and the cypresses bordering the white roads, nor of the bloom on roofs and walls. These ravished her senses and she felt a little drunk for most of the time.

While Charles was busy with his painting, she and George would lie about in the sun near by, or go for little strolls on their own. George was a placid baby and gave no trouble, unless one counted the crowd of admirers he was won't to attract. All Italians, it seemed to Roberta, were crazy about small children, especially fair-haired, blue-eyed ones. Once, when she and Charles were drinking their coffee on the Campo, with George in his portable pushchair close by, a young workman happened to pass. He stopped, scooped George out of his chair and shouting, "Oop, oop," tossed him up into the blue air as if he were a pigeon. He caught him as he came down and sent him up again, crowing with glee. It had happened too quickly for Roberta to feel fear; by the time she would have done so George was back in his chair and the workman, crying, "*Bellissimo bambino*," was disappearing into the shadowed calle; but the impression remained of the laughing peasant and the joyful baby, tossed towards the sun.

Another time she left George asleep on a rug at Charles's feet and wandered away towards a small russet-coloured church crouched among a metallic sea of olives. As she got nearer she could hear a thin sound of chanting, and soon she saw a cluster of children on the little piazza outside the church. They were gathered round an old priest who was beating time. It was late in the day, the sun was low and its long level beams shone on the children's dark little heads and black overalls and the rusty figure of the old man, enclosing them all in a glory like the gold background of one of those primitive paintings she had been looking at that morning. She tried to describe it to Charles.

"It's the quality of the light," he said, "the contrasts are sharper here than in England but there is a harmonizing fusion in the light if only I could get it right."

Roberta thought he had got it in the still life that he painted on their last day. Their friend had promised them fruit from the garden and there was an abundance of peaches, figs and grapes, all of which glowed in the picture. They had bought the pottery in the market and the fruit spilled out of the tilted, painted plate – some of the figs were split open to show their purple-pink flesh under the dark green-veined skin and, in the jug, a spray of pointed gothic vine-leaves set off the brilliant autumn flowers.

"Oh, Charles, it's lovely!"

"Third-rate Cézanne," said Charles cheerfully and had wanted to leave it behind; but she rescued it and had it framed and hung.

She had not really looked at it for years; now, as she considered it afresh, she thought that there was enough richness and glow from it to warm her for the rest of her life. She suddenly realized that she had chosen two of her husband's pictures that represented clearly the two contrasting sides of him, the puritan and the artist, and these had never seemed to conflict because they were harmonized always by the humour that, like the Italian sun, fused them into a finely balanced whole.

"So rare, so dear," she said to herself with pride and with pain.

Chapter 6

THERE WERE two corner cupboards at Rowanbank – one large and glass-fronted, the other quite small, perhaps a hundred years older, known as the Moses cupboard, with a door painted in colours which had faded harmoniously. It depicted a biblical scene. Pharoah's daughter, in a full skirt of yellow silk and attended by a page, stood imperiously beside a very blue stream bordered with spiky bulrushes, while Miriam, in peasant costume of green, red and white, lifted a stiff little swaddled Moses from a plaited cradle. In the background Pharoah's pennanted castle merged into billowy clouds. It was not a work of art but it was unusual and Roberta loved it because it made her laugh and brought again to her the vivid sense of her friendship with Rose at its happiest.

The whole story of that cupboard was pleasant. It had been left to her by an old man whom they had always called Punch – her father's coachman and then his chauffeur. She always thought of him as old but he was probably not so at all when she used to spend hours with him in the stables, which later became a garage. He was a bachelor and fond of children and Roberta loved to show off before him, reciting poems learned from her mother and telling him the stories of Robin Hood and Arthur and the Table Round, basking in his ready admiration. He lived over the stables and regaled her on peppermint humbugs and curly barley-sugar and when he died she was touched to find he had left her the cupboard in which he had kept the sweets. But then it had been a very ordinary though useful piece of furniture, its door varnished a dull brown, and no one knew anything about Pharoah's daughter until one day when she and Rose were fifteen years old.

They had been on an expedition together to the zoo, a favourite resort of theirs, and had coasted across London on the open top of a bus – oh, those lovely open buses where, if you were lucky and got the front seats, it was like being in the bow of a ship bounding along the rivers of the streets between the steep banks of houses. It had rained and they had buttoned on the waterproof apron that was attached to each seat. When they got up to rush down the winding stair before being carried on again, the rainwater which had collected in a puddle on their aproned laps tipped over and drenched them and, shrieking with laughter, they had stumbled on to the pavement. At home at last and dry again, they sat before the fire and toasted muffins for tea. The parents were out and they had the house to themselves. Roberta had gone to the corner cupboard for the "squashed-fly" biscuits that they both loved and then Rose had suddenly said:

"There's a chip on the top edge of your cupboard door."

"So there is. I'll have to get it repaired."

"It's a funnly blue colour where the varnish has disappeared. Berta, I believe there's something painted underneath."

"Oh, no, there couldn't be," said Roberta.

Opposition always fired Rose. "I bet you anything there is. Do let's try and clean a bit and see."

"What with?" said Roberta, becoming infected as she often was by Rose's enthusiasm and urge to action.

"Just soap and water and cotton wool might do it," said Rose promptly. "We hade a lecture on everything to do

with oil painting at our art class at school last term." Of
course, Rose would know, thought Roberta as she hurried
to fetch what was required.

They started off at opposite corners of the cupboard.
"Rub very gently," cautioned Rose. Presently she gave a
squeak of excitement. "Blue sky, birds and a cloud – I told
you so."

Roberta could hardly breathe from excitement. "Bulrushes and a stream . . . oh, Rose, you are a genius!"

Then Pharoah's castle and the baby Moses were
revealed and they were both silent with emotion.

"It's perfectly splendid," sighed Roberta, when the
whole picture had been uncovered, and Rose took hold of
her and whirled her round the room, then they both collap-
sed on to the couch and stared up at the cupboard in
admiration.

"I wonder why it was ever varnished over," said
Roberta.

"We shall never know, there may be thousands of
mystery pictures about – oh, Berta, let's be picture-
restorers when we've finished school," said Rose.

"Yes, let's," said Roberta, "darling Rose!"

Their friendship had begun when they were both seven
years old. "There's a nice little girl come to live next door,"
said Roberta's mother, "wouldn't it be a good thing if you
and she could be friends? Poor dear, she has no mother so I
think we must be extra kind to her."

Roberta was wary of friends chosen for her by her
mother and she did not take to Rose at first. She was a thin,
rather unattractive child with red corkscrew curls and skirts
too short for her and knobbly knees, and she actually still
had a Nanny. Roberta's Nanny had vanished when she was
six.

"It's because she has no mother," she was told and she
had overheard her mother saying: "I suppose it's her nurse
who thinks those awful curls becoming."

"Yes," said her father, "she's an ugly duckling enough with that hair and that queer little pointed face, but you have to look at her twice; and her father tells me she's remarkably clever."

The aura of pathos, combined with the repute of exceptional cleverness, was enough to mark Rose out from the other children Roberta played with and in spite of the Nanny she was impressed by sundry grown-up privileges Rose enjoyed and by a certain mature air that she assumed as a matter of course. For her part, Rose seemed to have decided from the first that Roberta was to be her special friend.

"It's quite unusual for her to take such a fancy to anyone," said the Nanny. "Miss Rose has always liked to keep herself to herself."

This of course, was ingratiating. Being half an orphan, Roberta thought, had its advantages. Rose was allowed by her father to do much as she pleased and apparently she paid no attention to anyone else. She gained further respect and interest too from certain dark hints she threw out about her mother's death.

"Actually she was poisoned," she confided at last to cement their friendship.

Full of pleasurable horror, Roberta enquired who had poisoned her and why.

"It isn't known, they couldn't discover but everyone knew she'd been poisoned. I heard the doctor say so – he didn't know I was there. I expect it was out of terrible jealousy because she was so beautiful *and* clever," Rose added quickly, in a way that made it clear that she knew that her mother had not been so beautiful as Roberta's, and so she had had to add that bit about her being clever.

But to have had a mother who had been poisoned was certainly something. "If only she could have been buried in Highgate cemetery with a beautiful monument so that we could have put flowers on her grave it would have been lovely," Roberta said.

Rose agreed, but she was buried in Egypt, which was no good to anyone. Rose had a taste for the macabre – there was that hit she had made as Lady Macbeth at school. This was much later, not at the day school they had attended together but at the big boarding school to which, fired by the stories of Evelyn Sharp and Angela Brazil, Rose had persuaded her father to send her.

"I want to see what it's like for myself," she had said.

Alas, it was not what she had expected. The school, a famous one, was bent on providing for girls an equivalent to the great public schools and it emphasized games and the communal spirit. Rose wasn't good at ball games, having no wish to "play up, play up and play the game", and she wrote miserable letters to Roberta in a vein of lofty self-pity:

> No one cares for brains here and you wouldn't believe how stupid and dull they all are. I shall not run away, which I have considered, and I shall not ask my father to take me away, because then they would think they had got the better of me; but I am reading Dante. I made Father let me bring his copy with me – the one with those lovely illustrations, and it must have been prophetic because he is a great comfort to me. I have put all the girls in my house and several mistresses into their appropriate circles in Hell. I have to take it into the lav to read it, because that is the only place in which I can be alone.

Rose was always an omnivorous reader, nothing came amiss and her memory for odd bits of knowledge picked up in her readings was phenomenal. She was too bossy and superior in her manners ever to be popular, but after her success as Lady Macbeth she was treated with respect and there was talk of trying for a university (by no means taken for granted then). But her father died suddenly of heart failure and it was discovered that he had left his daughter

373

very little to support her. She was just eighteen and until she came of age under the guardianship of an uncle who said university was out of the question.

"What will you do?" asked Roberta.

"I shall train as a cook," said Rose. "A good cook can always get a job. And then I shall go to America and marry a millionaire. You'll marry Rollo, I suppose." Her tone was pitying – she had never got on with Rollo and was undisguisedly jealous of Roberta's affection for him. When they were younger this had taken the form of open hostility. There was the time when she had stuck nails into his bicycle tyres to prevent him taking Roberta on an expedition.

"She's a little vixen, and she looks like one too – mind out that you don't get bitten one day, Bobs. I don't know why you are so thick with her; she'd devour you if she could."

"Oh, well," said Roberta apologetically, "she's Rose; besides she can be awfully interesting, you know."

The truth was that Rose lived her life with a fervour that both fascinated and nourished the more repressed and introverted Roberta. It was perhaps even more tiresome when Rose changed her tactics in adolescence and tried to vamp Rollo, which first amused and then annoyed him, so that sometimes he snubbed her unmercifully. Roberta tried to comfort her but she turned on her.

"I don't care, it's not as if I *liked* him, silly," she said.

But when she heard of his death she threw over her cookery course and came at once to Roberta, who clung to her as someone who belonged to past happiness.

For a period after this, Rose spent all the time she could at Rowanbank and Roberta felt her objective interest in life bracing. She made her read the papers, listen to the news on the wireless and go to concerts and theatres again. In the evenings they played chess, in which they were fairly matched, though Rose was a bad loser. It was something

Rollo had always had against her. Roberta was sometimes tempted to let her win. *She minds so much*, she thought with amused wonder, *but I can't do that; it would be like lying to her.*

In all that dark period Rose proved herself the most faithful and loving of friends, but as time went on Roberta began to suffer a sense of unease. Was it that she felt, in spite of all the sympathy, that Rose was too happy? She found herself wanting to argue, to object, to be generally unreasonable and ungrateful.

Rose had finished her cooking and catering course in London and was looking for a post somewhere on the coast – "To be nice and near," she said. "I mean eventually to have a guest-house of my own, of course – now Rowan-bank would make a good one, Roberta; there's the lovely garden and it's within easy car-reach of the sea. Don't look so shocked," she laughed.

"What about America?" said Roberta.

Rose laughed again. "That's as may be – we'll have to see, won't we?"

Roberta detected sometimes an assumption that Rose took it as a matter of course that they were to share this undefined future together and that nothing could be better. Why didn't she too feel this wholly satisfactory? The answer ultimately came with Charles. She wrote immediately to Rose about Charles, full of the naïve conviction that the two must like each other because they both liked her, for the experience with Rollo had apparently taught her nothing. The three met together for the first time for lunch at a London restaurant suggested by Rose. Roberta never went to it again.

"You paint landscapes, Roberta tells me," remarked Rose after the introductions were over, "realistic ones of Scotch mountains and cattle." She made it seem an odd, outdated foible.

"Well, yes," admitted Charles, "mountains certainly –

not cattle especially. I don't like cattle; they frighten me."

"Do you exhibit much in London?"

"Not really as yet." Charles looked to Roberta for help.

"He's hoping to make contacts in the near future," Roberta said.

"Oh, well, *you* can't help him much over that, can you, Roberta?" said Rose, and turning to Charles she explained kindly: "Roberta knows nothing about art; you must have discovered that by now. I try to get her to come to the most exciting contemporary shows but she much prefers concerts. What do you think of the London group?"

"I'm afraid I'm not familiar enough with their work to say," confessed Charles and was immediately treated to a concise, apt and informative lecture.

"Your friend is extremely well informed," Charles had commented later.

"And you always pretend you know less than you really do," said Roberta, annoyed. "You lay yourself open to people like Rose, you can't blame her."

Roberta had to admit that the occasion had not been very successful but she told herself that restaurants were hopeless places for first meetings. It would be different at Rowanbank. She decided to plan a joint weekend for them as soon as possible.

Meanwhile she pumped Kitty, who happened, at that time, to be seeing a good deal of Rose. Kitty's strong point was not tactfulness, and, besides, she was only a schoolgirl still, but this made her more valuable as a source of information.

"Did Rose say anything to you about Charles?" she shamelessly asked.

"Well, yes," said Kitty.

"What did she say then?"

"Well," said Kitty again, "you mustn't mind, because I like him very much."

"Oh, go on, Kitty. I could tell she hadn't taken to him yet, but she will later. What did she say?"

"She said she didn't know how you *could* after Rollo."

"That's pretty ironic of her, I must say," said Roberta.

The weekend at Rowanbank began as the London lunch had ended: in attack and retreat. On the Sunday, however, Rose seemed to be melting and actually proposed a walk with Charles after supper when Roberta said she had letters she must write.

On coming home, Rose seemed cheerful but Charles was quiet, so quiet that as soon as Roberta and he were alone together she said, "Is anything the matter? I hope you enjoyed your walk. Rose seems to have done so."

"She did, I think," said Charles, "she enjoyed telling me that I must accept the fact that I had caught you on the rebound, that I would always be a second best and your heart would always be with Rollo, that you had always belonged to him. She said she thought it would be kinder to let me know how things really were."

"Charles!" exclaimed Roberta. "You didn't believe her?"

"She's very convincing, your Rose," said Charles slowly. "I don't know . . . yes, I almost believed her *then*, but I almost don't now." He gave her a searching look and then quickly added, "No, I don't believe her."

She saw that his face had cleared and she now had attention for Rose. "But it was unforgivable of her," she said. "I shall tell her so at once."

"Must you?" said Charles.

"Don't you see that if I don't then this will always be between us?"

She found Rose in the room she always had when she was at Rowanbank and which had come to be known as Rose's room. "Rose, how could you talk such nonsense to Charles about Rollo?" Roberta cried at once. "You know it isn't true."

"I don't know it," said Rose. "Don't shout at me, and if it isn't true, it ought to be. I believe in loyalty if you don't.

377

Do you think I could put anyone in your place ever?"

"That's claptrap," said Roberta, "and, whatever you say, I know perfectly well that you knew you were not speaking the truth to Charles, and will you please go at once and tell him so."

"I shall do nothing of the kind," said Rose. "Good night." She walked past Roberta down the passage to the bathroom.

Has she ever admitted herself in the wrong? thought Roberta furiously. *She's not telling the truth to herself, that's what I can't bear.*

Rose was leaving early the next morning anyway and they hardly spoke to each other before then. They said a conventional goodbye on the doorstep and Roberta had gone back into the house but instinctively she glanced out of the window. Rose was still there standing in the drive, looking back at the house. *Why doesn't she go?* Roberta thought irritably; but she felt miserable that her chief feeling at Rose's departure was relief.

The estrangement lasted on. Roberta, giving herself up to her new happiness with Charles, didn't really bother herself about Rose. *It will come right sooner or later*, she told herself, *and it isn't my fault if she won't tell the truth.*

Her mother said, "Where is Rose nowadays, has she gone to America?" Her memory was slipping away but sometimes stray bits of talk or information would take root and unexpectedly trouble her. Rose had always been particularly good to her mother and on her visits had given up time to amusing and interesting her: "You said once Rose meant to go to America, it was only a joke, wasn't it? Oh, I hope she didn't really mean it."

But she apparently had meant it; for one day, out of the blue, there came a postcard which simply said: "I'm off to the States tomorrow, fearfully rushed and anyway I hate goodbyes. Will write from N. York, Rose." A second card arrived some little time later saying she had found herself a job and loved everything. "Why doesn't she give an address? How maddening of her," fumed Roberta, staring down at the card as if she could conjure one from the blank spaces.

But no address came, nothing came and nearly a year had passed. Her son was born with some difficulty and she was slowly regaining strength after George's arrival when, on a perfectly ordinary grey winter's day with no sort of warning, there was a knock on the door at Rowanbank. *How queer*, thought Roberta, *it sounds like Rose's knock, but it can't be.* Most people used the bell but Rose always had preferred the heavy old knocker, on which she would give a single resounding bang. Roberta flew to the door and there actually stood Rose on the doorstep – and extremely elegant exotic-looking Rose wrapped in white furs with a large bunch of violets pinned to them. Her face was glowing with excitement.

"Yes, it's me, Berta, I'm not a ghost, here catch." She tore the violets from her coat and hurled them at Roberta: "Oh, oh, to see you again, and I'm married to my millionaire, but it's all right, he's not here – can I come in, please?"

Roberta, hugging her, pulled her over the threshold, "Oh, Rose, Rose, you are dreadful. Why, why didn't you tell me, why did you never send me an address? It wasn't kind."

"No," said Rose, "it wasn't, kindness isn't for us."

"And now you've got a millionaire and I've got a baby," said Roberta, her voice trembling. "It's not possible!"

In due time Roberta heard more, but not much more, of Rose's doings. Her job had been in one of the leading hotels in New York and it was there that she had met her husband, who always stayed there on his business visits.

"His name is Vincent P. Primrose – silly, isn't it, for me, being Rose Primrose, but it can't be helped. I don't know what P. stands for – I've never dared ask in case it should be

379

Percy, but I dare say it's just P. Americans have got to have a middle initial, you know, it's the law. He's had two wives before me, one died, one ran off. Yes – he's getting on but I never liked boys and he suits me very well. He travels a lot; he's in the Middle East just now as a matter of fact."

"Oh, dear, I hope it's all right," said Roberta to Charles.

"I shouldn't worry," said Charles, "Rose can look after herself and is doing it very effectively, I should say."

"Now look here, Roberta," said Rose on the third day of her visit, "we may have babies and husbands, but we're still ourselves and I mean to take you away for a break. I've got a week more and you're looking washed out and old."

Roberta immediately felt washed out and old.

"We'll go to London, I think," went on Rose. "It's not as if you wanted country or sea; what you want is a complete change."

Roberta immediately felt that what she wanted *was* a complete change. It had not occurred to her before, but though domesticity with Charles and her baby was wonderful and lovely, of course, it was sometimes a bit weighty.

"Oh, Rose," she said, "I don't think I possibly could. What about baby?"

Rose, who had not shown the slightest interest in George, now brushed him aside as if he had been a little fly.

"You're not feeding him, thank goodness, so I'll lay on a trained nurse and you can phone every day."

"I'd have to see her first," said Roberta.

"I'll phone today," said Rose. "I know the best place."

"If Charles doesn't mind," said Roberta.

"Heavens, Berta! It's only for a week – after all, I've left my husband for you."

That's quite different, thought Roberta.

But Charles said, yes, she should go by all means, it would set her up.

Roberta had never stayed in London as a visitor before and found it a strange new city – a holiday city, a treat city.

380

Wealth and leisure and freedom from responsibility clothed it in a fresh garment of bright iridescent changing colours. She thought she would miss Charles dreadfully, but she didn't because the whole experience was so unreal, so like an Arabian Night's Entertainment; and because it was so ephemeral she gave herself up to it without reservation. Rose had taken rooms for them at Brown's Hotel.

"I thought American millionaires always stayed at the Ritz," said Roberta.

"I'm not an American millionaire – I'm his wife and English at that, and I've always wanted to stay at Brown's," said Rose.

Every night they went out to the opera, to the theatre, to a concert and all day they talked and laughed, it seemed without stopping, and were as light-hearted and silly and unreservedly happy as they had been in shared treats as children – sillier and happier, thought Roberta, for as children they had not known they were either. Yet for her there was something dreamlike and unreal about this happiness. The two of them exulted together in the ease that wealth ensures. The delightful days were padded with luxury – at the theatres, operas and concerts they had the best seats, they took taxis everywhere – no more bus rides – and Roberta had to stop Rose from buying her everything she admired in the shops.

"You are paying for my keep and transport and tickets," she said, "you must let me keep a little self-respect," and although she was full of amused delight at Rose's clothes and jewellery she was firm in not accepting any of these either. There was a topaz necklace in an antique setting which she especially admired.

"Do have it, Berta, it suits your eyes."

"But you said it was part of your husband's wedding present to you."

"He won't notice it and anyway I chose it," said Rose.

381

But Roberta wouldn't take it. "You can leave it to me in your will," she laughed.

One day they went to a sale at Sotheby's and Rose bid for some Chinese paintings on silk that Roberta admired. Triumphant when she got them Rose said, "You shall have these too one day." She knew all about Chinese art.

As always, Roberta was continually marvelling at what Rose knew and as always she found her unfailingly interesting. There was nothing to ruffle their relationship and Roberta felt the harmony between them complete and delightful until the last evening.

"I wish this could last for ever," said Rose, "and it could last another week, Berta; that nurse is perfectly adequate for the baby."

"But you've got to meet Vincent in Paris," said Roberta, knowing suddenly that for her part she must now go back to Charles and George at once, that she couldn't be parted from them for even a day longer – that a dream, however lovely and refreshing, was only a dream with no future and that dreams prolonged beyond their proper span go bad on the dreamer.

"He can wait," said Rose. "Do let's stay!"

"It's been perfectly wonderful," said Roberta slowly but Rose interrupted her:

"Oh! I can see you don't want to; you can't ever hide anything, Roberta – well, that's that then."

"If you can stay another week," said Roberta, "come home with me to Rowanbank."

"Sorry, no, a hundred times no," said Rose, "but we'll never forget this week, will we? And when I come back we'll do it again, promise!" and Roberta promised.

But, as it turned out, they never did it again and perhaps for that very reason this particular time with Rose was to remain quite distinct and jewel-like in Roberta's memory.

Rose's next visit coincided with the two-year-old George developing a feverish cold. As he was also suffering from a temporary mother-fixation, Roberta would not leave him.

"How you do spoil that child," said Rose, and spent most of her time with Kitty in Highgate.

Next came news of the break-up of her marriage: "It's not his fault," she wrote, "I couldn't deliver the goods; but don't worry, he's been generous and I've got plenty of plans up my sleeve." The plans involved starting up a business of her own, which seemed to absorb her completely for a long period.

"Rose is so fearfully capable," sighed Roberta, "she gets busier and busier, she's always saying she's coming over again but she never comes."

"She's got to make an outrageous success of things first," said Charles, "then she'll come."

But the slump followed and all Rose's energies were absorbed by financial alarms and excursions. Then, just as at last another meeting had been planned, war broke out and "Aunty Rose" became for young George synonymous with parcels containing butter in tins, chocolate, biscuits, packets of dried fruit, tea and coffee and a variety of strange and welcome additions to the healthy, sufficient but boring rationed home diet. Gratefully Roberta acknowledged these parcels and longed for another meeting as soon as life should have become normal again.

The Moses corner cupboard no longer contained squashed-fly biscuits. Instead, among other sentimental relics there was a tin emblazoned with stars and stripes – a tin that had come originally in one of Rose's war-time food parcels. Inside were Rose's letters, all of which Roberta had kept. She took them out now to destroy them – deciding that they must go with so much else of the past. It was silly to have kept it all; what she could remember she would remember and let the rest vanish. The two last letters were on the top of the pile and she fingered them gently – the first that had arrived after the war said she could not after all

make it to England but would Roberta *please* come to her –
"expenses paid, of course – come *soon*." But Roberta had
not gone. Of course, had she known Rose was ill she would
somehow have managed it, but since Rose was never ill
Roberta had thought it must be her business that was the
obstacle. It was just when the twins were expected and so
she wrote to say she would go later if it were really impossible for Rose to leave.

"Oh, it wasn't fair not to tell me, it wasn't fair," she had
cried afterwards to Charles; but Rose was never fair.

"She didn't want you to go to her from pity," Charles
had said, for the next scrap of a letter was enclosed with the
topaz necklace and the Chinese silks and the information
that Rose had died of cancer the previous month. It said: "I
have never loved anyone a quarter as much as I have loved
you, Roberta – don't be too sorry about me. I should have
loathed being old and I've had a good run for my money."

"I ought to have gone," cried Roberta. "There was that
young sister-in-law who could have coped."

"You couldn't have known," said Charles.

I never really understood, I was always failing her,
thought Roberta as she took out the bundle of letters and
replaced the empty tin (it was a good one and might come
in useful); though it would probably not have made much
difference. As often, when she thought of Rose she felt sad
and remorseful, but it suddenly seemed to her that to
indulge in such feelings was perhaps a form of egotism.

"And a betrayal of past happiness," she said, apparently
to Pharoah's daughter. She had spoken the words aloud to
impress them upon herself, as she shut the door of the little
Moses cupboard and entered it on her list.

Chapter 7

THE HOUSE agent had not been enthusiastic over Rowan-bank. "No central heating and only one bathroom," he commented sadly.

Roberta felt at the same time both apologetic and annoyed.

"We shall, of course, classify it as a fine period house," he said a little more cheerfully.

"But won't that give rather a wrong impression?" suggested Roberta.

He looked at her pityingly.

"The view," she murmured hastily.

He nodded. "Yes, the view is a feature certainly and the garden . . . though a garden, of course, is not necessarily a recommendation these days, Mrs Curling," the house agent told her. "Some people *do* still want one though and there's scope here – well-established flowerbeds and fine trees."

"Well-established too long ago, I fear," said Roberta, "and the trees are not on my ground, you know, in fact there's only the walnut tree actually *in* the garden."

But at the mention of a walnut tree the agent brightened up again. "A walnut tree's a distinct asset," he said. "Well, Mrs Curling, someone may take a great fancy to the walnut tree, you never can tell, but it is probably more likely to attract anyone looking for a place to adapt as a small guest-house or a select private rest-home perhaps than as a private dwelling."

Roberta felt depressed after this interview; though Alex had warned her that the house might be difficult to sell, she had not at heart believed him. She still hoped to be well settled in Coleridge Court by Christmas, but as the days passed she wondered. It wasn't likely, the agent said, that a sale would be made in the winter. Gradually she steeled herself to the unpleasant business of exposing her home to the possibly critical, necessarily curious gaze of strangers but so far only a few prospective buyers had called to view. These fell into three categories: the first comprised those inquisitive and leisured people for whom house-viewing is a hobby. They were easily identified by their perfunctory attention to details. Roberta resented these. The second category had been misled by the agent's description – "But we want a real period house," they wailed, or: "It will need a great deal spent on it." Towards these she felt apologetic. Then there were the hopefuls who called twice and even took measurements and of these she had at first great expectations, but so far these hopes had faded.

Meanwhile, however, she went stubbornly on with her turnings out and selections. Books! Roberta's heart quailed when she looked at her shelves, for hers had been a book-buying family. Her father, like most educated men of his day, had inherited and added to a fairly extensive library of well-bound classics, novels, biography, poetry and history. Roberta had started her personal collection with the Everyman series, whose price, at one shilling a volume, was within the reaches of her by no means lavish pocket money. There they were – children's stories in blue, fiction in red, essays and histories in brown and poetry in green. Inside each of them was printed:

"I will be with thee to be thy guide
In thy most need to be by thy side."

And so they had been and she was not going to forsake

them now. How well their stout bindings and good paper and print had stood up to the test of time, whereas her paperbacks, so many years younger, were mostly tattered and torn. She recalled her father's contempt for paperbacks – "Continental Flimsies" he had called them, for they were scarcely ever seen on British shelves until the Penguins and the Pelicans came to roost there – not before they were needed, she admitted, with the price of hardbacks soaring after the Wars.

Gradually every shelf in the house had become uncomfortably crowded. Roberta continually made vows to buy no more books, but she never kept them. Now, however, she must bring herself to select the limited number she would have room for in future, but how could she begin this miserable task? Her prime favourites she almost knew by heart, and though she hardly needed to reread them, it was unthinkable not to give them shelf space. Then there were certain classics which could not in all decency be left behind and there were all those authors who had been milestones in her development at different stages in her life: Samuel Butler, for instance, and D. H. Lawrence and H. G. Wells – she doubted whether she would ever open them again, yet she knew that once parted from them she might want them desperately, in fact so much so as to force her to replace them. Oh, it was hopeless, yet it must be done. The first thing she decided to work out was which shelves she could take and calculate how many books and of what size they would hold. Unfortunately those in her father's study library were too tall to fit into Coleridge Court and in the sitting-room there were alcoves with fixed shelves. There was a sizeable glass-fronted book-case in the hall that she must have, and she thought she could squeeze in one other. There were two possibilities both now in her bedroom, one was elegant, prettily shaped and finished but flimsy, and she thought that in any case she would have chosen the plainer but better made and more serviceable shelves, even

387

had these not also had associations which made them something other than mere pieces of furniture. They had been made by her son George as the occupation of his last school summer holidays – the summer of the fall of France and the Battle of Britain.

She was lying on the lawn in the garden listening to a robin, and also to the distant vibration of guns across the channel which, on fine clear days, you could feel rather than hear in that part of Kent. She thought there had never been a robin's song sweeter but poignancy was an added quality to beauty of every kind in that precarious summer, a sharpness and sweetness, a heightening of all pleasurable experiences. It was a golden late September afternoon and besides the guns and the robin, she could hear bees in the Michaelmas daisies and George's saw busy at his carpenter's bench in the stables. But presently another sound invaded her ears, the tiresome familiar whine of the air-raid sirens – "blest pair of Sirens", Charles called them. Soon, looking up, Roberta saw aeroplanes, a bunch of them swooping at each other in the clear sky, too far away as yet to be real. Near her the swallows were darting and swooping in imitation. She watched the planes lazily, but presently they grew nearer and bands of black smoke wove in and out of the white.

"Come along, George, we'd better take shelter. They seem to be coming this way," she called. "Here comes Father with the dogs."

They all went down into the Rowanbank commodious cellar, now fitted out quite comfortably for day and night accommodation. The spaniels, Gog and Magog, barked a little in protest.

"They must think us quite mad," said Roberta.

"Well, we are, aren't we?" said Charles.

George looked at his father solemnly. "We're not at all

388

mad, I think," he said. "You said yourself the other day it was the only sensible thing to do."

Roberta sighed; she found it strange that Charles of all people should be the father of the literal-minded, practical George, but her musings on the tricks of heredity were interrupted by the clatter down the steps of the old and young William Baxter and Joe Smith, a fellow farmworker. The fighting now was directly overhead and there was the loud noise of planes descending. They were silent until the sound faded.

"Just hope none of ours came down," said old William. "We can't spare 'em."

"Why don't those bloody Americans come in, I'd like to know?" said Joe. "We could do with some of their gangsters over here."

"Yes, but how to get rid of them afterwards?" said William. "Finish the job by ourselves, that's what I say."

The all-clear sounded soon, and they emerged again; the robin was still singing. George picked up a bullet from the doorstep and put it in his pocket.

"If you've nothing better to do," he said to young William, "be a good chap and bowl to me for a bit." The season was over, but George was loath to put his bat away and the practising nets were still up in the home field.

Roberta was wondering if the enemy planes had been turned back or had reached London again. She sickened at the thought. The sight of George putting on his pads was comforting. "You're like Sir Francis Drake, George," she said.

"Who?" said George. "Oh, wasn't he the Johnny who discovered America?"

"No," said Roberta, "he sailed round the world but when the Armada was sighted he went on to finish his game."

"Well, it couldn't have been cricket," said George, "for that wasn't played then."

389

"It was bowls," said Roberta.

"Oh, bowls," said George in disgust. "Why did you say it was cricket then?"

"I didn't," said Roberta – but he was off. If only he was interested in something besides cricket and carpentry, she thought. Charles had gone off to do his Home Guard duty and she brought out some sewing to do in the garden.

She felt impelled to spend as much time out of doors as possible, she supposed it was because she was suffering from a sort of claustrophobia from having to resort so frequently to the cellar. She could now hear the familiar sound of ball on bat coming up from the meadow, a singularly reassuring and homelike sound, and she felt a rush of love and pride in the village and all the people in it who were sharing their fears and hopes, joys and sorrows as never before. *There must be less loneliness about now than there has ever been*, she thought; *it is quite different from the last war because now we are all in it together. How adaptable we are. I would not have believed, for instance, that I could get so used to danger; not that I'm not still afraid, but I'm no longer panicky*. She looked back over the short months since France had fallen. *Then* she had felt desperate, had tried to get George away to friends in America, only he had refused to go, had herself contemplated leaving Rowanbank and, with Charles migrating to Devonshire, only he refused to go.

What had changed her? She believed it was simply Churchill's speeches. Yet she had not been before much of an admirer of his, almost the reverse; but yes, his words, just his words had changed her whole mood, and not even directly heard but coming over the air as they all sat round the wireless – such could be the power of the right words at the right moment, spoken in the right way. It had completely amazed her. Afterwards, of course, the confidence the words brought had been reinforced by the successes in the air of the "few". That confidence was still growing, but, although she was no longer in a state of terror, she was often very tired from the constant loss of sleep and the deep-reaching loss of security.

Sometimes, if tired enough, she managed to sleep through the noise, especially since they had moved their beds down below; she thought she would do so tonight for she had been to London the day before and was unusually exhausted. There had been a bad raid and the train journey had been circuitous and protracted and when she reached her destination at last it was through an indirect route past streets cordoned off and the rubble of ruined buildings. The air had been full of sour smells and tiny floating bits of charred paper. She took ages to get to the National Gallery where she was meeting Kitty and nearly missed the lunch-time concert; but, oh, the relief of Myra Hess playing Beethoven to the rapt grateful audience that had collected in the basement, clutching their sandwiches and gulping their coffee! And afterwards there was the picture to see – the one treasure which, selected out of the whole collection and changed at intervals, was displayed in the entrance hall in solitary splendour. The last time she was there it had been a Claude, prince of escapists, this time it was Chardin's bottle of wine and loaf of bread. Roberta thought how seldom she had seen a masterpiece isolated from its fellows, neither supported nor diminished by them, and the impact made the more direct and memorable as a result. This particular picture, in its profound selective simplicity, seemed to be conveying some message to her; it was demanding a reappraisal of her values.

She had some business to do after the concert and then there was the long uncertain journey home. An air raid held them up about half-way; the train slowed down and stopped and everyone in her carriage began to talk.

There was an anxious lady who was afraid she should miss her station – "They call them out, I know, but it's difficult to hear sometimes. Won't it be nice when the names go up again? I've got to catch a bus from the station, but do you think it's safe to go in a bus?"

"Safe as houses," said a man and they all laughed. "Well, you see, once the bus has started you won't know you're being bombed."

A porter came by with a megaphone: "Germany calling the British Isles," he called out, imitating Lord Haw-Haw, and everyone laughed again.

"I've got the last peppermint creams in the country here," said a girl. "Have one," and she passed them round, but no one took one – generosity could go too far.

"Save 'em for the kids," said the man.

Then they went on again but it was very late before Roberta got home.

Now she let her work fall into her lap and closed her eyes. She awoke to see George coming up the garden path towards her.

"I'll finish those shelves tomorrow Mum," he said. "I promised I'd get them done by the end of the holidays."

"They've flown – it always seems the end of the holidays," said Roberta.

She began slowly to sort out the volumes on George's bookshelves. As she did so she could see back through the years the figure of her schoolboy son, but with a pang she realized that she could no longer remember his features clearly; as a baby, yes, but beyond childhood – faceless. If only she had had more opportunities to know him, but his prep and public schools had robbed her of time. She sat and mourned for what she had lost and for what she had never had. George's education had been generously paid for by her uncle, Rollo's father, and he had gone to the schools he had advised, for Charles and she had been quite hard up. Also, because George was an only child they had thought it better for him to go away. But now she wondered. Immediately after school the Army had swallowed him up.

He was old enough to come in for the end of the War and after it was ended he remained in the Army, which seemed to suit him. He made an early marriage to a girl in the WAAFs – the Women's Auxiliary Air Force – and Roberta had not had time to get to know his young wife properly either. A drunken driver on a wintry road had seen to that and then she had become a substitute mother to their two babies, who were now nearer and more real to her than George. When she dreamed of her son, as she sometimes did, his personality merged into that of Alex; it was as if he had ceased to exist for her in his own right.

Chapter 8

AND YET they were not at all alike. George she remembered always in relation to some object: a cricket bat, a football, a saw, a bicycle, a gun, a car. Alex she saw as a figure in a void. Even as a little boy he seemed lacking in the common acquisitive factor.

"What do you do with your pocket money?" she had once asked him curiously.

"He mostly gives it to me," said Naomi.

"Then you shouldn't let him."

"But I need money so much more than he does," expostulated Naomi.

"Alex has too big a bump of altruism," she complained to Charles. "I don't know how he'll manage in life; he'll never dream of feathering his own nest. I doubt if he'd recognize a feather if he saw it."

Well, after all, he hadn't done so badly – it is seldom the things we worry about in the future that prove to be the real trials. He was good at his job and people liked him, though she suspected that they thought him an odd fellow; but they trusted him, just because he so queerly didn't want to feather his own nest first and foremost, and Clare saw to it that he didn't give quite all the pocket money to his causes. Patrick was turning out to have inherited George's practical turn, which was a comfort.

The phone rang. Roberta got up from the floor, where

she had been kneeling to read the titles on the lower shelves, and saw that her hands were covered with dust. *That just shows*, she thought ruefully, *I'm afraid Kitty was right, I am letting things go. Heaven knows when all my shelves last had a proper spring clean.*

It was Alex on the phone. "How often that happens," exclaimed Roberta.

"What happens?"

"I was thinking of you and then you rang."

"Oh," said Alex, "then I must think of too many people, Clare says the phone's always at it. Well, anyway how are you getting on?"

"Not too well," said Roberta, rashly, as she afterwards acknowledged. "I've begun to try and tackle the books. I never dreamt there were so many; they are all over the house besides the study."

"Yes," said Alex, "Clare was saying she thought they'd be a problem. Now, Granny, she and I have had a good idea." Roberta steeled herself.

"You remember Clare's cousin Morris, don't you? He's just retired from his librarian's job and he's at a loose end and we're sure he'd be very glad to come and help you. He knows all about books. He could list them for you and that would make it a much quicker business for a valuer – you'll be selling nearly all of them, I suppose."

"I suppose so," said Roberta sadly, and paused. She did indeed remember cousin Morris, a great talker, one who told you in detail about many things in which you were not interested. She supposed that if he were to list her books she would have to have him to stay, perhaps for some days. She quailed at the thought.

"It's very considerate of you both, my dears," she said at last, "but really I can manage quite well if I take it slowly."

"But why should you tire yourself out unnecessarily? Anyway, you don't quite know how much time you can allow yourself, do you, dear? A buyer may turn up any day and besides you'll be doing a really good turn to Morris; he'd love to be of use."

"Well, I'll think it over," said Roberta. "Are you sure there aren't any books you want for yourself? You didn't look at them much when you were here. At least take some for the children – I'll put some aside."

"None for me," said Alex firmly. "I get all I want from the library; but I'll run down soon again and we'll see about the children. And let us know soon about Morris, won't you?"

"Very well," said Roberta, "it'll be lovely to see you." She rang off rather abruptly.

It was typical, she thought, both annoyed and amused, for Alex could never resist a good turn and if he could bring off two at once was really happy. If she let Morris come it would probably be quite difficult to get rid of him. She was also conscious of the fact that she disliked the idea that Alex and Clare thought the job of dealing with the books too much for her. This decided her on walking to the village and back to see about some packing-cases she wanted to order from old Benson, the carpenter. It was the longest walk she had taken since her fall and, feeling tired on the way back, she turned aside to rest on a favourite seat in the churchyard, her mind busy with the problems of finding a good reason for declining Morris's help. The good reason was miraculously at hand.

Roberta had a weakness for churchyards. It was one of the attractions of Coleridge Court that it was close to old Highgate churchyard, through which she and her friend Rose and little Kitty used to walk together to school. They each had their favourite among the tombstones. Hers was a large family one – all those children, one after the other, fascinated her: John and Edith, Alfred and Frederick, Maria and Henry, Florence and Alice, Hester and Arthur and baby Samuel. She pictured all the children sitting at a huge dining-table with the father, John William, late of this

Parish, at one end, and Edith, beloved wife of the above, at the other. Rose favoured an earlier headstone with a skull and crossbones carved on it and Roberta remembered Kitty, who always lagged behind, calling out suddenly: "This is mine – oh, Berta, look! This one didn't die at all, she just fell asleep." Death was too far away, too alien to cast any shadow over the three little girls among the tombstones and even now the elderly Roberta at the back of her mind still thought of a churchyard as peopled with a quiet assembly of peaceable companionable folk. She never felt lonely in one and this village churchyard was a pretty place, well kept, with all its flowers of love bright upon the calm graves.

Thinking these thoughts, she felt put out by seeing her seat already occupied by a man, a stranger who, stretched out on it, was apparently dozing in the sun; but she was not going to give up her rest. She coughed. The man opened his eyes and at once made room for her. He was rather shabbily dressed – *But this means nothing nowadays*, she thought – a middle-aged man, rather good-looking, though he had boot-button eyes of that sort of opaque blackness which is singularly inexpressive.

"Good morning," he said, and his voice was educated and pleasantly pitched. "You caught me napping – it is so peaceful here. There is nothing like an English country churchyard for peace, is there?" As she sat down, he gave her a quick glance, smiled and continued.

"Beneath these rugged elms, that yew tree shade,
Where leaves the turf in many a mouldering heap
Each in his narrow cell forever laid
The rude forefathers of the hamlet sleep."

Roberta started, the quotation fell in so aptly with what she had been feeling, it was spoken sensitively too.

"Oh, yes," she responded, "the 'Elegy'. I often think of it myself here. The elms all gone, alas! But the yew is still with us and the forefathers, of course." Then she added with some hesitation, although they seemed to have made friendly contact so naturally, "You are fond of poetry?"

He laughed, "I set out to be a poet once but I found I wasn't one, so I made it my stock in trade instead: poetry and other books. I had a bookshop – until quite recently, in fact."

Again Roberta gave an inward start. She prided herself on a sensible view of life; coincidence, she held, was just chance, not "sent" or "meant" or whatever fanciful people like her mother liked to take it for. But there did seem something unusual, to say the least, in this meeting; first that quotation chiming in so exactly with her mood and now a book business. Her mind raced on, could it be that this stranger was the very excuse she was looking for to confound Alex and Clare?

She found herself asking all about his shop and hearing that it had been in Folkestone but now was no more. He had knocked about the world a bit, he said, but then wanted to settle down and had sunk all his capital in this shop in partnership with a friend.

"We were at school together and had scarcely met since. It was bad luck for me running across him again because, as it turned out, he was no good, a gambler who had cleared off with all he could lay his hands on, leaving nothing, but bad debts. Oh, well! That's how it is. I'm sorry to bore you with my troubles but you asked for it, you know. My old car's broken down and I just dropped in here to look at the church while the garage is patching it up, but it's locked up."

"Yes," said Roberta, "we've had vandals."

"You can't trust anyone nowadays," said the stranger.

Roberta had liked both his frankness and his lack of self-pity.

"You can get the key at the Vicarage," she said.

"It's rather late now," he said, "I'd better be pushing off. Well, it's been a pleasure to meet you."

398

And then Roberta heard herself saying, "But you know, it is rather extraordinary, meeting you here just now, I mean," and she began to tell him of her move and how the worst problem was the books. Now she wondered whether, knowing about them as he did, he could recommend anyone who could list and value her books for her.

"Arnold Hathaway," said the stranger with a little bow, "that's the fellow for you, at a loose end this very week and at your service. I could come over tomorrow if you liked and have a preliminary look at them anyway."

Roberta went home a little breathless but elated. She had of course hoped that he might offer to come himself. Arnold Hathaway – an unusual name and a pleasing one she thought, with two poetic associations. She had definitely taken to the man and hoped that evening that it wasn't all a dream and that he would actually turn up as arranged.

He did so, arriving at the time fixed and, after having looked round, said the listing and valuation would take about three days. He gave her the phone numbers of two references and having named what seemed to her a very reasonable quotation for the job, proposed, if she were satisfied, to begin the very next day. After he had gone Roberta made two phone calls, the first to a Folkestone doctor for the reference, which was satisfactory. *I shan't bother about the second one*, she thought and rang Alex.

"There's no need to trouble Morris," she said, "I've found someone locally," well, that was nearly true, "who is experienced and not at all expensive. I think it's really better to have it done professionally, Alex."

"Oh, very well," said Alex, "if you've made up your mind, though Clare will be disappointed. Who is this chap?"

"You'd approve, dear, he's down on his luck – a bankrupt bookseller but it's not his fault. He's a nice man and he loves poetry." *I sound just like Mama*, she thought suddenly and rang off.

"I can't think who this fellow can be," said Alex to Clare afterwards, "she never mentioned him before but she seems absolutely decided."

"Then there's nothing to be done – you know your grandmother," said Clare. "Bertram, if you go on hugging Boffin so tightly he'll scratch you."

"No, no," said Bertram. "He's a good cat, he's a nice cat." A moment later he dropped Boffin with a loud roar.

"What did I tell you?" said Clare.

Bertram stopped roaring in mid-yell. "No, no," he said in his ordinary voice, "it was an accident, he thought I was a tree."

Clare, annoyed at Roberta's summary dismissal of her cousin, and struck again by a certain resemblance between her youngest and his great-grandmother, said with an unusual firmness:

"It *wasn't* an accident, Bertram, he scratched you because you were squeezing him."

"A very normous tree," said Bertram.

Roberta, at the end of Arnold Hathaway's first day's work, was well pleased with her bargain. He had arrived punctually and had seemed to know his job. He had at once picked out some rare editions from her mother's collection of poetry.

"Yes," said Roberta, "my father delighted in procuring these for her – this little Donne, for instance. Are you interested in this?"

"Indeed, yes," said Arnold Hathaway.

They had a pleasant lunch together. He was a good raconteur and had travelled widely. Roberta congratulated herself that it was not Clare's boring cousin sitting opposite her. She had opened up the dining-room for his benefit (when alone she took her meals in her sitting-room) and he admired her view and was enthusiastic over her Georgian candlesticks and other silver.

"Forgive me," he said quite anxiously, "but I hope you

400

have these valuable pieces well insured. I came across a case only the other day of carelessness in that respect and in these degenerate times thefts are so deplorably common."

She reassured him.

The second day they discussed their favourite authors; he confessed to an unfashionable liking for eighteenth-century poetry, "Including the Churchyard School," he said, smiling.

Roberta found him most knowledgeable. That afternoon she had visitors who stayed late and she was not surprised that, by the time they left, Mr Hathaway's old car had disappeared from beside the dining-room french window where she had told him to park it. She glanced into the study and saw the neat lists lying on the table. *I shall quite miss him when he has finished*, she thought.

But the next morning he did not turn up and, rather put out at receiving no explanation, she went to lunch alone in the dining-room. There she found her explanation. What she did not find was the Georgian candlesticks, nor the cream jug, nor the salver, nor any of her spoons. The note Arnold Hathaway had left she read with incredulous horror. It said:

Dear Mrs Curling,

You have been very kind to me, I have enjoyed our talks and I am sorry to have to take your silver but my need is greater than yours. It was indeed a happy chance that brought me to your churchyard, where I was feeling so desperate when you found me that I actually wished myself with our rude forefathers beneath the sod; but your silver should save the situation. You see, it is a case of exchanged identity, such as was dear to the heart of the Elizabethan dramatists. My tale was true but it is my partner who is Arnold Hathaway and I am the bad lot and the gambler. I have nearly finished your inventory and you will not find any of your books missing, though I was sorely tempted to slip that little Donne into my pocket. Why I didn't, I don't quite know – perhaps you do. I don't much care for my own name so will once more borrow one.

"Autolycus"

As a child Roberta's worst dreams were of familiar and loved faces suddenly turning into mocking masks: the ultimate horror of any frightening fairy story was that of the witch or wizard or wicked stepmother disguised as a harmless peasant or beautiful Queen. Now her first reaction to this outrageous letter was not anger but a bewildered fear. Trust was betrayed and the foundations of a bearable world trembled. But she must ring the police. She had little hope, however; the thief had had twenty-four hours' start and was no fool – of that she was sure. Not that this excused her for being his dupe. Fury with herself now possessed her. How could she have been so credulous! She admitted with shame that it was more to get a rise out of dear good Alex and Clare than to escape Morris that she had leapt at this rascally stranger. She must indeed humble herself before them now and the worst of it was that they would be so kind. She was right.

"Don't mind so much, Granny," Alex said, "don't blame yourself so. I've been taken in many a time; but, you know, I think that's better than never taking a risk with people."

"Yes, Alex," said Roberta sadly, "for you it may be I can't feel like that. You see, it's like robbing you and Clare."

"Oh, Georgian silver doesn't really fit our way of life," said Alex, "so don't worry about that."

She felt still more humbled as she put the receiver down. It was a relief to be scolded thoroughly by Kitty and to be able therefore at last to find excuses for herself.

"But, Kitty, he really did like poetry, I'm sure of that. I think that's why he didn't take the Donne or any of the other books. He respected my liking it too; but, oh, how *could* anyone who loves Grey's 'Elegy' have stolen my silver?"

"Well, Hitler loved Beethoven and I dare say Nero played the fiddle quite well, and how many great poets and painters have been unfaithful to their wives – tell me that."

Roberta acknowledged once more to herself that the marriage of Heaven and Hell was an inescapable fact and it then seemed to her that the foundations of the world were steadying again. She had thought the "Elegy" would be spoilt for her but this was silly. Its beauty was undimmed. Light remained light and darkness darkness, though here on earth so often interwoven. There was one thing, however, that she would have liked to have known. If her silver had not been insured would it have affected Mr Hathaway? (She still thought of him by this name.) He had enquired so anxiously about this. She was very much afraid it would not, though she believed that he might have sincerely regretted it.

As she had feared, the police failed to trace the thief or her things. She grieved now over the personal loss – it was their vanished beauty, not their value that she minded and missed. Charles would have understood this but she thought he might have done what no one else did. He might have laughed. The thought of his possible amusement chased away bitterness. After all, she reminded herself, she had always had a soft spot for Autolycus and if this were not simply sentimentality it ought not to harden when she herself was a victim. It occurred to her too that really she had little or no right to the silver herself, for she had neither worked for it nor particularly deserved it and it was probably true that Mr Hathaway's need was greater than hers. "To each according to his need," and, though of course she knew theft was wrong, somehow a little of Alex's attitude to possession seemed to have rubbed off on her. It no longer appeared a matter of life and death which

403

of them she should keep. "Lay not up for yourselves treasures upon earth where moth and rust corrupt and where thieves break through and steal." She suspected though, that she might not be able to feel like this for very long, and meanwhile the practical necessities of the move must be attended to. Certain treasures, whether rightly or wrongly, had been acquired and were her responsibility and must be dealt with. She must continue with her lists.

Piano, she wrote down firmly, for, although it was seldom used and she knew the Village Hall was badly in need of one, she was not prepared to give up the piano.

Chapter 9

SHE ALWAYS thought of it as Naomi's piano for they had bought it when, with the realization that the child had undoubted aptitude, music for the first time had entered seriously into the family. The old Broadwood, with its pleated green silk behind the fretwork and side brackets for candles, upon which her grandmother had entertained the gentlemen after dinner with Mendelssohn and Chopin and the less difficult Beethoven sonatas, was not good enough for a budding genius. For so Roberta held her granddaughter to be, from the time when she had picked out melodies by ear at an early age, on through the steady accumulation of certificates and prizes right up to that unlucky journey to Salzburg. Indeed, she still did so, and cherished a secret hope that it was yet not too late for Naomi to make a comeback and to establish her pre-ordained fame as a solo pianist.

How thrilling it had been, that triumphant progress – almost without any setback, unless that rather difficult phase at the beginning of adolescence was to be counted, when the child had flagged a little and seemed to find the required practising wearisome. How to cope with this had been one of the few disagreements between herself and Charles.

"I think it's a mistake to put pressure on," he had said.

"But, Charles, she must practise if she is to do well in her next exam – it's crucial."

"Does it really matter all that much?"

"Of course it matters. Everyone knows there's so much competition nowadays."

"Pressure was put on me, if you remember, and little good it did."

"That was *quite* different. You never wanted to be a doctor, you weren't meant to be one; it was your father who wanted it."

"And don't we want this for Naomi?"

"Of course!" Roberta had cried, stamping her foot with irritation. "But only because it's obvious it's what she was made for, what she herself wants more than anything."

"Perhaps you are right," Charles had said, "it's difficult to tell with Naomi."

This was true. As a child Naomi did not easily or often show her feelings. Where Alex was exuberant she was withdrawn – he hugged, she submitted to being hugged, escaping as soon as possible. When, on one occasion, Roberta had to leave the children, he had cried: "I can't bear you to go away, Mummy, my life is wasted without you." Noami, on the other hand, was silent or, very occasionally, to Roberta's intense gratification she might mutter: "When shall I see you again?" Anyone she disliked she ignored quietly but firmly. She seldom cried and she did not laugh often, though she seemed happy enough. She had been a delicate child and Roberta had fussed over her and adored her as a rare little creature never to be taken for granted. Her reserve only intensified a certain quite pleasurable unease in the relationship. If she had ever analysed her feeling for the two children she might have said that she loved Alex but was in love with Naomi. She was not, however, jealous of Franz. No, it was not for being Naomi's husband that she found it hard to forgive him but because she held him to be the cause of her forsaking her career – and no talk either of any children yet to compensate, and she dared not ask about his or even hint, for fear of giving offence.

Naomi had not wanted to have the piano sent out to Austria. Franz had a Bechstein grand and it would have been superflous and a needless expense. So it remained at Rowanbank and sometimes when she was sure no one could hear her Roberta would stumble over a tune or two, regretting now that she had not kept up her music; but it had seemed unnecessary when Naomi was at hand to play so infinitely better than she ever could hope to do.

It was not strange that with her head full of the piano and its associations she should dream that night that she was playing it, not in her natural floundering fashion but as brilliantly as her granddaughter. In fact she was performing to a crowded and spellbound audience, at the Royal Festival Hall, it seemed. What was strange was that when she woke the music continued.

Opening her eyes, she saw the sun glimmering and shimmering through the leaves of the walnut tree to the sound of Mozart. She sprang out of bed as if she were young still and nearly fell because, strangely, she was old. Throwing a wrap round her, she went downstairs and there was Naomi at the piano.

"Darling, how lovely!" she exclaimed. "But why didn't you let me know? I didn't expect you till later on in my proceedings."

"Franz had a conference in Paris and we thought it would be nicer if we were both away together and I didn't think it would matter to you when I came. I can help with the clearing out now, can't I?"

"Indeed you can, but how did you get here at such an early hour?"

"I came by a night flight and I hired a car at Heathrow – I've got it for the week, they're not expensive if you drive yourself and I thought it would be handy – I want to get about a bit, see Clare and Alex and so forth." Roberta's heart sank a little. *Only a week and visits to be paid*, she thought, but immediately rebuked herself. Naomi was here now in the present moment and that was joy enough.

"You're looking well," she said. Naomi had too narrow a face and her features were too irregular for beauty but she had large very clear grey eyes which, when they were lit by interest or emotion, looked even larger from the thinness of the face and gave it a luminous quality which was very attractive. Her smiles came rarely but when they came they were delightful.

She smiled up at her grandmother now and said: "So do you. I hope I didn't disturb you; I thought you were usually up and about by now. I called in at the cottage and got a key from Mrs B."

"I'm afraid I've let myself get into bad habits of sleeping late," said Roberta. "I can't get off easily; I suppose it's having so much on my mind with the move."

"Yes," said Naomi, "it must be a great upheaval for you. You go and dress and I'll get us some breakfast."

After breakfast Roberta went to phone Kitty, who had been coming for the weekend. She had no intention of sharing Naomi's precious time with anyone else.

"Why didn't she tell you she was coming, the inconsiderate little toad?"

"She's not really inconsiderate, Kitty, it's only that her margin of communication is low."

"Well, it comes to the same thing. Yes, of course I understand and, yes, I can and I will put off my visit and, yes, I *do* know Naomi's perfect."

Roberta put down the receiver abruptly. Kitty never appreciated either of the grandchildren properly – a form of jealousy, Roberta supposed; but she forgot Kitty as soon as she got back to the sitting-room.

With Naomi's arrival the house had come alive again and the hours flew past. Together they set about tackling drawers and cupboards, an exhausting but no longer a grim task done in company. Naomi shared Roberta's love of

408

order and they made separate heaps of oddments: one for village jumble, one for Oxfam, one for a bonfire and one to keep for Coleridge Court. She was not allowed to linger, as she would have done if alone, over the seductive boxes of family photographs and letters, old theatre programmes, school reports, all the flotsum and jetsum of the past. Noami was ruthless.

"What a hoarder you are, Mother," she said.

"It's having had so much room," said Roberta, sighing.

"Well, let's get on – what shall we do with these old cameras?"

The weather behaved perfectly. At first it rained steadily, the insistent slanting drops beating against the windows, cutting them off from the outside world which indeed ceased to exist for Roberta. Then, when the back was broken of their allotted tasks, the still-warm October sun shone out so brilliantly that they took their lunch outside to the old summerhouse among the rampant sprawling Michaelmas daisies.

"Are you sure there is nothing that you want to take back with you?" asked Roberta a little wistfully.

"Well," said Naomi, "perhaps some of my children's picture books – Johnny Crow and the Beatrix Potters and the Caldicott Rhymes. There was a pile in the Nursery: I thought they would have all gone to Alex."

"He had his own old ones for the children, I kept yours separate," said Roberta, her pulse quickening. She at once saw an entrancing picture of Naomi with a book and a baby on her lap.

But Naomi went on: "You know I work two days a week now at Franz's Children's Clinic and I thought they would like them – the pictures are so good and I could easily translate the text for them."

"No, you never told me," said Roberta flatly. "Do you enjoy that?"

"Oh, yes, and I'm thinking I might take a course next

409

year so that I could be of more use. By the way, now we've got on so well with the turning out I think I shall run down and see Alex and Clare and the children, tomorrow perhaps. I'd better give Clare a ring now and see if it's convenient. Then I might spend a night in London."

"Very well," said Roberta. She sat on alone, holding on her lap a box of her mother's kid gloves, yellowing with age and with tiny pearl buttons. They seemed as melancholy as the little ghosts of white roses nipped by the early frosts that hung over the summerhouse roof. "Working at a clinic and about to take a course" – why did Naomi take up these things with which she had no business and why did she mention them so casually and not even talk them over with her? How little time there was left for talk now anyway, for she must send her off to Alex and Clare with a smile tomorrow, Roberta supposed.

"And like a sad slave stay and think of nought,
But where she is, how happy she makes those.
So true a fool is love that in her will
Though she do anything she does no ill."

She repeated the lines to herself partly for comfort and partly in admonition.

Naomi came bounding back over the lawn, looking amused. "It's all right for tomorrow, Clare says, but it seems that Becky keeps on and on about wanting a clock from you for herself, since Patrick is getting the grand-father . . . Clare's afraid she suffers from an inferiority complex because of Patrick being the eldest and Bertram being Bertram, so she wonders if you possibly might have another clock to spare and would I mind asking you."

"Why ever didn't she ask me herself before?" said Roberta.

"Oh, you know Clare, she'll have a dozen reasons – afraid you might think her grabbing, afraid that she might be encouraging Becky to grab, afraid lest you haven't

410

really a suitable clock or will rob yourself of one. Have you one, by the way?"

"There's the blue Staffordshire china one with the pink roses; it was to have gone into the sale but of course Becky can have it."

'She'll love that one. I always did," said Naomi.

"But I can't leave Bertram out," said Roberta, "he must have a special present too. I wonder what on earth he would like."

"I could ask now and then I can take it down with the clock tomorrow," said Naomi and disappeared again.

It seemed that Bertram would like the stuffed owl. He could not be found but Patrick firmly vouchsafed for this.

"It's moulting," said Naomi doubtfully, "we put it with the scouts' jumble, but if Patrick says so I expect it's all right."

The clock was a great success after a moment of disappointment as to its relative size.

"But yours is beautiful, Becky, Patrick's is just big," said Naomi, and Becky stroked the clock's overblown china roses lovingly. But when the owl was produced Bertram shouted:

"Take 'im away, take 'im away."

"Oh, dear," said Naomi, "Granny thought that was what he wanted." Patrick looked embarrassed.

"It's norrible Mr Brown," howled Bertram.

"Who?" asked Naomi.

"Stop it Bertram," said Clare. "What do you mean?"

"Mr Brown out of Squirrel Nutkin," explained Becky, "who pulled poor Nutkin's tail off."

"It's *not* Mr Brown, Bertram," said Patrick hastily, "it's Christopher Robin's Owl." But Bertram continued to howl dismally.

"Look here," said Patrick, "I'll have him, Bertram, I'll put him right away from you by my bed with his back to

411

you, so he can't possibly see you – then will you be all right?"

Bertram stopped crying abruptly, as was his wont, and nodded.

Patrick arranged the owl on his little bedside table with much satisfaction. He had always admired him greatly. But that night when they were both in bed Bertram sat up suddenly.

"Patrick," he said, "it's *my* Mr Brown what Granny sent me, Bertram, isn't it, Patrick?"

"Well, yes, I suppose so," said Patrick.

"Goodnight, *my* norrible Mr Brown," said Bertram.

After Naomi had got back from her visits there were only two days left. Roberta was haunted by all the things she had wanted to say and which she now felt would never be said. She longed for the forbidden fruit of emotional satisfaction but she did not dare destroy the delicate comfortable surface relationship between them. She was sure that Naomi would evade any intimate probings with displeasure, though she would not perhaps show resentment so much as slip away and hide behind some trivial topic, shaming her grandmother by turning into a faun or a tree or something equally detached and impersonal. Roberta thought, however, she might venture to ask her whether she intended to come back to Rowanbank again before the move.

"Well," said Naomi, "that depends upon when you go, doesn't it? We shall be going to Vienna to Franz's parents for the Christmas holiday. If you sell before then, I don't think I can come again so soon, unless you need me very badly."

Nothing on earth would have made Roberta press it.

"Oh, I hope to be settled in Coleridge Court by Christmas," she said, "so this is probably your last time at Rowanbank. Do you mind? Will you miss it?"

"Not really," said Naomi. "Well, the view and the garden perhaps, but I have the river and the mountains now instead – Rowanbank is my past." The dismissal was matter-of-fact and serene.

Well, do I want her to be miserable? Why should I mind her not minding? But I do, thought Roberta.

Aloud, and against her better judgement, she heard herself saying: "And I am your past too, I suppose." She meant it to sound like a playful sally, but to her disgust it came out in quite the wrong tone of voice, disgustingly suggestive of hurt. *Now I've done just what I resolved not to do, fish for a response*, she thought despairingly.

But Naomi only answered by one of her rare laughs.

She won't rise, said Roberta to herself, *and it serves me right; but what is to be done with the past then? Surely not simply to discard it like a snake his old skin.*

The following day, the last of Naomi's stay, they piled all the bundles into the hired car to be delivered to their various destinations in the village. At the Oxfam shop they were received by Mr Eliot with gentle courtesy. He was a retired solicitor and presiding over the shop assisted by his big poodle, Gigi, was his refuge from trouble.

"What a gracious day," he said as he took their sacks from them. "Gigi and I are taking our lunch down by the stream, we must catch the last treats of St Martin's summer while we can."

"Oh, dear!" said Roberta when they had left. "Poor man, he's so nice and his wife is so awful. I heard her screaming at him when I passed the house lately. She was drunk, of course; but, drunk or sober, she's a harridan. Yet I believe she was a very handsome woman once. If only she'd die . . . but of course she won't. He always reminds me of a Chekhov character."

"Everyone does, if you think about it," said Naomi.

"Oh, no! Think of Mrs Bun . . . and that reminds me, I must get some bread." Mrs Mugford, the baker's wife, served them. She had a round, brown, fat face and little black eyes like currants.

"Well, I'll grant you Mrs Bun," said Naomi, "but what about Bert Langford? He's straight out of Chekhov."

"Crossed with Dickens, I should say," said Roberta. "His old mother and his curiosity shop are pure Dickens."

"Does his mother still sit in his shop all day?"

"Certainly she does, I'm calling there next to tell him I'm having an auction, though I don't suppose he'll bother about it. He never seems to buy anything fresh and he hates to part with anything. I can't think what they live on."

Bert Langford's shop was at the end of the High Street. In its window was a Chinese vase containing some bulrushes the worse for wear, a huge tabby cat asleep on a carved stool and a small picture painted on glass. The picture was attractive, in soft blues and greens and entitled *The Pensive Shepherdess*; Naomi peered at it.

"I like that," she said, "I might buy it for Franz, he's fond of English antiques."

"But I can let you have something better than that!" exclaimed Roberta. "The whole contents of the big corner cupboard are going into the sale. I'd love you to take your pick. I didn't know you would like something for Franz."

"Oh, thanks, Mother, I'd have said if I'd wanted anything but this is different; I've found this myself. Isn't it rather pretty, don't you think, with the lamb on a ribbon and that dear little church in the background?"

Roberta did not reply. To acquire any fresh object at this moment seemed so unnecessary, even immoral to her; also, in spite of herself, she minded that neither Alex nor Naomi seemed to want or to care for the family things.

They went into the shop. Bert Langford was a frail, bent little man with wispy hair. He wore a very long purple scarf wound round his throat and trailing down his back. In a corner an even frailer and more bent old woman wrapped in a grey shawl sat busily knitting.

"Why, it's Miss Naomi," said Bert, in a surprisingly beautiful low clear voice. "We haven't seen you for a long while."

"How's that cough of yours?" quavered the little old woman.

"I'm very well, thank you, Mrs Langford," said Naomi, "I haven't got a cough."

"Your mother's always so anxious about your chest," said Mrs Langford. "Try two sticks of cinnamon in lots of water morning and night; my mother swore by that and she nursed with Miss Nightingale in the Crimea."

"Thank you very much," said Naomi.

Roberta had begun to turn over a pile of old gramophone records that lay on the counter.

"Oh, Mrs Curling, none of those will do for you," said Bert, shocked, "indeed no."

"I thought I might find one for my grandson," explained Roberta meekly, "but Naomi would like to see the little glass picture in the window."

Bert shook his head sadly. "I'm afraid that's not for sale, Miss Naomi," he said.

"Oh, Bert," said the old woman, "let Miss Naomi have it, now do."

Bert, still shaking his head slowly, removed the pensive shepherdess from the window, dusted her, and at last let Naomi carry her off in triumph.

"Do you think he does it on purpose?" she asked. "To make people want the things more, I mean."

"No, he really loves them and can't bear to part with them. If it wasn't for his mother he'd close down, I believe."

"However old is she?" enquired Naomi.

"No one knows. Now one more call at the scout's hut and we're done."

On the way home they continued their game of allotting villagers to different authors. Miss Murphy at the Post

Office, Roberta decided, was an Agatha Christie.

"She's too sinister for a Christie," said Naomi. "With those pale eyes and her twisted smile, she's more Simenon."

"It's too bad," said Roberta, "she's really a very good daughter to that old paralysed father, but I do admit she is frightening. I'm always giving her the wrong change."

Soon, she thought suddenly, *all these people will become characters in my book of memory*. The vicar was obviously Trollope and they agreed that Mrs Baxter and old Bennet the carpenter were both from Hardy, but they argued over Mr Spires, the schoolmaster.

"You only say he's Lewis Carroll because he looks like the Mad Hatter," said Roberta, "but I assure you he's really Henry James."

They reached Rowanbank in a hilarious mood and Roberta reflected a little sadly, as she got tea, that they met each other more easily and more closely in the world of books than in real life.

The previous morning they had discovered a pile of old piano music in a small tin trunk, gilt-edged volumes of Mendelssohn, Clementi, Chopin.

"Who did these belong to?" Naomi had asked and they had found an inscription in faded ink: "Louisa Mary Willmott – 1860."

"I think that must be your great-great-aunt," said Roberta. "I don't remember seeing them before – it's extraordinary what turns up."

Now, this last evening, Naomi brought down one of these albums and started playing. As Roberta sat down to listen, it was immediately borne in upon her that she had heard this particular melody before, long years before and never since, and that it was connected with some unpleasant experience. Then, as it continued, she was no longer at Rowanbank.

*   *   *

It was autumn and she was not even in England. She was a girl again in Bruges, walking the cobbled streets by the side of Sister Marie from the convent school and carrying a basket for her. They came to a tall narrow old house on the Quay de Marbriers, knocked on its door and were let into a lofty, dim room where a white-haired lady wrapped in a black and silver shawl greeted them and was presented with the bottle of home-made wine from the basket.

The lady, who in spite of her hair did not appear old, looked at Roberta so strangely that she felt shy and when Sister Marie rose to go she said, "If you have some other calls to make, dear Sister, perhaps you would leave your pupil here with me for a little while, I do not often have the pleasure of seeing a young girl's face now."

"Of course," said Sister Marie. "You will gladly stay with Madame, will you not, Roberta? I shall not be long."

When they were left alone Madame looked at her again with that curious searching attention and said abruptly, "Do you like music?"

"Yes," answered Roberta.

"Well, I will play for you, but not here. Come with me," and she led the way up great stone stairs until they came to two rooms leading out of each other.

The first room was hung with pale tapestry and seemed full of musical instruments: there was a grand piano, a cello in an open case and what looked to Roberta like a lute decorated with faded ribbons propped against a gilt chair. There was also an easel with a half-finished portrait of a girl upon it. The lady sat down at the piano.

"You will hear me better from my daughter's room," she said, "you are too close to the piano here – go in, please, she will not mind."

Roberta obeyed; there was no question, she felt, of not doing as she was told. The inner room was luxuriously furnished but she had no eyes for anything but a swift impression, for she was riveted by the figure of a girl seated

417

at a second piano, very still and silent. The girl wore a red velvet dress that swept the floor and her black hair was tied back with a red ribbon. She did not move and Roberta faltered on the threshold, wondering what she should do. The light was filtered through the lime trees outside the narrow window and it was only after a long minute or two that she realized that what she was looking at was a life-sized wax figure.

Then the music began. The notes fell softly in slow succession on the air. To Roberta, who had retreated to the window, it seemed as if they turned into the small yellow leaves that drifted down one by one, "brightness falling from the air", to the grey waters of the canal beneath. She stood motionless till the music ceased. Then she tiptoed back into the outer room again.

Madame looked up from the piano. "Did you enjoy it?" she said. "It is my favourite Étude. My daughter plays it also," and Roberta knew somehow that the music in front of the wax figure was the same.

With relief she heard Sister Marie's knock at the front door.

"So she played to you, did she?" said Sister Marie as they went back to the convent. "She must have taken a great fancy to you, poor dear soul. Since her daughter died in an accident she has not been quite as others. She took you to her daughter's room, you say? You are a little upset, I can see. It comforts her, you must understand, that figure. You are Protestant and of course are not used to such dear images – the figures of Saint Cécile and Saint Theresa in my sewing-room, how I would miss them! And the music that Madame played, it is always the same, I believe; it was what her daughter was playing that last morning of her life, you see. Ah, well, she has better music in Heaven, I am sure."

But Roberta had shuddered. The rooms, Madame and the wax figure had been recurring images in troubled dreams for some time afterwards, but she had not thought of them for many ages past.

Now the music had re-created the whole experience for her in startling vividness and she found it still had power to disturb her. Naomi had finished before she had quite recovered the present. "I don't think I have ever heard you play that before," she said. "What is it?"

"One of Chopin's lesser known Études," said Naomi. "No, I don't think I have played it – it isn't Chopin at his best, is it? A bit cloying."

"Yes," agreed Roberta. "Won't you play something else?"

Naomi turned over the pages. "It's not what you'd call a very inspiring collection, but . . . oh, here's some Beethoven."

A serene and timeless little theme washed over Roberta, freeing her from all her tangled emotions. *How foolish to want Naomi to express herself in words*, she thought. *She is a musician and the music says it for her and for me too – it says all I want from her and all she wants, I know, to give me. We know each other perfectly in this.* A deep peace and happiness flowed through her.

Naomi closed the piano and said, "Poor old piano, how I used to hate you, though of course it wasn't you I really hated, it was music."

"What did you say?" asked Roberta.

"I said I hated music," remarked Naomi lightly, and then seeing her mother's face she added: "Oh, it's all right now, it was only when I had to work at it and worry about it so."

"But I don't understand what you are saying, Naomi," said Roberta, "you couldn't hate music."

"Yes, I did," went on Naomi's clear matter-of-fact voice, "especially the piano – not my flute so much, because that was only secondary."

419

"But you always wanted to be a musician."

"You wanted it," corrected Naomi.

"But you were so good at it."

"Yes that was the trouble, I couldn't help that; but I really wanted to be a doctor, a surgeon. I think I would have made a good surgeon." She looked down at her hands.

With a struggle to get out the words Roberta said, "Why didn't you ever say so?"

"Oh, you would have minded so much. Besides, when I was a child I didn't care, and then I took it for granted that you and Father knew best, and later I thought it was my duty because I knew I was good. I went on thinking it was my duty until I met Franz. I can't tell people things or talk about them until they are over. It's really lovely, Mother, not to have to hate music any more."

It was perhaps the most intimate confidential talk Roberta had ever had with her granddaughter and it was an incredible one.

She lay awake that night tossing uneasily trying to come to terms with it. Uppermost was the sense of loss – to have been so mistaken seemed to change the past into a hollow place of false echoes. Then there was self-reproach too to be dealt with. How could she have been so insensitive – was it vicarious ambition that had blinded her? She was afraid it might have been so. She began to talk to Charles as she often did in emergencies. In life he had been her conscience, and the habit of referring everything to him persisted. Sometimes he answered. Reason told her that this was only the natural outcome of their long close relationship, her heart said otherwise.

"Yes, I remember you warned me against pressing the child but I don't believe you guessed what she was really feeling and, oh, the irony of it, Charles! Wanting to be a doctor, I mean. Oh, how strange – and it's not the same Naomi. Oh, Charles, I wish she hadn't told me, I want my Naomi back again."

420

"Like Madame in Bruges," said Charles.

She lay still for a while after this. "Yes," she admitted painfully, "a wax figure of my own making, dead, in the past. Oh, well, I shall have to be like the snake after all and discard my old skin."

"Not like a snake," said Charles. "Remember Alex's *Wonder Book of Nature* – like a toad, swallow the past and let it nourish the future."

"It's hard," said Roberta, "so hard."

In the morning there was no time for more talk.

Naomi said: "I'll come to Coleridge Court as soon as I can, at Easter perhaps." Her eyes were bright with the anticipation of seeing Franz again. She kissed her grandmother lightly on her forehead and it was if some winged creature had brushed her in passing, then she was gone.

Roberta sat down and wrote a note to the caretaker of the Village Hall, offering the piano and promising to arrange for its removal.

Chapter 10

IT WAS now the end of October; the clocks had gained their hour and the days suddenly seemed closed in and Roberta more than ever before disliked the thought of the long, lonely evening hours. She began to be really anxious about a sale. She had been obliged to find the money for the Coleridge Court flat or she would have lost it, "And heaven knows when another will come your way," Kitty had said. Her bank had been accommodating and had managed a bridging loan, but Roberta was not happy about this and Mrs Baxter was another source of anxiety. Her daughter Betty's baby was due in December and she wanted to be settled in with the family in good time to help.

Viewers were now falling off as the agent had predicted; lately, far from resenting their intrusion, Roberta had welcomed them. She was learning sadly from experience not to build on false hopes. She had had one actual offer only so far. It was from a cheerful weather-beaten lady, only interested in the garden, and that solely in its potential capacity to nourish and amuse two goats, a donkey, four cats and two dogs, all of whom she had rescued from neglect and general misery. Roberta warmed towards her but when her offer proved really too low to be considered, she was relieved that the threat to her father's beloved flowerbeds was removed. Then there was a charming American couple, to whom the Edwardianism of Rowanbank especially appealed. It was apparently quite period enough for them and they enthused over its "art nouveau" alcoves, the fireplaces with their beaten copper hoods and fenders, its leaded windows and gables. They began to plan where to install the extra bathrooms and the radiators for the central heating, but she never heard from them again. There was the large family party who arrived without warning and rushed about as though the place belonged to them already, allotting bedrooms and disputing as to north and south aspects, but though they said they would phone her agent immediately, they too departed for ever.

At last an acceptable offer materialized. It was from an elderly couple, accompanied by a younger, vaguely related pair with whom they were proposing to share the house. All four had looked at the famous view in silence and any comments as they walked from room to room were quietly unfavourable.

"Curious shape this bedroom, isn't it?"

"Does your kitchen face south? That must make it rather hot in summer."

"Mary, mind that awkward little step, this passage is so dark."

'Roberta was therefore surprised when the offer came, but she felt she must accept it at once. It was subject to a surveyor's report but this did not worry her unduly, for she believed the house to be structurally sound. She began to hope that after all she might be settled by Christmas.

The surveyor arrived in due course. It was a cold day, and, as he had spent quite a time outside, she invited him in to the sitting-room for a cup of coffee.

"A good period for building, this," he remarked pleasantly. "Not likely to find any dry rot here, that's the worst enemy. Victorian homes are full of it." He made no other comment, but he was a jovial man and his manners confirmed her confidence.

She confided the good news to Mrs Baxter when she

arrived the next day with a big bunch of chrysanthemums from the cottage garden – "To cheer things up for you a bit."

"They're lovely," said Roberta, "but I don't want cheering up so much today, Ellen dear. I think I've sold Rowanbank at last – I didn't want to say anything before but I'm almost certain it's going to be all right."

She arranged the flowers in her mother's old blue jug – *though I can't make them look as she did, the witch*. They smelt appropriately of wet autumn leaves, she thought. How stupid of people to grow them in pots all the year round; flowers should keep to their proper seasons. Chrysanthemums actually were not among her favourites but she was grateful for them now; they certainly brightened up the doleful look of the rooms where the removal of various objects showed discoloured places on the walls and threadbare patches of carpet. A bookseller from Tunbridge Wells, offering her only a little less than Arnold Hathaway's valuation sum, had taken away the books, and the piano had been promptly removed to the Village Hall. Willow was very concerned and stalked around, waving his tail and smelling the emptiness. Roberta congratulated herself that she had not to show any more viewers over a house with such a tatty interior. The board by the gate now said "Under Offer" and she herself now felt "under offer" too, in a sort of no man's land between past and future.

She was by this time down to listing the choice of essentials such as chairs, tables, beds; since these were dictated more by necessity, size, and general utility than by association and sentiment, they were easier to select. But there were many regrets. She would, for instance, have liked to have kept her rocking-chair but it took up too much room; and the pretty round table was discarded in favour of a folding Pembroke one which could be put away when not in use. She was also taking over the dull but still serviceable floor-covering of the flat which she meant to enliven by a couple of her favourite rugs; but Kitty, who was paying her postponed visit, insisted on new curtains.

"It seems an unnecessary extravagance," said Roberta. "I am sure I can cut up some of the old ones to fit – besides, I'm fond of them."

"They're all faded and most of them dreadfully worn. Don't be so stingy and sentimental, Berta. You want something much lighter and brighter to fit those small rooms. Let's send for patterns."

Roberta gave in and compromised by choosing for her new bedroom the old William Morris thrush pattern which had been in her sitting-room, but in yellow instead of red, for the room faced north.

"Are you going to give a farewell party?" asked Kitty.

"What a dreadful idea!" said Roberta. "I don't like parties any more and I hate farewells."

"Well, I don't think you ought just to slink away from Rowanbank," said Kitty. "After all, Uncle built it and you've lived in the village most of your life."

"Who's being sentimental now?" said Roberta. "There's very few left that remember the parents and those few I mean to go and see separately before I leave. But a party. . . . No, I want it all to be over as quickly and quietly as possible, like a death."

"You take it too seriously," said Kitty. "Think how many people are on the move nowadays. All over the world people are moving house; people just don't stay in the same place now, whether they want to or not. I enjoy a move myself; it's a challenge. By the way, I saw a rat yesterday in the attic sitting on that pile of old studio magazines of Charles's that you thought I might like for my hospital."

"Oh, dear!" exclaimed Roberta. "Willow won't go up there any more, in fact he spends more and more time with Mrs B. in the cottage. She keeps a special brand of tinned pilchards that he's partial to. She says he'll settle down much more easily when he has to leave Rowanbank if he gets broken into it gradually by a change of scene now, but rats! I'm glad it was you and not me."

"I said: 'Hullo, Rat, what are you doing here?'" continued Kitty. "He said, 'What are you?' and I said: 'I'm a portent, you'll have to look out for new quarters soon, I can tell you; there'll be changes here, no more nice musty heaps of papers in corners and a younger cat than Willow, I shouldn't wonder, and probably a dog too – a terrier.' He was a sensible rat, if cheeky. He said, 'OK, OK, not to worry – the world's all before me.'"

"I bet he was a young rat," said Roberta. "I take your point, but I'm not you. Unlike yourself, I like to take off my coat and get out my slippers and feel settled. I don't think I'm a natural traveller, at any rate not now, and I devoutly hope I shall never have to move again. And, Kitty, I'm sure I'm not peculiar in hating it all and feeling it traumatic. You know how when you've got an illness everyone cheers you up with horror stories about it; well, Charles's nephew has just had to move because of his job and his wife's had a breakdown and the Mitchells' marriage came to grief because of their move and Alice Rose died when she had to give up her cottage, the one I might have bought.'

"Stop it, Berta," cried Kitty. "It's just the reaction from having actually sold the place. Now, do give a party, it'll do you no end of good. Oh, here's Mrs B. – what do *you* feel, Mrs B.? Aren't you glad that you will soon be rid of your cottage and that big garden of yours and starting a new life?"

Oh Kitty! thought Roberta – but Mrs Baxter only smiled and, to make room for a coffee tray, bore away the jug of chrysanthemums, still glowing though not now at their best.

"I'll bring you a fresh lot tomorrow," she said, 'but they'll be the last, I reckon. These are all William's plant-

426

ing; he always did well with his chrysanths. Now Betty's Norman, he's got no use for flowers, grudges them every bit of room he does. Still, there's always window-boxes."

"So there are!" exclaimed Roberta gratefully. It seemed suddenly to her that window-boxes symbolized a humble hope such as surely she could count on for her future. She found them more comforting than Kitty's philosophic rat. Yes, she decided then and there, she would have window-boxes, but she would *not* have a party.

Fate, however, decreed otherwise, for though one can decide not to send out invitations, one cannot prevent them from arriving.

Not long after Kitty had departed, Roberta met the vicar in the Post Office, and he asked her to take tea with him the following afternoon. Charles and she had never been regular churchgoers, in fact Charles, still suffering from his upbringing, had rarely attended except at Christmas and Easter. But Roberta had a deep affection for the church itself and had become fond of the present incumbent. The Reverend Hector Simmons was scholarly, sensitive, conscientious and kind; he was also exceedingly absentminded. This had not mattered greatly while his wife was still alive, for she had kept him in order, but since her death he had become even less reliable. He was self-reproachful and sad about his shortcomings. "I feel I am grieving Marian and letting her down as well as being a nuisance," he confided to one of his long-suffering churchwardens. But his parishioners, who loved him, combined to make good this failing whenever they could and to hide his lapses from him.

The village grapevine functions swiftly, thought Roberta, *he's probably heard already about the sale and wants to know more about it and to show me a little extra attention, bless him.*

She decided to take him George Herbert's *Country Parson*, which she had discovered among her father's books,

427

as an appropriate parting present. It was a nice little facsimile of an early edition and she hoped he did not already possess a copy.

His eyes lit up as he opened it eagerly, "My dear Mrs Curling, how very kind, but can you spare it?"

Oblivious of her polite assurance and of his housekeeper Mrs Spence, arriving with an ample tea-tray, he began to read to himself – murmuring at intervals: "What a treasure, what a treasure!" but soon broke out aloud with: "Listen to this now, my dear Mrs Curling: 'When men have nothing to do then they fall to drink, to steal, to whore, to scoff, to revile and all sorts of gamings.' Poor dears, poor dears, how true. Human nature doesn't change much, I fear. Let's see what Herbert advises as a remedy, for it looks as though work for everyone was not the rule even then. 'Husbandry' – well, perhaps, 'the study of mathematics and fortifications' – hmm, hmm, 'the family man has his hands full if he do what he ought to do' – very true, 'for John the Baptist squared out to everyone (even to soldiers) what to do.' Did he now? Indeed, I must look into that, but what's this? 'Love is the Parson's business, wherefore he likes well that his Parish at good times invite one another to their houses and he urgeth them to it and all dine and sup together.' Ha! How very right that I should light upon this in your exceedingly kind gift, Mrs Curling, for it is just the subject I wanted to talk to you about. So if you have had all you want we will draw up our chairs to the fire."

Poor Roberta complied, cast a wistful glance at the untouched tea table and wondered anxiously what was coming.

"I hear you have disposed of Rowanbank," said the vicar, "I hope to your satisfaction. It seems then that you mean to leave us all shortly. It goes without saying that we shall miss you very much."

Roberta, only wishing that it *did* go without saying, murmured that she would miss everyone too.

"Now taking old George Herbert's advice, even before I had read it, I have been thinking that this is one of the times he refers to when we ought to meet together to sup or dine, for there are many I know who would like to say their goodbyes to you and give you their good wishes. So we have planned a little gathering in your honour and I've been asked to invite you and to find out what date and what time would be convenient."

Oh, my, oh, my, thought Roberta, *what a bore and how Kitty will crow, but I must be gracious about it, for it is meant so well*. Aloud she said, "How very kind, but I feel I don't deserve it; it's a long while since I've been much use in the village, I'm afraid."

"Don't you think that perhaps we are never the best judges of how much use we are?" said the vicar. "But talking of use, are those fortunate people who have bought your house likely to be of any? So many newcomers nowadays are with us but not of us."

"I really couldn't say," said Roberta. "Actually they were not very communicative, but that's no guide – I hope at least they will prove a better substitute for my ageing bones."

They went on to discuss other matters. Before Roberta left, however, a date was fixed for the party – the first convenient one, for she felt she would like to get it over as soon as possible. As she was opening the garden gate on her way home, Mrs Spence came running out after her.

"I saw that you didn't get no tea at all, Mrs Curling," she said, "and I'd made a cake on purpose, but as soon as I saw him with his nose in a book I feared how it would be. Now, won't you step round to my room and I'll make a fresh brew? He'll never notice."

Roberta laughed. "It's very kind of you, Mrs Spence, but I want to get home before it's quite dark – it's foggy tonight – though I'm sorry to miss your cake."

She walked back quickly. The village had now almost

completely disappeared, she might have been walking on the moon, but even if the mist and the gathering darkness had not obscured the well-known landmarks, Roberta would not have noticed them, she was too busy with thoughts of the party which seemed to bring her departure nearer and confirm its reality. *At least I haven't to worry about whom to invite, which would have been dreadfully difficult*, she thought, *and there won't be room for very many at the Vicarage anyway.*

She found that Mrs Baxter knew all about it already. "I'm to help Mrs Spence with the refreshments – there'll be me and Florrie Mugford and Mrs Spence's niece Doris, and Mercy Brown."

"Surely Mrs Spence doesn't need so many helpers," said Roberta.

"It's well to be properly provided," said Mrs B.

"But the vicar won't be inviting all that number of people," expostulated Roberta.

"There aren't going to be *any* invitations," said Mrs Baxter serenely. "Vicar thought best to let all come who wants and it's not going to be at the Vicarage, it's to be in the Hall."

Oh, the old rascal, thought Roberta. *With his talk about George Herbert's little friendly meetings in each other's homes and all the while plotting to use the Hall, which'll be cold and half-empty and dreadful. Oh, my, as if moving house were not bad enough without all this fuss! Well, I simply shan't think about it any more – "time and the hour runs through the roughest day."*

Yet on the day itself, in spite of telling herself that Kitty would say it was she and nobody else who was making the fuss, and though she felt she was behaving exactly like Clare, she was full of nervous apprehension as she set out.

Afraid of being late, she started too early and spent what seemed an uncomfortable time making halting conversation with old Colonel and Mrs Brandon, who were always the first to arrive anywhere. Roberta had turned her back on the door and tried not to look over her shoulder at the trickle of fresh arrivals. The vicar, who was always late, she thought might well forget to come altogether and she was relieved to hear his greetings. After that it was soon all right; the trickle became a steady stream, the Hall began to fill up and to buzz quite loudly and she was able to relax and to welcome the guests. There were many more than she had expected, which was gratifying after all, though she knew that certainly some only came for the outing and the refreshments – old Joe Banks, for instance, whose wheelchair had been pushed within easy reach of the sausage rolls and who, she was sure, was very hazy as to why they had been provided. Not that this mattered in the least; Roberta was relieved to sense that the atmosphere was full of a diffused geniality, not particularly directed towards herself. She felt easily and naturally drawn into it warmth and began to enjoy herself. The heating of the Hall was functioning satisfactorily for a wonder and the place felt comfortable. She thought that Charles's two pictures of the High Street in summer and winter, which she had donated, looked very well, and there was a big pot of autumn berries on Naomi's piano, about which Rachel Lewis, the village organist, was now purring: "Such a generous gift, dear Roberta, and so greatly needed."

By this time Roberta felt she could even do justice to the excellent spread. Mrs Mugford, alias Mrs Bun, the baker's wife, conjured up an easy-chair from somewhere so that she could sit and eat and drink and chat in comfort. *Why really, what angels they all are; you couldn't wish for nicer people*, she said to herself. She knew that such golden thoughts would not persist, but at least she would have had them and this she felt was important. What was it George Herbert had said, "Love is the Parson's business" – well, wasn't it everyone's business?

But now a general lull in the talk occurred and the vicar

stepped forward and Roberta realized with horror that he was about to make a speech. She looked away in confusion as he expatiated on her long association with the village, of the sad severance of old ties that would occur when she left them, of the debt of gratitude they owed to her and her family, that their thoughts and good wishes would go with her to her new home and that he hoped she would accept a small token of those good wishes.

He then advanced towards Roberta and handed her an envelope. She opened it and found inside a list of hymns for the next Sunday's service. She glanced up in bewildered amusement but the ever-wary Mrs Spence was at her elbow.

"It was Mrs Baxter who put us up to it, Mrs Curling," she said quickly. "She told us it was no use giving you a book or such like, you were getting rid of so much, but she said you might be going in for window-boxes in London and a garden token for them and some plants to go in them might be acceptable."

"Quite so, quite so," said the vicar, beaming.

"Oh, you shouldn't have," said Roberta, thrusting back the hymn list into the envelope, "it's very very kind of you all. I *do* mean to have window-boxes and what a lovely reminder of you they will be, if I needed reminding, which of course I shan't."

There was a sound of clapping and then Rachel Lewis went to the piano and a group gathered round her. They sang "Jerusalem" and "There is a Tavern in the Town" and "Good King Wenceslas", though it was only November, and ended up inevitably with "Auld Lang Syne". Meanwhile Mrs Spence had slipped away and returned with the token which she had found, as she had expected, on the vicar's desk, and an unperceived exchange was made.

Then Roberta went home. On musing over the evening, she thought how ageless was the sense of a village community and how strong the filaments that bound them together, which she was about to sever. Fearfully and lovingly, she put aside the window-box token and prepared for bed.

Perhaps it was because she was still under the spell of the farewell party that when she opened a totally unexpected letter from her solicitor the next morning her first thought was "a reprieve". For it stated that the surveyor's report on the house had not been favourable after all, that extensive work on the roof and gutters was necessary and in view of this her price must be substantially reduced or the sale was off. Dismay and annoyance, however, soon drove out every other emotion. That traitorous surveyor whom she had refreshed with her best coffee!" That one can smile and smile and be a villain. . . ." Her roof was perfectly sound, she had slept under it in comfort all that year; she didn't believe there was extensive work required. It was an outrage. "They can think again!" she exclaimed as she read the letter through once more, but then she thought of the uncertainty of the future, of being plunged back into that no man's land again and, foolishly perhaps, one of the things that worried her most was the anti-climax it would be to stay on in the village, perhaps for months after that farewell party. Of course she shouldn't have counted her chicken before it was actually hatched. Clare, she remembered, had warned her once, but she had brushed aside the caution as merely Clare's habitual over-anxiousness; now what should she do? Oh, "the slings and arrows of outrageous fortune"!

Kitty, ringing up to know how the party had gone, was for capitulation. "You can't keep Mrs. B. away from her daughter much longer and the flat won't improve by being left empty all this time."

"But I can't afford to drop the price so much," wailed Roberta.

"Oh, I expect they'll come round if they really want the place," said Kitty. But, remembering their lack of apparent enthusiasm, Roberta doubted this.

Alex and Naomi were for holding out. "There's as good fish in the sea, or better," said Naomi, and Alex pressed her to come to them when Mrs Baxter had to go.

Roberta was ashamed that the thought of this was so unwelcome. Why why had she ever consented to move? Well, it was not too late, she could take the house off the market. But Mrs B. was going, the empty spaces in her rooms mocked her, and, if the roof and the gutters were really in such a bad state, they would let the rain and the snow in on her, she supposed, throughout the coming winter. In the watches of the night she could hear Kitty's rat making merry overhead.

Chapter 11

In the midst of this sea of troubles a raft appeared; that same cousin of Clare's, the retired librarian, the once-rejected Morris, wrote out of the blue to say that he found his enforced leisure unsupportable and that he and a sister had decided to join forces and invest their savings in acquiring a suitable property to run as a small guest-house and was Rowanbank still available? Letters and interviews followed and the outcome was that Roberta accepted his offer. She would be slightly better off than if she had reduced her price as demanded, and to sell to Morris would have several advantages. It would please Clare and Alex, it would keep Rowanbank almost in the family, Morris and his sister would, she believed, prove an asset to the village and lastly it gave her some satisfaction to be able to discontinue negotiations with those unenthusiastic conjectural purchasers. Moreover, Morris was willing to adapt his plans to her convenience and this left her free to choose her own time for the move. She found she could accept the idea of Rowanbank as a guest-house without repugnance and could even feel pleasure at the thought of how many people in the future would be able to enjoy her lovely view and her father's garden. She had come a long way since the day when Rose's suggestion that this indeed would be a suitable fate for her home had filled her with horror.

She thought at first that she might, even yet, be in

Coleridge Court for Christmas; but Alex and Clare were so insistent that she should spend her first Christmas away from Rowanbank with them that she gave way, and the more readily because both Alex and Kitty would be more free to help her with the move after the festive time was over. So it was settled that as soon as Mrs Baxter left her cottage she should also leave, but that after Christmas she would return for a couple of nights with Kitty for a last pack-up. The removal would then take place, followed by the auction, and then the workmen would move in for repairs and alterations so that Rowanbank Guest-House could open for the summer season.

The weeks now flew by and the morning of Mrs Baxter's departure arrived. Nothing could persuade her from coming round as usual "to see to things".

"Oh, Ellen," cried Roberta, "I'm sure you're too busy at home."

"It's all done, dear; I've only got to go along to the churchyard with a bunch of my Christmas roses. I don't quite know how it is," she explained. "I know William's not there, but it seems something I can still do for him."

"Of course, I understand," said Roberta and she suddenly envied Ellen Baxter. But would Charles have liked her to put flowers on his grave? She doubted it and anyway he didn't have a grave, only a little memorial plate inside the church which was there for her satisfaction not his. "Oh, Ellen," she said after a little pause, "I can't begin to thank you for everything and for being my friend for so long. It's hard to say goodbye."

"Things must change, it stands to reason," said Ellen, "but there's no sense in goodbyes. I'll be thinking often of you, dear Mrs Curling, and you'll sometimes be thinking of me, I dare say."

"Indeed I shall," said Roberta. She watched Ellen Baxter sail majestically down the path, through the gate and across the lane to the cottage for the last time. Then she decided that the best thing she could do straight away was to take the bus into Hastings and buy Christmas presents.

She bought a new paint-box for Becky and a painting-book of her favourite Flopsy Bunnies, in the fond belief that she had inherited her great-grandfather's talent – Becky was still painting her ferocious vermilion houses, Clare wrote, whenever she got the chance. For Bertram, Roberta brought a seductive picture-book containing much useful knowledge about an ant and a bee, and for Patrick, whose latest craze was carpentry, a proper carpenter's measure and a chisel. She believed in useful and edifying presents for children and in frivolous ones for grown-ups; so for Alex she chose a pair of luxurious slippers lined with fur and for Clare, whose shabby grey dressing-gown she had noted with disapproval, she found a glamorous house-coat of tomato-coloured silky material which would set off her dark hair and eyes.

She returned home pleased with her purchases; she had spent a lot of money but felt the better for it and set about the preparations for her visit with improved spirits.

These were dampened on her arrival by finding that she was not to be the only Christmas guest, though she had feared this might be the case, since Alex and Clare were only too prone to indiscriminate hospitality. Jock (she never discovered his other name) was a dour Scotsman, friendless and homeless, Alex explained. On further acquaintance with him, Roberta did not find this too surprising. He smoked, even at meal times, a particularly noisome brand of tobacco, coughed incessantly, occupied the bathroom for an unconscionable period and switched on the television set as frequently and as loudly as possible, so that Roberta felt it a judgement on her for having foisted it on the household. The children, however, had tired of it, she was glad to see.

Patrick and Becky were very busy making Christmas presents and cards and Bertram had invented a new game for himself inspired by the preoccupation of his elders. It was called "Moving House" and involved packing up his toys and books in all the cardboard boxes and plastic bags that he could lay hands on and conveying them from one end of the house to the other. It was difficult not to trip over these, as they were frequently discarded on the stairs or in the passages, but it employed him satisfactorily.

Christmas was observed as a strictly demythologized festival in Clare and Alex's household.

"I'm sure you understand, Gran," said Alex, "we can't tell the children what we don't believe ourselves."

And Roberta, thinking of her mother, felt: *Who am I that I should not understand?* Yet, as in the case of television, she believed that Alex and Clare did not allow enough for outside influences. Patrick and Becky seemed to her to be very muddled and she considered all three children deprived.

They had not been allowed even the brief midnight magic of Father Christmas, let alone the shepherds, the Wise Men and the star. Becky had once asked: "Why does Father fill our stockings instead of Father Christmas – is it because we are bad? He comes to *all* my friends." *Well, Father Christmas must take his chance*, thought Roberta. *After all, he is only an inhabitant of Looking-Glass Land; but for the rest I'll go surety.* And partly from worthy motives and partly, it must be confessed, from unworthy – for her dear Alex and Clare always seemed to arouse in her a spirit of opposition – she decided to take the children to see the Crib in St John's Church down the road. This was a huge, grim Victorian building usually kept closed for fear of vandalism but because it was Christmas week it was open for several hours each day with a custodian on duty. Becky and Bertram, who had never been inside any church before, were at first abashed by its sheer monstrosity and Patrick was in a mood of benevolent interest, so no one spoke till they got to the side chapel, where there was a large well-peopled stable.

438

The children stood in a row and stared, then Patrick said, "That sheep's much too big, I think . . . why, he's almost as big as the ass, and the ass oughtn't to be the same size as the ox. I wish I had my measure here to measure them."

"Hush," said Roberta, casting a look behind her. "Don't speak so loudly." But her own voice was drowned by Bertram's shrill one.

"Are they going to eat the baby?" he enquired eagerly.

"No, of course not." said Roberta, hoping against hope that the custodian was out of earshot.

"When I grow up," said Becky dreamily, "I'm going to have two dear little babies, one called Flopsy and the other called Jesus."

"You can't call them that, silly," said Patrick, "Flopsy is a rabbit's name – you're always mixing up animals with people – and nobody's ever called Jesus."

"But animals *are* people," said Becky, "and Jock's got a dog called Bobby, and why doesn't people call their babies Jesus? He was a very nice man."

"He wasn't exactly a man, that's why," said Patrick. "Do explain, Gran."

Roberta hesitated. She thought she heard laughter in Heaven, explain the eternal divine paradox! Should she give them a dusty answer? – "You'll understand when you're older." But she did not really believe that understanding was required or even possible. She put up a swift prayer, which to her astonishment was answered no less swiftly.

Suddenly and magically the organ burst forth above. Unperceived, someone had come to practise for the carol service. As the great notes of "Adeste fideles" rolled gloriously out over their heads, the children were startled into silence and also, at last, into something like awe. The sound ceased as abruptly as it had started while the organist found his next score and Roberta hurried her flock away. Becky and Bertram ran noisily down the aisle but Patrick

439

came slowly. He did not resume his questioning and Roberta thought that the music was a better answer than any she could have provided.

She did not expect to enjoy her Christmas Day very much, and nor did she. In the first place, she was really a little sated with Christmases which, as she grew older, seemed to recur more and more frequently, another coming up before the chimes of last year's carols had died on the air. Then she had to fight the nostalgia for Rowanbank and the past that threatened, unless she were careful, to engulf her. With the children around she could not count on much peace but at least they brought with them the compensation of their own excited happiness. The same could not be said of Jock, whose addiction to tobacco and television was telling progressively on her nerves: but a mild complaint was met by Alex with the shocked response: "Poor fellow, he has so few pleasures."

There is, however, such a powerful compulsion on Christmas Day itself to please or to be pleased, that the hours generally pass benignly. So Roberta managed to sustain with commendable grace the dawn chorus of children, the fraught ceremony of giving and receiving gifts, cousin Morris and his sister to dinner and an interminable evening's entertainment provided by Patrick and his friend Martin.

She took herself off to church in the morning, though not to St John's (where she feared to meet the eye of that custodian), and hurried back after the service, so as not to keep the family waiting for the present-giving ceremony. Everyone seemed pleased with what she had chosen for them and she herself was touched by Patrick's gift, over which he had obviously taken much trouble. It was a large collage neatly framed in plywood, depicting a bright blue sea with white crinkly paper waves into which a huge scarlet sun was setting, while a ship with a fine sail was entering the brown tweed harbour walls. Underneath was

440

written in bold, though somewhat unequal letters: "SAFE HOME."

"It's an alligator," said Becky. "Patrick, let me do the sun – isn't it beautiful!"

"She means an allegory," said Patrick hastily, "about your moving, Gran. I did most of it at school in art and Miss Brown helped me a little but I did the frame at home all by myself. Do you like it?"

"It's splendid," said Roberta, wondering what on earth she should do with it. She decided it must live under her bed, to be brought out and give a place of honour whenever the children came to Coleridge Court. For the time being, she bore it away to her bedroom and propped it up against her looking-glass. She trusted it was a good augur for the future – *I only hope I shall feel "safe home" again one day*, she said to herself and lay down for a little rest before dinner.

Clare was busy in the kitchen. She had refused help – "It only confuses me, thank you all the same," she had said to Roberta – and was having to concentrate resolutely on what she was doing, as her mind was perturbed on three counts. First her guests, unfortunately not being vegetarians, might sadly miss their turkey, bacon and sausages.

"Oughtn't we to provide them with the horrid stuff?" she had said to Alex, but he had answered:

"Not on our lives."

So, secondly she was anxious that the substitutes should do justice to the family's principles and, indeed, was not without hope that they would prove delicious enough to convert at least Morris and his sister. She had no hope of Roberta. Lastly she was praying that everyone would get on with everyone else, that Bertram would behave nicely, that Jock might, with luck, not show up at all and that Morris would not talk too much about Rowanbank, which might upset Granny. This, however, she need not have feared.

Roberta, though she still found him tedious and ceased to listen when he held forth on all the possible and impossible heating systems in vogue, was touched by his enthusiasm and also, as she looked down at the undistinguished cutlery and thought how her lost silver would have embellished the table, she was overcome with self-reproach that she had rejected him in favour of that specious rogue Hathaway. Laura, Morris's sister, was a small, bright bird-like woman with a habit of clicking her false teeth at the end of each speech, which added a peculiar emphasis to her otherwise mild remarks. She was in her mid-fifties and had lately been released by death from a life of subjection to a fierce invalid mother from whom, of course, Morris – though the adored one – had early freed himself. No one had thought this unfair or strange. Roberta hoped that Laura was not now exchanging one thraldom for another, but she decided this was unlikely unless it had become a habit, for Morris was a gentle man and also used to looking after himself. They were both full of eager plans and had already two prospective long-term guests in view.

"We mean to attend your auction (click click)," said Laura, "for even between us we find we haven't enough furniture for all your lovely great rooms. Mother and I only had a small flat at Putney, you know. You wouldn't object to us buying in some of your things (click click)?"

"Of course not," said Roberta, "I'd like to think of them being still there."

"That's what I told Laura," said Alex. "The sideboard, for instance, you'll need a good sideboard for a guest-house and it would be a pity to move that one, it fits in the recess so well."

"We may not get it," said Morris, "in fact you ought to be hoping it will catch the dealer's eye, but you don't know much about such things, I believe, Alex. It all depends on the demand, of course; large furniture isn't so much sought-after these days. Now our grandfather, Clare, if you remember, was quite an authority on period pieces – he told me that you must always look at the back and the inside of drawers. I'll tell you why."

Oh, thought Roberta, *he's off again;* but she felt that for both Morris and Laura moving house was romantic, an alluring adventure, an expansion of their lives, and this was in every way a complete contrast to what she herself was experiencing.

Clare brought in the Christmas pudding in triumph. She was feeling relaxed at last – everything had turned out well after all, the children's behaviour had been exemplary and Jock was mercifully still sleeping off his Christmas Eve revels in the boys' bedroom.

The evening was devoted to Patrick's ENTER-TAINMENT. Becky and Bertram could not remember a Christmas without this event but in reality of course it was only since the six-year-old Patrick, after having been taken for his first pantomime, invited the family to an ENTER-TAINMENT, consisting of a rapid recitation of nursery rhymes given in varied and elaborate costume which involved long intervals between each item. This had been repeated each year with steadily increasing ambition, until now it included Becky and Bertram and his best friend Martin, and had taken on the semblance of a play. It retained, however, the same characteristic lengthy prepar-ations and intervals with the briefest of scenes and dialogue.

On the whole the elders welcomed the ENTER-TAINMENT as employing the children happily while they were left in peace, all that was asked of them being free access to the "dressing-up" chest and enthusiastic applause. *Are there any creatures who at the same time manage to be so boring and so interesting as children?* Roberta wondered to herself as she gazed at Patrick who, with an army cap that had once belonged to George falling over one eye, waved a cardboard sword over Martin, wrapped in Bertram's scarlet bed quilt, lying slain at his feet. Becky, in an old white lace curtain, cheered from a tower of perilously piled stools. It was clear that a romantic rescue was in process, but it was difficult to know who Bertram was or what he was supposed to be doing. He wore a green paper crown from one of the morning's crackers and a spangled evening cape long ago discarded by Clare and sat silently and apart under a red umbrella. Perhaps he was a fairy.

Roberta, gazing, considered her great-grandchildren anew. In their grotesque garb they presented a fresh aspect, and she caught now and then a hitherto unsuspected family resemblance flitting momentarily across their faces. This fascinated her. They looked flushed and serious. The distillation of absurdity and charm in their performance held her spellbound and she felt a sudden wave of protective tenderness towards them. If only she possessed an enchanter's wand she would have waved it to keep them as they now were, safe in the present. So soon "the painted birds would cease to laugh in the shade", so soon the play would be over and Patrick's ENTERTAINMENT no longer be one of the wonders of the world. But she shook off the thought at once. As if that would keep them safe! What a mockery all this silly sweetness would be if they were never to grow out of it, to be "on the move" from innocence to experience.

There was a sound of clapping round about her. The actors were leaping across the room – "Did you like it? Did you like it?" they cried. "It was much the best yet, wasn't it?"

Boxing Day is not generally one of the easiest in the year's calendar. Perhaps it was better when there were twelve days of Christmas; as it is, it must always be something of an anti-climax and, besides, has to contend with hangovers, indigestion and the reaction from the extra good behaviour of the previous day. Clare was thinking

444

gloomily along these lines as she opened the sitting-room window as wide as it would go, to let in air after Jock's nightly occupation. *Granny will hate it smelling like this.* It really was rather a nuisance having him with Gran in the spare room and she wished he would at least fold up his blankets. She hoped Alex would take him off for a walk soon and she would send the children out and that should secure a little peace. Just then Roberta, who meant to spend the morning writing to Naomi, came into the room. She had not slept well and felt low and as she opened the door a chill north-easterly blast met her.

"Gracious, Clare, it's December, must we have the window open so wide or even at all?"

"I thought you hated the smell of smoke," said Clare, "that's why I opened it."

"Well, yes, I do," said Roberta. "It's a choice between two evils then, I suppose, but it really does feel very chilly in here."

"I'll leave it open just a crack, shall I, and turn up the heating?" said Clare, soothingly.

But Roberta, sensing the soothing and resenting it, said, "It will take some time for that to be effective. It seems to me that radiators are always too hot or not hot enough; you never get the comfortable warmth that the old fire gave. I hate the idea that I shall only have radiators in the flat. It is a pity, I think, that you and Alex didn't keep just one open grate."

I know you think it, said Clare to herself, *and have said so several times, dear Granny, but surely we can do what we like with our own house*. Her patience, which that morning was not of first-class quality, was wearing a bit thin and she had to remind herself that old people were usually touchy about temperatures. "I'm just going to turn out the children to get some fresh air," she announced brightly.

"I should have thought they would get enough of it in here," said Roberta and immediately commented silently:

I shouldn't have said that, I really am rather a nasty person I'm afraid.

But Clare only said, "I'm afraid it may rain later. I hope Alex has taken his raincoat."

Yes, that's what annoys me about Clare, thought Roberta, *that's what I find depressing: she's the sort of person who always thinks it's going to rain.* She sat down to her writing, hoping that in describing Patrick's play and Laura Morris's curious clickings to Naomi she would recover cheerfulness and good behaviour.

Clare, by means of bribes and threats, persuaded the children to get on their outdoor things and go into the garden. She then returned to the sitting-room with some sewing. *I'm really very fond of Gran*, she told herself firmly, *but being fond of a person doesn't always seem to be enough. Perhaps I didn't thank her properly for that lovely present. . . . I wish I knew what to do with it. I'm not the sort of person that wears housecoats, and my dressing-gown is still quite good and much warmer. I wonder if I could make it into a dress; I need a new dress so badly and it's a lovely material, though a bit bright. Yes, I shall try and do that.* The thought pleased her and she set herself to think of something to say, for the silence had lasted too long and her grandmother was folding up her letter.

Roberta, too, felt that there should now be some comfortable conversation. *Clare and I have the best intentions*, she thought a little sadly, *but we don't mix chemically very well. I don't suppose it matters much, however, for we are both nice people, or at least fairly nice.*

The children's voices in the garden were clearly to be heard in the quiet room through the slightly open window and suddenly these became louder and disputatious.

"I'm going in now," Patrick was saying, "I've got work to do."

"No, no!" shouted Becky and Bertram. "We can't play Old Man without you."

"You must play something else then."

"Shan't," roared Bertram.

"Hi, Bertram, where are you going?" cried Patrick.

"To fetch Gran."

"Gran can't play Old Man; she too old, she can't run."

The garden door slammed and then Bertram shouted: "Stupid Old, stupid Old!" and burst out crying.

Clare jumped up. "Oh, how naughty!" she exclaimed. "Really, Bertram! I'm so sorry, Granny."

"Don't fuss, dear," said Roberta, "Bertram's absolutely right, 'stupid old' it is. I wish more people saw it like that. *I'm* as eager and willing to play and run as ever – *I* don't mind about draughts and fires, I can jump over the moon – it's just 'stupid old'."

But Clare was not listening, for she had already left the room.

Roberta, however, continued the conversation with herself: *That's what I must always remember, I must never let "stupid old" become me.* With this blessed sense of detachment the burden of the day seemed lifted. She became charitable and, till lunchtime, entertained a pacified Bertram with a fourfold reading and rereading of the Ant and the Bee.

Clare, thankful to leave them together, retired to her kitchen, deciding to avoid thinking about either of them for the present. Feeding her family and her guests over the holiday had its problems, but they were not complicated like some.

The next day, Kitty arrived to convey Roberta back to Rowanbank. She had been busy with Christmas at her hospital, but was as usual cheerful, energetic and tactless, either by nature or design. Roberta could never quite make up her mind which.

"You look washed out, Clare. I always say give me an institutional Christmas rather than a family one. Roberta, I hope you at least are in good shape – you'll need to be."

447

"Why do you say such things?" she demanded as they started on the homeward journey.

"What things?" asked Kitty.

"Well, for instance why depress me by the awful shape of things to come?"

"You looked too happy to leave poor Clare," said Kitty. "You and Alex never notice how she slaves."

"She was born a slave," said Roberta with guilty emphasis, "and no one could possibly call Alex selfish."

"He doesn't remember that charity begins at home," said Kitty.

"You're not fair, Kitty, it's just that he thinks of Clare as part of himself."

"Exactly," said Kitty. "But I didn't mean to depress you about the move. It will be fun."

Roberta reflected. Yes, it was true she was happy to exchange Clare for Kitty, for with Kitty it did not matter whether it rained or no.

She found her bracing companionship invaluable over the following week, for it proved a traumatic time. Each morning she woke in a panic which resolved into a pattern of apprehension: how was she ever to be ready in time? What had she to do that day? What vital detail had been forgotten? But by breakfast this whirlpool had subsided and was succeeded by the merciful sense of unreality which had, at intervals, taken over ever since she had first decided on the move.

She spent the days busily on packing, finishing off her new curtains, giving and receiving last goodbyes and making and losing and remaking her beloved lists. Kitty bought three sets of coloured tickets, red for the articles to be removed to Coleridge Court, blue for the goods to be auctioned and green for the few pieces to be sent to Alex and herself. It was while she was fixing on the red labels to one after the other of the objects she had chosen to take

448

with her that the thought occurred to her: *These are all bits of my past – childhood, my parents, friendship, lovers, marriage, children. Why, I've been moving house all my life.* She sat for some time musing on this and it seemed to her a momentous enough idea to share with Kitty.

"Very fine and metaphysical," said Kitty, "but now please confirm the time the removal van will be here and phone Coleridge Court about the keys, and don't forget you promised to see if the young couple in Mrs B.'s cottage will be of any help to Laura and Morris."

Ellen and William Baxter's successors had moved in just before Christmas and Roberta had hardly seen them yet. Now she braced herself to call and it needed some courage for she was missing Ellen at every turn. A large smart car blocked the cottage path and she had to step on to the flowerbed to round it. On the further side a young man was busy cutting down the old pear tree. True, it was long past good fruiting and obscured the light, but – "Change, change in all around I see," Roberta muttered as she rang the door bell. A fair, top-heavy girl in tight jeans and an enormously wide thick pullover answered it.

"Mrs Forbes?" enquired Roberta. "I'm Mrs Curling from Rowanbank."

"But she didn't use surnames, of course," said Roberta to Kitty afterwards. "They're Samantha and Don and I was Roberta in no time and Ellen's kitchen is bright red and the stairway's got stars painted over it."

"Well, I think that's rather nice," said Kitty. "And as for names, away with barriers I say. You couldn't expect a young William and Ellen, but I bet you did, and a couple of their babies playing in the garden, but the point is are they going to be of any use?"

"Not much, I'm afraid, she's got a job in a shop in Rye, but she said she'd do what she could at weekends. She's friendly enough, seemed pleased that Rowanbank is going to be a guest-house. 'Bring some life to the place,' she said."

"Then that's another thing off our minds," said Kitty. "Don't look so glum."

Roberta laughed. "I suppose everything being so different ought to make it easier to leave. Nothing can stay the same, I know, but why then does one mind so much that it changes?"

Chapter 12

ON THE day before the move was to take place, Roberta had slept late, tired out by all the endless unforeseen details that had to be attended to. She woke to a strange white light and an unearthly stillness and, suspecting what she would see, she threw a shawl over her shoulders and went to the window. A charm of snow lay over the country-side – it was the first fall of the winter and, as always, seemed to Roberta momentous and fantastic. The familiar landmarks were transformed or altogether blotted out, the low round hills melted into the sky, paths had disappeared, hedges bowed low, distinctions of tone and colour were non-existent. This withdrawal into anonymity of her beloved view seemed to Roberta like a gesture of farewell.

She sighed and hastened into the warmth of the sitting-room. Telephone bells began to ring.

"At least we are not cut off," said Kitty.

"Clare always said this would happen if I moved in January. I do wish she wasn't so often right," said Roberta. "Will everything have to be put off?"

But it appeared that, if there were no further falls and no disastrous thaw followed by a freeze, all would go ahead as planned: Alex would arrive at nine o'clock the next day to take Roberta to Coleridge Court, leaving Kitty to follow with the men and van.

"Are you sure you'll be able to manage, Kit?"

451

"Of course. I'm an old hand. They're certain to be nice men, you'll see."

"Alex has taken the day off," said Roberta. "He's going to help me get straight."

"Good, you'll need to feel at home as soon as possible in this weather. And won't you be glad of the central heating, you old Spartan?" said Kitty.

No further snow fell and Roberta did not know whether she was glad or sorry. The hours of waiting now seemed endless, as waiting so often does, yet she clung to them; as long as they lasted, she was still herself – still at home. During the brief daylight the sun failed to pierce the gun-metal sky and any light there was seemed to come from the snow-laden earth.

Kitty cleared a space in the garden upon which to scatter crumbs for the birds. "It isn't deep," she said, "it ought to be all right." Later Roberta caught her coming down from the attic. She looked guilty and was carrying an empty saucer.

"Kitty," Roberta exclaimed, "don't tell me you've been putting food out for that rat?"

"Well, I expect he's terribly hungry," said Kitty, "it'll keep him from foraging below stairs. You were too fast asleep but I heard him last night. Besides, don't you want him to have lovely last memories of Rowanbank? He'll be off as soon as the builders move in."

"Oh, Kit!" cried Roberta and suddenly wanted to laugh and cry at once.

The next day, though the snow remained, the roads had been cleared and the removal men arrived punctually, but when Roberta opened the door for them she was dismayed to see two frail-looking little gnomes grinning up at her. Even Kitty was taken aback and rushed to the kitchen to put on the kettle, muttering: "Best fatten them up a little before anything else."

The gnomes, however, seemed both friendly and capable and, after consuming mugs of strong sweet tea, set about their work without delay. The smaller of the two seemed to be in charge. He assumed at once a fatherly attitude towards Roberta.

"Now don't you worry, lady," he said, "the weather's OK, there won't be much on the roads this morning, and so we'll get along all the quicker, but we can't have you catching cold. You leave everything to me and my brother, we've never hurt or harmed a piece yet, have we, Ned?"

Ned nodded and patted the frame of the mirror. "Nice bit here," he said appreciatively.

"You do understand, only the things with the red and green labels are to go to London – the blue ones are to stay here."

"Yes, lady," said the chief gnome. "Pity, though, I don't like homes broken up, see? Fanciful, I know, but seems as though all these pieces have got used to living together."

I never expected removal men to be so human, thought Roberta. *Perhaps it's because they're such small ones – I do hope they'll be equal to lifting and carrying everything. It's a good thing they haven't got to cope with the piano.*

Actually, however, once they set to they began to deal with the furniture so rapidly that she was relieved when Alex's car arrived for it was certainly time to be off if she was to arrive at the flat before the van, so she drove away at last in a bustle and had no time to think or to feel.

There was no snow at all in the London streets, only in the garden of Coleridge Court little patches of irrelevant whiteness showed up under the bedraggled bushes. It all appeared rather sordid and desolate. "Get a kettle on as soon as you arrive," Kitty had said, "tea's the priority in a move," and she had packed a basket with the necessities and thrust it at Roberta on parting so that, obediently obeying instructions, she did not stop to consider anything but that the flat seemed warm, that the gas cooker was functioning and that the rooms looked too small for anything but dolls' furniture. This dismayed her, but almost at once the van drew up before the door and Kitty marched in.

"Here we are again," she announced loudly. "Have you got tea ready? My dear, they're twins, Fred and Ned, absolute pets."

The gnomes, who had followed close behind, looked gratified and accepted their ritual mugs with pleasure and soon all once more was in rapid motion.

"Let's get lady's bed in first and make it nice and comfortable for her," said the fatherly Fred.

Does he expect me to jump into it here and now? thought Roberta. *I only wish I could.* Instead she found herself breathlessly busy. Ejected from the van with remarkable rapidity, each object demanded an immediate resting place. The larger pieces presented no difficulty; it was the little articles and worst of all those unwanted, forgotten shamemaking bits and pieces – a shabby wastepaper basket unaccountably still full of rubbish, old boxes with forgotten rusty tools, an incredible pair of Charles's wellingtons – where had they been hiding and what on earth should she do with them? Fred and Ned carried each bit of rubbish tenderly in and set it down carefully in the tiny hall. *Surely that must be all now, thank Heavens*, thought Roberta, for there was a lull at last. But it was *not* all. She looked out of the window and saw, blocking up the whole approach, the large old garden seat. It looked enormous out of its context.

The gnomes, having lowered it on its side, edged round it and called to her, "Where shall we take this, lady?"

"But it ought never to have come!" exclaimed Roberta.

"I told him," suddenly spoke up the hitherto subservient Ned, "it didn't have no red label. I told him but he don't listen to me."

"Easy now, Ned," said the other, "it didn't have no blue one neither. It was like this, lady, see, this here was lying

454

on it and this had a red one on, OK, so I took it that both was meant to come together."

He held out a small bundle of gardening tools, a little weeding fork, and trowel and a pair of secateurs and a pair of gloves, all of which Roberta had put together with her window-boxes in mind. She remembered now having left them on the bench after labelling them and she supposed she had overlooked the bench itself – perhaps the snow was to blame, but it was no use bothering about that now.

"Yes I quite understand," she said to Fred, "but I can't think what we can do with it."

"Oh, well," said Alex, "something like this was bound to happen. It'll just have to go back again, that's all."

Fred scratched his head. "That'll be arkard," he said, "we got another move on today before we finish, down Essex way; just in time for it, and we'll want all the room in the van we can get."

They all stood and looked at the seat, which lay there obstinately asserting its right to exist.

"Wait a sec," said Kitty suddenly, "I've got an idea. Your phone's connected, isn't it, Roberta?" She vanished but reappeared again very soon.

"It's all right, I got on to the warden at once and she says to put it in the square garden for the time being, and your garden key is hanging behind the kitchen door – oh, and she says she hopes everything is all right and will you let her know if you want anything."

The gnomes' faces cleared and they carried the seat across the road. It was set down under a big old lilac tree where it at once took on an air of permanence. "Pity it can't stay there; it looks at home, like," said Fred.

"Well, who knows," said Alex, "it might be possible. I should think the tenants would welcome it and it would make it seem more like your garden, wouldn't it, Gran?"

Roberta assented vaguely; she did not at the moment feel that the square could ever seem like her own garden,

455

but she was too tired to care. She was conscious only of relief that a crisis had been at least temporarily resolved and that soon the men would go and she could relax. This, after a final round of tea, they proceeded to do, taking Kitty with them.

"Fred says he'll drop me at the Angel," Kitty said. "I've got to be at the hospital by four today, but I'll come round as soon as I can tomorrow to help get you straight."

"I can't be grateful enough to you," said Roberta. How kind everybody was being, she thought, and what a nuisance she was. Now here was Alex starting already to hang her curtains and pictures.

"I'll just get these out of the way and then perhaps we could have something to eat," he said. "Tea's all very well but I'm starving."

"I've got enough food here somewhere," said Roberta, "only I don't know where anything is."

"We'll go out then," said Alex. "Is this where you want the mirror? There! That's a good job done!"

But Roberta, who had carefully planned her walls beforehand, now saw that the total effect was wrong.

"Oh, Alex!" she exclaimed. "The *Still Life* – I thought it would fit nicely there, but it's crowded by the door, and the landscapes are too high, and the mirror too low – oh, why am I such a fool?"

She was in a daze of exhaustion, exasperation and grief.

"Come and eat," said Alex.

When they got back she certainly felt better but the pictures still looked wrong.

"The Japanese say about their gardens: 'If you place stones in the wrong order your house will fall down.' So it is important," she pleaded.

"Well, I'll alter them then," said Alex cheerfully; "not to worry, but then I must be going."

"I've kept you too long already," said Roberta. "Clare will think there's been an accident."

She sat back and watched and saw that she had been right and wondered why the correct placing of objects mattered so much. It was of immense comfort, she felt that it should be so, a sort of reassurance about the universe.

"There's more snow forecast," said Alex, drawing the newly hung curtains, "we've been lucky it's held off today. If we're in for a bad spell now it'll be such a comfort to know that you're snug and warm here instead of shivering away at Rowanbank."

"I'll fetch your coat, dear," said Roberta without comment.

After he had gone, she sat motionless before the place where the fire ought to have been and stared round at the strange little box in which, unaccountably now it seemed, she found herself. She sought some assurance of continued identity from the few household goods she had brought with her but, removed from the surroundings she had always known them in, they appeared unfamiliar, as if she were seeing them for the first time. She realized that it was long since she had actually looked at them at all – that queer little cupboard, for instance, that really handsome mirror, that rug, nice but worn. . . . Her eyes travelled over them critically as objects existing in their own right, unencrusted by associations. She herself felt curiously weightless and empty and a little dizzy. "Lawks a mercy, this is none of I," she quoted fearfully to herself.

Presently she made an effort to find the necessary equipment for a meal, which was a difficult and lengthy process. Then she went to bed. She was tired out but she could not sleep. It was neither dark nor light, for a lamp outside could not be satisfactorily excluded; neither was it noisy or quiet, since through the window, open because of the heating, came the unremitting roar of London which sounded even more clearly as, hour after slow hour, the nearer noises were hushed. Every now and again the radiator gave a gurgle and Roberta listened for it and hated it.

457

The sense of lost identity grew stronger and she began to panic.

"I've made a mistake, I've made a great mistake," she said aloud, "I must go back." But she knew she couldn't.

At last she fell into an uneasy doze in which she was searching feverishly for something, she did not know what, that was gone beyond recall. She was wakened by the ringing of her telephone and stumbled out of bed to answer it.

"Roberta Curling speaking," she said, and hoped this still was true. There was no reply but she distinctly heard a sound of deep breathing. "Who is it?" she enquired anxiously.

Silence – then a high shrill voice proclaimed: "It's me, Bertram, me!"

"Oh," said Roberta with relief. "Oh, darling, how lovely to hear you! How are you? How clever of you to phone."

No reply, only another long pause and then rather faint and far away; "Goodbye . . . goodbye."

But Roberta did not ring off, for she could still make out the breathing and at last, just as she was giving up, there came a loud triumphant "Hullo" and then the receiver clicked back into place.